Dear Target Guest:

It was a real thrill to learn that my new novel, *Flat Water Tuesday*, had been chosen for the Target Book Club. *Flat Water Tuesday* has made friends with readers in North America, Europe, Australia, New Zealand, and South Africa. To have it selected by this prestigious reading group is a marvelous new chapter of what has been quite a journey.

Flat Water Tuesday began as an effort for me to capture on paper the tension, beauty, speed, and thrill of rowing at an American boarding school much like the one I attended. I grew up in Buffalo, New York, and the experience of going away to school was my first taste of independence and the allure of travel. Over the years, as I revised the manuscript, the story changed to become much more than a memory of the water. *Flat Water Tuesday*'s main character, Rob Carrey, is a former rower who faces one very emotional week. Like I once did, he works in the world of documentary film. He spends half of his time in New York and the rest in other parts of the world. When his relationship with his New Yorker girlfriend, Carolyn, begins to crumble, the two of them struggle to find one another in the shadow of loss. In the middle of all this comes the news that a former rowing teammate has tragically died, and Rob needs to return to the school to finally put to rest the ghosts of his past.

Much of Rob Carrey's identity is wrapped up in being a rower, and I have been lucky enough to hear from oarsmen all around the world who have identified with his efforts on the water. But he is also deeply in love with Carolyn, and his love for her has been equally resonant with readers. Only a few people ever feel the speed of a fast rowing shell in their lifetime, but the need to find the one person who is meant for you is universal. Ultimately, *Flat Water Tuesday* is a love story. It's about how far we go to hold on to our dreams and the people who touch our lives.

After living with the characters of *Flat Water Tuesday* for so long, it is a pleasure to share them with you.

I am delighted that *Flat Water Tuesday* will be available at Target, a store I invariably visit whenever I am in the United States because it has a wonderful selection of useful things I can't find overseas, and I am greatly looking forward to hearing from Target Book Club readers. Warm regards and happy reading,

Ron Irwin
www.ronirwin.com

Praise for Ron Irwin's *Flat Water Tuesday*

"Irwin's descriptions are observant and intimate—readers become immersed in the Darwinian cruelty of the young reflected against the loneliness of a lost, jaded teacher, then confront a man finding purpose, and close the book after bathing in a deeply evocative, hope-filled conclusion. An elegy to love and loss and reconciliation." —*Kirkus Reviews* (starred review)

"In taut, muscular prose Irwin details the punishing training regimen of the God Four, a crew of competitive oarsmen who commit themselves body and soul to the pain and glory of their sport. *Flat Water Tuesday* is a powerful consideration of the exhilarating love of competition and the high cost of victory." —Amber Dermont, *New York Times* bestselling author of *The Starboard Sea*

"A gripping read. If you've ever marveled at the fluidity of a quadruple scull cutting through water in first light, and wondered what makes its four-man motor work, this book will provide the answers, and then some. Irwin is adept at revealing the tricky bonds between rowers, and the way those bonds can shape—and misshape—a life." —Tom McNeal, author of *To Be Sung Underwater*

"*Flat Water Tuesday* is the best debut novel I've read this year, a compulsively readable dark drama that weaves multiple story lines toward one marvelous denouement. Ron Irwin writes with confidence and skill and authenticity in this exploration of identity and the poisonous fuel of ambition. It will call other books—*A Separate Peace*, *The Art of Fielding*—to mind but stands alone as an original and powerful work. I'll read anything Irwin writes after this." —Michael Koryta, *New York Times* bestselling author of *The Prophet*

"In Ron Irwin's capable hands, past and present fuse into a haunting meditation on class, guilt, and the perils of victory." —Eric Puchner, author of the Pen/Faulkner Award finalist *Model Home*

"With echoes of *A Separate Peace,* Ron Irwin's wonderful *Flat Water Tuesday* is a masterful coming-of-age story about making one's place in the world, about the sacrifices love asks of us and of the rewards it may give us, about friendship and responsibility and so many other aspects of being human. It's compelling, moving, and often heartbreaking—all of the things we want good novels to be." —Joe Schuster, author of *The Might Have Been*

flat water tuesday

RON IRWIN

THOMAS DUNNE BOOKS 〰 ST. MARTIN'S GRIFFIN NEW YORK

This is a work of fiction. All of the characters, organizations, and events portrayed in this novel are either products of the author's imagination or are used fictitiously.

THOMAS DUNNE BOOKS.
An imprint of St. Martin's Press.

FLAT WATER TUESDAY. Copyright © 2013 by Ron Irwin. All rights reserved. Printed in the United States of America. For information, address St. Martin's Press, 175 Fifth Avenue, New York, N.Y. 10010.

www.thomasdunnebooks.com
www.stmartins.com

Designed by Steven Seighman
Map by Jane Heinrichs

"Mending Wall," from the book *The Poetry of Robert Frost,* edited by Edward Connery Lathem. Copyright © 1930, 1939, 1969 by Henry Holt and Company, copyright © 1958 by Robert Frost, copyright © 1967 by Lesley Frost Ballantine. Reprinted by permission of Henry Holt and Company, LLC. Boat diagram copyright © 2014 by Cameron MacLeod Jones

The Library of Congress has cataloged the hardcover edition as follows:

Irwin, Ron.
    Flat water Tuesday / Ron Irwin. — First Edition.
        p. cm.
    ISBN 978-1-250-03003-0 (hardcover)
    ISBN 978-1-250-03002-3 (e-book)
    1. Rowing—Fiction.   2. Contests—Fiction.   3. Faith—Fiction.   I. Title.
    PS3609.R93F53 2013
    813'.6—dc23

                                                              2013003730

ISBN 978-1-250-05982-6 (Target Book Club Edition)

St. Martin's Griffin books may be purchased for educational, business, or promotional use. For information on bulk purchases, please contact Macmillan Corporate and Premium Sales Department at 1-800-221-7945, extension 5442, or write specialmarkets@macmillan.com.

First Target Book Club Edition: May 2014

10 9 8 7 6 5 4 3 2 1

This novel is for my mother,
Donna H. Irwin, who told me to
get it all down in writing.

The Fenton School believes that the sport of rowing boats encourages Discipline and Fellowship and builds young men of Good Character.

—Letter to parents, The Fenton School, 1905

The Fenton School reserves a limited number of places for students who wish to take a postgraduate year in a boarding school environment. A postgraduate year of study at Fenton is a repeated senior year of high school that offers, in many cases, more rigor and discipline than the average student has become accustomed to at home. Postgraduate students at Fenton are often attracted to our extensive sports program, and each year they play important roles on our varsity football, hockey, and rowing teams. The postgraduate student receives a certificate of attendance upon successful completion of their year at the Fenton School.

Extensive financial aid is granted to PG candidates on a needs basis.

—*The Fenton School Handbook* (current edition)

Behind every beautiful thing, there's been some kind of pain.

—*Bob Dylan*

Mr. Rob Carrey
c/o National Geographic Television
1145 17th Street NW
Washington D.C. 20036–4688

Dear Rob,

It's been fifteen years since we last saw each other, one month to the day. Can you believe it?

I'm sure you wish it was longer.

In six weeks it will be our fifteenth reunion at good old Fenton School. A milestone! And they want us all to come on back and reminisce. I am positive you have no plans to attend. But I'm sitting here trying to tie up loose ends. Trying to knock off unfinished business I thought would go away by itself.

When you are rehabbing you are told to get in touch with people from your past. To apologize for the things you did while you were hammered. They give you a little model letter *you can send if you don't know what to say. Some people in my group just photocopied it about a hundred times and sent it on to all the people whose lives they screwed up on the way down. My group leader insists that you can't just send it via e-mail. I don't know why. E-mail appears less genuine, I guess.*

I have the letter here in front of me. It says I ought to tell you that thanks to some spiritual principles, I have been able to get my life on track. I don't hold with all that about "spiritual principles." But you do get some time to think when you've lost your job. When your wife leaves you. At the end of the letter you're supposed to tell the recipient how long you've been sober. In my particular case that's about three and a half weeks, give or take.

Anyways, Rob, I have nothing to apologize to you about. I have about ten more people on my sorry list (second smallest list in the group, I kept track) but you are a guy who does not need my groveling.

Here's the thing. Somehow we all decided never to talk about what happened during the last year at that school. I have no idea how it affected you guys. Maybe your memories are better, more useful, or more selective. But I've been talking to people. People in the group, mostly, and a therapist who says I should express my feelings instead of acting out because of them. She also says, over and over, that whatever emotional energy you waste on feelings of guilt, rage, and emotional pain, your body will reclaim in self-destructive behavior. She says the things I tell her about the past are surely tragic but that I have to "seek closure."

We all know something more happened back then than just a simple everyday tragedy. I should know, because I'm living a simple everyday tragedy. Hey, here's a secret: A few months ago I started to think people were following me when I was really drunk. The therapist informed me I suffer from "paranoid segues" (she also uses another term, "mild delusional psychosis"—my vocab is increasing in direct proportion to how crazy I get). But one day somebody might ask me some hard questions about what happened to me when I was eighteen years old. It could happen, right?

I swear, Rob, if they ever do, I'll tell them I forgot it all. I'll claim with my trembling hand on the Bible that I blanked it out. The whole year.

It might even be a little true.

I've been forgetting lots of things. Forgot to drive on the road a month ago and totaled the BMW—flipped it twice. Those German fun bags deployed perfectly. Pull one of those stunts and you wake up hours later, wondering where the hell you are—in my case, it was in the emergency room in Sharon, Connecticut, with a nurse snapping her fingers over my face, catching a contact buzz off my breath.

So, anyways, the nitty-gritty details of what went on during senior year at Fenton are a little fuzzy, but the basic memories are intact. I bet they're pretty intact for you, too. And for the rest of the crew. If you're like me, you think about it. Maybe you think about it at strange times. Like in the shower, when you're sneaking shots while your wife brushes her teeth. (You fill a shampoo bottle with vodka; it tastes a little soapy but gets you through breakfast. Know where I learned this? Fenton, of course.) Or like when you're washing dishes with your third or fourth scotch on the windowsill. Pissing in your own Jacuzzi with a beer in your hand. Pissing in your bed after.

Maybe, if you're like me, this stuff comes back when you're sitting in a rented condo, five miles away from your house in Greenwich, and just a hop, skip, and jump away from that school. Just sitting here on somebody else's furniture eating pizza and smoking cigarettes with a rented Ford out front.

I admit it: I have taken up the wicked weed in this last month. It's awesome. You can smoke all day and still drive somewhere. If you have somewhere to go, that is. Try doing that on G&Ts. I'm eating lots of candy. And drinking milk shakes. Remember milk shakes? I order them from the place down the road because I don't trust myself with a blender.

Try to imagine being the kind of person who can't have a blender in the house.

I'm feeling pretty sorry for myself, I know. The first rule you learn at Fenton is to never feel sorry for yourself. Same thing in rehab. So let's say it loud and proud, Rob: "I am the one at fault for everything that has happened to me."

I also know this: If things hadn't turned out the way they did at Fenton, you might actually be heading back to the reunion this year. Me, too.

I told my ex-wife (that word looks weird on the page, Rob—it's the first time I've ever written it, I'm not even sure if it's supposed to be hyphenated) about all of it a few years ago, after we were married, just to be on the safe side. She told me to drop you an e-mail and I got pretty fired up to make contact for a while, but . . . You know how it is. Georgia (my ex—it's getting easier to write) thought it was pretty dumb that we never kept in touch.

None of us have, I told her.

Stupid people, she said.

I regret it now.

Do you know the school has no record of you? I bet that's the way you want it. You are listed as an alumnus who is Missing in Action, but I Googled your ass off and got your producer's address, finally—after seeing your name on a credit for some film called The Disappearing Mountain Gorillas of Uganda *that you can get (on deep discount) via Amazon, if you're interested. Finding you took me about an hour. But that's okay. I've been spending lots of time surfing the Internet. I found everybody on the team sooner or later, but you were the hardest.*

Carrey, did you really move to South Africa? It had to be you on the Web site. You look pretty much the same, but you've gotten bigger and you've lost all that hair. It says on your filmmaker's bio on the National Geographic homepage that you divide your time between New York and Cape Town. Good idea. I've always wanted to see Africa. Send me a ticket. I'll fly down and we'll sit on a beach and drink beer. Well, you'd have a beer. I'd get a Coke or a lemonade or Kool-Aid or a virgin banana daiquiri or whatever they serve ex-drunks with ex-wives and ex-careers over there.

Anyways, Rob, I'm writing all of you. Everyone who was on that team.

I saved this letter to you for a good while, though. I really did want to contact you for years, even when most of what I had to say was scribbled on the back of cocktail napkins. I battled to write this, wondered if I even have a right to say anything at all to you about that year, even if you are reading this letter in some rainforest or whatever. But for what it's worth, here it is: Make peace with the past. Figure it out.

If you do, drop me a line.

Fifteen years, Rob. Sitting here in this room, it feels like two minutes ago we were gods.

I'm so sorry for everything, after all.

Your friend,
John Perry

SoberJohn@gmail.com
1-860-564-7165 (Call now. We never close!)

PROLOGUE

I folded the letter in half so I could look at the embossed name on top of the stationery. I laid it on the airplane's tiny tray table. It was the twentieth time I had read it, at least. It had been forwarded to my Cape Town apartment while I'd been on the eastern coast of South Africa on a marine shoot; two weeks of sitting on a boat with a diver, a fisherman, and two cameramen in the middle of a shoal of sardines, waiting for the game fish and the sharks that would pile into the melee. Now I was flying home with a hard case full of Beta SP tapes as carry-on luggage and the half-finished script for the documentary I'd spent six weeks putting together. I had promised myself I would do some writing on the airplane, but by the time the nineteen-hour journey was two hours gone, I gave up and watched a movie and then ordered a drink, knowing I'd feel it upon landing in dawn's brutal light at Kennedy. I was tired from the moment I boarded the plane in Cape Town and settled into my seat, thanking God the 747 was only three-quarters full and I'd been given a full row on which to throw down my chewed-up leather briefcase and the magazines and newspapers I'd bought to get back up to speed on world events. I was dreading New York and what was going to happen there.

I ran my fingers over the postmark on John's letter. It had left Greenwich, Connecticut, over five weeks ago and done a detour in DC until *National Geographic* had sent it on to me. I had found it when I got back from the shoot along with a crumpled pile of bills, junk mail, fast-food menus, and traditional healing ads that had been jammed into the metal box in the foyer of the crumbling art deco apartment block where I lived. I had immediately thrown it away when I saw the return address, just before I locked up the flat and ran down to the street to meet the taxi. But as I opened the back door to the whimpering yellow Mercedes-Benz, I signaled "hang on" to the wiry kid tapping his fingers to a Kwaito riff on the beaded steering wheel and climbed back up the three flights of stairs. I cranked open the dead bolts and unlocked the alarm so I could scrape the envelope from the bottom of the wastebasket and stow it in my bag. I almost trashed it again at the airport, came a hairsbreadth to stuffing it in the overflowing orange bin by the X-ray machines along with the other contraband passengers jettison before getting screened. But I kept it, even though I didn't tear it open until I was halfway across Dakar.

John's was one of the few personal notes I had received from anyone in a while. I almost decided to call him when I landed. I'd say hello and tell him I was too busy to see him, which was true. I had a film to edit, a script to finish, a Jeep to sell, and I had to get more work. Over the next few days my personal and professional lives were going to be rejiggered—this week I was splitting with my girlfriend, Carolyn Smythe. My heart clenched at the prospect. We had a business to hammer out and a contract to renegotiate. So I'd wish John well. I'd tell him to hang in there, that alcoholism is a rough row to hoe and I could sympathize.

Or maybe I'd just e-mail him and be done with it. Say it was good to hear from him—no matter how random and rambling his letter was—and not even mention I was in the city and planned to be there for three weeks before I flew back to Cape Town to start life again, single.

I pressed my aching lumbar vertebrae into the seat and twirled the plastic South African Airlines tumbler. They had turned out the lights and tucked us in over an hour ago. The passengers in my section sat glaring at the tiny screens in the backs of the chairs. Some of us were draped in our flimsy blankets, trying to sleep, lines of seated mummies in the mausoleum darkness. We'd entered the dozing purgatory of the tourist-class long-haul flight. Another eight hours of stifling boredom lay ahead.

The flight attendant drifted through the darkness to me, took away my tiny menagerie of Johnnie Walker bottles, and brought a new one, with new ice and a small bottle of still mineral water. As she placed them on my tray she gave me a quick, commiserative look that might have been a warning or maybe something else. I examined the dark porthole beside me and saw only my reflection under the orange reading light, a ghost of a face looking back at me with Jack-o'-lantern eyes.

None of the others who were close to me at that school had tried to contact me, ever. John was the first.

I squeezed my eyes shut, hard, trying to picture him, the John Perry I knew in boarding school. To my mild surprise I could not summon an image of his face; I could only remember how physically big he was and I wondered if he had aged well or if all that hulking muscle had slowly turned to fat. I imagined him over the intervening years; at his college graduation, at his wedding—he had forgotten that he'd invited me. I remember receiving that invitation, belatedly, from my brother Tom, who lived in my parents' old house in Niccalsetti, New York. I had opened it in Cape Town and folded it away guiltily after seeing his name and that of the girl whose parents were proudly announcing her impending union.

I had stashed the thick, ivory envelope in my desk and told myself I'd send him a picture of one of the lions we'd spent an agonizing month filming in the Ngorongoro Crater in Tanzania. I assured myself that I'd go online and send the couple a gift off their hopeful wedding registry site and follow up with an e-mail, one lousy e-mail saying congratulations. If I'd actually done that it would have been the first time I had contacted anyone from the Fenton School since the day I walked out of there.

But I didn't send him a photograph, or an e-mail or a gift or even fill out the RSVP postcard.

And I was damned sure none of the others did, either.

FALL

I.

My fragile rowing shell was moving fast and light down the river. It surged forward, then coasted while I recoiled for another stroke. I felt the pull of the sculls in my legs, then in my back. I heard only the splashing and the *zing* of the water dripping from the blades as I slipped by the ancient school. The endless lawns to starboard turned into soccer fields and then into the practice football field. The freshly painted goalposts marked the end of my practice session, and passing them I tasted my speed, closed my eyes and inhaled it, the vibrations of the boat in my spine.

I leaned back and the shell ran out beneath me, gliding over the water like a bird. A million trees up, the mountain threw rippled reflections across the water. The blades of my sculls kissed the smooth surface as I neared the Fenton School boathouse. I could turn and see the dock floating four inches above the waterline. Even this late in the season I could feel the heat rising up off the banks, as if the valley had kept part of summer's warmth for the fall. I hunched over and drew a stopwatch from my sweatshirt and did the daily math, looking at the digital numbers through watery eyes. The calculations were easy. I knew how far two thousand meters was down the course and I allowed some time, because you rowed with the current to get down the river and fought it coming back. I was shaving off seconds, all right.

I had a notebook stowed under the foot stretchers and I pulled it out after I slid off the boat's sliding seat onto the dock. I flattened the pages on my damp thighs to pencil in my new times, saw the improvement and shut the book fast, slid it in the waistband of my rowing trunks. I flipped the scull out of the water to my shoulders, then settled it on my head and waited while it dripped, balancing, my body the fulcrum as the boat gently teeter-tottered against my scalp. Holding the boat steady with my left hand wrapped around a rigger, I bent my knees and picked up the sculls with my right, straightened, and began the careful walk up to the boathouse. When I had negotiated the fifty-seven steps to the dark entrance, I aimed the bow into the straps hanging from the rafters within, then strapped in the stern. I popped open the deck plate and used a crusty, grease-stained towel to wipe the river water from the hull. I pulled the ropes that raised the boat to where it settled into a sliver of reflection in the gloom and tied up, still a little out of breath. I set the sculls upright in their wooden rack and pulled the great sliding doors shut.

As I steamed my way through the clear, early-morning cold of fall toward the school, my knees would start to ache by the time I reached the first buildings. The muscles in my back would tighten and my fingers would begin to burn. It didn't matter because, thinking about the times in that notebook, I believed I had an edge.

———

Fenton was one of the few high schools in the country specifically planned to be a rowing school. As I made my way from the boathouse toward the neo-Gothic school buildings, I could see the dark trees and deep green autumn grass beside the water. Although the river ran slow here, its current was still stronger than anything I had experienced in the Black Rock Canal in Niccalsetti where I grew up and where I learned the sport.

The magnificent Schoolhouse overlooked the section of river we raced upon. The Fenton School's founder had been a coxswain at Yale. Ignorant of, or more likely indifferent to, the muddy slog required to sink foundations in such soft valley soil, he had insisted that the school have this very vantage point beside the water. I could imagine my father walking along these old buildings thinking about this, toying with the idea of putting in a bid himself to drive down the reinforced rods you used to keep old piles like these standing. Busted-out buildings had kept him employed for twenty years in Niccalsetti, a place where they hadn't replaced the museums and reform schools and prisons for a century and a half. My father still employed stonemasons, skilled second-generation Italians and Brazilians who brought their wives' cold fettuccini and *feijoada* to the sites we worked.

After a quick shower and change, I hustled myself through the bright morning sun, my abraded hands held down, stiff and away from my body. The oar handles had torn into my palms, as usual, and I could feel the blisters forming. As I joined the throngs of students already on their way to breakfast I realized I was hungry. Ravenous. I could feel the sheaths of muscles over my gut, hard against my belt buckle. The smell of fresh cut wet grass and the trees just losing their leaves was almost overpowering. I stopped and looked up at the mountains behind the school, willing a sudden wave of nausea to pass. My lungs felt raw.

I was mesmerized by the trees exploding out of the valley, the river snaking slow and thoughtful by the buildings. I always regarded this beauty with a sense of awe. And also anger and disbelief. I'd spent four years slugging it out at the Niccalsetti

Senior School where a freight train ran right behind the one ragged football field we had. I'd never considered the existence of schools with this immense, unending, perfectly manicured splendor. It seemed to me that the entire season—all the trees and the grass and the perfection of the water—had been created just for us, the four hundred or so Fenton students who knew for sure they'd live forever.

They had been dropped off here two weeks before along with their trunks stuffed with catalogue clothes and their stereos and their cube fridges and duffel bags and backpacks and suitcases and computers, all of which had been hauled into the dorms by kids and parents with good forehands and firm handshakes. Bank accounts had been opened and topped off and dozens of credit cards had been handed out. Framed posters and Indian tapestries had been taped, nailed, stapled and fun-tacked to the dorm walls. Ratted furniture, passed down from generations of Fenton students, was hauled out of deep storage and deposited in rooms where it would get yet more battered and suffer the stains of hormone rages, late-night binges and furtive blow jobs. Once the parents were gone, the contraband had been unpacked: Ziploc bags of dope, pills, condoms, porno, video games, junk food; more exotic drugs, knives, bottles of pilfered booze. These kids would deposit their youth here, and then move on to other beautiful campuses.

I was still trying to find my way around the place, trying to accept that a high school could have so many corridors and buildings and sub-buildings. Senior year at a boarding school was a bad time to be an outsider and I was a postgraduate rower—a scholarship one at that. I only had nine months of this kind of living and then it would be snatched away again and I'd be sent back to where I came from unless I was very, very fast on the water. Which was just fine by me, because I was dead sure that I was the fastest thing these bastards were ever going to see.

I didn't even hear Connor Payne approach, quiet and lithe as a panther, and stand just behind me, out of my peripheral vision, in the fashionably wilted Brooks Brothers blazer, Fenton School Boat Club tie and pressed trousers he always wore to class. He fell into step soundlessly alongside me and waited for my reaction. My first thought, when I did notice him and tried to stay cool, was to picture him on the podium wearing his Junior Olympics medal in Belgium. How had he survived the Junior National training camp, skinny as he was? I'd seen pictures of him on the news board at home in the Black Rock Rowing Club's boathouse, his fists punching the sky in victory. In the newspaper clippings he had seemed bigger, darker, more menacing. I'd been at Fenton for two weeks and he hadn't even bothered to say hello. I'd learned enough about him to know that he'd choose his time to greet me, and of course it would be now, with my hands looking and feeling like they'd been put through a cheese grater. Like all predators, he had a nose for weakness and wounds.

"What did you do to your hands?" he asked, glancing down quickly and then away, as if I was already embarrassing him.

"I was out sculling today."

"Let's see."

I held them up and he grabbed the side of my right hand, studied it as if he were thinking of bidding on it. The pressure of his bony fingers made my eyes water. "I'm Connor Payne, by the way." He turned his attention back to the wreckage of my palms. "And you're Rob Carrey," he continued, "from Niccalsetti. I voted to have you brought here. It was you or some rower from Philadelphia who'd been caught stealing cars last spring." He continued to examine the red, sticky ridges of my hands methodically. "These hands are no problem. Bad, surely, but you're going to be fine." He let go and checked the watch inside his delicate wrist, a stainless Rolex on a leather band held together with a strip of pink electrical tape.

The sun caught him full in the face. His skin was impossibly pale. In profile his nose was almost a perfect triangle. He was perhaps an inch taller than me but I must have had him by ten pounds. He had long, sinewy limbs, a shock of blond hair—coarse hair, like an animal's—and his eyes were dark gray, animated only for a second as he looked around furtively, a fellow rule breaker. "Come to the Rowing Cottage and I'll fix you up."

I felt ambushed.

"Your high erg scores were the reason I voted for you, by the way. No one else's came close." He glanced at me. "Did you fake them? You did, right? I mean, obviously."

"I didn't even send them in. Back home, they make about six coaches sign the scores."

"It doesn't matter now. You're here. You'll have to pull them again for Channing, though. I don't care if you and your coach lied to us. What's a few seconds on an application if it gets you out of a place like Niccalsetti? I'd understand your lying to us. I'd respect it. I would." He nodded encouragingly.

"Want me to pull those scores right now?"

He shook his head, grinned. He had a salesman's smile. It made you like him even if you knew it would cost you.

My hunger momentarily forgotten, I followed him away from the waking school, across the grass that was wet enough that we made two trails as we went along. He didn't look at me as he ambled toward the small cottage, a cottage I'd passed every day, sculling. He pulled off his blazer and swung it over his shoulder. He was wearing four-hundred-dollar handmade shoes from England and they were getting covered in tiny grass clippings and stained with dew as he went. He surveyed the river and the buildings and the road into town and even the mountains beyond the school, inspecting it all as if he owned it. He moved with an easy, sleepy slouch you can't fake or copy. He was enjoying being at boarding school, enjoying every day of being a champion rower who was well known even in Niccalsetti, New York. Connor would be the first millionaire's kid I'd ever befriend, and probably the richest person I'd ever know. And the most gifted.

For almost everyone else at Fenton, things were different. After two weeks of confined dorm life you started to think about revolt and mutiny. The school was laid out like a little prison for privileged teenagers, and I don't think the parents who put up the tuition—a year's pay on my dad's work crew if you scored a bonus—knew it. I'd visited the Scadondawa Prison with my father to pick up workers who'd called him when they were paroled because they had nobody else to spend the fifty cents on. He had pointed out its design; even if the whole place burnt you could lock it down and come in on the ground and over the top with riot gear, soften the convicts up for the screws in their white helmets and face masks who would charge in, ready to bust skulls. You could seal us up in Fenton's dorms and bring down the cream of the east coast within a few minutes. Maybe those three dorms, each with a service road leading right into the quad, were constructed as they were so you could save the kids if there was a fire, but I doubted it. The guys who built those buildings knew who they were dealing with.

All that didn't apply to the captain of the rowing team. Connor lived by himself in the Rowing Cottage. It was the first house you came to when you rowed down the river from the boathouse, a sentry standing on stilts. With its stern white clapboard siding, its dark shutters and brooding, heavily sloped roof, it looked like an island retirement house for a whaling captain, the kind you find outside of Niccalsetti on Lake Erie, for the wives of customers who sent my father pictures of houses they'd seen in *Architectural Digest* with three-page spreads and titles like "Hideaway in Martha's Vineyard" or "Nantucket Dreaming." My father liked having his crew doing the demolition and grunt work on those houses, houses that were meant to be on the ocean but were instead perched on that frozen lakeshore, built by people rich by Niccalsetti standards but not rich enough to get out. My father never kidded himself about those jobs. Most of what he did would never be featured in a magazine and after we had dug the foundations, or ripped the guts out of some ramshackle heap, another company would come in with its own architect to build somebody's dream home. He would leave his card, CARREY'S JOIN-ERY, and maybe a few pictures of kitchen cupboards he'd built for the few clients who cared about that kind of work, one of them being my mother. Half the cupboards in those pictures were in our kitchen. He would wait for the call that never came from families who didn't care about wood, people who wanted brushed-steel kitchen appliances, pre-made fiberglass cupboards and granite counters. Day after day we'd load into the truck and drive to the next subcontracted demolition job or the next gutting. Never to build a kitchen or a bookcase. Still, my father refused to call himself a wrecker, or even a builder. Always a joiner, or a cabinetmaker. And no one he hired or begat ever questioned why.

2.

The Rowing Cottage was built right against the river and there was a sunken dock in front of it for the eight-man shells of long ago, before the school switched to fours. Connor's father had bunked here thirty years before, and his grandfather and great-grandfather decades before that. He could look at the faded photographs on the walls lining the stairs and see his ancestors' younger selves looking back at him; three generations of Payne manhood trapped in time. Connor's great-grandfather, Cyrus Payne, was hardly recognizable as human. His team picture was browned and creased, the names scrawled in purpling ink beneath featureless, sepia bodies standing before the same river we practiced upon.

If I had been in Connor's shoes I'd have taken those pictures down and hidden them in the attic crawl space, first thing. You could feel the heavy weight of expectation in them, the uncompromising demand of the past for an undefeated present. In another twenty-five or thirty years, Connor could fully expect to see his own son take his place on that wall. The Payne men all looked out at the world from behind their upturned oars with an identical arrogant gaze, a gaze they'd keep for the people who cleaned their stables, washed their cars and built their vacation homes.

After that day I never looked at those photos again.

Upstairs, the landing opened straight into the dilapidated living area. Connor's blue-and-gray captain's oar was mounted on pegs above the small bay window that overlooked the river. The sleek, carbon fiber oar looked strangely new in the antique surroundings of the cottage, which were war-room Spartan. The furniture consisted of an ancient couch hemorrhaging stuffing, two scuffed and mismatched tables and a worn cabinet with trophies and medals crammed inside. There was a threadbare rug that was most likely worth something once. He had hung a few pictures on the walls on nails that had been there for decades; they looked skew and small and out of place. The low ceiling had brown water stains blooming along its edges. A long-dead grandfather clock was propped up in the corner.

He sat me down on the window seat and I looked directly out onto the water, which reflected the morning sun on my torn palms. A heavy layer of dust covered the windowsill along with a few mummifying summer flies. Whistling tunelessly, Connor ducked into the small bathroom opposite his own, monkish bedroom and brought back the instruments of torture: a razor, a brown bottle of rubbing alcohol, nail scissors and a Zippo lighter. He dragged the smaller table over to us. The wooden oar handles had sucked the moisture from my palms and scraped away the dead, soft flesh. My fingers were burned, reddened and blistered. The heels of my palms would be split soon and the thin bones of the hands themselves would ignite into phosphorous sticks.

Connor shook his head, eyes down on my palms. His face looked almost translucent, the bones under his eyes and along his jaw oddly feminine. He flicked the lighter, held the edge of the paper-thin razor blade directly into the flame until it glowed. I could smell the carbon blackening the steel. He snapped the lighter shut. "We'll do the right hand first. That's the worst." He found the biggest blister on the middle finger and carefully positioned the blade over the exact center. He sighted it, then shook his head. "I can't see. Hold your hand closer to the window."

"Just do it."

He smiled, amused. "Getting scared, Carrey?"

"You think I haven't done this before?" I took a sharp breath.

"You rowed well today. Really. I watched you coming back down the river. Did you make it to the covered bridge?"

"Almost." I grit my teeth and looked up at him, trying to ignore the hot edge of that razor hovering over my fingers.

"Nice. I haven't been out since I came back to school."

He sliced into the soft belly of the first blister and I felt the skin contract with his touch and the heat. A tiny puddle of clear, sweet-smelling pus drooled out around the wound. He quickly put the blade down on the desk and snatched up the brown plastic bottle of rubbing alcohol. He poured a few drops over the hole in my hand and I ground my teeth through the chemical freeze that made my fingers curl. I had to hold my hand still with the other. He looked up at me. "You're not going to throw up, are you? If you do, do it out the window."

I forced myself to look away from the red hole in my hand. I focused on the trophy case moldering by the bedroom, counted the cups over the Henley plates and the medals sitting in pools of decaying ribbon. I stopped when I got to thirty and then started into the brass hardware and the plaques, some of which were piled next to the case, waiting their turn. The FSBC hoard. The alcohol fumes were making my eyes mist over. Connor leaned farther over my hands. "Did I slice the skin below?"

"I don't think so."

"It looks like it hurts." He said it with what sounded like satisfaction. He picked up a cotton swab, held it like a pencil, and carefully daubed away the open blister's germs. He put the nail scissors to the flame of the lighter and began snipping away the damp flaps around the cut. Soft white caterpillars of dead skin floated to the desk below us, where they curled. He patted the open blister with alcohol again and I bit my lip through the second burn. Four more blisters to go on my right hand, but he was working quickly and expertly.

He drew the blade across the next blister and I wanted to howl as it split open. "Channing was once the best coach in New England. He could have coached at Harvard. Exeter and Andover wanted him. He had a firm offer from Dartmouth five years ago. Now, I doubt he could move if he wanted to. He hasn't won the Warwick Race in five years, hasn't gone to Henley in six. The alumni aren't happy about it, of course. But he's good. He's always had winning seasons, but Fenton hasn't had such a dry run in the school's history. Warwick's really upped its game and we just haven't had the right combination of rowers." Connor burst the last two blisters one after the other—*pop, pop*—I swore I could hear it. He put the blade next to the clippers on the desk and made me make a fist. "Does that feel all right? It feels like your hands are in ice if your blisters are getting infected."

"I know. I'm fine." But I could feel the pain now, hot and strong.

He switched his attention to my left hand. Although the pain was not nearly as bad, I had to force myself to swallow the bile that kept rising in my throat. I had cauterized my own blisters at least a hundred times—all rowers routinely perform this minor surgery—but had never shared the ritual. It was an uncomfortably intimate experience.

"Done. I won't bandage them; they need to dry out. Don't get them dirty. You'll be okay for tomorrow."

I cleared my throat, but could not bring myself to actually thank him. It was taking all I had not to look at my hands. They felt as if they were on fire.

"You should know something. The Harvard coach called

Channing asking about you. One good thing about Channing is he's friends with that coach. They were on the same freshman crew, you know, like, two hundred years ago."

He knew he had me. You listen to that kind of thing when you train alone. You like to hear people are talking about you.

"You understand that Harvard only cares how you do in the God Four, right?"

"The God Four? You mean the varsity four—first boat?"

"Yes. It's called the God Four because for a long time God himself couldn't beat us—this was years ago, obviously. The name's stuck, though." He nodded as if confirming something to himself, then turned to me. "You can row out there in the single all you want, but you need to prove yourself in the four."

"Prove myself in the *four*? Why?"

"I told you—we haven't beaten Warwick School for *five years*. That's the most important thing for you to think about right now. We go to the National Champs no matter what, but that takes place at the end of the year—*after* the colleges send out acceptances. So Harvard and the other schools look at the Warwick Race instead." He nodded toward the stairwell. "My family has seven Harvard grads, dead and alive, who have rowed against Warwick and beaten them. It's all I've heard about for the last ten fucking years of my life. I've lost against them for the last three years and it's not happening again, believe me. Now I'm captain and we're going to win. And I guarantee Harvard will know about it two minutes after we crush Warwick."

"Well, good luck with that, Connor. Really. But I don't get what all this has to do with me. I'm a sculler. I don't row in a team and I can't afford to go to Harvard."

"You don't *get* what all this has to do with you?" He looked genuinely nonplussed. "The only reason you're here is to row in the four. Why else? I've watched you. You have a self-taught form, no finesse. But you've got the power we need." He grinned.

I could feel the blood rushing to my fingers. "I've won a lot of medals rowing with no finesse. You don't understand. I'm not rowing with three other preppy kids. Or dragging some coxswain down a race course."

"You should see your face. You look ready to hit me."

"I came to Fenton to scull. I'm a sculler. A sculler who wins. I don't want to relearn this sport and lose with your team, no disrespect."

"You really *don't* get it." He laughed. "You don't get it at all."

"Get what?"

"The point of the Warwick Race. It's not . . . you know . . . just another race. It's how they select the freshman crew at Harvard. Do I need to paint you a picture? Channing and the coach are old friends. Do you think there's some kind of, I don't know, *selection camp* for Ivy League rowers in high school? If we win this race, we all get in. The whole team. That's their deal."

"Channing thinks you're that good? What's so different about this year? Who are the other rowers?"

"He has me and Chris Wadsworth and John Perry. And Ruth Anderson, that chick in your chemistry class who's the coxswain. And now he's found *you*. And, yes, he thinks we're good."

Everyone knew John aka "Jumbo" Perry. He was the noseguard on the football team, one of those kids who looked like a hit man even when he was wearing a letter jacket. Wadsworth was from Maine and hung out with the squash jocks. I didn't know he rowed. As for Ruth Anderson . . .

"We all go to Harvard, just like that? After an eight-minute race?"

"Channing and the coach cooked this up years ago. They have a gentleman's agreement. That's the way it works. I can't believe nobody told you all this."

"Well they didn't. And what's the deal, by the way, if you lose this great race—again—this race you haven't been able to win in five years? What happens then? Let me take a guess. All of you guys go to college anyway and I get sent home, and thanks for the memories. What about our grades and SAT's and all that?"

"You mean does the coaching staff at Harvard care if you delivered newspapers in Niccalsetti and sang in the choir and know how to do the algebra on the SAT? No. Not when they are dealing with a kid who can beat the Warwick boat. Maybe they'll give you special classes or something if you are really, you know, like, *primitively* dumb. God knows I'll need them. Channing called his buddy and told him that things may finally change this year and that Warwick is going to face a harsh challenge. He said he'll watch with interest."

"That's it? He'll *watch with interest*? That's not much of a guarantee."

"They don't put agreements like this in writing, Carrey."

"I wouldn't believe it if they did."

"Carrey, win the race and you'll be a blue-chip recruit from Niccalsetti, New York, who broke Warwick's winning streak. They don't expect you to have much money. They have a few billion lying around to help you out."

"A few billion."

"This deal with Harvard is common knowledge around here, Carrey. Ask Ruth. Ask Wadsworth, or even Perry, who, if he doesn't win, will probably have to go to trade school. Or maybe prison."

It was time for class. He stood in front of me with that grin on his face. The kid was already used to telling people what to do. Standing in his own house in high school, with his earnest face and his expensive, ruined shoes and oppressive pictures on the wall.

"Want to hear something ironic?"

"What?"

"Half the kids Harvard accepts blow them off. Ruth is all about Yale and she has the grades, too. Wadsworth already wants to go to some dinky school like Williams or whatever. It would be you, me and Perry from our crew. We could share a room on the Yard."

"What yard?"

"Nice. Classic. You'll figure it out."

"So just answer my question."

"What question?" He waited.

"What happens if we lose to this superboat from Warwick? Then what?"

Connor grinned at me again, like he'd taken the serve off me on the tennis court. His was the safety of a kid with generations of Harvard-educated men behind him whose money and power would protect him from the things that struck down the rest of us mortals. "I haven't given it any thought. If you think about things like that, they tend to happen."

My hands were really burning. It was getting hard to hide it. I wanted to scream. I'd been told that one year at Fenton would open doors for me. That's what my father said again and again on the rides back from the site over the summer. My coach at the Black Rock Rowing Club told me the same thing: one year at Fenton and you can write your own ticket. But I hadn't heard about the Warwick Race and what it meant until now. The Warwick Race results were engraved on a long wooden plaque in the dining hall, above the headmaster's table, like homage to crews lost in battle. I should have realized their significance, but you can't spend your whole life reading plaques.

"I'm not rowing in the race, Connor. I'm going to scull and kick ass and then we'll see what coach is interested in what rower. You can take your chances with your friends. I don't have a dog in this fight."

"Rob, how can I put this so you'll understand? The God Four is the top boat in this school. There is no sculling program. You row in the God Four against Warwick, if we select you, or you row in the JV. Or you can play baseball. Or foosball. But Channing won't let you row one race in that scull. Not one."

"We'll see."

"We will *not* see. Because Channing is the coach and I'm the captain of this team and this is how the school does things and—"

"Hey Connor, you know what? Fuck you, fuck your school and fuck the Warwick Race. How about that?"

I tried to elbow my way around him in that close room. He made a quick sidestep to block me, surprised that somebody would give up an audience with him so easily. I just wanted to shove him aside but I wound up running into him, and the air whistled out of his lungs. He stood his ground, managed to push me back against the wall with his shoulder, an instinctive reflex to put me back where I had been standing, back in my place.

My right hand balled into a fist and the pain was horrible. It occurred to me that the close warm air in there, the stink of alcohol combined with my own wounds and anger and hunger, was going to make me puke after all. Or pass out.

"Carrey, if you walk out on me I'll blackball you and you can go back to wherever they found you."

Then I really did try to push him aside and at the same time he tried to hit me, swung at me hard enough so that he just missed when I stepped back and swatted him, going for the face, but hitting him in the neck with the side of my hand, an oblique karate chop that sent liquid fire up my wrists. He struck me in the chest and it was hard enough to hurt and I lowered my shoulder and drove it into him, pushed him off his feet. We danced awkwardly across the room, into the banister, pressed close, face-to-face. "Carrey, cut it out," he managed to gurgle, and there was that one second of satisfaction when I heard panic in his voice.

But it wasn't me he was frightened of.

We were shoved up against a one-hundred-year-old banister that cracked under our weight, then shattered in an explosion of splintered wood. We fell into space along with the wreckage of the railing and there was a moment of stomach-clutching descent before we smashed into the stairs, sweeping off the photos lining the walls in a shower of glass and paper, the two of us twirling downward to land in a bloody heap at the bottom, me crammed against the door and Connor against the last two stairs. I pushed myself away from him gingerly.

The stairs were littered with the remains of the banister, and Connor had been cut up pretty bad on the way down. His forearms were covered with bleeding scratches and there was a nasty-looking tear behind his ear. For that matter I would be carrying bruises with me for weeks. I watched him pull himself up to his feet and lean against the wall. His teeth were reddened and he had to steady himself against the stairs. I tried to get to my feet and felt the skin against my ribs stretch. Then he surprised me. He looked at me and said, "Are you all right?"

I nodded. "You?" I doubted I would have taken that fall without breaking something.

"You almost broke my neck." He said it with a sense of wonder. Admiration. "That was fast."

"I didn't want to break your neck, I had no idea this thing was going to—"

"Let's hope you can react that fast on the water." He brushed the dirt and paint and shards of dried wood and glass off his shirt.

And then I puked. I spat up water and bile and what looked like blood, kneeling over the wreckage and dust. Connor stepped back and waited until I was done. He helped me to my feet and I closed my eyes against the rush of blood from my guts to my brain. Then he said, "Keep this quiet. If Channing finds out, we've had it."

But it was too late. Mr. Roberts, who was on duty that morning, knocked once and opened the door into the tiny foyer where we were standing. He was one of the geometry teachers, short and blinking in a wrinkled corduroy suit he wore even on that sweaty fall day. We loomed over him out of the mess. He took in

Connor's bloody mouth, ear and arms, my ripped clothing and the utter destruction of the banister and pictures scattered and crushed all over the stairs. The sour reek of my vomit made him step back out into the driveway. We both took the minute he gave us to catch our breath, but Connor didn't say anything else to me. He was too busy blotting the blood off his perfect teeth. Fifteen minutes later I was in the dean's office with Connor, and ten minutes after that I was on my way to first period, with a note calling for twenty hours of punishment work to do, over two weeks, after school.

Later I was told Connor had paid for the damage to the stairs himself. He had the banister restored perfectly, hired a company from Hartford to do the work. He sent out all the pictures to be reframed as well, and paid for it with a personal check. He never mentioned any of it to me at all. I heard it from some kid on the freshman club team who didn't believe I'd actually hit Connor Payne in the face.

3.

I walked through the orange arrival halls of Kennedy in a dazed, jet-lagged fog, past the tired airline crew and into the guts of the building. I rode the escalator down past the jaded, post-9/11 security and then stood in line with my fellow travelers under the cameras budding out of the low ceiling above the corrals leading to the customs desk. I'm the type of person customs agents, maître d's, bouncers and doormen don't seem to like. I get detained, I get things confiscated, I get thrown out, declined. Carolyn once told me, "It's because you always look like you're ready to hit people. Even bartenders don't like you. Just relax, can you do that?"

When it was my turn for inspection the wired-down-tight customs officer took a look at all the stamps in my passport and gave me a glance, this man possibly a year older than me, hyperalert for this time of day. He was in short sleeves, his badge hanging off his breast pocket. "You've been in and out of the country a few times," he said. He paid special attention to the stamps from Rwanda and Uganda. He squinted at the crude signatures under the stamps from Zambia.

"I've been working as a freelancer." I half smiled, tried to be ingratiating.

"What line of work?"

"Television. Documentary films."

He just looked at me, professionally blank. I added, "You know. Video. TV."

He glanced at the passport and the clearance material again, like he was looking at a bad poker hand. Then he pushed it back to me. "Make sure you clear your baggage, especially any electronic goods. Welcome home."

And with that I was through to baggage collection, where I picked up my overweight bags that had been vomited onto the carousel. Including my carry-on, I had four heavy Pelicans and a duffel. I pushed it all on two trollies to a makeshift table where two customs agents, a man and a woman, both in white gloves like old-time traffic cops, first opened my carry-on case to reveal my shoot tapes lined up in a row, each one of them plastic wrapped. The inspectors examined all of the Beta tapes and mini-DV tapes, then the separate Beta SP camera and the Canon XL. Everything else was locked up in Cape Town—all the lights, the boom, the zeppelin, the fuzzies and the small edit suite. And a cage full of diving gear that took up the entire front room of the apartment.

"Haven't seen a Betamax tape in a while," the woman agent commented.

"They're for professional playback."

"Yeah, that's right, uh-huh?" She had stout, no-nonsense forearms and she was carrying a Beretta 9 mm high on her hip, clear and accessible. "What would I see on these tapes?"

"Sea life."

"Do you have journalist credentials?"

"Do you need to see them?"

"I would appreciate that, sir."

I showed her what I had. It wasn't much, just a manila folder with a few printed e-mails, an ID and a fax from Washington. They could call *National Geographic* if they wanted to and confirm who I was if my work rang any alarm bells. She went over each paper, running down the lines with her finger, her lips pursed. "What exactly were you filming?"

"Sharks and game fish."

"Nothing that might be politically sensitive or inflammatory?"

Not unless one of those Zambezi sharks had a thing against Americans, I thought, but shook my head. I was too tired to get into an argument about freedom of speech and artistic expression. I had interviews in there with some people making fairly general negative statements about the propensity of rich American tourists to come to South Africa and Kenya wanting to fish a threatened species like the black marlin. The woman, who was obviously in charge, looked over the papers and then back at the tapes again as if she was considering opening up a few, then thought better of it. She thanked me and the duo moved on their way, leaving me to rewrap everything and lock up the cases.

I pushed one trolley ahead of me and pulled the other along behind me and came out through the customs tunnel into the drab receiving area, to be put on display for the inspection of the people crowded against metal barriers waiting for passengers. Families. A tour group leader in a loud yellow shirt hanging over his black trousers. Two skulking limo drivers in tight mortician garb doing some scavenging. I scanned the faces because maybe Carolyn would be out there. I told myself it was possible she could have fired up the Jeep and come out to greet me. She'd be in the waiting throng somewhere, ready to put her arms around me.

But I didn't waste too much time looking.

Instead, I made my way out to the taxi ranks alone, chose a yellow and green station wagon that I managed to fill and sat in the back waiting to see that butchered skyline as the car chugged out of the rank. The driver was rotund, slack jawed and ashen, wearing a black turban. He had slapped a bumper sticker on the dash that read, "I AM A SIKH, GOD BLESS *AMERICA*."

New York was its mammoth self, dark and grimy. The roads to its innards were packed with American cars and Americans on the way to work. American billboards glowered down at me. As we crossed the Williamsburg Bridge the city loomed up as we circled onto the roadway, the bridge bigger than almost anything in Africa, built on a huge scale like the city itself, like the country.

Looking out over the water I felt a rush of vertigo before we plunged into the Lower East Side, toward the loft on Broome Street. By the time we got there, I was nodding off. It was early summer, already hot and steamy, and the wide street in front of the building was clogged with people. The driver and I unloaded my luggage in front of the cavernous door to the warehouse where Carolyn and I lived.

"You travel heavy," the driver puffed accusingly, his round face wet with sweat.

"Just wait a second while I make sure somebody's home, okay?"

"We wait too long I turn back on the meter."

I pressed the buzzer and Carolyn's voice crackled though the intercom instantly. "Rob?"

Maybe she had been looking out the window, watching the traffic, anticipating my taxi, I thought. "I'm back." My voice sounded thick and strange.

"Hang on." An exasperated sigh.

I handed the driver a fifty and watched him heave open the door to the station wagon and churn the window down. He whipped the car into the surly, crawling traffic and acrid smoke burped out of the exhaust when he mashed the gas. Then the freight elevator doors groaned open—a steel wall of graffiti sliding into the building—and I horsed the bags in, scraped the plastic cases on the hot cement and pushed myself in on top of it all.

The loft was on the fifth floor of a warehouse that had been partially renovated. Below us we had a real, honest-to-God sweatshop; illegal Asian immigrants working sewing machines twenty-four hours a day, all with a wonderful view of Teddy Roosevelt's old police station. I could hear the machinery and the shouts in there as the elevator lumbered upward to the wooden barn doors that opened into her apartment, Carolyn waiting there with her tentative hug and her diplomatic smile. She stepped halfway into the elevator and picked up the tape case, left the rest for me. "You look like death," she said, sighing, and gently touching my wrist, as if trying to steady me. *You look exhausted*, I thought, *but still so beautiful*. She kissed me, a formal touch of her lips against mine. There was the brief press of her hipbone against my leg and then she was away before I could pull her to me. She stood against the elevator doors while I slid everything else onto the wooden floors, the silence of the apartment an unexpected relief.

"I made coffee," she announced. "And bought croissants and the *New York Times*, if you want to read." She pointed to the wide kitchen area where a bowl of daisies, surely from Confucius Flowers down the street, was bursting into color. She was wearing a white oxford shirt that hugged her too tightly to be mine, cargo pants and one of the malachite necklaces she'd bought when we first went to South Africa. Her rhinestone ring matched it, and her blond hair was pulled back from her face. She seemed smaller. Carolyn pushed five ten in her socks, and she was almost my height in heels. She'd obviously been up for a few hours; the loft smelled of coffee and the cigarette she'd smoked to prepare herself for my grand entrance. She had her contacts in, which possibly was a good sign, although when I thought of her I pictured her wearing her new, wire-rimmed glasses that made her look older and wiser than she was. She'd lost weight while I was away. It didn't suit her. It was weight loss from being up too late and not eating. She looked me over as if I was a paying guest. She seemed ready to kick me out right away if I decided to pick up where we had left off six weeks before, already irritated by the mess I had made in the living room. "Do you want to sleep?"

"Is that a trick question?"

"I thought you would. Was the flight bad?"

"Just long. Not crowded."

"I wondered if they would hassle you at customs again."

"They definitely considered it. It's a new world."

She looked me up and down one last time. I should have reached for her then. She would have let me. But I hesitated, and the moment was gone. "Have a shower and get some sleep. Give me the tapes and I can start digitizing them. Have you done anything with the shoot tapes?"

"They're in the black Pelican, in pretty much the same order the customs woman left them."

"How many hours?"

"Twenty, I think." I flipped open the case and pulled out the tapes, brought them over to her editing table, the Mac already on, the Beta player humming in the tower.

"We don't have much time. It may be a day lost to jet lag for you but it's another day at the office for me. Go on. Take a shower." She hadn't moved from the door. "Change your clothes. Have something to eat and go to bed." She waved at the partition under the fogged, warehouse windows. Behind it lay the sleeping area, you couldn't call it a bedroom. "Take my bed, okay? We'll figure everything out later. I don't want to tiptoe around you all morning while I do this."

"It's *your* bed now?"

"Mine when you moved in, mine when you move out. Are we doing this now?"

I raised my palms in surrender.

She helped me lug all of my things to the section of the studio where we used to sleep together. I removed my leather shaving kit from my briefcase and went to the industrial sliding door of the bathroom. "I'll help you sort through the tapes later."

"Did you number them?"

"You know I numbered them, Car."

"I'll get into it now. Go. Seriously. You stink."

She'd laid out a freshly laundered, folded towel on the toilet lid. Hers hung primly in the middle of the long rail we had once both shared. She'd put down a bath mat, but that was not hospitality, that was prudence. I stepped into the cavernous shower that had been built for two by the previous owner—we'd found that convenient, once—and showered in lonely silence. The hot water streaming down my back felt obscenely luxurious, and I had to hold on to the brushed metal handle over the soap alcove to stop my knees from buckling. I cranked the heat up as hard as it would go and felt dizzy in the furious gush, then shut off the water. I stepped out into the haze of steam. I shaved and wrapped my towel around my waist and padded back out into the studio, where she was already busy across the room at the computer, her back to me, watching the screen as the machine digitized six weeks of work.

"I have the shot list in my briefcase," I said, stoned from the humidity in the bathroom.

"That would help. Do you have the time codes of the interviews?"

"Yeah, yeah. Printed. I have them on the flash disk, too. Hang on." I sat on the bed, lost the towel and slipped on some shorts. I ruffled through the case, found a sheaf of notes, then lay back on the pillow and started pawing through them. And fell fast asleep.

———

It was dark out when I opened my eyes. Carolyn was covering me with the duvet when I woke up. She, who had slept beside me in this bed naked or close to it for five years was wearing a baggy white T-shirt and white boxers. My boxers, yet another piece of clothing she'd colonized, along with my cashmere coat, numerous hats, sweaters and a pair of mirrored sunglasses.

"What time is it?"

"It's eleven at night. Your body clock's going to be a mess."

"You should have woken me up."

"I tried. You were a ton of bricks."

I lay there listening to somebody downstairs moving something heavy and metal across the floor. A television was on somewhere; a buzz of noise, a pause, a buzz.

She lay down beside me. "The tapes are good. What I've seen. I skipped around. The footage is really . . . yeah . . . top notch."

"I hope they think so at the channel."

"They will."

I rolled over on my side and looked at her, reached out and touched her face and she blinked. She took my hand and held it between us in a neutral soul brother handshake. "The water was cloudy in some of the shark sequences but I've already seen the shots we can use. It's better than we could have hoped for. Really."

I pulled myself closer to her and she didn't move away. I went to kiss her and she put her hands up, shielded herself. "No, Rob. Don't."

She rolled over in the bed and turned off the light, plunged us into the cold, blue glow of the sleepy city, the sounds of the cars and the trucks outside new and unfamiliar and invasive after weeks on the Durban coast. I looked at the outline of her neck in the dark, and then came closer, pressed myself against her and rested my hand on her waist. She shifted slightly, quickly, claimed her half of the bed, more than her half of the quilt. "You get to sleep here just for tonight. Tomorrow you're couching it. We have things we need to talk about, Rob. So keep that hand where it is."

Silence reigned.

Then she exhaled heavily. "If you do that again you'll be on the couch right now. I'm not kidding. You are *so* not getting laid tonight."

I rolled over on my back and looked up into the darkness. I closed my eyes and willed sleep to return. I listened to the sounds of the loft. The push-out window creaked, and the faucet dripped. Water slushed through the pipes in the wall. The dishwasher whirred and hummed in the kitchen. The fridge kicked on, kicked off. A siren began to whine a block away. These city sounds. These American sounds.

She yawned and then said, "You were talking in your sleep, by the way."

"What was I saying?"

"Something about rowing."

"What about it?"

"I don't know." She rocked back and forth, claimed yet more of the duvet from me. "You were going on about somebody named Channing. Who's he?"

I smiled in the dark. Then I thought about Perry and his letter and stopped smiling. "It's a long story, Car. Go to sleep."

4.

The boathouse looked like a barn with an elongated top floor. It stood back from the river and was built to appear intimidating. The heavy outside sliding doors opened to the boats and the oars and you walked by them to get to another set of sliding doors that led to the tanks—two stagnant troughs of water with sliding seats and outriggers next to them. Here was where a rower's form was hammered into him, where unforgiving mirrors reflected back every weakness in a place that smelled of dankness and mold and waterborne rot. There was only one window, high up and filthy, that barely let in any light. The way up to the attic rooms was easy to miss, just a simple wooden door, like a cabinet door, that opened to a narrow set of stairs.

I arrived early, before the others, to the first meeting of FSBC to get my bearings and not look like such a newcomer. At first I thought that the ergometers and weight machines would be up here, but soon figured out they were in the basement, a sequestered hell I would come to know all too well. The top floor consisted of the meeting room, such as it was, and Channing's office. His real office. He had a carrel in the English department, but this was where he existed. The office looked over the river, and it was the kind of functional room you'd find in an army HQ. A wooden desk. A longer table near the desk. A computer that Channing obviously never turned on, steel filing cabinets. Pictures of the English Henley, banners, posters of races gone by and a crimson and white wooden oar suspended in the darkness—Channing's captain's oar from Harvard. The pictures and trophies in one of the cabinets looked neglected. He had one entire shelf just for tools. And above and around that, books. Hundreds of them. Huddled black paperbacks, waterlogged leather-bound classics, yellowing cloth-bounds, worn hardcovers. The wisdom of the ages moldering away.

I looked, but didn't dare step inside. Amazingly, his office door just hung open. I had come from a school where everything was locked against the students; offices were protected by steel-clad doors and teachers walked the hallways with keys around their necks. Feared and hated as he was, it probably never occurred to Channing that a student might be insane enough to invade his personal space.

Nothing in his office, aside from the books and that oar, said anything about Channing himself or indicated he had a life outside the school. There were plenty of rumors. One was that he had been a criminal lawyer before Fenton and had quit for any of a thousand reasons: a client had committed suicide, he had insulted his boss, he'd been sued, he'd been disbarred. He lived off campus in an old white farmhouse—that was a fact—and his wife from the scumbag lawyer days was long gone. That was another fact. He had inhabited that office for thirty years and had either never thought to, or purposefully declined to, put anything personal in there.

The meeting room was all raw timber and rising damp and had the distinct feel of a fortress about it. It seemed intentionally stripped of any extravagance and was the kind of room that was always hot and close in the summer and bitterly cold in the winter. Uncomfortable by design, it had been built using the same architectural philosophy that went into constructing a monastery, or an interrogation room.

John Perry, Chris Wadsworth, Ruth Anderson and Connor came stomping up the stairs for the inaugural meeting. No one said anything to me, but Connor lifted his chin in acknowledgment when he saw me. His mouth was still swollen from our fall and his torn ear looked crusty and painful. I unconsciously touched my bruised ribs. They were followed by the returning JV four and about a dozen more kids who were going to try to make the team in the spring—sophomores and hopeful juniors from the club boats who only rowed at a recreational level, not competitively against other schools. Other students wanted to be here, but Channing was only interested in the contenders for the JV and Varsity boats. Mid-September and he was already calling us together for a sport that wouldn't start officially until March. For top-level rowers, there was no off-season. Crew was always a reality.

When Channing stalked in, rumpled, mistrustful and radiating contempt, the room quieted down immediately. He looked like something that had stood up to the elements too long and was starting to fall apart. He was the best coach at Fenton. And the most despised. The way he looked at you, you knew he wasn't missing anything. He was tall, still limber and easy in his movements for his age, which must have been early sixties. He taught a vicious AP English class and was a master of the pop quiz and the brutal exam.

He slapped his briefcase down on the long desk at the front of the room and removed his sheaf of notes, thumbed them for a full minute while he gathered his thoughts and made us sit there scratching, coughing, trying not to look at one another. That torn bouquet of yellow legal-sized papers had been stapled together enough times so the top corner looked like it had been chewed. He held these notes by his side while we waited and I could see lines and lines of his penciled handwriting. Even I could see he carried those notes just for show. They hadn't made the school big enough for him. And so we looked at Mr. Charles Channing and he looked back at us and beyond us to the world outside the boathouse and I'm not sure which he liked less.

Seated in a folding metal chair in front of Channing's desk, facing us, was Ruth Anderson, the coxswain of the God Four and the first girl to make the team ever, flouting eighty years of history. She was small, and her hands and wrists were those of an aristocrat; blue veined and bony. The bird-wing ridges of her collar bones were prominent and she had long, dark, feline hair. That year she weighed ninety pounds during the winter and dropped to eighty-four in the racing season. Connor sat next to her and the message was clear. Only the two of them had secure seats on the team. The rest of us would have to fight for them. Nothing was guaranteed.

Channing finally cleared his throat and set the notes down on the table. The gangling bodies in the room hunched forward, as if we were at the start of a session of prayer to a higher power. He began.

"I've called you together to remind you of some of the things you might consider before we gear up for the spring term. It is right that I let the students from the club boats understand how we work here. Some of you may think this meeting is premature. I assure you, it is not."

No other teacher talked like Channing. It took me weeks to realize that he was not being ironic, that this was really the way he spoke. His was the dialect of a lost aristocracy.

He sighed, glanced at Connor and Ruth, rested his eyes on me. "Understand that the first boat at Fenton is a four-man shell

with cox. As is the second boat. There are no eights, as there are
in the clubs." The kids from the club boats—the lower orders—
looked on without reaction. They knew this. So did the returners. I wondered if this homily was for my benefit.

"This means there are only eight places in the Fenton School
Boat Club. One club rower will be named our spare, but will not
row with us. So if you do want to make this team, you will have
to compete against one another."

I raised my hand as he said this and he smiled. "We should
also get to know Mr. Robert Carrey. Whom I had almost forgotten. Please stand, Mr. Carrey. Let's see you."

I stood up and he pulled his spectacles from his jacket pocket.
"Mr. Carrey is one of this year's PG recruits and hails from Nic-
calsetti, New York. He is a single sculler, a very successful one.
We believe this has prepared him well for rowing in a four."

"That's just it, Coach. It has not," I said.

Channing paused and the room tensed. "Excuse me, Carrey?"

"Rowing in a single is not good preparation for rowing in a
four, Mr. Channing. I don't know anything about rowing in a
four."

Channing straightened combatively. "Is that so, Mr. Carrey?
Could this be an oversight, do you suppose? Let us see. In a single,
a sculler—an oarsman—uses two oars. But in a four, the rower
uses one large oar. This is the essential difference. Yes, I can see
how this might be initially difficult for you to adjust to."

"I didn't mean—"

"No, no, please, this is important. In a four, the coxswain
steers from the stern and the oarsmen each have one oar. We also
do not row pairs by the way. Students flip pairs, you see, and
drown, which is always irritating. Fours are more stable."

"Nobody told me this before and I—"

"Nobody *told* you that we only row fours at Fenton? Even
after you were *accepted*?" And then I knew for sure he had
prepared this. That Connor had told him about our fight and

that Channing meant to finish the argument once and for all. I'd walked right into it.

"Carrey, did you not carefully consult the admission package that was sent to you *to learn what kind of boats were rowed here at Fenton*? Or call the school to enquire? Or examine the school catalogue, which we print at great expense and send out to anyone who asks for it? I am quite sure there are only pictures of fours in that catalogue. We do mention this little affectation of ours. Very clearly."

I waited. I could feel the blood rushing to my head and my hands and willed myself to calm down, to not blow up and have a tantrum. He sensed it and prepared himself.

"Coach, the letter that was sent to me said that I was accepted because of my wins in the single. That was very clear. I could even bring my own boat, it said."

"Well, I am glad we can clarify this for you, Carrey. You are *permitted* to row your single from time to time on my river, when I say so, but my top team is a *four*. It is referred to as the varsity four and some may call it the God Four but there is *only* the four. We have a JV four. We have a club four, yes, and an armada of eights for the clubs as well. But the varsity four is the *only* team that we offer up for competition at Fenton at the varsity level. Is this clear, now? Is there anything I have left out?"

"I won't row in a four." This came out almost as a whisper, because I was trying to keep my voice down.

Channing put a hand to his ear. "Excuse me?"

"I don't row in fours, Coach. I don't row with other people. I'm a single sculler."

"Carrey, I believe you mean you haven't *yet* rowed in a four. Do not be overly concerned. You can easily learn. We have faith in you. We believe you can make the transition from two oars to one and row as part of a crew. Connor Payne, for instance, is a fine single sculler, too, but he is also the stroke seat in the four. I assure you, this is not difficult. Sculling will be a boon."

"Coach, the problem is not me being *able* to do it. I don't *want* to learn to row with three kids I don't know. No offense, but that's not—"

"None taken, Carrey, none taken. Do you think you are offending *us*? You are only offending yourself. We are trying to clarify things for you."

"I'd like to race in the single."

He slammed his hand down on the table. "*In what race*, Carrey? Against *whom*? What boarding school will you race against? Shall we have a special race just for you?"

"I'm sorry, Mr. Channing, but I just don't want to row in the four."

"Then you are welcome to leave." Channing pointed at the narrow staircase. "There's the door, Carrey. Go. You can go right now. But I warn you if you leave this room, you will not be coming back." He said this mildly but he kept his eyes on me. I found myself scooping up my bag to leave and then forced myself to stop. Because Channing meant it. I knew it and everyone else in the room knew it, too.

"If you want to row with us, Carrey, you will have to learn to row in the four. This could be a good change for you. A welcome change. Many single scullers row in the team boats. It is expected. It is not difficult. So think carefully about your next move and *do not sit down*." He turned to the rest of the crew. "The God Four will again be facing Warwick this year."

He took a breath and visibly composed himself. Our exchange had rattled him. He began again. "Every year, as most of you know, we formally challenge Warwick School to a race. And for the last five years, to our perpetual shame, Fenton has failed to win." He said this in the same way he might announce that we had all been diagnosed with terminal cancer.

"For the benefit of those present who were . . . elsewhere . . . last year our disgrace took place at Warwick. This year we race at home and we will not, I repeat *not*, be humiliated on our own

river again. Channing waited while every rower shifted in his
seat. "As always, we face Warwick on the third Tuesday in
April. You should know that the FSBC alumni have made it clear
that they hope to see us win." Channing paused. "But they are
not us. They are not here. History does not wait for the verdict
upon them. All of them wish they had one more crack at victory
on the water against that hated place Warwick. This chance
is reserved for we few." Another pause. He was quite the show-
man. "Listen."

We listened. Outside, you could hear the shouts and whistles
on the fields around us, pulses of noise. "The armorers, accom-
plishing the knights, with busy hammers closing rivets up, give
dreadful note of preparation."

I had no idea what Channing was talking about, but I had the
sense of it.

"And preparation for rowing is indeed dreadful. Mr. Perry,
let's start with you."

John Perry was riding his chair backward. He sat like a
chained beast, his blue letter jacket buttoned precariously over
his bulk. He looked up at Channing with tiny blinking eyes.

"You *are* John Perry, yes?"

Perry looked at all of us for support and we looked back at
him. Connor interlaced his fingers behind his head and examined
Perry while Ruth looked politely away, at some spot on the floor
to my left.

"Coach?" Perry was flustered. "I mean . . . you know who I
am Mr. Channing—"

"John Perry from the losing first boat of last year? This is
you?"

Perry tried to smile. "Yeah, okay, it's me—"

"I ask because you look like his fatter, slower twin. Perry, you
are too heavy for my boat. Your task is to lose weight and become stronger and gain endurance. This does not mean eating

pizzas at the Fenton Pizza Garden or grappling with idiots from Taft on the football field."

Wadsworth snickered under his baseball cap. Seated in a window seat, he was framed by the late afternoon light, his legs dangling into space. Channing turned on him immediately. "Chris Wadsworth. Another survivor from the disastrous boat of last year. Have you been thinking how you will make amends? You have work to do."

He turned to the board and wrote the number 7 in the middle. "You have seven months, gentlemen—and lady—until the Tuesday race against Warwick School. Less than that until the season starts." He took off his glasses. "I cannot call formal practices until the spring but Mr. Payne and Ms. Anderson will be keeping track of who is working. This means that while I cannot *force* you to begin training now, I can *ask* that you start thinking about the fact that no rower's position here is secure and I can *urge* you to make every preparation necessary for what lies ahead. You will all be tested and some of you shall be found wanting."

He turned the full force of his gaze on me and I knew he was getting ready for his final delivery. "Carrey, you have never seen what awaits you this spring. You need to understand that right now you are just . . . the raw material. You are merely breathing potential. The tabula rasa where Fenton's history will be written. Did you seriously think we would tremble before your abilities? *You*, a PG mercenary who is already a disciplinary case two weeks into the start of the school year because—"

"Come on. That was not my fault, I—"

"We do not care to give hearing to your explanations or alibis, Carrey. We care about getting ready for a race that will define us. Will define you. We care about crossing the finish line ahead of the other boat. We care about winning. This is all we care about. And we cannot win if you are being disciplined, or if you have been expelled. So, Carrey, I ask that you be not afraid of greatness: some are born great, some achieve greatness and some have greatness thrust upon them. Don't query the form in which greatness comes. Am I clear?"

"Yeah."

"Yeah? Do you mean 'yea'? As in, 'Yea, though I walk through the valley of the shadow of death, I will fear no evil: for thou art with me; thy rod and thy staff they comfort me?'"

"Yes."

"No, Carrey. No. I offer none of you comfort. I offer you no protection from evil. This you will fashion yourself or be beaten. Opportunities for glory are flying around all of you like bullets. And some of you, Carrey, are crawling upon the ground with helmets on. Have you made your decision? We all await."

My head was spinning with rage. *Do it*, I thought. Leave this crap. Walk out the door.

I grit my teeth. Screw this for a laugh, as Wendy would say. Walk out.

Walk out and go . . . where?

Home?

I took a breath.

"I'll do it." And felt like I was betraying everything I'd come from and suffered through to stand there. A Judas for a bunch of prepsters.

"You will do what, exactly?"

"Try out for the four."

"And suffer the slings and arrows of outrageous fortune with the rest of us?"

"Whatever."

Triumphant, Channing stared at the others, all of them looking away from me as I stood there, defeated. "Seven months. Connor will be ensuring that you begin your preparations. Dismissed."

You never saw a room full of kids clear out so fast, all shoulders and gangly arms squeezing through the door and pounding down the stairs. Connor and Ruth conferred briefly then got up and left. I put my bag over my shoulder and started to follow.

Channing caught me at the door. "Mr. Carrey. A word."

Connor glanced back at me and grinned, shut the door behind him.

Channing put his glasses back on and it occurred to me they might also be a prop. He dug around in the mess of his briefcase and pulled out a folder, licked his thumb, opened it. He read for about three seconds to himself, then looked at me. "It says, in summary, Robert Carrey. PG student. Championship-level rower with decent grades. Hails from the Niccalsetti Senior School, an institution of learning I was unfamiliar with until you appeared here. Your grades are surprisingly high—are you hiding a brain from us, young Carrey?"

It was my turn to look out at the trees sloping up the sides of Mt. Algo and just breathe. There were millions of those trees. I was barely holding it together. It was a farce—being my age and dealing with this crazy old man.

"Mr. Carrey, a recent missive from our mutual friend the dean informs me you have been caught destroying school property and fighting with one of our associates in the Rowing Cottage."

"I tried to tell you. Connor deserved it. If you start in on me you might as well go get him, too."

"Connor Payne might have deserved it but you have both been punished for it. Did you deserve to be punished?"

"He was asking for it."

"Connor Payne asked you to hit him and you complied?"

"I didn't hit him, I just wanted him to get out of the way."

"Be that as it may, you now owe the school twenty hours of work, and you will be working for me. Off campus. I happen to need a painter. Can you paint?"

"I can paint."

"Are you sure? The school does offer free labor to its senior teachers but I have found in the past it is often not the most qualified or intelligent or diligent labor."

"I've painted stuff for my father since I was eight. If I finish early, will you let me out of whatever's left?"

"There will be plenty for you to do."

"All right. I get it."

"Meet me at my home at four next week on Monday, once you have recovered from your injuries sustained in your . . . altercation . . . with the captain of my first boat."

"What about Connor?"

"What about him?"

"Does he have to paint your house?"

"He does not. I am not his advisor. I have no idea what he will be doing to work off his hours. He may wind up raking leaves, or shoveling mulch, or cleaning bathrooms."

"I hope he gets the bathrooms."

"I shall keep you appraised."

"I'd hate to think you'd make me do a job like this because I'm a scholarship kid, Mr. Channing. Just to put me down."

"No, no, Carrey. Rest assured we'd have contempt for you even if you paid full fees."

"Does the school supply you with paints, too?"

"No. But I do have the use of its sandpaper and tools."

"Free labor and equipment."

"Teaching is notorious for its many benefits. This is why I entered the profession."

"I thought you used to be a lawyer. Plenty of perks there."

"You are misinformed."

"They say you got fired."

"Fired or disbarred? I never can keep track."

"Is it true?"

"With all this free labor and sandpaper and such at my disposal, Carrey, why would I ever consider the law as a profession? Meet me at my house on Monday. Four P.M. sharp. Wear your work clothes. Try not to assault anyone on your way."

"Where do you live?"

"Walk down River Road until you see a white house. Can you remember that?"

"I can."

"Good. Go. Learn."

5.

My father showed up at the school a day later than he was
supposed to, on the same Monday I had to start work at
Channing's. He arrived in his ten-year-old immaculate Ford
F-150, drove right to the boathouse doors and threw down the
brake. My scull was strapped to the truck bed, the stern sticking out. He had built a carrier for it himself, a padded cradle that
held the scull in place down the New York State Thruway. He
had taped the outriggers together and stowed them underneath
the boat and had made brackets for each oar that he could lock.
He had driven alone, left my mother behind to keep an eye on
my older brother and the house. When he arrived at the school
he jumped out and inspected the boat, no doubt the tenth time
he'd done it during the whole eight-hour drive. Then he walked
over to the dean's office and handed over the balance of the tuition my scholarship didn't pay for, in cash, and made the dean,
Mr. Owen, make up a receipt then and there.

When I got out to the boathouse, my father was looking down
at the riggerless scull, long and sleek and green, tied with nylon
belting against its cradle. He ran his finger over the top. "I should

have found a tarp for her but nothing fit from the workshop and I didn't have time. Didn't want it flapping around back there either. I figured you put anything on a coat of varnish slick as that, you wind up scratching it."

I touched the bottom of the scull, the boat representing a cool month of mowing his lawn and lugging wood up from the lumber yard every morning in my brother's station wagon and hauling it into his shop out back of the house, then sweeping out the scrap and bagging the off-cuts while he and Tom worked. My father paid me fifty cents below union wages then, when I was training hard every afternoon. He wound up paying for the last twenty-five percent of the boat anyway.

He'd driven to Fenton along Route 7, a map neatly cut from the back of the school catalogue and taped to the road map of the state thruway. He'd arrived to find the boathouse doors open to the late afternoon sunlight. It looked and smelled like a workshop in there and my father felt at home, I could tell. I knew he would have looked over Channing's tools and the fittings and riggers on the wall. He would have noted with approval the neat boxes of screws and the endless cans of paint and varnish and caulking and sealant and cleaning agents and itched to touch it all but wouldn't have done so because it wasn't his workshop and he'd no more touch another shop's equipment than fly to the moon. In his worn chinos and work shirt and baseball hat he was all work, all business. He understood how to bend steel and wood and people, if he needed to.

He wouldn't go back into the main school with me, have a look around or maybe something to eat. He just wanted to sit in the truck and talk before moving on. But I knew he didn't want to park the truck in the visitors' area, next to the Volvos, Jeeps and BMWs. He didn't want to embarrass me. I hated that. I felt a surge of protectiveness toward him that I didn't want.

He believed that by encouraging me to spend a year at Fenton he was depositing me at the gates of a better world. Years later, after I had failed to make any more money than he had, he and I would argue. It was inconceivable to him that a person with my education—so agonizingly hard won—would choose to do anything else but make money and embrace the life that generations of us had been denied.

Once my father had established that the boat was indeed secure, that his handiwork had not failed him, he looked over the long sea of green around him, the manicured fields and glowing white lime in front of the modern field house. He squinted over the soccer and lacrosse training fields, acres of lovingly, expensively maintained grass. The football goalposts held his attention, and the stern blue bleachers rising out of that luxurious emerald sweep. "They play good ball at this school?" he asked.

"They lost their first game to this other school, Taft, because they have no kicker and the quarterback kept overshooting the receiver."

"Bob Wiley says the Niccalsetti Lions might be undefeated this year. They promoted the second string quarterback. Wiley says he isn't as good as your brother was."

"They'll never have another Tom Carrey on that team."

He grunted, gazed out at the field, as if seeing my brother—graduated from school, home now, jobless, aimless—backpedaling into that perfect green carpet. "Did you talk to the rowing coach yet?"

"At a meeting."

"How'd it go?"

"Not as well as it could have."

"These guys as good as they say they are?"

"They could be. Some college coaches think so, that's for sure."

He nodded. "You cleared the scull with your coach, right?"

"Yes. They don't scull as much out here. He wants me in a four-man boat. They call it the God Four."

"Is that right? The God Four? Just remember that the sculling is what got you here."

"The races that mean anything aren't going to be in the single. I have to row with other kids."

"So, what you're saying is, you're going to have to row in the four and there's no two ways about it."

"Pretty much."

"And you got all hot under the collar as usual because you thought you'd just come up here and do things your way and everybody else, why, they can just go hop."

"I'm not a team player, Dad. Come on, you know that better than anyone. Single scullers don't *need* to be team players. I'm not used to depending on others. The whole reason I like the sport is because it's all about *me*. My decisions. My fitness level. My strategy in a race. If I lose, it's down to me. Same when I win. It sucks needing other people to win."

"Then why not just pack it in and come home, Rob? You can row in the Black Rock Canal until you're my age and I'll see if you can get a place on my work crew in the meantime."

"It crossed my mind."

"It didn't cross *my* mind. Or your *mother's* mind." He looked at me hard then around me, as if he wanted to kick something. "For four years you push yourself harder for this sport than I've ever seen a kid push himself. You go out in your boat in the snow for crying out loud, and then you have the sand to tell me you don't want what they have here because you can't abide the thought of rowing in a team? Goddamn it, Robby, there's a time for being a stubborn fool and there's a time for going with the flow and this sounds like it's one of those going with the flow times."

"And what if I lose? What if this boat loses, if they aren't as fast as they need to be, then what? Then I came all this way and got down with some kids who can't move a boat."

"Then at least you joined in and didn't wind up sitting on the shore waiting for nothing. It appears this scull has given you all you're going to get from it. So try throwing your dice on another table."

"It's not that easy, Dad."

"Things are sometimes a hell of a lot easier than people think they are. Go and row in the four, or the eight, or whatever they say. And don't look at me like that. How about you just say you'll do it so I can cross it off my list of idiotic things to worry about."

"All right. I'll do it, then. I'll row in their four. But I won't like it."

"Your liking anything is the last of my concerns, son." He squatted and sighted down the smooth hull of the boat. "Might as well get this unstrung and in the boathouse. This building looks almost new. I thought the book said they'd been rowing here for a hundred years."

"The old boathouse was further down the river, about a mile away. They closed it up a few years back when they bagged a few million from some rich alumnus to build this one."

He glanced up at me. "Are you telling me that one man gave the school the money for this building?"

"That's right."

"What'd they give him in return?"

"Put his name up over the door."

"Well, that's something."

We walked into the dark cold. He looked down at the wooden floors, grunted. "They could treat these. You kids marching in and out of here all day, all wet, you'd think they'd treat the wood. Or maybe they just put in new flooring when the old one wears out, they have that much money." He looked at me. "You're going to need the rafter racks for the boat. I guess I can drill one in right up there." He focused into the gloom above. I looked around and saw that there were scull trolleys underneath what I later would learn was one of the club eights. "They want me to put it on those. We're not supposed to drill holes in the walls around here."

He looked at the rolling racks and grunted. "All right. Saves me some work."

"I didn't mean it like that."

"I sure do know you didn't."

We unbuckled the cradle. He had put cotton pads under each buckle, tied them with string. The scull looked great, there weren't even faint scuff marks from it moving on the cradle. It had been kept perfectly still for five hundred miles down that road. He worked methodically and slowly as usual, laying back each strap one by one, making sure I saw him do it. He pulled the riggers from under the boat and walked them into the boathouse while I untied the bow ball. "I saw some pretty girls while I was driving through town. I expect they haven't slipped under your radar."

"They haven't."

"You'll want to be careful."

"I'm always careful."

"You got your mother's looks on you and girls are going to take notice of it. I'd imagine a fellow can get in a whole lot of trouble not thinking straight, and trouble isn't what you need right now."

He helped me lift the boat out of the cradle, set his jaw and inched it into the house, then opened up the passenger door to the truck and pulled his tool belt out, strapped it around his waist and picked up the riggers from inside the boathouse door. Kneeling by the boat, he selected a wrench and pulled out a bottle with the screws inside. He handed me a palm of screws and another driver. "You take the right-hand one."

"Starboard."

"What is?"

"On a boat right is starboard."

"We're not on a boat."

"I'm just saying."

"All right. And what's left?"

"Port."

"And the front?"

"Bow. You know, bow ball."

"I didn't make the connection." He held the rigger to the splash-board, began screwing in his side, smooth, quick turns that didn't scratch the protective plate.

"The back's the stern."

"I know it. And you've got the bow deck and the stern deck and the slide and the seat. The oars are called sculls, right? But the boat's a scull, a single scull. Explain that."

"I can't."

"But you know the difference between all of it."

"I do."

"Good man."

<hr>

We sat in the truck's cab while he ate part of the lunch he hadn't bothered to eat on the drive down. He'd lost weight since my sister's death. Three years ago he would never have skipped lunch, would definitely have stopped for it. He'd brought along a bag of my mother's sandwiches and a thermos of black coffee, both of which he passed to me. When he was finished he lit a cigarette, pushed the pack back in his pocket, lifted his chin. "I know, I know, go ahead, make sure the door's open. You don't need any of this smoke in your lungs."

I rolled down the window instead, looked out over the water. It was getting plenty late. Channing was going to start to miss me already, not that I truly gave a damn. My father reached under his seat, picked up a copy of *The New York Times*, set it between us. "I bought this in Mohawk, on the thruway. There's not much news you need outside *The New York Times*. Take it. I looked at it already, got the general gist of things."

"I appreciate it."

He rummaged under the seat again and shook out a brown manila envelope, the kind he sent invoices to his customers in,

Carrey's Joinery up in the corner. He placed it on the dashboard. "That's cash for your bookstore account."

I reached out, placed a finger on the envelope.

"You don't need to fall over yourself thanking me."

"Thank you." I looked at him when I said it.

"I went to the dean and we had a little talk. He told me they give you an option to buy tuition insurance. You pay them some extra money and they give back the balance of what you've paid in if your kid manages to get himself thrown out for any major infractions. You want to hear what they consider to be major infractions?"

Here it comes, I thought.

"Drinking's up there at the top of the list. Right next to it is smoking, any kind of smoking. I figure a kid with your ability would be out of his mind to smoke, but I may as well remind you."

"You smoke."

"No boarding school or college is interested in me for anything and never will be. And don't be a smartass."

I looked out over the river while he took an angry drag on his cigarette. Then he started in again. "The school also lists premarital intercourse as a rule infraction. And being AWOL. And driving a car. And taking drugs. And showing disrespect to those in authority. This place isn't fooling around is what I'm saying."

"Did you take out the insurance on me?"

"I figured since you already did all the things they don't want you to do while you were back at home, you might consider retiring from your old life and focusing in on the job at hand."

Lines of students were filing out from the field house. He sipped his coffee, agitated. "Another thing they don't tolerate is fighting. I thought I'd bring that up as well, all by itself, as another issue altogether."

"Half the fights I get in aren't my fault, Dad. And it's not a big deal."

He smacked the steering wheel. "Do you *know* how many times I hear that? It's never anybody's fault. You send some millionaire's kid home with a busted jaw, son, and get kicked out, understand you'll be signing up somewhere in town as I certainly don't need a hothead on my payroll and, on top of that, I can't afford a lawyer to protect you. That's the way it works."

"How do you know Connor Payne is rich?"

"I took a *goddamned* educated guess, Robby." He flicked the cigarette out the window, where it tumbled, sparking, into the grass. Then he looked at it angrily, furious at himself for littering. "You think eight or nine months of your life is a long pull, don't you? It's not even a year, kid. You haven't been drafted. You're not carrying a weapon and calling anyone 'sir.'"

I let him sit there for a beat and cool off. "I'm not planning on getting in trouble, all right? I'm going to be okay."

He reached into the glove compartment, pulled out his leather wallet and it fell open in his hands. He extracted some notes, all new and crisp. They were held together with a paperclip. "Take this. You ought to have some walking around money."

"I can't take any more of your cash, Dad."

"Go on." He coughed, hard and deep in his chest.

I picked up the bills, slid them into my pocket. They were fresh from an ATM somewhere on the I-90 and they cut into my leg. He'd been driving up here and thinking about the money in the envelope and figured it wasn't enough so he had drawn more at a rest stop. He drove me nuts.

"What time is it?" he asked suddenly.

"After five."

"I wish I could have sent you kids to a place like this when you were younger."

"Wendy would have been kicked out inside an hour."

"Wendy would've been running the place inside fifteen minutes and wouldn't have to crack heads to do it." He grabbed his cigarettes, a reflex, contemplated the last one and returned the box to his pocket. "Ah, hell, I didn't mean to say all that other stuff to you, Robby."

"I'm not keeping score."

He nodded, settled it, had to cough a couple of times before he could speak again. "I'm driving into Hartford. I'm staying overnight so I can see a doctor tomorrow morning about something. Then I'm heading back. I have a job to finish. I won't be able to stay."

"That's fine."

"If you think of anything you need, you just call home. I'll be checking in with your mother and Tom before dinner."

"I won't need anything. Thanks for the scull, Dad. You didn't have to go to all the trouble."

He rubbed the bottom of his chin so I heard the scratches of his one-day beard. "One of those college coaches called a week or so ago. A man who claimed he was from Harvard. Your mother almost had a heart attack in the kitchen. They sent through some information. A catalogue or something like that. It's in the bag of stuff your mother packed for you. They asked to be sure you saw it." I watched him run his fingers over the worn steering wheel, counting the indentations, dividing them. "You get on that Harvard team and you're my first blood relative to make it to college."

"They're only interested because I'm a good rower, Dad, not because I'm smart."

"The way I calculate it, you get in, you're smart enough."

I didn't tell him I had just received a postcard of my own from them with a picture of the Newell Boathouse on the front and a scrawled message at the bottom from the freshman coach telling me he hoped my grades would improve while I was at Fenton. And congratulations for my Canadian Henley win. I hadn't told anyone. I could have told my father and he'd have it to chew over on the drive home, but I didn't. Instead I said, "They figure just hearing from them will make you drop everything."

"They're right, aren't they?"

"They either take me or they're going to be rowing against me."

He turned in his seat. "You won't tell them that, will you?"

"I'm sorely tempted."

He laughed. "Don't let your mother hear. You be sure she doesn't catch wind of that little proposition."

"Even if it's true?"

"Especially if it's true."

He grinned. He looked pretty tired. Then something occurred to me. "Why are you seeing some quack in Hartford? What's wrong with the doctors in Niccalsetti?"

"Nothing's wrong with them."

I didn't press him. I thought at the time, stupidly, that he'd have the sense to tell me if there was anything I needed to know. So I let it pass and said, "I have to meet a teacher off campus for something."

"The teacher you're going to go work those punishment hours for, like a skivvy?"

"He wanted to know if I could paint."

He laughed. "You think you can handle this place?"

"It's a bunch of preppie geeks. How tough can it be?"

"No tougher than anything you kids have been through. I can guarantee you that."

I reached over to shake his hand and he took it, then pulled me to him, his chin rough on my ear. We gave it a few seconds.

6.

Carolyn got up very early, showered and dressed in the bathroom. I was still asleep when she started up the coffeemaker and cleared out the dishes from the night before. She smoked a cigarette in the dawn light coming from the line of windows over the kitchen appliances, ate two grapefruits, section by section, drank a bottle of Evian and sat in front of the computer with another cigarette. She would have turned off her cell phone before she started working. She was pouring herself into this documentary for me and I think at some level she thought I at least deserved a good, finished, edited piece of work before she tossed me out. Either that, or she was throwing herself into work to avoid a final confrontation.

I woke up and smelled her in the sheets and walked barefoot across the cold wooden floor to the boundary of the kitchen tiles and looked in at her working, nodding in time to something harsh and loud in her studio headphones. I watched her from my post by the door, the way she hunched over the keyboard like a man over his food, working with a pencil in her mouth and another in her hand that she picked up and put down in-between bouts of typing. She'd edit like that for hours and then would need a massage, need to feel somebody's fingers—my fingers—drilling into her back, finding the ropes of tension and rubbing them away, the muscles along her spine taking the most strain, her deltoids and traps needing at least forty minutes of attention. I could massage her at night for over an hour and in doing so my hands would grow numb with the pain of it, my wrists would start to cramp, and she'd half-doze through even the hardest, deepest massage and fall asleep like a cat at the end.

I went back to sleep for just a few more minutes. Carolyn dragged me out of bed two hours later. She put on more coffee and we pulled the croissants out of the fridge that I hadn't touched the day before, and I consumed them sitting on one of the stools that hid under the long, stainless counter sweeping into the living area of the loft. Carolyn drank black coffee with sweetener.

She didn't need the rigorous diet. She was a woman of beautiful planes, defined by the sweep of her hips, her sharp, high cheekbones and her swept back blond hair. Carolyn had her own toxins. Too much coffee. An on-again, off-again cigarette compulsion. Wine.

She wanted to go over the script for the shark piece with me so that she could start editing the digitized footage, chopping and changing on the editing suite. She needed my input about which of the many tapes had the footage we'd be using. I had a fairly good script already that indicated where the footage should go in, but it was a laborious process nonetheless and would consume all of her time for weeks to come. I trusted her work implicitly and so did *National Geographic*. We were cutting what they would refer to as a "fat" piece so their editors could do further work and provide professional narration, although I would wind up doing a scratch track—a primitive recording dubbed into the tape—that would give the channel something to work with when they removed my voice and put in their own narrator's.

I had worked with Carolyn for years like this. In fact, we had met because I needed somebody with an editing studio in the U.S. to handle my work once the channel stopped taking raw footage from me and started commissioning finished pieces. Much of my work was not profitable for her—her real money came from editing corporate videos. I met her at the New York Documentary Center on Maiden Lane during a conference I had attended just for the hell of it. She had been handing out cards and we'd fallen into a conversation after sitting through a presentation by the wife of some Hollywood director who'd helped fund the place. That was five years ago. When Carolyn had learned what I did she immediately offered to do some editing for me, I could name the price. She'd made the offer over beers at a Front Street microbrewery under the Brooklyn Bridge that everyone had repaired to by the late afternoon and by that night we were having dinner at an Italian restaurant nearby, which was a long, drunken, romantic stroll uptown.

I remembered walking next to her and feeling her hand inches from mine. She was talking about her work, I suppose. When she finally brushed my hand with hers, my heart ground its gears and I was lost.

Sitting in front of her edit suite, the script spread out in front of us, I watched her carefully sip her coffee, set the mug down, start zipping through the material on screen. Carolyn and I in one sense had nothing in common. Even while she worked from home she was dressed fashionably by my standards. The filmers I worked with, including myself I guess, were a scruffy looking bunch. Carolyn worked with corporate clients and her place was what I once bitterly described to her as "executive-pseudo-artistic." But I secretly loved having access to this cavern of space at the bottom of the city. I liked the repolished wooden floors, the iron studs in the walls and the naked steel pillars and girders, the wide warehouse windows. Even the freight elevator was charming in its dirty, utilitarian way. She had put in a kitchen near the living area and upgraded the bathroom. The fixtures were flagrantly expensive—brushed stainless steel German faucets and spouts that she had installed after an entire year of saving. She had found oversize, white modular couches to stand on a massive afghan rug, and pedestals and floating shelves displayed the masks and statues I had brought her from Africa, South America and Canada. I regretted getting her that mask collection, though. More than a few lovemaking sessions had been interrupted as I moved us away from the leering gaze of all those contorted wooden faces.

She'd been to Africa and South America with me a few times but she preferred the city and, I felt, work that really paid. Her clients were mostly in New York. She had never romanticized the career of a documentary filmer: the cheap life of third-class flights and overweight baggage and meals on the fly and forced interviews and extreme weather. She liked the cachet that working for *National Geographic* gave her, and liked to help me, but that was it. I had once, in a rage, accused her of being too corporate-minded, said that money was the driving force behind everything she did. She had conceded the point. She had also wondered aloud if anyone really did anything without thinking about the back-end, and reminded me that she could write off the work she did for me as charity.

She sounded like my father when she said that.

Six weeks ago, just before I had flown to South Africa, Carolyn had announced that our relationship was finished. It was an impossible relationship we had, she said. Two people our age had to start making something substantial out of their lives. We agreed on that. It was more than the simple fact we were unmarried, which she claimed didn't bother her. If I wanted to shoot film and edit, I could do it anywhere. I could do it right here in New York. Anyway, I should be doing more corporate work, she insisted. It was easier, it was fun sometimes and it paid more.

Yeah, I had replied, I could just see myself filming the inside of a new bank. Or doing training tapes for sales teams, or filming exterior shots of new offices. I hated the idea of spending weeks shooting restaurant and travel inserts for cable TV channels. Why not? she'd countered. It pays the bills and people care about where they work and where they eat and doing their jobs well.

But there was more to it as well. Our fights had started occurring more and more regularly, almost immediately after I came back from a shoot, with flare-ups through the ensuing weeks until I left again on the next assignment. The very fact I had an apartment in Cape Town irritated her. My Cape Town place was a small, one-room bachelor studio, I had told her, a place to sleep and get mail and lock up my equipment. I wasn't going to live in a hotel for half my life. No, she'd said, you could live in *our* place. I reminded her it was *her* place. I just helped pay the rent.

And then there was yet more to it, another layer that we couldn't touch. Even when the arguments came to the point of her throwing things out the window, of her going so far as to demand I leave the loft and find another place to sleep, we never bore down to it. The last night she threw me out, I walked over to our restaurant and got drunk at a table near the kitchen and then returned and begged her to let me in, freezing my ass off on the sidewalk because I'd stormed out of the loft in a T-shirt and jeans and boots into SoHo in February. I had wound up sleeping on the stairs leading up from the factory entrance. Even when she let me in at 5:00 A.M. and showered with me and brought me to bed, fucked me, and let me lie next to her in drunken silence, shivering, we didn't talk about it.

The *Titanic* had sailed on after it skidded against its iceberg. It had traveled a couple of miles after it was damaged, water creeping up the sides of the ship. Our tear was deep, under the waterline. I knew when it had happened and so did she and the other stuff was just excuses, really. They were the tribulations you could work through when your things weren't awash all around you. We just made our plans for abandoning ship.

———————

Channing's white farmhouse with its overgrown driveway was right after the main town of Fenton and was pressed too close to River Road. The front shutters were peeling but otherwise it seemed in good shape, bigger than I thought it would be. It was a long building and when I walked around the back I realized it was built on a hill and he had a good few acres of property, all of it gone wild. He'd kept his back screens up for too long and they were rusted and bowed crazily in and out from winter. I saw what he was building and what I would be working on: a new shed. The garage right next to his house was obviously too small to store anything in—it was one of those old carriage houses they still had in New England that you swore was slumping over to one side when you looked at it long enough. A hundred years ago there would have been a barn somewhere close by but that was long gone now. The surrounding land and houses were owned by movie stars and investment bankers from New York, who every so often drove out to Fenton to look at the leaves.

I called out Channing's name a few times and then stepped up to the front door of the little shed. I turned around and looked at the main house; from that angle it was maybe the loneliest looking place I'd ever seen in my life. He'd gone out and bought a stack of pressed wood—too much, I thought, just eyeballing it—and two wine boxes of paint were stacked on top of it. An A&P shopping bag full of stiff old paintbrushes balanced right on top of the gallon cans of paint. There was another box full of the shingles you get at those big outlets for people too cheap to call a custom roofer, who figured building a house was as easy as buying a video on the subject.

Sawdust was all over the ground and dusted the floor and

sills of the shed and I knew without walking in there he'd been ripped off by a crew of bozos. I could see the old mugs and dirty rags left in the corners and the coffee rings on the finished sills that they hadn't bothered about. They'd screwed the job up good and proper. I wished for a second I could give my father a tour. He'd have a laugh. He'd walk in there and kick the walls hard enough to buckle them. I wondered if Channing had only recently wised up and fired everyone once things had progressed to this condition, or if he just didn't know any better. Boat work and building work were two different animals, I guessed.

"Carrey. Only an hour and a half late, I see."

There he was now, in the doorway to the porch of his house, without a tie. He walked down the sagging steps, crossed the ragged lawn. "What do you think of my addition?"

"I'd call it a subtraction."

He made a sound and his deep-set eyes flashed briefly. His hair was tightly curled, fading. He wore brogues, khaki pants that were spattered with flecks of wood stain along the sides and a parchment-crisp shirt that had been ironed thin. Channing had the faded tan you get working outdoors every day. His hands were manicured and clean but beat-up and raw, too. I'd discover it was hard for him to pick a pencil up off the floor, or dig a piece of chalk out of the tray in front of a blackboard. He'd built a sailboat once, he'd tell me, and being the coach of the crew he did most of the work on the shells. But Channing didn't have woodworker's hands. They looked like they belonged to a meat packer.

"I thought at first this was going to be a storage shed but now I'm thinking you're building an office?"

"Possibly; also it will serve as a guesthouse."

"How much did you pay the morons who built it?"

"Isn't it possible that I built it myself?"

"Not unless you're the kind of guy who litters all over his own little playhouse."

He frowned, looked in at the mess. "I paid them a fair price. And you are exceptionally insulting, Carrey."

"Straight talk is no insult in this business, Mr. Channing. I can make a recommendation or I can be polite."

"All right, then. Give me the hard truth. Lay it on me, as they say."

"The sashes aren't set right and your wiring's too low and they've spaced the framework wide to save money and they used the crappiest wood they could find."

" 'Crappiest' won't even make it through a spell checker."

"Flimsiest."

"The plans were drawn up by some friends at a very good outfit in Millerton."

"The plans might be great but your builders are killing you. Ten bucks says those nails will be rusted out in the wood by the end of the month and they overbought and overcharged you for materials and then left the site looking like a pig sty. You go get a measuring tape and measure the distance between those wall studs and I'll tell you now it's wider than on the plans."

He grunted. "I had a few reservations . . ."

"Did you cut them a check?"

He didn't answer. He ran his hands down the door frames and windowsills, which you could bet had been leaning against each other in a Walmart somewhere downstate a few weeks ago. "Do you think you can put a layer of paint on this?"

"I can do more than that."

"I need you to paint. That's all. Let's keep things simple."

He stood on the half stoop they'd made for him and looked down the hill leading into a creek by the house, the whole thing weeds and shrub now. I stood in the shade of the house, smelling wood and sawdust and glue and mixed plaster and felt at home for the first time in weeks. "You don't have to supervise me. It's not like I'm going anywhere."

"I'm not supervising you. I'm thinking of how to advise you. I've been chosen to be your advisor."

"What do you mean, like a counselor?"

"I don't want to counsel you. Every student is assigned an advisor. One who advises."

"Do you have any advice for me?"

"Don't get drawn into fistfights or the destruction of school property and you won't have to paint houses."

I heaved the cans of paint onto a makeshift table his crew had set up inside the shed using milk crates and one of the sheets of plywood they'd stiffed him for. Channing at least had bought good paint for the outside, an off-white, and two bottles of thinners with a bundle of brand-new, honest-to-god stirrers taped together. He'd also remembered to get sandpaper and new brushes.

"Rowing with others takes a certain kind of determination, Carrey."

"Doesn't seem like I have a choice."

"The sport is not just about brute power. Or endurance. Or the ability to suffer. Rowing in a team forces you to respond to what other men do in the boat. To adhere to a strategy. To follow commands. To put your petty gripes and prejudices and fears aside."

"It means putting up with three rowers I don't know or trust and a girl who could steer us into the rocks. My experience working with other people has been pretty disappointing."

"Carrey, eventually you will learn to be pleasantly surprised when people do *not* disappoint you. You're going to stir that paint, I suppose."

"Unless you have a mix machine around here, yeah I'm going to stir it. When it's time to open the can. And that only happens once the prep work is done."

"You mean when the preparations are finished. My second piece of advice to you is to stir that paint well."

He was trying to make sure I knew what I was doing but I think he had confidence in me already. I picked up the sandpaper and looked around for scissors, finally just tore a piece off and began on the wood outside the door. It was late already and he'd have to let me go in fifteen minutes. The sandpaper's scratching shut him up for a while. He took a step away from the door and stood in the evening's sun, looked up at it and blinked, as if he'd never noticed it before. He looked at me again. "It's already been sanded."

"Whoever sanded this did it so half-assed they shouldn't have bothered."

"Carrey, I might have sanded this house. Did that occur to you?"

"You want the job done right or what?"

"I want it finished."

"Then give me a day to prep this surface or else you'll be skewering me in front of the whole team again. I'll never hear the end of it."

He looked at his watch. "Almost time for you to go back."

"You don't want me to stay? Are you going to count these hours?"

"Hours? By my estimation, Carrey, you were here for only a few minutes."

"I was held up. You can check with the dean."

"Don't be held up tomorrow." He gently touched the side of the shed, ran his hand down the wood as if he couldn't understand how this half-built thing had appeared on his property.

"You have a lot more than twenty hours of work owing to you on this place. You know that, right?" Talking to Channing now was like talking to a man who almost wasn't there. He was gazing with some worry at the porch jutting out of the main house that needed almost as much work as the shed, collapsed as it was, its foundations covered in moss—fingers of it—old age clawing the bricks and wood.

"You're nineteen years old and as raw and brash and rude as they come and the best team in the world is interested in you," he said. "Amazing."

"I'm a PG recruit. I'm here because it's a free ride."

"It won't be a ride of any sort. I can assure you of that. You're not the first rower to want a place on this crew. Others have come before you."

"Who says I want it?"

"You'd be a fool not to. And you didn't walk out of our meeting, as I partly expected you would."

"Do you really think I'd be a fool not to look forward to seven months of training with kids who will despise me because I don't get my clothes from the right catalogue? To relearning a sport I'm already pretty good at? Trusting my future to Connor Payne, who hasn't won this magical race in three years of trying and a coach who hasn't won it in five? All so I can help a bunch of rich guys beat another bunch of rich guys in a race that I don't care about?"

He nodded, his eyes flickering at my mention of the Warwick Race. "Yes. Exactly right."

"I'm starting to think this isn't just strange. It's insane, that's what it is."

"Rowing is a pastime for people who enjoy winning at all costs. You are among this cohort, or you would not be here." He hummed to himself, checked his watch again. "And, Carrey, the others won't despise you. They might begin to hate you, at least as much as you seem to hate them, but they won't despise you. Maybe you could settle for a mutual disdain."

I ran the sandpaper over the door frame and it tore. It was getting hard to see what I was supposed to be doing.

"Tomorrow you can clean this place up. And finish sanding."

"I'll be here at 3:30 P.M."

"Don't let yourself be delayed."

"I won't."

7.

Walking back down River Road to school I felt the temperature drop the minute the sun fell behind the mountain. Winter was lurking, you could feel it in the air, just under the warmth. I thought about what my father and Channing had said to me. I had taken enough time to get my bearings, figure out where I stood. You always had to know where you stood, or so my sister Wendy—three years dead now—once told me. I reckoned my position was pretty clear.

I arrived back at North Dorm too late to change for dinner. They made you wear a coat and tie and I was in my work clothes. Anyway, I liked the quiet. Everyone was in the dining hall and I had the place to myself. I sat on one of the benches outside and figured I'd get some candy bars now and hit the snack bar after study hall. I was burning calories like a machine and I could eat anything. I went down the battered steps into the rec room, which always smelled like dust and rotten fruit. It was a pit, with a twenty-year-old TV and furniture that looked like it had been caged with wild animals. The place was littered with junk: book bags, sports equipment, books, old magazines that had been eviscerated, a Nerf football in shreds, as if it had been rescued from the jaws of a particularly vicious dog. I went to the vending machines along the far wall and started feeding in dollar bills from the wad my father had given me, watched the candy bars and chips fall from the racks inside to the trough below.

That's when I heard Ruth's voice. She was furious, yelling at someone to go to hell. I walked back across the rec room to the stairwell and peeked out, saw her in the dark phone booth—the bulb long dead—her hair pushed back and two anger marks on her cheeks. Her knuckles were sharp outlines where she gripped the phone. She was looking right at me but I'm not sure she saw me, or if she did, she found it easy to pretend that she did not.

Ruth had an aura of another place about her, like Fenton hadn't managed to touch her in the whole three years she'd been here. We shared a chemistry class and we had definitely noticed each other. At least twice that I was aware of, when we were supposed to be learning how to balance equations, I had sensed her watching me. When I glanced at her the second time she didn't look away. Her eyes were so intense and clear green as a tiger's—that I couldn't hold her gaze. But I gave it a second before looking down. She seemed fragile and tough at the same time—she had to be. Ruth had steered the God Four to victory after victory last year and then been denied the Warwick Race. She was intriguing.

The other chicks in the school hated her, of course; too good looking, too confident, too indifferent. From what I could tell, the guys on the team tolerated her. And feared her because she had to know them at the most elemental level. It was the coxswain who called out the final strokes of the race, who set the training, who raised the rating until you ran into a wall of exhaustion. Every time I looked over at her, I remembered that there was something almost satanic about every good coxswain. She was friendless like me and she didn't care.

And I'd die before I gave her the satisfaction of saying hello first.

"I'm asking you if I can come home for one weekend. One." The person answered, a long answer that she didn't like. "Mom, you promised me you would not do this. We had an agreement."

Another answer, and you could tell from the way Ruth set her mouth it was pretty feeble. "I have to go. No. I have to go." She slammed down the receiver and stood up in the cramped space. She picked up her bag. It wasn't a student's backpack—a scuffed, torn nylon job like mine with the names of doomed rock bands scrawled across the bottom and a dope blossom drawn across the logo—but a leather satchel, a mail pouch. She flipped it open. Her books were carefully lined up in the first section and she had another pocket in there with a brush and a bag of chick stuff.

She rummaged around until she found a hard pack of Marlboro Reds, tweezed one out with her fingernails and mashed her lips around it hard enough to flatten the filter. She felt inside the bag for a lighter and had to almost tear the thing apart again. She finally found it and flicked it twice, lit the end of the cigarette and frowned, got two puffs in, holding the cigarette away from her face, blinking and swallowing hard.

"What are you looking at, Rob Carrey?"

"Is that your first cigarette?"

"Were you listening to me on the phone? Don't you have anything else to do other than eavesdrop on people's conversations?" She took a deep breath, looked around, checked her watch, fanned the air. "Better stand back, I wouldn't want to ruin your crew jock lungs, Rob."

"Give me that pack." I was right, it was the first cigarette she'd taken from the pack, you could see them all still bunched together in there. I flipped it over, gave it a tap and a cigarette popped out. I took the lighter from her hand, her fingers cold in mine for a millisecond when she handed it over. I torched the

Marlboro and gave the lighter back to her. I sifted a Coke can out of the garbage and held it out between us. "Go on. Ash in this or you're going to burn the building down."

She managed to push about half the burning end in the opening and smeared cinders down the side of the can when she pulled it away.

"This cigarette is stale."

"Well, my goodness, that's gratitude."

"It tastes like you've had it in the bottom of a drawer for a year. Feels cool to be holding, doesn't it? Except who is ever going to suspect *you* of anything?"

She looked at me, softened for a second and then recalled how pissed off she was. "Since when do rowers smoke? You should be paranoid about your health." She was doing better with it now, taking smaller puffs and not looking like she was going to choke to death after.

"I'm almost a pack a day at home, if you count secondary smoke as smoking. All the best science says you should. If they catch us doing this, it's twenty hours of work. A black mark on your perfect record, Ruth."

"My record isn't perfect. Please stop saying that." But she flushed and looked away and I knew I'd scored a point.

"So you want to take up smoking? That's the best rule you can break?"

"I've been giving some thought to taking up a lot of things." She tried to inhale and then coughed on it. You had to feel sorry for her but I wasn't going to put mine out and give her an excuse to bag hers as well. She held the cigarette away from her face, straight up, like she'd seen on TV. She let it burn. "I've seen you on the water a few times." She looked away from me. The hallway was dark and close, too warm and humid from the ancient heaters. I heard banging in the walls, heat struggling upward. "Can I say something to you? And you won't be offended or take it the wrong way?"

"Half of what people say to me I take the wrong way and I wind up in trouble."

"When I heard you were the PG rower I didn't believe it, not at first. I really didn't. You seem so different. I think you are, anyway. You were supposed to be in Channing's English class but he transferred you out. He can't stand rowers in his class. Everyone knows that."

"Why?"

"Because rowers usually aren't smart. They're idiots. He's the rowing coach, he should know."

"Who was on the phone?"

She waved her cigarette at the pay phone and the ash fell onto the little steel writing ridge where she rubbed it in with her finger. "My mother. She's supposed to live in this country. She should be here now but decided to go to England when I wanted to see her for a weekend." She threw her hair back and changed the subject. "So, you're from Niccalsetti, New York. Upstate New York. The Black Rock Rowing Club, right?"

"You're the first person I've met here who knows about it."

She looked at me evenly, like she was inspecting me. "You'll make the team if you want to—Paul Wendt's place from last year, the number three seat. I didn't think you stood a chance at first. I do now."

"Why didn't you?"

"Because you're not arrogant enough. You're something else, but not arrogant. You need to be arrogant to make the team."

"Are you arrogant?"

"I'm the first female to coxswain the God Four in the history of the school. When they elected me to the team, twenty of the rowing alumni sent back their colors."

"Did you keep them?"

"Channing gave me their ties and I used them to stuff two throw pillows."

"Don't exhale like that."

"Excuse me? Like what?"

"Like you're blowing a fly away from your face, out the side of your mouth. If you're going to smoke, do it right."

"Like this?"

"Now you're not inhaling."

She just went on as if she hadn't heard me. She regarded me through all the smoke. "I want you to be a good rower. I'm hoping you'll help us beat Warwick. It was dumb to stand there in front of everyone and tell Channing you weren't going to try out, that you only want to row in the single."

"I'm really not psyched to be rowing on a team."

"That's ridiculous. Just get over your hang-up, get on the team and start rowing—and winning. We can't lose the Warwick Race again, we just can't. The dumb alumni will blame me and say it's because I couldn't steer. Paul was good last year. But you have to be better. You can't just be this cocky boy from upstate New York. You have to rock."

"I've never had to rely on others to win. Never had to trust somebody else to steer a boat I was in. I mean, seriously, the whole idea around a coxswain is . . . what? So you steer, and . . . ? You're really sort of the coach's spy, right?"

She flushed again. "That's not true! I'm a member of the God Four. I hate Channing as much as you guys do."

"But it's not like he's ever going to cut you. And if you're so important to the team why isn't it called the God Five?" I was winding her up because I liked the way her eyes looked when she was mad but I could see I had gone too far.

"That's just the sort of sexist crap I have to put up with all the time. You guys can't see where you're going when you go down that course. I can. I steer you. I can see the other boat. I'm the one who pushes you through them. You? What do you do, genius? You look at the back of the guy in front of you. I have to see everything, judge if the other team is dying and when we make a move. I'm the brain of the boat. Without me, you guys wouldn't even get the boat down to the water. I give the command for hands on, to lift it, to lower it to the water and hold. I get you out there so you can do one thing: row. At the rating I tell you. And until I tell you to stop." She was pretty riled up.

"Yeah? And what about the seven months of daily training we have to put in?" I thought I might as well go for broke.

"What about it? You don't need to drop almost a fifth of your body weight and half starve yourself to do it, Carrey. And still be able to run with you guys in the freezing cold. You try running those miles on an empty stomach. You don't need to keep track of the training schedules for a dozen rowers, or organize every session in the rowing tanks, or monitor everyone's erg scores and weights records. You just have to show up."

"Okay, okay. Channing just gave me the big teamwork lecture."

"It's not about teamwork. It's about something else that's like it."

"Why do you do it?"

"Why do I do what?"

"Why be a cox for some retro guy's rowing team? I mean, what's the point if you think it's so awful?"

"Oh, God. What's the point in anything? I'm good at it, I guess."

We had to get out of there sooner or later. But she was on a roll. She looked at me sideways, as if she was aiming her words. "Why do you row?"

I waited a second and it was my turn to change the subject. "I was getting tired of seeing you in class and wondering what you're like."

"Am I what you expected?"

"Put the cigarette in the can and let's get out of here before they bust us."

"Let them."

"Do you really want to finish that? You don't." I held out the can.

She took one last drag, slid the rest into the can. I heard it fizz when it hit bottom. She waved away the smoke between us, as if she was waving at me, trying to get my attention and also saying good-bye. She turned and started walking away. She knew I was watching her go, too, watching her walk the whole hall until she disappeared through the door to the stairs. I couldn't drop my cigarette fast enough into the can with hers. I felt like choking. You had to wonder what people were thinking, smoking those things.

———————————

Carolyn thought this might be the best work I had ever done for the channel. It consisted mostly of underwater footage I had snagged with pan-cams over the course of eight dives with some of the locals. I had also gone into the cage with a digital camera in plastic waterproof housing and stayed there as long as I could each day. The Durban water was warmer than the water near Gans Baai, where everyone went to film the Great Whites—there was so much Great White footage among the filmers in South Africa that we all traded it like baseball cards. But the Zambezi sharks look nearly as fearsome—and the tens of thousands of sardines in the water made the sea look frenzied—especially as they ripped into the tiny silver fish that swarmed around them. Each night back at the hotel I'd go over the day's footage with the divers. They'd be pumped up, fast forwarding to the sharks. They had named some of the bigger ones that looked suitably menacing on camera: Bugsy, Mugsy and Bart. Carolyn told me that it seemed incredible that a little over a week before I had been underwater in that carnage. It may have looked exciting but I had felt at peace in the cage, panning the area for Bugsy's next appearance or Mugsy barreling out of the dark like a jet fighter and banking around me. For every one minute of shark footage I recovered, there must have been an hour of less interesting sardine footage. And eighty percent of the shark footage was unsellable because of the light or a camera jump or the ambient sound of the edge of the camera lens hitting the side of the metal cage. Carolyn's major job was finding the minutes of wheat in the hours of chaff.

The two of us ate in front of the computer, separating segments of the video into smaller chunks we could mix and match with the interviews and the scenery shots. By the time we were finished consuming the goodies from the SoHo House of Thai and Asian Cuisine I was bushed again. I managed to stay up until nine and then I took a shower and went to bed, fell into the dreamless slumber of a deep-sea animal.

I woke up with a jolt about three hours later and for a heartbeat had the terrible feeling I was in a hotel. I lay on my side and looked at the heavy sliding door to the bathroom in the dark, letting my eyes adjust, hoping as I did I was really back home and not in the Heathrow Hilton or a windowless hotel room in Schiphol Airport or in a Holiday Inn in Botswana. When I made out the familiar outlines of the room and the dim line of light from under the shades, I swung to my feet. Carolyn wasn't in bed. I heard somebody shout something ugly and drunken far down below on the street. I felt my heart writhing in my chest and walked out, barefoot, into the living area, then to the suite. Carolyn's chair was empty; the plastic pods of food were abandoned. I called her name a few times. The shot where she had downed tools was a cutaway I had snagged on the last day of filming of a mother and baby at the beach, the mother holding the baby closely and protectively, the kid squinting into the sun, pointing out at the water, a blue beach hat flopping over her chubby face. It was a close-up shot.

I felt my heart plunge inside me.

I threw on my sweatshirt and jeans, found my leather jacket in the closet and pulled on my sneakers. I went out the kitchen door into the narrow service hall and took the concrete factory steps up to the heavy door leading out to the roof. I pushed the door hard and it groaned open. The night air was cool on my face. The old police station was lit up, displaying all the yuppie apartments with incongruous dormer windows and skylights poking through the chateaulike exterior. I walked around the roof, and finally found her sitting on one of the air-conditioning units, smoking a cigarette. She had a big scotch in an insulated plastic *#1 Yankees Fan* tumbler next to her, straight up, with ice, and was already halfway through it.

"What are you doing up?" she asked. The minute she said it I figured she was working on drink number two or three. There'd be a bottle up here somewhere.

"I've been looking for you."

"I'm taking a break. Is that okay? It's midnight. I like looking at the lights out here."

"Maybe you should drink downstairs."

"I'm sick of downstairs. I spend my whole life in that place. God, do you snore. I always forget."

I sat next to her, carefully, hoping she wouldn't get up or start pacing or maybe throw something, like that heavy plastic highball we had gotten on a rare afternoon out to Yankee Stadium shortly after I moved to the city and was in the mood for the touristy attractions. That cheesy souvenir was proof that we once had shared carefree times. Carolyn hugged herself, her breasts pushed together as she shivered. She drank from the cup and set it down. "Once I thought about jumping off this roof. Right down onto Broome Street." She was speaking to her feet, as if in confession.

I put my hand over the small of her back, my fingers just touching, so I could feel the heat off her body.

"I wanted to do it. I don't know why. Then I thought I wouldn't die, I'd just get really, really hurt. That was too terrifying. Maybe I should stay alive and then die from natural causes and be found alone in my studio, in front of the computer. They'll have to pry the mouse out of my hands."

"You're just tired, Car. Take a day off; take two. Let's go somewhere. Anywhere."

"Maybe bad people deserve to die alone."

"You're not a bad person. You know that."

"How can you be sure?"

I touched her gently, felt the strength there, and she leaned against me just for a moment. "I'm such a wimp."

"You're not."

"I saw that footage of the woman with the baby and I thought of you filming it. I ran it about ten times. What do women and babies have to do with sharks, I want to know? I even asked you and you didn't move. I was yelling at you from the desk. How the hell are we supposed to edit that in?" She looked at me. "Was that little moment a message to me? To us?"

"It wasn't a message. It was me not thinking. Come on, you know that."

"I'm so sad now. I'm sad and I'm so mad at you." She leaned against me again and didn't pull away. We sat there for a long time. Finally I stood her up and led her toward the door. I left the glass up there. It was part of the consideration one irresponsible drinker shows another—lifelines of strategically forgotten drinks, two years of surreptitiously abandoned glasses that would be found by other people, relics of a lost civilization of love. I brought her downstairs and locked the door while she watched me, biting her lower lip. I led her to the bedroom and left her there in the dark while I turned off the lights in the living area, left the computer glowing and pulsing by the desk. We undressed in the pale city light, methodically, in the cold apartment, each one at either side of the bed. We lay down and clung to each other and she held my upper arms, pressed her palms and nails against me like she was trying to push me away. When we were finished she asked me to sleep on the couch. I didn't argue. She hated me to hear her cry.

8.

I woke to the sound of the phone bleating. Carolyn picked it up in the bedroom just before the voice mail switched on and I heard her mutter something and then the bed creak and she padded through into the room naked, the morning sun washing out her skin and eyes. She had pressed her nails so deeply into my biceps that they hurt. Rubbing my arms, I felt a vague sexual thrill. She held out the phone like an offering; savage morning goddess.

I gave her an open-handed look and she shrugged, dropped the handset on me and I fumbled it.

"Rob?" The voice was dimly familiar. "It's me. Ruth Anderson. Can you hear me?"

"Ruth Anderson from Fenton?"

"Yeah. Wow, what a bad connection."

"It's a crappy cordless," I said. It actually wasn't crappy at all. It was just a little wonky because Carolyn had thrown it against the wall once or twice. Trying to hit me. "How are you doing? What a surprise."

Carolyn, dressed now in her sweatpants and a soft, white,

belly-baring T-shirt, walked past and glanced down at me, then away, making a point of not being interested. I watched her, hungry again.

Ruth asked, "Um, hey, look, did you get a letter from John Perry?"

"I read it a couple of days ago, on a flight in from overseas. I've been away. He sounds bad. I was going to call him." I sat up, wrapped the blanket around my shoulders. I smelled like sex and dust.

Ruth breathed into the phone in what might have been a half laugh or an expression of mild disbelief. "So, you haven't heard?"

"What?"

"God, I was hoping I wouldn't have to be the one to tell you this." I heard her take a breath. "John's dead."

I didn't say anything, felt myself tear up for just a millisecond before I blinked it away. When I did speak my tongue felt heavy and sticky in my mouth and I told her that was terrible news.

"Yeah. He killed himself. About a week ago. He jumped off the George Washington Bridge. They were fixing it and some worker saw him go over. It's too awful."

I closed my eyes and thought of him falling. A figure plummeting off that giant expanse into the Hudson. I looked up at the grimy window framing our living area and saw the silhouette of a strolling pigeon.

"Are you there?"

"Yes. I think you caught me a little flat-footed. I don't believe it."

"I know. I'm sorry. I was stunned, too, when I heard. The school called me, Rob, and asked me to contact everyone on the team from our year. There's going to be a memorial service for him at the reunion this weekend. It would be good if we all made an effort to attend. It seems his family asked for all of us to be there. You've been kind of out of it, though. I haven't been able to get hold of you."

I nodded into the phone, realized she couldn't hear that, and said, "Yeah. MIA. That's me."

"I called Niccalsetti and tried about four Carreys until I got your brother or your cousin or something. He said he didn't have an e-mail address for you because he doesn't own a computer."

"You got my brother, Tom. I didn't even know his number was listed."

"Do you think you can make it, Rob?"

"I don't know. I haven't spoken to John, to any of you, in fifteen years."

There was a pause, and the line crackled. She could have moved away from her desk to speak to me, or switched the phone to the other ear. "Look, I'm not crazy about going back there either but his family has specifically asked. Fenton's close to the city. You could just take the train."

"I know it." I looked over at Carolyn at her desk. "I suppose I have to, now that you've found me."

"It's this Saturday. At noon. I'll e-mail you the information. I also have a newspaper article you can read, about, well, you know. Give me your e-mail address, okay?"

I spelled it out: rcarrey@natgeochannel.com.

"Wow. Do you really work for *National Geographic*?"

"When they let me."

"Do you write for them?"

"Film."

"Oh. How cool." She thought about that for a beat, and then said, "At least we can catch up. Anyway, I have to make another call so I can't chat now."

"Ruth?"

"Yes?" She sounded like she was used to closing business on the phone. She sounded achingly professional.

"Where are you calling from?"

"My office. Oh, I'm *sorry*. I'm in the city. In a law firm."

"That's interesting."

"Not really, Rob." There was a pause. "But an interesting sounding woman answered the phone. Are you married?"

I glanced over at Carolyn, who was at her post in front of the computer, her back to me. "No. You?"

"*There's* something we can talk about when I see you."

"Fair enough."

Her voice took on that firm tone again. "I'll see you at the school. Read your e-mail, I just sent it off to you."

We said our good-byes and she clicked off. I lay the phone down, went to the bedroom and pulled on my pants and shirt. I walked into the kitchen and poured myself some coffee that the machine had brewed automatically an hour ago. I thought about John Perry. It was Thursday. Carolyn stood up from the workstation, finally, walked to the couch where I had slept. She picked up the handset and looked at me expectantly.

"That was a woman I went to high school with."

"In Niccalsetti?"

"No. Fenton School, in Connecticut. Where I rowed. A guy I knew from the crew died and they're having a service on Saturday."

"Was he a friend?"

"He was, in a way." I took the phone from her, set it back in the charger, gently wriggled it until it fit. "He killed himself. Jumped off the GW."

Carolyn's eyes widened.

"I hadn't spoken to him in years. He wrote us all notes but I didn't get mine until I came back from the shoot. His life had gone a little crazy."

"That's awful, Rob."

"I haven't seen him since before college."

"That school has had its share of tragedy." Carolyn had gone to a girl's day school in New York before she went to NYU. The idea of boarding school seemed arcane to her. It seemed arcane to me, actually. Carolyn regarded me for a second more and then examined the counters. "I guess I could finish the opening parts of the edit myself, if you help again today."

I went back into the bedroom, the floor cold on my bare feet. I sat on the bed and flipped open my notebook. Carolyn sat at the table, watching me. I downloaded my e-mail account and it took a while. I hadn't even looked at the computer in weeks and the usual spam came through and then the messages from the filmers in Africa and three e-mails from Kevin, my editor at *National Geographic*, all of them with headings like, *Where are you?* and *Earth to Rob* . . . Ruth's e-mail came in last, with the text of the article copied in the body of the message.

MAN JUMPS TO DEATH FROM GEORGE WASHINGTON BRIDGE

A thirty-three-year-old man abandoned his car on the George Washington Bridge on Friday and jumped to his death from the south sidewalk. Port Authority police sources said a workman painting the New Jersey tower last saw Jonathan Perry, of Greenwich, Connecticut, at approximately 11:00 A.M. on Friday. "He had one leg hooked over the guardrail . . . appearing to go over," said Port Authority Police Deputy Dan DiMarchi. A Coast Guard crew pulled Perry's body from the Hudson River on Saturday. "There was no note," said Lieutenant J. D. Forbess. Perry had apparently been taking antidepressants, police said.

I read the article twice and then shut the computer. Ruth hadn't added anything at the bottom of the message. I went back into the kitchen and poured myself half a mug of coffee and sipped it, the taste milky and sweet and a little stale. I drank it standing over the sink and washed the cup very carefully and set it in the rack, watched the water drip from it onto the rubber beneath.

Behind me, Carolyn said, "Are you okay? It's awful news and I kind of think it might be good if you went up to the service. We have to start thinking about what happens now. With us.

I'm sorry about last night, Rob, but I don't regret it. It doesn't change anything, though. It'd still be best if we stick to our plan of your moving out."

I turned and we faced each other in the kitchen like boxers too tired for the last round. "Not *our* plan. *Your* plan. What if I said I didn't want to go?"

"You're going to go anyway, Rob. To South Africa. To Europe. To Brazil. To fucking Zambia." She said the last place with a bite. "You don't really live here. This is pretend. This is . . . convenient."

I went over to the window and squinted down into the city light. It was a gorgeous day. Down below the cars nosed their way around each other, and the galleries were putting up their sidewalk boards. There was a new exhibition on two buildings over entitled *Eggshell Mantra: A Pop Art Collection*. I scooped up the keys from the granite island between us—her keys, with the frayed, beaded fertility doll fob—and went to the door.

"Where are you going?" she demanded.

"Out. I don't know, Car. Out."

I slipped into the cool stairwell and took the elevator to the bottom floor, stepped onto the street and walked for a long time.

———————

The primitive ritual of human sacrifice, otherwise known as formal ergometer testing, began with twelve rowers jacketed against the fall cold, running down the morning-gray highway like motley cattle, stamping and chuffing and spitting. I ran in the middle of the throng listening to the grunts and hawks of the contenders for the God Four pushing themselves through the crew's first dawn run. We had left the dark school buildings behind us and had stampeded down Route 7, past the sports fields and the hulked building of the hockey rink. The average Fenton rower was too big, too malformed and heavy in the shoulders, to run with any grace. We were meant to move boats. Our road running was a study in careful inertia, of piloting rangy muscles, oversized feet and bodies meant for leverage and not velocity.

Connor led, cap pulled low, ignoring us. Ruth ran behind him for a while, then dropped back to move among and around as we lumbered along; an agile sheepdog keeping the herd in line. She constantly checked her tiny digital watch as she ran, an irritating reflex that betrayed her obsession with time and pace. "Faster, guys. Coach will be waiting."

The football jocks lagging at the back trotted a bit faster in response as she pushed us on up the road, barely out of breath, in her sunglasses, blue sweatsuit and knit gloves. As she ran guys would flip her off, but she was ready for it. "DeKress, you're slower than my mom."

DeKress grinned. "That's not what I hear, Ruthie."

"Wadsworth, can't you even keep up with a girl? Perry, John Perry, you need to move those arms."

She glanced back at me, red-faced, her breath making quick puffs of vapor in the dawn. "Carrey, I could take you over two miles. Ten dollars says I could."

"Not a chance," I replied, trying not to let her hear how winded I was.

We circled back, still following Connor, moving now in a brutal solemnity, each runner's eyes cast down to the road or into the back of the rower ahead of him. All the bantering and wisecracking ended as we focused instead on breathing. We stopped near the river and walked off the warm pain, our breaths fogging up the cold air. A dust of frost had settled in the trees that were brightening and reddening. Mist rose from their depths into the new, deep blue morning sky, the light outlining the mountains.

If any of us saw beauty there, none commented on it as we walked and stretched and mumbled to one another on our way to the brooding boathouse and its basement where the appraisals would begin. Channing had been waiting but looked at our steaming throng as if surprised to see us. He was dressed for labor in worn khaki pants, a checkered shirt, heavy sweater, scuffed brown waterproof boots. He was carrying his leather briefcase and a clipboard and was wearing a faded baseball cap that at one point had the national team rings emblazoned across the front. He was completely impervious to the cold. The casual air he adopted before ergometer tests was a deliberate tactic meant to allay our fears.

I walked into the wood-and-oil darkness, set my heels with each step hard enough to shake the wood boards. Connor switched on the lights and they flickered to cold fluorescence above us. The boats, stacked upside down on their wooden trestles, shone blue in the hollow light. Connor glanced at them as he headed for the basement stairs. "The weapons of war," he murmured.

"Time, now," Channing said as we passed. He glanced at me once, briefly and without recognition.

Connor reached the bottom of the basement stairs and took a long, satisfied breath. In the gloom there were eight ergometers lined up in two symmetrical rows of four. Like huge, patient insects, they had lain in wait for us in the darkness. The stink of sweat and oil and steel hanging above them was mixed with the odor of human bodies in distress; human effluent. Eight machines, each one connected to a tiny computer, the ergs stood as reminders that our speed and beauty on the water were functions of brute force and endurance.

By the time we entered the room we had gone silent, more silent than any of us were in class or in chapel. The hollow dripping from the showers echoed. We collapsed against the walls, sat with our feet splayed out in front of us in the dust while Channing, Connor and Ruth went through the motions of zeroing computers and checking seats. Channing worked wordlessly down here. When he was finished he stood toward the back of the room, his hands behind his back, relinquishing control to Connor and Ruth.

Each erg was a steel monorail with a sliding seat on two squat legs. Two boards and two sets of straps for the rower's feet were bolted to the front. A bracket extended straight from this same end of the monorail and it held a heavy fan protected by a black cage. A black bicycle chain snaked out from the innards of the monorail, into the cage, over the gears of the fan and back out of the cage to a mock oar handle that the rower pulled while sliding on his seat, just like in a boat. Screwed onto the cage was the small square computer that calculated the energy you used to spin the fan and the distance you had traveled. You rowed on this thing. It tallied the strokes you poured into it, kept a tab on your slow but sure capitulation. An erg test measured how long it took to row two thousand five hundred meters. A good score was around eight minutes.

We began to prepare for the ordeal, throwing off sweatshirts and baseball hats and nylon pants and spitting into the sinks, gulping from water bottles, trying not to look at each other, or the machines. Or at Ruth, who moved around our farting, hawking bodies with some nimbleness. Ruth was partly one of us, partly not, because she held the clipboard. How many girls could deal with being in a room where guys were stretching and burping, scratching their balls, cracking their joints and generally getting ready to experience pain? She did it with a clinical detachment: checked us off her list, assigned us our test slots, all the while moving indifferently between that mass of human meat.

Phil Leonsis stripped off his shirt and stood towering in front of her, all muscle and hair and bravado. "What do you think?"

Ruth looked him up and down. "About what?"

"You and me, Ruth. In the shower room. I need to warm up. Let's go. Five minutes."

She looked at him sharply and then the look changed to something between aversion and pity. It was the same expression a nurse gives a patient on a gurney before surgery. "You're asking for five minutes with me before an erg test, Leonsis? You'd be ruined."

He laughed. "Not if you blow me, babe."

"Shut up, Leonsis." Perry glowered at him from across the room. "Stop messing around, dude."

Ruth smiled sweetly up at Leonsis and turned away, two red spots high on her cheeks. She called Connor to one of the end ergometers. "Connor wanted to go first this morning. The rest of you can warm up on the other machines. All times from now until final selections are made will be recorded. You can come back and retest but this is the fastest way to cut you guys. The top four rowers will form a training group. The rest of you will train with John Hinkle." Hinkle, the second boat coxswain, looked up at the mention of his name. He sat in a bright yellow climbing jacket in the corner looking ill. Ruth looked us over. "Stretch your backs, your legs, your arms. I repeat: we take down *all* times today, no matter how pathetic."

So Connor had the responsibility of setting our benchmark time and he had to do it right there in front of us. Some of the rowers stood and began their own preparations. Five left to stretch and stamp in the next room to avoid seeing what they themselves would soon endure. But most of us stayed to watch. The exertion required for an erg test was almost unreal. Anything could go wrong. You could cramp, pull a muscle, throw up, perform poorly because you were coming down with a cold and didn't know it yet or because your body was tired from training too much or too little; myriad reasons could contribute to an embarrassing score.

Connor stripped off his sweatshirt and sweatpants. Beneath these he was wearing his worn racing trunks and a white undershirt. He had wrapped a piece of toweling around his head and adjusted it carefully, a crude sweatband that looked like a bandage. He coughed, settled onto his machine, strapped his feet into the foot stretchers. He crouched, extended his arms and grabbed the handle that rested against the fan's cage. He pushed down on his legs and leaned back, pulled the handle toward him. The fan in the cage began to whir and then growl as Connor snapped his arms to his chest. The bicycle chain snaked out from its coiled home. It ticked back into the machine as he came back up the slide. The fan spun and slowed as Connor crouched and caught it with a stronger push from his legs. The computer lit up and the numbers began to churn on the screen.

I hugged my knees.

Let him be weak, I thought. *Let him not be equal to his bullshit*.

Connor balled his body, reached and pulled. The machine snarled, whirred and ticked back. He brought up the pace, and the machine began to hiss, its numbers reacting to every second stroke. His rasping breaths came quicker, the hissing turned into whines and then screeches. A blue vein stood out on his forehead, rose and pulsed into the sweat towel binding his hair. One minute went down. Connor exhaled and gulped the air as the machine rasped.

Two minutes. Anyone could slam down two good minutes. What's two minutes?

His legs crushed the white boards of the foot stretchers; he spewed spit at the machine's cage before gulping in more air. Connor was pulling hard and evenly and the numbers flickered, changed, and his times began to weaken, but only slightly. Three minutes, then four. One hundred and twenty strokes counted on the screen, one hundred and twenty crouches, pulls, hisses, whines and screeches. Then it was five minutes and now one hundred and sixty. The muscles lacing his forearms were straining, shifting over one another. One hundred and seventy crouches, one hundred and seventy releases. One hundred and ninety strokes now, the pace brought up, the stakes higher.

I sat in the dust of the boathouse, watching, my stomach filled with a black acid of fear. It was horrible to see how good he was. How easy it would be, I thought, to relent. To give up a few strokes. By now Connor's body was revolting against the pain, his veins were filled with poison, his head was thrumming. What compelled him to seat himself to this feast of agony? Two hundred strokes passed, his blond hair was a wet blur. How many meters were rowed now?

Two thousand.

Five hundred to go.

Just under fifty more strokes.

Now two thousand one hundred and the screeches came faster. The blue vein wormed deeper into his skull, and the striations down his legs went pink, then red. Two thousand four hundred meters, and then four more shuddering screeches and quick rasps and two thousand five hundred meters rowed. There was a last snarl from the machine and Connor slumped over, eating the air, pushing the handle away, his eyes shut, their white lids covered with sweat. The otherworldly presence in the room was gone now. Left behind was Connor's collapsed, spent body, merely human again.

He stood up, finally. The room had gone silent and Ruth, not looking at him, marked his time, the best time I had ever seen a rower pull. Wiping his eyes, he looked at me first. "Your turn, Roberto."

9.

We realigned the ergs so that I rowed with Wadsworth, Leonsis, DeKress and Perry, all of us in a line with Ruth pacing beside us. On my right, DeKress did the entire test wearing a baseball hat backward. He and I settled into an easy pace, maybe twenty-eight strokes a minute, but halfway through I ticked out to thirty-two and he just looked over at me and blinked through his sweat. Leonsis, next to him, tried to power through the first hundred strokes and made it to seventy-five before taking it down to a slow twenty-five strokes a minute. His style went to hell, but he was powerful enough to pull through it anyway. At the end, wearing a Fenton squash shirt and shorts, Wadsworth rowed to stay near the top and simply outpaced DeKress. He didn't look at us while he did it, just gazed at the computer over his horn-rimmed glasses, scored a decent time and stopped, packed up, left. I admired that. As for Perry on my left, he conducted a tug-of-war with his machine. His test began badly and only got worse.

My time was three seconds behind Connor's. A world apart. But still second best in the club, enough so I was assured a place on the senior training squad. I was furious with myself though. I had known the time to beat, knew exactly what I needed to do, but started out too hard and couldn't make it up at the end. The last thirty strokes saw me lose three seconds. I willed the numbers to flicker in my favor, but they wouldn't. The basement air seemed to cling to my lungs and the wind from the other fans and sobbing breaths from the other rowers distracted me. As did Ruth's closeness to me while I tried to pull through it. Even though she didn't flaunt it, she was a fierce feminine presence in this morass of sweaty testosterone.

Toward the end she just said, calmly, "Your last twenty strokes are coming in two and you can beat Connor. You're good for it, Carrey." Her voice so close it seemed like it was in my head. I looked over at her and only saw her in profile, her dark eyes looking at my fading numbers. "Don't look at me, Carrey, look at the computer. Seventeen strokes in. Don't get distracted." And I tried to jam it for the last ten, but the numbers would not obey. The pain became so unbearable I knew I had to settle or risk passing out. Losing consciousness chasing Connor's score was not what I needed, but there was something else. A rage at seeing those numbers stand still while I poured everything I had into it. The feeling of hatred running up my spine and boiling beneath my brain blurred my vision. Connor had felt the same pain but had rowed through it, alone, knowing what he had to do to make himself more untouchable than he already was. I knew that if I stood up after that test I'd scream. I had no idea why. Maybe it was the way Connor lost interest in my test before I hit the last twenty strokes, turned away knowing I'd never make up the time. Ruth watched me finish impassively, took down my score and moved off. Before she did she gently touched me, part congratulation, part something else.

Three seconds.

Half a boat length.

Connor's universe remained undisturbed.

Just about everyone witnessed John Perry collapse on his machine. He rowed next to me on one end of the row. We had tapped hands before the test, not a handshake, not a slap, just an assertion of a mutual presence. We had moved his ergometer away from the rest to accommodate him and he had rowed with an uneven fury, slobber hanging out his mouth while he worked. The ergometer test was about two hundred and fifty strokes and he survived only the first one hundred and twenty, and then his pace went slack. Ruth felt it before I did, and stood behind him, cursing at him, swearing at him, appealing to his pride and his strength, then mocking him, shouting at him to move the numbers up, to pull harder, to punish the machine. But still Perry faded. By the end of it, he was hunched over the oar handle, rowing in a weak frenzy, the handle barely clearing his knees, his tremendous body depleted of oxygen. Humiliation and pain rose off him in equal measure as he tried to row through it. Ten strokes, fifteen jagged strokes, then a series of whipping strokes over the knees. His breathing sounded like groaning.

Channing had taken a seat against the wall on a battered wooden bench that looked like it might have once served as a pew in some country chapel. He watched Perry as if he had finally found out what we as a group had been hiding from him. Connor stood silently next to him the entire time. Perry, eyes squeezed shut, threw himself into the machine.

Ruth's voice cracked over all of us, "Now you come back on this and show these guys what you can do. You are dying on me Perry, *dying*, don't you die." But Perry did die, and Ruth's voice rose to a screech and then sunk into awful silence. I had finished my piece two minutes ahead of him, sat gasping over the monorail. The rest of the oarsmen finished within forty seconds of me, but Perry chugged on, our eyes on him, some of us attempting pity. When he was done Perry collapsed, covered in sweat and snot and watery vomit, his face turned away from Channing and Connor. Ruth took down his score. An eternity later, Perry stood, red-faced and blotched, and reeled drunkenly to the door.

Connor turned to him and spoke, loud enough so we could all hear. "You didn't finish. You stopped at two thousand meters."

Perry nodded in response, unable to look up or talk.

"Mark that down, Ruth. Write 'Did not finish.' Put it in big letters by his name so we'll remember." He continued looking at Perry in disgust. "Get out. Hear me? Get out of here and come back when you are ready to train."

Perry walked to his sweatshirt, unsteady and spitting, and pulled it on under Connor's unrelenting gaze. By now no one in the boathouse was even pretending they weren't watching him get cast out. As Perry left I felt a sickness inside me. A clammy feeling of guilt and apprehension. I heard Perry labor up the stairs, then listened to his heavy plodding steps across the floors above, the creak of the door. I looked once at Channing, who regarded us as if we had confirmed something elemental about human nature that he had almost forgotten.

Connor was not about to let Perry quit, though. He never invited Leonsis to train with the returning God Four and Leonsis never asked why, either, was simply told to keep working and come back for the group tests. It wasn't because Connor liked Perry. It was because Leonsis would never take Connor's shit. And Connor also knew that Perry's sprint times were deadly. He was a brute at the start of a race, nobody in that room could match his first fifty strokes. His endurance could be built back up—he was playing football now, moving in short bursts. On a good day, Perry could kill Leonsis with his bare hands, and Connor wanted that kind of power in his boat.

But Perry might also have been salvaged because Ruth never forgave Leonsis for asking for a blow job in front of the JV returners. Even in jest he had overstepped the mark, and Ruth was not afraid to wield her power.

———————

I walked all the way to Washington Square Park, snagged a lone bench and tried to cool off. By this time in my life I had learned not to do anything important when I was in a rage, certainly not to argue with Carolyn. I knew as well that I could not think about John, although I wanted to. I watched two people doing t'ai chi. NYU kids sitting under the trees and by the fountains, nodding into iPods over books. Some kids on the kind of modern swings undreamed of when I was a child in Niccalsetti.

I moved over to the game tables and sat down close to the fountain. It was warming up but the serious grifters were still sleeping. I practiced what I would say to Carolyn when I returned, how I could get us back to where we were eight hours ago. I had brought my cell phone, shoved it in my pocket when I left the loft. It was, hands down, an unfashionable phone. It was one of the flat metal ones that opened and were cool a decade ago, and I had never traded up because I always told myself that I would simply put the phone I used in South Africa to roam when I came back to the city. But I always wound up using this one, which was verging on being a collector's item when I met Carolyn.

She kept it in the same basket that she kept her iPhone, my charger wrapped around it. It was a good sign.

I checked the message window, idly hoping she might have texted me, but of course she hadn't. I flipped open the phone, thought, finally punched in "bagels/coffee (?)"

And then I waited obstinately for ten minutes, knowing (bitterly) that Carolyn would have picked up the text right away. She kept her iPhone next to her wherever she was in the loft, refused to leave the place without it, woke up to it, told the time with it. The wait was part of the message to me. The trick was not to get irritated, not to follow up with a "wtf??" despite knowing she could be back to me in thirty seconds if she wanted. There was no arguing with this procedure. If I called her, she'd put me to voice mail. If she was truly pissed off at me, of course, she would not reply. This was possible.

So I sat and watched an old woman in a cashmere suit playing chess against her granddaughter. The woman was sitting primly on one of the green benches in front of the permanent chessboards, and the granddaughter was standing on the other, moving pieces with care, laughing when the grandmother thought, moved, lost a piece and smiled. Each time one of them moved they would bow their heads over the board. Every move of the girl's was a revelation for both of them. The old woman was once tall, now frail, still impeccable. The granddaughter was wearing loud pink overalls. Sneakers that lit up when she moved. Dressed, obviously, by a mother with different tastes.

As I watched I found myself tearing up, and I wiped my eyes quickly on my shoulder, looked furtively around me to make sure nobody saw. I set the phone on the bench next to me. Seven minutes had gone by since I texted Car. Rowing had left me with an excellent sense of time.

The granddaughter had put her grandmother in a tough position. I imagined filming it, a long shot from here, then close-ups of the game from the grandmother's perspective, then the kid's tiny hands on the chess pieces. I couldn't see what color the granddaughter was playing, but I imagined she was playing black, had taken her grandmother's bishops and rooks and knights while losing only a few polite pawns. The grandmother's queen would be cornered in the back of the board by a relentless march of the childish army, the child's defenses ever secure. I'd do a profile of the knowing look on the grandmother's face as her queen was wiped off the board and the king was boxed in, then get a table-level shot of the king being ceremoniously knocked over to a scream and a hug from the victor.

My phone vibrated, buzzed, spun halfway round on the wooden bench and started to slide downward.

I goalied it. Flipped it open.

"whatev."

I didn't look back at the two chess players. I stood and walked toward Lafayette Street. I had a plan. A kid wearing a blue Columbia University rowing windshirt and sunglasses steered a silver mountain bike around me. He had on Nikes and black rowing trunks and a backpack. It could have been me a decade and a half ago. It could have been Connor.

I know that whenever I imagine Connor Payne I am unfair. I represent him badly. The fact is, whenever I thought of Fenton, I thought of him. Of the privilege of being friends with him. It gave you a kind of grace that I had never experienced back at home. There was simply no equivalent sport to crew in a regular high school. Not even the football players are part of the kind of aristocracy that the members of the top crews at the top rowing schools in America enjoy. Fenton students admired the rowing team, they admired Connor. And Connor was arrogant. He was the most arrogant person I ever met, and he encouraged us to be arrogant as well. The school, in his mind, had been divided between rowers and the plebes, most of whom he referred to as "tools" or "dorkage."

In his mind, you had to succeed without any effort. Striving, working, was in bad taste. Connor told me this, the hardest working person I have ever known. Most of the teachers at Fenton were tools, in his mind, except for about five or six of them, the really hard-core teachers, most of whom failed him mercilessly. He failed with a grim sense of pride. Case in point: He refused to prepare for the SAT. He obstinately refused to take it seriously.

The SAT was for kids he called "power tools." Geeks and pure dorkage took the SAT review course the school held.

Never mind that the college guidance counselor solemnly told us during that year that no Ivy League school would consider family connections when making an admissions decision. It was a new era, we were warned. I brought this up with Connor, whose GPA hovered around a 2.5, whose SAT scores were a joke, who did no extracurricular activities other than row like a demigod. Connor snorted. "There's family connections and then there are *family connections*, Carrey," he told me. "Get real."

For my part, I slaved at Fenton. Or at least I thought I did. True slavery in my life would come when I was assigned to a film crew in northern Canada, when we hauled our own editing equipment up to some hellhole near Saskatchewan and worked until midnight every day, and partied at a bar called The Zoo until three and woke up to film the next day. At Fenton I did my homework, which was a big deal for me, given that I had passed through four years at Niccalsetti Senior School without bringing books home at night, working instead for my father after sculling, or going to bars with my brother. I worked at Fenton because I needed every advantage I could get. I tried to do it secretly. I tried to hide it, but Fenton was harder than Niccalsetti. I envied Ruth her good grades, which, in retrospect, I'm sure she bled for as well.

But on the water I was different. I felt the chains fall off, felt the power I had over the others, the kids who had worked their way up through the ranks, year after grueling year under Channing. Kids who would row for U Penn and Brown and maybe Princeton or the University of Washington or the Naval Academy. I beat them on the water and off the water without really trying—the only real competitor I had was Connor. I couldn't help admiring him. Not because he could beat me—that was unspeakable—but because he made it seem so easy. His acceptance of me, I knew, depended on me being as good on the water as he was. Everything else was secondary. And back then, this seemed worth it all. Rowing at Fenton was all about discipline, and the ability to withstand pain. That would be the measure of my youth. Rowing through it all.

By the time I was approaching Bleecker and Mulberry and moving away from NYU, I was among the kind of people I had grown up with. I liked that I identified not with the other camera-wielding types that infested this part of the city, but with the working guys, some of whom I, in my never ending naïveté about Manhattan, believed might be connected.

The men who worked for my father thought my going off to Fenton to try and attract a big university was a scam, of course. They understood the idea of kids getting basketball and football scholarships because those were real sports that people played on TV. But a scholarship for rowing? Even the guys who drove along the expressway beside the river and saw the eights from the Black Rock Rowing Club didn't think it was really difficult. It was distant, it happened on the water, it wasn't spectator friendly, it looked too graceful. Rowing wasn't a real sport to them.

Football. Now that was a real sport, a sport they could understand. My brother Tom had done them proud, even though he'd never see the inside of a university. Tom had captained the Niccalsetti Senior School to victory against every other school in the county. When he came to work the guys treated him like an all-conquering hero, a Roman legionnaire back from the front. My sport—rowing alone for medals—they did not understand; it was merely tolerated because I was the boss's son. Year after year, through fall, through winter training, through spring, the guys on my father's payroll rarely asked me what I was doing.

So when they found out a school in New England—a prep school—wanted me, they were suspicious. Prep schools were already suspect enough, storage places for rich kids. When I told them Fenton wanted me for crew, that I was idiot enough to do an extra year of high school, the questions finally came. "They have school teams for rowing, you mean?" I said yes and they'd think about that. "And all the big colleges have rowing teams?" Lots of them did, sure, I told them, they called them crews. But the colleges my father's guys knew about were the Big Ten colleges that formed the bulwark of the football pool, and schools like Georgetown and Notre Dame, which they saw on TV during basketball season. Did *those schools* also have crews? "Yeah," I'd say, "but they don't give you scholarships to row on those teams. Just the Ivy League schools. And then only sometimes." Ivy League? "You know, Yale, Harvard, Princeton." And the guys would shrug and say those were cool, too.

At first I didn't want to go when Fenton contacted me through one of the sculling coaches at the rowing club and asked me to repeat my senior year there. The offer came just when I was trying to figure out how I'd pay to go to the State University of New York at Niccalsetti, which was pretty cheap, but still going to be a push for my parents. I was looking at working my way through college and then the letter from Fenton arrived at the Black Rock Rowing Club after I won the Canadian Henley Sculls. One year at Fenton and I could get a break on tuition at a rowing school. My father pushed me to do it. "You liked Niccalsetti Senior School and you have lots of friends there and girls and all that, but what did they do for Tom? These rich-kid schools can get you into places. It's nine months. Then you can come back here and spend the rest of your life with your buddies if you're that dumb. But take the opportunity."

Shouldering my way into the coffee place on Lafayette, Fenton seemed like another universe. A dream. I wondered what my younger self—fanatic that I was—would think as I ordered extra-large cappuccinos, bagels, fresh bread for toast, green lemonade and the rest of the supplies I'd need to buy myself another morning with Car. What would that kid make of me walking back to Broome and finding my awkward way up to the loft where

Carolyn would pointedly ignore me as I threw my keys and cell phone down in the kitchen and placed the food on plates?

How would that Fenton student of a decade and a half ago like to see his older self set these things down like graven offerings beside this woman in calculated silence? Would he watch in bewilderment as Carolyn flipped off the lid to her coffee, took a sip and then noticed the vegan cookies I knew she could not resist? Rob Carrey of fifteen years past would wonder what I was doing as I crept up behind her—while she tried to ignore me lugubriously, gazing at the computer screen while crunching the cookie—and sank my teeth into her shoulder hard enough to make her yelp and laugh, truce flooding into the room for an exquisite moment.

10.

The first really cold snap that blew through Fenton that year caught us all by surprise. I woke up and saw the clouds of condensation on my window and felt the icy floor after I rolled out of bed. Walking down the boardwalk to the dining hall I faced the rest of the students in the morning silence, most of us unable to even contemplate winter term yet. Chris Wadsworth and John Perry were drinking coffee while looking over the river that was now a sad, dark gutter of water dividing the frosted grass. Wadsworth caught my eye and said, "Coach is going to want road training now. Connor will, too."

Behind his glasses, Wadsworth had pale blue eyes that made him seem lupine and pitiless. He was dressed for class already, wearing a long camel coat, leather gloves and a neon blue skiing hat. In less than ten years he would be a lawyer in New York. He was one of those guys who was ruddy and healthy year round, and who also always seemed a little stoned somehow. It was a look many aspired to at Fenton. He played squash—very well—a sport that would be useful to him for the rest of his life, unlike crew. You met lots of kids just like Wadsworth at Fenton, guys who were already thinking a decade ahead, almost living it. He rowed in the bow of the God Four. Was known for pulling all-nighters studying con-law cases in the attic of North Dorm. He squinted at me. "Do you think we're going to get a chance to row before spring break, Carrey?"

Perry looked at me evenly. "Carrey has other aspirations."

Wadsworth grinned. "So I hear."

They had been friends since freshman year and the easy back and forth of their joking had the touch of a well-rehearsed performance about it; a finely choreographed two-man act. Perry was dressed for the final assault on Everest wrapped in a Gore-Tex climbing vest and Nepal knit cap. The tassels hung down ludicrously next to his ears. He examined the river and the haze of cold rising from it that would dissipate later in the morning in the weakening fall sun. Perry was a valuable and well-liked football player and had been on the varsity team since his freshman year. His folks lived in Darien, Connecticut, where his father owned a trucking company. His last name was on the same trucks I used to see delivering frozen food to the supermarket on my street at home.

"I think Carrey's after Ruth Anderson," Wadsworth continued to goad good-naturedly. "Queen Ruth. Now that's aspiration in its purest form."

Perry grinned shyly at the water. The hardest part of adjusting to this life was dealing with the constant insults, the bantering. Guys said things to your face here you'd kill them for at home. It was all we had in a world where you didn't ever express affection or friendship, where to be overly committed to anything was considered in poor taste. This was as friendly as these guys could be.

It was impossible that Wadsworth knew what I thought about Ruth. It wasn't like anything was happening between us. I sat behind her in my chemistry class and had only really had one real conversation with her. But the fact that these guys knew about this meant that she had told somebody about it.

And that was very cool.

Wadsworth glanced nonchalantly over the railing. "Carrey's getting laid. Time somebody did."

Perry looked at me, startled. "Are you, Carrey?" There was sincere surprise in his voice. And envy.

"Jumbo, do you really think I'd tell you?"

Perry winced. "My name's John. I hate being called Jumbo."

"Jumbo, everyone calls you Jumbo."

Wadsworth laughed. "It's like, on his birth certificate. 'Jumbo. Fifty pound baby boy. Mother deceased.'"

"It is not." Jumbo looked nervously down the boardwalk. "What chick wants to go out with a guy named Jumbo? You guys need to stop calling me that name. I'm a senior now. I have rights."

"There are worse nicknames, Jumbo."

"There are not! Being called Jumbo sucks!"

"There's that sophomore everyone calls Pumpkin Head."

"You mean Georgie Panousis? Okay, yeah. But that's because he had to endure a pumpkin *drop*. Not because his head is pumpkin *shaped*."

"A pumpkin drop?"

"Last year he wouldn't get this crazy senior, Bruce Harmon, a pizza during study hall, so Bruce and some of his friends dropped rotten pumpkins on him while he was, like, sleeping. Pumpkin drops used to be a tradition around here."

"Nice. If anyone tried to do that to me I'd break his arm."

"They only did it to freshmen. Seniors were exempt and everything. And you're a rower."

Wadsworth smirked. "Georgie's might have been the last official pumpkin drop ever. Pumpkin drops are extinct now. The headmaster told us the next time we held a pumpkin drop there would be an expulsion. Georgie's dad threatened to sue the

school, the dick claimed Georgie got a concussion from it or
something. The headmaster has no sack. An eighty-year-old tradition. Gone. It's a crying shame."

"Are you a virgin, Wadsworth?" I asked, trying to catch him
off-guard.

"No, Carrrey, I am not a virgin. I mean, technically, no way."

"The rumor is, you're a virgin, Wads. And you have it all
over you. Chicks can smell it. Ask anyone."

Wadsworth set his jaw. "FYI dickhead, next weekend I'm
taking a college visit to Yale. I'm staying with Jill St. Pierre."

Perry laughed. "Carrey doesn't know who she is, dude." A
blast of wind came whipping down the boardwalk and blew
Perry's cap tassels in his face. "Jill graduated last year. She and
Wads used to go out but Wads never scored. So, anyway, word
is Yale has suddenly thawed her out. She's apparently transformed into the Whore of New Haven. Maybe he'll finally get
some serious action."

Wadsworth shrugged. "Nicely put. Nice. I appreciate that,
Jumbo. Jill will, too. Very nice."

"Dude, everyone knows this."

I looked at Wadsworth with pity. "That's kind of sad, Wadsworth. I mean, it's really sad."

Perry rubbed his stomach and changed the subject. "I've
been running, Carrey, can you tell? And practicing on the fucking erg. It's hard to get my head into rowing this early in the
year. We have months till the racing season starts. Ruth sent me
a note and told me I had to lose, like, ten pounds. And whenever
I see her she gives me this look. Like she knows I'm slacking."

"Perry is scared of her," Wadsworth said.

"You are, too, man. She's like, the Devil."

Wadsworth looked at me. "She is. We are mean to her because we fear her."

"Dude, I'm not mean to her," Perry protested.

Wadsworth giggled maliciously. "That's because Perry secretly wants her. He asked her out once. To this dance at Hotchkiss. And she said it 'wouldn't be appropriate.' Talk about getting über-negged. Poor bastard."

"Dude, shut up, dude. It wasn't a *dance*. It was a *social*." Perry punched Wads in the arm and Wads had to take a step back to absorb the impact. He rubbed his arm and shoved Perry back. Or tried to.

"Don't tell Connor that Ruth shot Perry down. I know you guys hang out. Connor would never let Perry forget it. Seriously. We're taking you into our confidence."

"I don't hang out with Connor, Wads. I don't even like him."

"Nobody *likes* Connor. We tolerate him. Like taxes and death and all."

"We gotta go, Carrey," Perry cut in. "Tell Captain Connor we don't want to run today. Tell him to take a break for once in his life."

Wadsworth grinned. "Fat chance of that. Connor's a psycho. Carrey, you, too, are a psycho."

Perry pushed him down the boardwalk. "Give our regards to Ruth."

Wadsworth put a gloved finger in the air and made his final pronouncement. "Now, speaking of virgins . . ."

I watched them go, Wadsworth tall and lanky, Perry shuffling beside him in his untied, clownishly oversized Bean boots. From behind they looked like two busted-out boxers on the bum. The future leaders of America.

———

Wadsworth was right. Soon after our exchange on the boardwalk, Connor and Channing wanted roadwork. By late afternoon a few days later, the sun was weak and pale beside the mountain, darkness falling ever earlier. We jogged stiffly down the road against the wind. Channing drove behind us, his war-torn Chevy burping exhaust from its busted manifold. The gas fumes were eye watering even at twenty yards in the brisk cold. Connor ran behind the herd, next to Perry, who was wearing a filthy brace over the yard of cloth covering his right knee. Ruth ignored us, staying just out of Connor's range of vision, pacing the crowd in her heavy sweat clothes, her mirrored sunglasses making her look like a bug.

Perry was puffing hard, hawking, plodding forward with his head down. His face was red right to the tip of his nose, as if he was cooking from his own internal combustion. Basted in his own sweat, he wiped his nose with the back of his hand as he ran, then smeared snot on his chest like streaks of mucosal war paint. Connor kept hounding him. "Run. Go, load."

Perry wheezed, spat, pushed his knees up and bunched his massive shoulders around his head. "It's all muscle, Connor. Pure muscle."

"Dead weight. All dead weight for this team to haul over the finish. Run."

Perry coughed and tried to pour on some speed to get away from him, loping now toward the rest of us. Connor just lengthened his stride a fraction, not even breathing hard, and was all over him again. I could hear Perry's meaty footfalls and smell him: a musty, elephant pong. "I'm benching three hundred even, dude. Free weights. Three hundred even." Perry gasped this out to the general crowd, but mostly to irk Connor. Connor shoved him and he almost lost his footing. It always irritated Connor when Perry brought up weightlifting. Connor maxed out at two hundred ten on a good day—on a day when that's all he was focused on. He hated the free weights bench in the boathouse and always put his book bag and sweatshirt on it when he trained down there, as if that ominous equipment was only good for hanging clothes. "You're not lifting the boat," Connor spat out. "You're rowing it. Run it off, fat boy."

Perry had a Buddha's patience, his meaty bull shoulders

dropped and rounded against the cold and strained against the wet cloth of his sweatshirt. I couldn't even hear Connor's footsteps as they bickered. "Where did they find you, Jumbo?" he asked, running easily and lightly, not the slightest bit winded. "Seriously. I really want to know. The admissions committee must have interviewed you and somebody actually had to say, 'Okay, John Perry's a good candidate for this school. He's the right stuff.' I mean, Carrey I can just about understand. We have to help underprivileged people in this world, but there's no excuse for you, Jumbo. None."

Perry took it and took it. I wondered what would happen if he just turned around and swung at him. It was all he had to do. Connor wouldn't last a second in a fight with Perry. One smack from that moist, fat fist and Connor would wake up in summer vacation needing therapy to relearn his name. Maybe Perry thought taking shit from Connor was good for him. Like it was character building or something. Back home, where kids routinely fought out of sheer boredom, Connor wouldn't exist. Somebody would have killed him.

I upped my pace and broke away from the group, started lengthening my stride when I saw the boathouse. I wanted to leave all of them behind me for just a minute, hit the road in front of the boathouse at full speed. But Connor shadowed me, staying just out of my peripheral vision. I could hear his footsteps striking the ground with mine and I pushed it a little harder. I couldn't lose him. By the time I saw the boathouse peeping over the fields, I put my head down and charged it, figured I had two hundred yards to shake him, but he stayed right behind me, and then he was next to me. I laid it on and he kept it up. "Nice pace, Carrey. Very nice."

I ignored him, kept the speed up until we had twenty yards and then I tried to lose him again. I took a breath and dug in, sprinted as hard as I could, thinking I'd beat him to the driveway by a stride, but he was already pouring on the juice and just managed to cross next to me. It took all my self-control to resist the urge to hit him down to the water. I turned away from him and walked it off.

He hadn't beaten me, but there was no way I could have pulled away from him. I turned and looked up at him and he was doubled over, wheezing, gasping, then stood up when the rest of the team stampeded onto the boathouse drive. He quickly turned and looked at me, grinning, his breath short clouds of vapor. "Sweet one, Roberto."

I jogged by him toward the boathouse.

Ruth caught up with me. "Good run, Carrey."

"He still almost beat me."

"You don't have to compete with him for everything, Carrey. He's not the enemy." Sweat glistened in her hair. Her sunglasses had slid down her nose.

"I can't help it."

"Just be cool, all right? Can you do that for me? Play nicely with the other boys." She grinned wickedly. Punched my arm. "Don't make me mad at you, Carrey. Or make me do something I'll regret."

Ruth herded us back into the unheated boathouse for another hour of training. Channing had posted the workout up on the bulletin board on an index card written in his jagged script: *Work on the ergometer, a weight circuit, bench pulls circuit.* He didn't come into the boathouse with us, simply drove off and left us to our own devices.

We descended into the catacombs beneath the boats and set to work on the machines. I rowed next to Perry, who started gasping for breath after a seven-hundred-meter piece—just a few minutes of effort—and bent double against the foot stretchers with his eyes bulging. Ruth sat next to him, wrote down his slightly improved time. Perry studiously ignored her, knowing that she was paying attention to him at Channing's request because the erg was his special weakness. He glanced at me. "You okay, Carrey?

"You don't need to take that crap, Jumbo."

"You know how he is."

"I know how he is."

He rubbed his knee. "This sucks. I want to get out on the water."

Ruth spoke, finally, looking down at her clipboard. "Spring is months away, John. You still have to deal with a whole winter in this place."

Two machines over, Connor finished his second seven-hundred-meter piece and rowed it off on the machine, then laid the handle against the cage gently, as if it were alive. He leaned over, looked at Perry and me sitting there and shook his head, checked his watch. Then he stood up. He came over and looked down at Perry's knee, Perry's leg as big around as both of mine, pale and hairy. Connor looked at it as if something had suddenly occurred to him. "You're going to be able to row on that, right Jumbo?"

Perry nodded, stood up, eye to eye with Connor. His head was perfectly round, and his hair clung to the sides of it like a helmet, thick and bushy as a dog's.

Ruth looked up at both of them, a diminutive referee. "Perry, seriously, should I have you booked in for treatment on that knee?"

"Nah." Perry was breathing hard, I realized. His recovery off the machine was awful. "My knee is cool. It always eases up after a while."

Connor pointed at the weight bar we kept in the corner of the room. When we'd cleaned up the week before somebody had stacked the extra forty-five pound weights on either side of it, three on each side.

"How much is six times forty-five, Perry?"

Perry's mouth worked as he thought.

Connor made a disgusted sound. "It's two hundred and seventy pounds, you *goof*. Add an additional forty-five for the bar and we come to three hundred and fifteen. Do you think you can clean that?"

"Hell, yeah." Perry sounded just a tad too eager. The repentant zealot, wanting to make amends with the high priest of crew.

"That's impossible." Connor wiped his mouth, looked Perry up and down. "Don't lie to me."

Perry sized up the bar. He slowly rolled it from the corner and stood in front of it. Even the guys on the ergometers stopped rowing. Perry looked over at Connor. "I can lift it. Yeah, I can."

"To your chin?"

"I can lift it and throw it, if you want me to."

"Ten dollars right now says you can't."

Ruth was watching this with increasing alarm. "Wait. This is dumb, you guys. John's hurt, I don't think—"

"Shut up, Ruth. Jumbo is fine. He needs to toughen up. That erg is kicking his ass."

"John, you don't need to do this. Coach hasn't called for any heavy lifting yet. It's not on the program."

Connor laughed. "Who cares what's on the program? This is just a wager. Between gentlemen. Jumbo says he can lift it and I want to see him do it."

"Connor, I really—"

"Shut *up*, Ruth."

Ruth's face set in anger and she looked up at Perry. "John, you don't need to do this, okay?"

Connor's eyes flashed. "He damn well does, Ruth."

Perry shrugged. He set his eyes on the bar. He licked his lips and wiped his wrist across his nose, stood over the weights, reached down with his fleshy palms and tested the bar, released it. Then he rolled his neck, shook out his paws and circled his shoulders, breathing hard the whole time. It was a transformation. He looked like the work of a sculptor who had been asked to carve a huge human figure and not bother with the details.

He was menacing, indestructible. His was a body meant to lift and work and absorb pain.

He was squaring off over three hundred and fifteen pounds. Dead weight, clean and jerk. I considered what would happen to me if I tried it with even two hundred. I'd been on a job back home with an ex-army guy named Quayne McAllister, who'd tried to roll a sixty gallon drum full of silica gel out a loading dock and had caught its full weight when it rolled back in on him. He'd hit the floor clutching his twisted spine and howling; raspy, high-pitched screeches of pain that had brought my father running into the room yelling at me to call an ambulance. I still remembered my father rolling him on his stomach while the grown man with two sons older than me lay there snorting in the dust like some animal he'd found gutshot in the road. After that McAllister was just another guy at work with a back brace and tape on his wrists who walked with a limp.

Perry wrapped a leather belt around his kidneys and pulled it tight. He pushed the bar out farther, so it was between Connor and himself. "You want to try it first, Connor?" Perry looked like he meant it. As if skinny Connor Payne, with his measly one hundred and eighty-five pounds, was going to have a chance even moving the thing. Perry smiled ingratiatingly. I willed him to needle Connor just a little more. Remind Connor he was asking him to do something he himself could not.

Wadsworth, who had been watching all this from one of the weight benches, broke in. "Call it off, Connor. This is grotesque." There was a fault line of fear in his voice.

Connor didn't even look at him. Seemed not to have registered that Wadsworth had spoken.

Perry swung his arms out and then practiced getting into position, leveling the bar, finding just the right spot for his drive. He breathed low, from his stomach, as if sucking energy in from the close, rank air. He pursed his lips, swallowing some idea about the weight, some concept about leverage we didn't know.

Then, in one blur of movement, he seemed to almost fall on the bar, to collapse over it and catch himself as his hands found the metal. Hunched over the bar for only a second, he drove with his legs and stepped forward at the same time. The bar came off the floor just a shade unevenly, and Perry puffed his cheeks, looking right at Connor, and ripped it upward to his shoulders, the weights rotating slightly, his knees bent just a touch, the left leg taking the greatest strain. Finally he rose, the weight parallel to his shoulders. He grinned, his face tight and florid with the effort. He sucked in a chestful of air, a strained contortion that showed his teeth. He exhaled hard and took a quick inhale. The boathouse was dead silent. We could hear Perry's feet sliding on the floor to keep his stance, his tendons red and pulsing over his socks.

Connor leaned forward, almost into his face. "Can you get it over your head, Perry?" he needled. "*Can you?*"

And for that one second Perry thought about it, thought about trying for that last push and getting his body beneath it. Wadsworth tried to spot him but he was too slow. Perry gave it one last heave and stood, wavering under the strain, legs apart. Finally, he pushed the bar outward and it crashed down with a loud clatter leaving two deep indents in the blue wooden floor. Perry rocked back so his shoulders were straight. Wadsworth pounded his back, "You okay?"

Perry nodded, making fists, rolled his neck again and turned away. Wadsworth turned around furiously and pointed at Connor. "What the hell was that?"

"I thought he could do it. If you get it to your shoulders, the rest is easy."

Wadsworth shook his head, hearing something he wasn't sure he could believe in Connor's voice. Connor took a quick step in his direction and spun him around. "Wads, you know what? I can't lift that weight. Can you? Don't even answer me. Perry's the only one who can."

"So fucking leave him alone, for—"

"But I can tell you something. If I *could* get that bar up to my shoulders, I would get it over my head. That's the difference between Jumbo and me."

Connor seemed to dismiss him and turned to Perry, waited while he caught his breath. "Well done," Connor said. "I'm impressed. Very impressed." He held out his hand. Perry didn't take it. Connor left it there between them and I willed Perry to hang tough. After a few slow seconds Perry brushed Connor's fingers with his.

I had to look away.

Ruth pushed by the three of them and clumped up the stairs. I heard her kick open the door above and stomp past the boats and outside. Connor smiled. I got off the ergometer and pulled on my own coat and my *Carrey's Joinery* hat. "Come on, Jumbo. Let's get out of here, man."

Connor laughed. "Screw you, Carrey. Jumbo's fine. Look at him."

I turned and stared at him. Jumbo was right next to me and Wadsworth was standing behind us. Connor looked at the three of us, standing his ground. Fearless.

"Where's Jumbo's ten bucks?"

"What?" Connor looked like he genuinely didn't know what I was talking about.

"You bet him ten bucks he couldn't lift that weight. Where's your money? You owe him ten bucks."

Perry said, "Rob, man, it's cool—"

"It's not cool. He owes you ten bucks." I kept my eyes on Connor. If he was going to hit me, it would be right now. I damn near prayed for it.

Connor smirked. "Don't you think I'm good for it, Roberto?"

"Pay him, then."

Connor shrugged, walked nonchalantly to the back of the training room, fumbled through his backpack and extracted two fives from his prissy black leather wallet. He straightened, sauntered back across the room, ignoring everyone looking at us. He handed Perry the money and somehow managed to make it look condescending; like he was tipping a bell hop or something. Perry stuffed the bills in his sweatshirt. I punched Jumbo's heavy arm. "C'mon, man. Let's get you some air. You need to walk that off." I turned to Connor. "You couldn't even get that weight off the ground."

"I don't have to, Carrey. I have the best time on the erg of anyone in this room. Including you."

"That's all you have, asshole."

Connor grinned, turned away.

Jumbo followed me upstairs and we walked through the boats to the sliding door Ruth had left hanging open. I looked around for her but she had disappeared into the last light of the day. Perry walked next to me and I could swear he was limping, just a little.

"I did it, Rob. Jesus. I've never done that much weight. That was badass, right?"

"It was total crap, Connor asking you to do that."

"Naw, man. I called his bluff."

He was walking heavily, smiling broadly, as if he'd just been given a bag of popcorn.

"Jumbo, you don't need to take Connor's bullshit. You could tell him to go to hell and what's he going to do? Hit you? Not let you on the team?"

"You know it's not that easy. And it's cool I'm still training with you guys after quitting the erg test. I owe him for that. He could have blackballed me. Leonsis could have my place."

"He's not God, Jumbo."

Perry stopped at Route 7, looked across the road. "Rob, I've been here for three years. I came here as a freshman, like Connor did. Like Wads and Ruth. Back then all the seniors hazed the crap out of us. Even Connor. I must have delivered a hundred pizzas into the senior garret. Connor was given a wilderness every night."

"A wilderness?"

"He had to wait on all the kids at the rowing table. And do the whole cleanup. Without help. That's called doing a wilderness. He was like the wilderness kid."

"So? It didn't make him humble."

"But he still made the God Four. He still did it. He was the first freshman in years to make the God Four. Like, since World War One or something, when all the seniors went off to battle or caught polio or whatever. At the end of the year, somebody was waiting on *him*."

Perry coughed, spat, jogged across the road and when he got to the other side he was almost winded. All I had to do to keep up with him was lengthen my stride. My *walking* stride.

"Last year they held the Warwick Race over at Warwick. Every year Connor's parents come up for it. They come up in a real limo. This big silver Caddy with smoked glass windows. So, anyway, last year, they didn't even get out. They just had their chauffeur park it near the finish line."

Perry covered one of his huge nostrils with his thumb and blew. A stream of snot sprayed out onto the road. I tried not to puke.

"It was their message to us. They had watched two God Fours lose and they weren't going to bother getting out of the car for the third race."

"You want to know something, Jumbo? I didn't know real people drove around in limos. I thought they were for, like, foreign dignitaries and kids on prom night and rock stars. A limo. And you feel sorry for him? Nice."

"Dude, Connor is from New York. Do you think his dad, like, hails cabs and stuff? Or takes the subway?" Jumbo laughed. "Anyway, we almost beat Warwick. We had them by half a boat length into the last twenty strokes. And this guy who graduated last year, Paul Wendt, caught a crab. His oar jut sliced under the water and yanked him out of the foot stretchers. It smacked him in the jaw and he was just laid out. One more inch and he would have been tossed out of the boat."

"Believe me, I've heard about it."

"Do they call it 'catching a crab' where you come from?"

"Where I come from? Jumbo, Niccalsetti is just eight hours away. It's not another country. We use the same language."

"Niccalsetti is only eight hours away? Really?"

"It's New York State. The state isn't that big."

"So, you get summer and all? I thought it always snowed there. Like, you know, Finland or Alaska or whatever. Seriously. No offense."

"Finish the story, you ignoramus."

"So we still pulled it together. Came back over the line a boat length and a half down. By the time we'd let it run and were spinning the boat to go back to the dock, the limo was gone. They just drove away, man."

He started lumbering toward the school. "Wadsworth's parents took us all out to lunch after, including Channing. Connor didn't say anything the whole time. And he never spoke to Wendt again. We won every race after that, but we lost to Warwick, and that's all that counts to Connor because that's the only race that counts to any of them."

"That doesn't excuse the fact that he's a prick."

"I know, Rob, dude. But it kind of explains it."

We walked on in silence until we got to the entrance of North Dorm. Perry lived in West Dorm, still had a hike ahead of him. Students were pushing by us on their way to dinner. I was starved. Perry looked at me earnestly. "Do you think Ruth is pissed off at me?"

"I think she's pissed off at all of us."

"She always is. It's kind of cool."

"Good luck, Perry."

"Don't need luck. I'm stone cold, bro." He grinned, put his hands in the air in victory, punched the sky. "I got three hundred and twelve pounds up to my shoulders, man! Can't beat it, even on a good day!" He strode away, all the freshmen giving him a wide berth. I watched him cut across the field toward the chapel, alone, still waving his arms and making a racket.

I cupped my hands over my mouth and shouted, "You lifted three hundred and *fifteen* pounds!" My voice echoed against the mountain.

That stopped him. He turned, shouted back, "Really?"

"Do the math!" I couldn't help smiling. The dork.

He stood for a second, adding. Then he whooped. Performed a ludicrous jig.

At home we had a neighbor named Feldman, back before my father had restored the house my parents currently lived in, back when we were really poor. Feldman was a drunk boilermaker who had a big St. Bernard. The dog lived in the yard of the house we shared, had his own doghouse, and during the muddy season in Niccalsetti he was covered with muck and his bushy fur clung to his great shoulders and forepaws. Some nights the dog used to stand out at the end of its chain and bark at nothing at all, big ferocious barks that woke my brother and me, who slept in the back room over the yard. The dog was so strong that he sometimes managed to pull the doghouse sideways, so Feldman had to drive a steel pole into the ground and chain him to that instead.

Feldman came home from the bar one night and the dog started up, straining at the end of his chain, barking for all he was worth, until Feldman started kicking him. You could hear Feldman swearing and kicking the dog, dull thuds and chops, the dog barking back strong and loud through each kick. I got up and watched through our bedroom window, the dog taking each kick and barking, just barking, and the man wailing out there in the dark, his head jogging up and down. My brother woke my dad, who went downstairs and out the back door and pulled him away from the animal. Feldman was bellowing and sobbing and my father helped him up the stairs.

Looking at Perry hiking across the quad I could hear that dog barking at the night, asking the starless sky with great fury why such a good, strong animal could be chained and kicked in such a small place.

11.

When Carolyn walked down the street with me I some-times felt an aura rising off her. She strode on supple legs through crowds, a leopard on the prowl, consumed people's eyes, men's eyes. It was strong erotic juju. Men did what Carolyn wanted. They gave her tables in restaurants and made room for her at the bar. Being with her gave you instant alpha male status. I'd look at her at a party, with a glass of wine in her hand or an-gling a glass of scotch to her lips and feel ill with desire. We had sex across the world. In France. In Spain. In Africa. Up until two years ago, sex between us was like breathing, and we became careless, as careless as you can be about something essential that you take for granted, like sunshine or air or sleep or blood or your heart pumping.

"I think I might be pregnant," Carolyn whispered one Satur-day morning while we were making love, just as I was coming. I reared back from her in shock but when I saw the anxious, needy look on her face I felt myself melt into her. She confirmed it with a home pregnancy test and we spent a long morning talk-ing about it in our robes, sitting in the summer sun streaming through the warehouse windows, a stained paper wisp with its magic purple lines between us. This pregnancy was a sign we were meant to be, she felt. We were going to have the child. We were going to make it work. That was that. Somehow I'd have to change my life and she'd change hers.

Part of me was desperately adrift but another part was satisfied. Her pregnancy made me feel possessive of her, and protective. That talk, that agreement at the kitchen table (sealed with yet more sex in the adjoining bedroom after she had gone online, naked, at the computer, to make sure sex was kosher when you were about four weeks and a day pregnant, we were *that* ignorant) was the most important agreement I have ever made.

In the following months we did things newly pregnant couples do. We read the books. We shopped for pregnancy clothes for Carolyn, most of which she despised and returned. We looked at pastel-colored Lilliputian table and chair sets, sleigh-shaped cribs, changing tables with outboard rubber bins for used diapers. We started to adjust our lives. I had one big shoot to do, in Zambia, in a nature reserve called the Luangwa Valley. The money would allow me to take some time off when the baby was born and get us into a new apartment. That was the plan.

The two of us started thinking about changing our living arrangements. Should we still live in the city? The studio had been great, but it wasn't a living space for a mature couple like the two of us, with a kid on the way. The studio was also drafty, she pointed out, and it was loud—everytime you walked across the bare wooden floor you'd wake a sleeping infant. Especially if you were wearing boots or heels, she added. The kitchen echoed, the cars down below on the street sent noise up through the push-open factory windows, which, she pointed out, were so filthy from decades of grime they'd never come clean. The pigeons in the morning would wake up the baby, too, not to mention the sweatshop downstairs. We could never have guests or do much work at home, because the only private space was the sleeping area and anyway a baby needed its own bathroom, next to the nursery, which was right now the spare room that was filled with film junk, boxes, and her clothes and shoes.

The baby was always referred to as "she." I have no idea why. "If we were trying to work here, Rob, she'd hear every word," Carolyn would say, in a voice I had never heard. "And we have to push the volume on the edit suite pretty high to hear the ambient, you know? She'll hate that."

I told her the Zambia shoot would be one of my last assignments outside the country. Part of the good vibe of her being pregnant was that both of us were terrified and we didn't care. Anything was possible.

———

"Smooth out, Robby." Connor's voice sounded controlled and patient, the voice of someone out to test me. I had been avoiding him ever since the episode with Perry and was taken aback and immediately irritated to find him on the water. He sat hunched in his own flat, thin craft, watching me. We had been enjoying a few temperate days—a last respite before the really cold weather blew in—and I was sneaking in this dawn practice because I doubted I'd have a chance to scull again. Connor was the last person on earth I wanted to see right now. He was waiting for me where the river bowed after the bridge, had to have started out in the dark at least twenty minutes before me in order to catch me off guard like this.

I grit my teeth, the rubber ends of my oars slippery in my hands. Balancing, I crept forward, the fragile wooden scull precariously gliding across the water, my arms outstretched for another stroke. I dropped the oars in behind me and pressed with my feet and then my legs, fell back into the stroke and the boat surged, water running around the bow. Connor was just ahead of me now, eyeballing my bladework.

The muscles across my chest tightened as I tapped the oars out of the water, gently feathering them for my next stroke. I saw the stern of Connor's shell as I passed. He was still crouched languidly in his seat. I caught another stroke, and the boat ran free, losing me in a familiar sensation, the feeling of speed and hypnotic rhythm. I fell backward for a second into that mysterious rush.

"Decent, decent." Connor leaned forward and pulled his boat to me. "Not bad."

I sincerely wished he would vaporize.

Connor rowed the *Morrison*, christened after a Fenton old boy who had been shot on Sword Beach. It was a Vespoli racing shell, blue and black, banged together from carbon fiber and aluminum, light as an arrow. Connor reached forward, dipped his oars into the water and snapped off a swift, level stroke. He fell back into the coda of each finish. He feathered his blades and torpedoed away from me. "Let's see what you've got."

I spun my craft and dipped the oars into the water, flung down a few quivering strokes, then settled into a smooth set that left me feeling as if I were being borne down the river only inches above it. I shot by him, then slowed down to wait for him to catch up. I watched Connor's back as he leaned into his own oars, his eyes level, the black shafts extensions of his long arms.

As he drew even, his blades disappeared into the river and his boat began to really move. I drove into my oars. When I floated forward into my recoveries, I could hear his breathing and the splash of his oars. I heard the tiny drops of water falling from them as he gathered for each new stroke. Lungs burning, I glanced over my shoulder at the dock, a blur just visible over the waterline less than eight hundred meters away.

My long, slender oars bowed a tiny bit each time I drew them through the water. The living bones of my forearms and wrists and the birdlike ones of my hands were flexing as well. Bones and wood snapped back into shape at the end of each stroke. My lungs began to smolder and I found myself gasping for air. Matching my every movement, Connor gave me a quick glance, noting the distance to the dock. Our oars were almost touching one another, our blades sharing the same swirling whirlpools.

Then, unexpectedly, he leaned into his finish and paused, granting me some time. I slipped by him, leaving him tense and poised, carried along by the river and his own flowing inertia. I pounded through ten more strokes, then I paused as well. My speed carried me forward. Was it over? Abruptly, his glistening back bowed and his oars sank into the water again. I glanced behind me, the dock maybe only twenty strokes away now, then focused once more down the river. Connor was charging toward me, his oars smooth and low and quick, the *Morrison's* bow ball claiming giant increments of water with his every stroke. I could clearly see the rigid muscles of his back straining through his wet shirt. By the time I reckoned the dock was beside us, the bow ball had vanished and Connor himself appeared in my red vision, gliding, face contorted, a great silent bird of prey falling upon its quarry. Mouth open, eyes bulging, arms outstretched, he snatched the final stroke from me and drew it to his chest.

Unbelievable. He was just unbelievable.

We paused mid-river, inside the dank shadow of the bridge. Our breathing echoed hollowly. We tapped the boats back to the dock gently. Connor didn't look at me as he pulled his feet from the foot stretchers, heaved himself out of his seat to stand beside his boat dripping wet, his face red beneath his bone-white shock of hair. "You'd go faster in a better boat," he said.

Please. Shut. Up. I took a deep breath, my lungs scorched from the race. "Have you ever rowed in a wooden boat? Ever used wooden oars?"

He still wouldn't look at me, and it was satisfying to see how exhausted he was. He was struggling to fight off the pain, to stand straight on his red knees. I held my shell a foot away from the dock's edge. "The oars flex, like a tree flexes in the wind. The boat gives against the water. My father used to ask people if they'd want to play a plastic violin, or a plastic guitar, or a steel piano."

"Do you plan on playing music with that thing?" Connor looked at the boat dubiously. "Did your father make those repairs to the bow deck?"

"Yeah." I waited for the insult.

"He worked the wood right in. He had to strip it, huh? Re-varnish?"

"Everything."

"You can barely see the joins."

"He's pretty good."

"How old's that thing?"

"Thirty, maybe forty years old."

"My father keeps a wooden sailboat on Cape Cod. You sound like him, getting sentimental about wood when it's just a liability on the water. A pure liability and lots of work to keep up. I still beat you. I even spotted you seven or eight strokes."

"You gave me nothing. You were just messing with me. Plus, you took the outside lane around that bend. I figure you must owe me a length anyway, considering we only started about a thousand meters down."

"I'd say maybe half a boat length. The river's not that high."

"You weren't going to mention that though, were you? You wanted to let me think you had me."

"Wouldn't you?"

"I'm just wondering if you were going to be honest about it."

"I'm not about to talk to you about currents and details like that when you're bashing away with those oars. You'd have found that extra stroke easily if you'd used good old American carbon fiber."

"I'd have found it if I had that outside lane."

He bent down, braced himself, flipped the scull out of the water, balanced it on his head, then steadied it. "I'm thinking that if you can do what you did today in the God Four, maybe you'll stand a chance at greatness. Because you're pretty damned good."

"What makes you think I had any doubts?"

"I'm just informing you."

"You want to go out and race again? For real?"

"You'll have plenty of time to prove yourself." He began walking the boat back up toward the boathouse. I watched him balance it as he reached the incline, finding his footing carefully on the ramp. His dirty white socks were soaking wet, making the trip all the harder. He stopped, his back to me, and steadied the boat one more time. "You're good," he said. "I'll be the first to admit it, Carrey. That was not easy."

I hated how he felt he could pass judgment on me. Despised it. He knew he had a right to, because he had won—no matter by just a second, unbidden and unfairly. He was just so incredibly powerful. I watched him walk up the ramp and into the boathouse, waited for five cold minutes until I got out of my boat. I flipped it up and knelt easily for the sculls with the boat balanced against my scalp. I picked them up, wet wood slippery and heavy in my hands, the sculls balanced in my palms. I had twisted open the scuppers and airholes and the warm, living smell that breathed out from the innards of the boat calmed me. I kept my neck straight, felt the press of the weight against the bottom of my spine. Water dripped off the bow, along the sides of the boat and from the splashboards. The boat felt light, and I held it far down on the port outrigger, walked carefully so it wouldn't tip and smash the stern or the new rubber bow ball.

Had I looked down the shoreline, I would have seen Channing turning his stopwatch in his hands. He'd walk to where he believed we started racing and gauge the distance properly. He'd gaze down the river humming softly to himself, check the distance against the times he had scrawled inside his diary and slip his stopwatch into his trousers. He'd walk through the long river grass to the fields, then across to the road, whistling.

12.

I had an old rolltop desk that Carolyn's uncle once had in his house in Sag Harbor and sent down to us when his second wife went on a redecorating binge. It was a hulk, with tiny post boxes and letter files and a key to lock the entire thing up. It was an easy eighty years old and when I first got it I saw myself working at it late into the night on scripts alongside Carolyn. Except there wasn't really space for a desktop PC on it, so I'd use my notebook and that became a royal pain because it was easier to write where she was working, sitting next to her with the notebook on my lap. The desk became the bill storage center, a place of waiting for newspapers, junk mail, menus shoved under our door, invitations to gallery openings. The piles quickly became fearsome. Our files and our paid bills were shoved into the drawers. Important documents, like passports and film permits and visas for me and letters from *National Geographic*, were stacked in the little letter boxes in no particular order.

Carolyn's desk wasn't a desk, it was a black, faux ebony counter I'd built into the bricking of the loft and bolted in with industrial-size plugs and supports. It was ten feet long and it was always clear. Her personal files, as well as anything related to the business, were neatly packed away in a series of matte stainless steel file cabinets. My behemoth desk was pushed aside and always looked a total mess. Her area was pristine and it irked me, but she did point out that organizing *my* crap wasn't *her* job. Yes, I argued back, but she would *never* leave so much as an open envelope or a Coke can in the Sacred Sanctorum of the Temple to Apple, Inc. while *my* work area, unused as it was, was *her* dump zone.

Carolyn would roll her eyes at this.

As Carolyn edited I started the process of emptying out my desk. I wanted to do it casually—not look like I was boxing everything up, angry that I had to start making plans to leave the apartment and that some of the documents under the piles in that desk were three years old and probably important. Insurance documents for the car ranked high here, as well as documents relating to its long-term parking, not to mention all the receipts for the camera gear, plus, of course, my bank statements and credit card bills. I took the piles of papers and letters and bills, as well as the rubber-banded returned check envelopes, and stacked them on my chair. It took me almost half an hour to clear down to the actual wood of the desk and then start moving out the stuff that she had cubbyholed. Two steel cans of pencils and pens, three packs of Post-Its, a box full of stained, dusty business cards, more cups, two coffee mugs—mismatched orphans from Carolyn's first apartment that didn't jibe with the sand-colored ones hanging in the glass fronted cabinets of the kitchen. And then a picture of us taken in DiSoto's Bistro, another snapshot of the two of us kissing at an opening for my friend Alex Thompson's *Canoe Diaries*, a documentary on northern Canada canoeing that was a surprise hit here in New York.

As I sat clearing out all that stuff, it became clear that the detritus, the real junk, had been unceremoniously shoved into the desk, but that my most important documents—bills, permits, tax receipts, plane ticket stubs, hotel vouchers, dead checkbooks—had been organized by date, and carefully labeled. Carolyn had taken the trouble to do that for me, perhaps over a long period of time, perhaps only over the last few weeks as she prepared to jettison the relationship. I piled all of these records on the floor, and knew that Car was watching me do it while she worked, her lack of comment a giveaway. Now that I was working under her gaze I was more careful. I piled each stack on top of the other and casually dumped the rest in a couple of grocery bags. I was whistling while I did it, trying to camouflage my first act of retreat.

Still whistling (and I am not a whistler, and Car knew this, yet I whistled on through this knowledge), I rifled through the letter holders, noting that there, too, my passes and cards had been stashed away with some care. And then, lo and behold, packets of receipts from jobs I had completed here and overseas and claimed as expenses to the accountant and of course the channel. Each packet was neatly organized and double clipped. Then, amidst all of that, I found a picture I had not looked at for some time . . . a framed picture from my parents' house in Niccalsctti. The frame's soft, felt prop had been torn off years before. I gently wiped away the dust from the glass with my thumb and there we were, Tom, Wendy, myself on the dock of Miller's Point.

I squinted down at the picture, amazed at how young we all looked. We were children, despite Wendy's knowledgeable, challenging gaze into the camera (held by my mother, the person who took all of the pictures in the family, my father uninterested in posterity, and rightfully so, given what it held for him). Wendy was wearing a one-piece bathing suit and Tom and I were in cut-off jeans, Tom thrusting his skinny chest out, his eyes dark and jovial and sharp. Wendy's hair was wet, she had been swimming that day, had beaten us both back to the dock and regarded the future she would never see with a bemused arrogance, her chin lifted slightly, her face girlish and pale under her weasel's coat of hair. Her skin glistened in the sun. I stood slightly apart from them, shading my eyes, squinting so my mouth was forced into an awkward grin. I had swum in last behind John. I still remember his white feet kicking the brown water into a froth next to my head as we tried to reach Wendy, who swam into the sunlight with her head down, her arms whipping lazily out of the water while we thrashed behind her.

We had climbed up the dock after her while she stood over us. There was no ladder. The Miller's Point dock was meant to be a boat slip, but you could haul yourself out of the lake if you were young and light and strong and didn't mind the wood cutting into your stomach while you did it, or risking bites from the dock spiders that occasionally lived below.

The picture was taken in early June. I was sixteen years old, Wendy was nearly fifteen, Tom was eighteen. Even standing flat-footed on the dock, you could see the beautiful woman she would have been. She was already moving from being skinny to being willowy, her breasts swelling under the suit, her shoulders thrown back to give them the best effect for the camera. Yet she still had a defiant, tomboy poise. She was still the type of girl who would climb fences or agree to play the all-time-no-tackle-or-free-kick quarterback or join in on a snowball fight or a loo-gee contest. Even in that picture you could see Tom's unconscious protection of her. He was standing as if he was blocking her from time, one foot forward, settled on his back heel, one shoulder almost jutting between her and the camera.

Yet to the casual observer, to the person not sitting in a quiet room holding the picture up to his eyes and trying to look through nearly two decades into the faded colors, to that observer, Wendy looked older and more mature and certainly not in need of protection. She was the composed face in the picture, the child who knew herself well, and to whom the camera gravitated. Had I been doing interviews with doomed Niccalsetti families, I would have set the shot just like that, with the striking girl/woman in the centerpiece. I would have interviewed her while the two brothers smirked and looked on, because the camera would have liked her better, because just looking at her, you knew she'd have the kind of answers that would count and could be edited well into the documentary. If she could be interviewed today, speaking through time from out of that photograph, she might say, "Look at the three of us as we stand now." Her voice would be light but full of that mimicking gravitas she used with Tom and me. "We're as perfect as we will ever be. One of the boys beside me will be sent away by a broken father, the other will break himself. I will die fifteen feet from where you see me. Look carefully at these people."

Wendy drowned a few months after that photo was taken, on an Indian summer day during Tom's last season as quarterback for the Niccalsetti Lions. She'd been outside with my father one Sunday afternoon doing support work for him for extra cash. She wanted to go for one last swim and Tom came with her, drove her in my father's truck down to Miller's Point and let her out for that quick dip in the river. He sat in the truck in the small parking area, the radio set to the football game. She had worn a swimsuit to the site because the whole week had been unseasonably hot and she had known she would want to cool off on the way home. My brother had been emphatic about that, that she wanted to jump in the water *just to cool off*. And so he hadn't bothered to get out of the truck, had stayed in the cab because the football game was on. It was a late afternoon and the Bills were coming back on the Colts and there were rumors this would be the year the Bills might hit the Superbowl—they had a new quarterback and things were turning around. Tom took this as an omen, believing that if the Buffalo Bills could actually win the conference, then anything was possible, such as, for instance, the Niccalsetti Lions hitting and winning the state championship. So he sat there with Wendy's door open, drinking the one beer our father allowed him (and not me, never me, Dad was already worried about me, and not Wendy), sipping it with his sun-glasses on and his shirt off, looking out into the sun and the endlessly sparkling lake and listening to the Bills actually take it to the Colts, just squeeze them like they had the Dolphins and the Raiders. And just as the last downs were being counted he stepped out of the truck and shaded his eyes and looked for my sister and called her name, and then walked, and then ran down to the dock and to the end, not really terrified yet but definitely scared, with a cold feeling in his stomach because Wendy was supposed to be *just cooling off*, but where was she? And he scanned the little park where I'd come a million times in the night with my friends and there was nothing to see.

Later, they'd find her and the doctor would say she was probably pulled under by a cramp. The water was cold with the impending fall and she might have drowned swimming up for air after that first, bracing dive. She just dove into the water and disappeared. It seemed impossible. The doctor was sure to tell us that it was nobody's fault, that whoever was watching her would have had to have been right on that dock and very fast and a strong swimmer to have saved her. All of the things, of course, that Tom was. But the truck was parked yards from the dock. Whoever was sitting in the truck could really not have been much help on that bright day, especially some distracted under-age kid drinking beer.

I set the picture aside. "Thanks for putting that stuff away for me, Car."

She nodded at the computer. "Somebody had to do it."

"How many cigarettes do you have left in your bag?"

"I quit. This you know."

"That's not what I asked."

"Maybe half a pack of stale Camel lights."

"Can I have one?"

"You don't smoke, either."

"I'm asking as one non-smoker to another."

"No. Get your own."

The compulsion would pass in a minute. What I wouldn't mind, in fact, was a drink, but we had strict rules about opening bottles in the daytime. Pretty soon there would be nothing to stop me from pouring myself a cold one at eight in the morning if I wanted. The thought wasn't comforting. Now she was leaning forward and nearsightedly squinting at the rough script, then looking back up at the computer and doing the math on the time in and out for each sequence.

"Stop looking at me work, Rob. It's creeping me out."

"I'm never going to be able to take this desk with me, wherever I go. In case you were worried about that."

She paused. What was going to happen to the desk hadn't occurred to her. She shrugged. "I don't want it here. After, you know, whatever."

"It doesn't fit the décor, right?"

"It's not that. It's not mine. Sean gave it to you, not me. I have a desk."

"You could sell it."

"You sell it. I don't want strangers coming here to look at how I live. Go to eBay right now, if you want. Or take out an ad."

"I don't want to sell it."

"I don't either."

"Okay."

"Okay."

"So, then, you'll hold on to it for me?"

"I'll hold on to it. Yeah."

"It won't offend your minimalist, postmodern taste?"

She threw me a filthy look.

"I'll just store it here for a while and get it later."

"And while we're on the subject, there's not much point in boxing all those invoices and bills that took me hours to collate."

"I guess not."

"Then leave them there. It's not like I'm going to vaporize just because you're leaving." She turned back to the computer, muttered something under her breath.

I piled the bills neatly back into the desk, squared them off on the work surface, tucked them into the letter galleys. She kept her back to me while I did it, and I took my time. When I was finished, that desk was ready for some serious inventory, the records were right at our fingertips. It was not a dump zone anymore. It was a filing area, a depository of records, a history of our life together. I gently rolled down the articulated cover and locked it. I ran my hand over the smooth oak and slipped the key into my pocket. I was smiling. It was something I had in reserve.

13.

My first practice in the tanks. I entered the dank and musty cavern to find Channing in the semidarkness conferring with Ruth and Connor. Wadsworth and Perry were already perched on their respective sliding seats located on the island that divided the water troughs, Perry at port and Wadsworth behind him at starboard. They were rowing at a slow rating, about twenty-three strokes per minute, I guessed. Like theirs, the two empty sliding seats in front of them had crude adjustable foot stretchers with black sandals bolted to the bottoms. The seats had been pulled from dead boats past. The oarlocks extended over the tanks and we used carbon fiber oars that had been shortened so that we couldn't rip the water channels apart. The tanks themselves were just wooden corrals with their own brackish streams. On each opposite wall was a row of streaked, filthy mirrors, so even a rower practicing alone could work on his stroke. I watched Wadsworth and Perry, already covered in a film of the water's slime and their own sweat, breathing dust as they rowed. It smelled like a place more suited to slaughtering animals than to rowing.

The tanks set the oarsmen up on a high plane so that their form could be scrutinized and picked apart. I had never felt so exposed as I climbed up, shook out my arms and rolled my neck, telling my heart to stop clenching up in my chest. I breathed deeply through my nose. The air was ripe with the odor of growing, vegetative things. The humid heat of the room did not appear to bother Channing, who finally noticed me and nodded at the two empty seats with some irritation. "Let's go, gentlemen."

Wadsworth and Perry held up their rowing and waited while Connor climbed into the stroke seat—the front seat we all followed—and I slipped in behind him. Connor pushed his oar into place and took a tentative stroke. Channing turned to Ruth and nodded, then took a step away from the tanks. Ruth stood on tiptoe by the video camera mounted on a tripod and focused it on us. I watched the red eye beside the lens blink, blink, blink in time with my heartbeat and tried to look impassive, not wanting my fear to be recorded. I focused intently on Connor's neck.

Ruth was dressed in her usual blue sweat suit and her ridiculously small running shoes. She climbed up on the edge of the tanks and squatted down, ensuring that Connor and I were tied in properly. "You guys have ten minutes, okay? An easy pace, maybe twenty-five strokes a minute, I'll track you on the watch. Connor, Coach is going to be watching you. Rob, your finishes have to be smooth today, hear me?"

I jiggled the oar, nodded. I watched the stiff, precise movements of the others and refused to believe that I, too, looked that regimented behind an oar. Without the motion of the boat, the wind and the speed, we were robots.

"Ready? We'll start with the pick drill, that's arms only, on my command . . . and go."

Connor began the curt, chopping strokes of the drill using only his arms, his back straight, pulling each stroke to his chest and slowly recovering the blade.

"Don't feather your blade," Ruth yipped. "Square blades. Come on, Connor, square 'em up."

Connor flipped the oar up. Ruth hadn't looked at my strokes yet.

"Connor, your outside elbow's too high. Rob, slow down that recovery. I said *slow*. Are you deaf? No. That stroke's not slow. Still not. That one is. Yes. Thank you, Rob." Ruth narrowed her eyes. "You two aren't together today. Get it right, or I swear I'll make you do picks all day. Don't look at me Rob, head in the boat."

Ruth may have looked like a child bundled up in huge sweats, but her voice was harsh and low and she made a point of being cruel to Connor. She jumped off the ledge of the tank and walked over to him, put her hands behind her back and watched Connor rowing in silence. Then she leaned forward slightly and said to him in a stage whisper, "Your timing's off, Captain. Way off."

She took a step back, "Add the backs in three, and one . . . and two . . . and three . . . and now with the backs, come on, keep it sharp."

Adding the backs lengthened the recovery. I felt a tug in my legs as I caught each stroke. I bowed forward, pushing the oar over to the middle of my shins and snapping off the catches in time with Connor. The splashes from the four of us were louder now. I could hear Perry breathing harder with the exertion.

"Knees down, Carrey. Come on, that's it. Follow Connor. Connor, head up. Concentration starts now."

Channing came over to the tanks, his hands shoved in his pockets, and stood behind Ruth. Ruth glanced back at him, and Channing nodded once. I could not see his eyes in the gloom. Ruth turned to us. "Let's go half slide gentlemen, in three, on my count, and one . . . two . . . three . . . and half slide. And half again, don't get lost in it, Carrey."

My half slide mimicked Connor's exactly. My knees bent

slightly, my outside arm plunging between them, gathering length. As we moved into the half slide strokes, water began to slop over the side of the tank.

"Move the rating up two on three. One . . . and two . . . three . . . and up two." Ruth reached into her sweatshirt, brought out the rowing timer and clicked each stroke into the little computer. "Twenty-seven on the dot. Nice."

Channing shook his head. "You're erratic, Rob. Smooth it out."

Ruth stepped right back up to me. "You heard the boss." Ruth held up the timer again, in front of my face, and clicked in three strokes. "Coach is right. Twenty-eight now, what's wrong? Am I bugging you, Rob? Smooth out, full slide, full strokes on three, and that's one . . . and two—lengthen . . . three—lengthen . . . full now, thank you." A single spot of sweat sprung out in the center of Connor's back. He was pulling flawless strokes, one after another. He was dropping the oar perfectly into the water, creating a quick backsplash that wet my inside arm and the length of my blade. Water was running down the mirrors to our left, splashing out of the tanks behind us.

Channing said, "You look strained, Robert Carrey. Relax. We're all friends here." I tried to loosen my shoulders, to breathe easy under his gaze.

Ruth clicked two strokes into the timer. "Still at twenty-seven, Coach."

"Try him now," Channing said.

Ruth clicked in the strokes. "Yes, twenty-eight."

"Carrey, slow the hands. I'll only ask you once. Slow them."

Ruth stepped up to me. "Slow down, Carrey. Make it up on the slide." She was just out of my line of vision. I put all my concentration into my hands, willing them to slow.

"Ruth, keep track of Mr. Payne. He thinks we've forgotten him." Channing's eyes hadn't moved from me.

"Is that right, Connor?" Ruth shuffled over to him. The tanks were high enough so that Connor was sitting at waist level to

Ruth. Ruth crossed her arms and watched him. "I'm putting this stroke in the computer, and this one, and this one. Sorry, Coach, they're at twenty-eight." Connor cocked his head for a moment, took a deep breath in exasperation as he rowed.

Things were going wrong.

"Slow down Mr. Carrey for us, Ruth."

"Eyes forward now, Rob. I want one stroke off this timer." It wasn't easy. A slow, even rating is as hard as a fast, high rating. Connor's head was forward now and his slide slowed only a fraction. The backsplash of his strokes spattered me with tiny, distracting showers as I tried to focus. The slow rowing made me vulnerable. My shoulders had stiffened and I could feel the panic beginning and was trying to quell it. It was a desperate scream in the back of my mind. *Stay focused. Stay clear. Stay focused. Stay clear.* Ruth clicked in three strokes and said, "Now you're low, Rob, twenty-six."

"This is very interesting, Mr. Carrey."

"Now you guys are about right. Twenty-six and a half . . . and now you're on." Perry was breathing hard, but he was ripping the oar through the water. Our movement created its own ionic breeze.

Mr. Channing moved toward me. "It looks as if our new recruit doesn't like our low ratings."

I didn't move my eyes or my head. I kept them focused on the growing spot in the center of Connor's back. Eye movement in the tanks was instant death.

"Rob's on track now, Coach."

"Really? Bring them down to twenty-five, Ruth."

Ruth turned to Connor. "Down two in three. And that's one . . . and two . . . and three . . . down now, Connor."

Ruth clicked us in. "Rob's good for it."

"He's shaky, if you were to ask me."

"Rob, smooth it out. Nice and easy."

"Find out if Carrey can follow this stroke rating."

"Carrey, steady now, you're looking good."

"But not strong."

"Hands, hands, Rob."

"These two oarsmen are not rowing together, Ruth."

"Stay with Connor, Rob," Ruth hissed. "Come on. That's a good stroke. That one's good. That's a bad one. Good stroke. Good. Good. Bad. Bad."

"Rob's off again."

"Rob Carrey, fuck, twenty-five and steady."

"He's not doing it, Ruth. And watch your language, my dear."

"Rob, follow smooth now, Connor, up one, still low, up a stroke, still low, now you're high, that one's just right. Stay there. Good. Good!"

Channing didn't think it was good. "I've had enough of this. Have them stop. I have other rowers to take care of. Carrey, if you can't slow your hands and follow Mr. Payne, you're no good to us. You're wasting everyone's time. Ruth, please stop the film."

We stopped rowing, our oars askew over the swirling water, and I realized there were two others in the room—Perry and Wadsworth—who had rowed evenly throughout the ordeal, through Channing's chastisement and Ruth's relentless criticism.

I didn't look at Connor when I hopped off the tanks. I yanked my sweatshirt over my head and pulled on my sneakers. The hot, furious feeling was boiling up inside me and the disgusting stale air in there made me want to throw up. Channing glanced up at me and I ignored him. Connor turned in his seat, his face red, and said, "Practice isn't over, Carrey."

"It is for me."

───────●

Outside it was already gray. I was breathing hard and shaking. Connor pushed through the sliding doors still sweaty from the tanks and started right in on me. "You have the classic sculler's problem. Fast hands. You'll get through it. You'll see on the video tonight. Watch your hands."

Go away, I thought. I stood in the cold blast of wind coming off the river, realizing just how hot it had been in there. The leaves on the trees leading down the drive hadn't been stripped yet, but they soon would be.

"You thought this was going to be easy, didn't you?" he said. "It's not. You're going to have to get better. You don't have to take it like such a baby. That's what these sessions are for. If you storm out of a room like that it sets a bad example to the rest of the team. There's months of this ahead of you, Carrey, before they even select a boat. This isn't Niccalsetti, where a little luck and some brass balls will win you your races."

"That's not the point."

"Grow up. Pull yourself together. Channing is going to be harsh *every day*. He's like that with all the recruits, all the kids from Boston and Philadelphia who come here thinking they're hot stuff and find out they're not as great as they thought. If you want to succeed here, you have to do better than that, and not get frustrated." He grabbed my arm, spun me around, and I came close to outright hitting him. "You're in a whole new world. Adapt to it. Try to live up to the reputation you have. Do you think you're the only guy they're going to abuse down there? You know what really blew it for you? Look at me. Do you know what it was? It wasn't your speed on the slide, or the way you were leaning out of the boat on the recoveries."

"What was it then, oh guru of the river?"

"Your stomping out of there like a little kid. Do you really think these people are out to get you? They're not. They don't care one way or another so long as the boat wins this spring. So stop getting emotional about it and get better. Go build some character."

"Like yours?"

"Yeah. Like mine." He looked at me clearly, searching my

face. "I have to go back. I'll clear your stupid stunt with Channing. Go somewhere and cool off. Be there tonight for the playback. And don't lose your temper again. This isn't just about rowing. It's time you noticed that."

I'd hit a wall back there. And he knew it. I'd choked, and formal training had barely begun. Connor turned, slid open the door to the boathouse and disappeared.

I walked into the clear cold of New England, found my way down to the road, crossed it and made it halfway up the walkway to the school. Leaves were already falling and being blown in swirls around me. I sat down on a bench inside the school gates and leaned over on my knees. I thought for a second I was really going to puke but the feeling passed. The sweaty, jittery feeling didn't. I held my hands in front of my face, watched them trembling. Made two fists and felt that warm, rushing sensation in my palms, then opened them, willing them to stop shaking. They didn't. I tried to take a deep breath and couldn't do it. And then I started to laugh. I have no idea why.

"What the hell are you laughing at?"

It was Perry. Without me noticing, he'd somehow gotten all the way down to the gates in his navy sweatpants and huge, clownlike running shoes. His face was red and he was still really sweaty. It was as if steam was rising from him when he sat down heavily next to me and kicked his legs out so his feet were resting on their heels. "Are you going nuts already?"

"I might be."

"They let you have it down there, dude, but I've had it worse than that." He reached into his pocket and pulled out a Mars Bar, bit off the top of the wrapper and spat it into the wind, took a wet bite out of it and offered some to me. I shook my head, looking at his big horsy teeth marks in the candy.

"Why do you do this, Jumbo?"

"Call me John, okay? Could one guy call me John on this team? Do you think I want to come back here in fifteen years for some reunion and have my kids hear that everyone called me 'Jumbo'?"

I leaned back, watched him chewing, just shoving the chocolate in his mouth. He was like a bear in the zoo eating a piece of candy a kid had given him. He looked at me and wiped his mouth. "They hassle everyone, dude, make sure nobody feels singled out. Didn't you know that? And the worst thing you can do is get mad."

I was getting cold sitting there.

"I'm telling you. You can always get back in their good graces. They'll test us again this week. Weights and ergs. You know what bench pulls are, right?"

"Yeah, Jumbo. I know what bench pulls are. Believe me."

He slapped me on the shoulder, hard. "Good. Then you can get back in their good books."

"It's worth a shot."

He nodded. "There's a guy named Tony Brickman at Warwick. He set a record last year for the bench pull. Connor doesn't like to talk about it. The guy also went to the Crash-B Sprints. Competed against college kids on the erg. He did okay."

I had a sudden vision of a big, red-haired version of Connor on an erg. A kid bigger than Jumbo who could run and had endurance and was as much of a psychopathic freak as Connor. A kid with a million dollars and a hundred years of champion rowers in his family who would kill him if he lost. To anyone.

"Jumbo?"

"What?"

"Do you know what happens when you put a bunch of weights and an ergometer on the water?"

"No?"

"They sink, Jumbo."

He thought for a second, and then his face cracked into a grin. And then he laughed and then choked while he coughed up a golf ball of snot. "That's an old one, Rob, man."

He punched me on the arm and it hurt.

14.

Carolyn was entering her second trimester and visibly, proudly pregnant when I left for the Zambia shoot. I'd be away for about a month and for the first time in my life I was reluctant to leave for an assignment. But there was no getting out of it. The special we wanted to produce was an ambitious one about traditional medicine and involved coordinating shoots in Zambia, South Africa, Madagascar and Brazil. Filming in Brazil and Madagascar was in the can—shot by crews I had subcontracted out to—and most of my South African work was also complete. Only the Zambia footage was outstanding, and it was important.

After doing some preliminary interviews in Cape Town, I flew into Lusaka to film traditional healers on location in a small village north of Kitwe. These highly esteemed medicine men and women hated to be referred to as witch doctors and preferred to call themselves sangomas. The traditional healers—the sangomas—across many of these far-flung, rural communities had what some researchers believed might be workable, cheap treatments for AIDS. The interviews I would be conducting, most through an interpreter, were going to be aired on the channel along with footage of the western doctors and several drug company reps who had come out to meet with the sangomas and some of their patients. It was a unique experience walking around rural Zambia with a doctor who lectured at Columbia University, a woman who had never been out of New York. I followed her with the camera every day while she met with the sangomas, some of whom begged us for money and quietly accepted small gifts in return for interviews. The channel never pays interviewees; I was bribing these guys with beer and a few dollars out of my own pocket.

We were lucky enough to be invited to witness a three-day indoctrination ceremony for a new sangoma. We filmed the grisly business of the bloody slaughter of chickens and goats and then a furiously bellowing cow, as well as the endless ululating praise recitations. The Big Pharma reps and the American doctors with us found the first offering of chicken feet and the meat peeled off a goat's head—called a "smiley" because the skin pulled back from the teeth when the head was cooked—to be gastronomic revelations. The doctors and pharmacists were struggling to figure out how to isolate the alkaloids that had helped many of these healers bring the fight against AIDS to a new level. Because the simple fact was that some of their patients were living and nobody knew why. We all know that the drugs we now use to fight cancer owe their existence to the alkaloids found in the plants of Madagascar and the redwoods of California. So the cure for HIV might very well lie behind the all-night ceremonies of certain Zambian sangomas sipping bloodred tea and tearing apart humble potatoes that seemed to prolong the life of the hopelessly ill indigenous people who met them only in that strange context. As one sangoma told me, "Your body remembers these herbs I give my people. They are part of the medicines your spirit craves." He took a pull from the expensive scotch bottle I had bought in Heathrow and pointed at the uncomfortable executives sitting nearby on folding chairs. "They know this, yet they do not want to know this."

Healing and belief. In Africa they went hand in hand.

Ten tapes later I wrapped up the shoot and drove my rented Toyota Land Cruiser, packed with my equipment and American doctors and reps, to the Kenneth Kaunda International Airport outside of Lusaka. I dropped them off and headed straight to the Taj Pomodzi Hotel in the center of town, the only really decent hotel in the city. My flight left the next day. The Pomodzi was comfortable in a washed out, '70s, African revival way, and positively luxurious after two weeks of filming in the bush. It had a green pool and a bar where air crew from British Airways flights hung out with drunk journalists and NGO workers watching satellite TV and drinking semicold Zambian beer, each bottle a different shade of amber, thanks to the vagaries of African brewing. Exhausted, I headed straight to my room, locked up my equipment, took a long shower and collapsed on the bed, the air conditioner turned all the way up, beckoning sleep. There was a knock at the door just as I was dropping off and I groaned, got up in my towel and opened the door a crack. A young woman from the front desk was standing there deferentially, her eyes down, holding a piece of hotel stationery which she proffered to me with both hands. "Telephone message for you," she said. "This lady who calls, she says you must telephone her right back."

The message was from three days beforehand when we had been filming the raucous celebrations of the new sangoma graduate. I sat down on the bed. It was a New York number I did not recognize. I called through on the credit card and a woman answered, "Lennox Hill Hospital."

I almost put down the phone. Then I realized what must have happened and I crossed my fingers against it. "Yes. Sorry, I'm calling from overseas. Is a patient registered there by the name of Carolyn Smythe?"

There was a flurry of typing and the brusque voice came

back on. "That patient was in ob-gyn. I'm putting you through to the nurse on duty."

Another nurse, another flurry of typing, and I was transferred yet again. An exhausted voice came on the line. "That patient has been discharged." She refused to reveal any further information.

I called the loft immediately and Car picked up after one ring. Her voice was flat and tired, as if she had been sleeping for a very long time. When she heard me, she started to cry. Long, sniveling howls. Racking sobs that rattled the phone line across the Atlantic and shattered our love.

———

The Schoolhouse basement was a common room off-limits to underclassmen, which, for obvious reasons and not very imaginatively, was referred to as the coffee room. It was nothing special; just a spare room with some tables and chairs, a couple of sad couches, a coffee urn and a guy in a stained white coat listening to a radio and collecting dollars into a Tupperware bowl. Still, it was one of the few places on campus you could escape to other than your dorm room, and it had the added bonus of being a co-ed zone where seniors could freely hang out and flirt with each other outside of the classroom. Somebody had tried, unsuccessfully, to counter the room's starkness by putting up a few posters on the walls, the usual ones of old bands and rap singers and animal pictures that upperclassmen had left behind after graduation.

The coffee guy's name was Al but everyone called him The Coffee Guy, and he hated all of us, not without reason, I have to admit. He must have been one of the most persecuted individuals in Connecticut. He looked like one of the union truck drivers they put on load duty rather than behind the wheel: an ex-drunk short timer with six months to go before being pensioned out who didn't want to break his back before that first check came in. He sat heavy and rumpled on his folded chair, his legs pushed apart by his belly. He was notoriously impervious to both insult and flattery; no amount of taunting or buttering-up could get a rise out of him despite the earnest efforts of many.

Except for The Coffee Guy, Ruth was alone in the corner reading and sipping coffee when I walked in. Al took my order, drew me a cup and accepted my dollar, all without looking up from his newspaper.

She was reading through square, mannish glasses that she took off and folded closed as I approached. But she kept the book open in front of her I noticed. I sat down and pushed it up. "What's this?"

She pushed it back down, hard. "Ionic Greek, if it's any of your business."

"You speak Greek?"

"They stopped speaking Ionic Greek about three thousand years ago, give or take a few hundred."

"How come you're not studying any languages you can use?"

"What are you studying?"

"Spanish. Because they make me."

"Are you doing well?"

"I've been able to speak it since I was ten. It's a blow off. Some of my father's workers are from Mexico. I was thinking of taking up French."

"Why?"

"It's pretty suave."

"You're pronouncing it wrong. You don't say 'swave.' "

"How do you, then?"

"Do you plan on flying to Paris after graduation?"

"You never know. I might. The world championships are in Belgium. They speak French there."

"They speak Flemish, dummy. And Paris—okay, forget Paris. I hate that city. It's not worth it. And you'd get along without

French anyway. My mother doesn't speak the language and she has a pied-à-terre there."

"A what?"

"You know. An apartment. She got it from her first husband as part of the settlement. Lucky her."

"So you speak French. You could have helped me pass."

"I had a French tutor until I was sent here."

"Why didn't you stick with it?

"I had learned enough. And he kissed me in my mother's living room. And I hate Paris. You don't listen, do you?"

"What did you do when the guy kissed you?"

"I hit him where men don't like being hit. Then I ran downstairs and had the doorman come up and throw him out. Then I called his wife." She closed the book softly, kept it before her with her fingers gently upon it, like a hymnal. "What do you want?"

"I came down here to apologize for being such a jerk in the tanks."

"Am I supposed to be impressed? Is that what you thought? Connor covered for you, you know. Channing was pissed. You just can't do that stuff, Rob."

"I know it. I screwed up. I nearly didn't go at all. Seriously."

"Don't be dumb."

I picked up the little bowl of sugar envelopes sitting before her, ripped one open and made a pile in the middle of the table, stirred it with the red stick from Ruth's coffee. I drew a boat in the sugar, made marks for every oarsman.

"Oh. I get it," she said. "You wanted to make a statement. You wanted to be a rebel." She leaned over and gently exhaled, scattered sugar across the table. "I don't like that kind of attitude. Can I ask a stupid question?"

"Go ahead. There are no stupid questions, or so they tell me."

"Do you really think switching from a single to the four is going to be so hard? I watched you in the tanks. Your problem isn't your rowing. You know exactly how to use that sweep oar. Your problem is that you're angry. You started out angry. At Channing, at Connor. Maybe you're angry with me, too. It's as if you think we want to take something from you."

I scratched the table with the stick, tried to etch in my initials. She cupped her hand and brushed the sugar into it, poured it into her empty mug. "You came here to row with us, so you're going to have to be on our team. And you're going to have to go to our training sessions. And wear the tie and observe all the silly traditions. Anyway, you were only asked to the tanks. You weren't asked to race. Not yet. There's a difference."

"I wasn't mad down there. Channing, Connor, you, the others . . . rowing in the tanks . . . I don't know, you were all only a few feet away. I was . . . afraid I guess. I kept thinking that Channing was going to look real close and see that I'm a fraud. That he'd know there was no secret sauce."

"What secret sauce? What are you talking about?"

"You know, the secret sauce at McDonald's. The secret herbs and spices in KFC, the secret formula in Coke. The whole reason people buy that stuff is there's a secret ingredient that makes it better. Even the scientists can't figure out what it is. But it's in there."

"There's a secret sauce in McDonald's and KFC food?"

"Yeah. I mean, no. I mean, nobody knows. That's the point."

"Carrey, you aren't making any sense."

"How could you not know about the Colonel's secret recipe? That's what doesn't make sense."

She blushed. "Here's what I do know. Boys who row in the God Four are cooler than scullers. That's what I know. So, good luck."

"I don't need luck. I told you that. I don't need them to like me, Ruth."

"But you want them to. Everyone wants to be liked."

"You don't."

She scowled into her book. "Winning isn't everything. I never thought I'd say that, but it isn't. And no one likes a sore loser."

"Winning *is* everything here. At least as far as crew is concerned. They want to win the Warwick Race so badly it's like an obsession. Nobody has said they'd be happy with a loss. That's for sure."

"We want to win against Warwick, yes. But you don't need to win at *everything*, Carrey. You don't need to beat Connor on the water every time you two go out in your dumb sculls. Or sprint faster than him on every single training run. Or kill yourself trying to better his erg scores. Or act like a prima donna in the tanks. Talk about an obsession . . . I mean, what is it with you and him anyway? The guys on the team *like* you, Carrey. But they're starting to think you're kind of a jerk. Like, worse than Connor. And that doesn't work for me. I have enough jerks to deal with."

"So what do you think I should I do?"

"Calm down. Just calm down. Be cool. Like when you first got here, before you even knew there was a Warwick Race. Before you met Connor and he started running around in your head. You seemed much nicer then, okay?"

"I'll give it a shot. I can't guarantee anything, though."

"Well, that's the best I can hope for, then. Now, go away. I need to study and you're distracting."

I checked her out, this fragile-tough chick with her Greek book. Wendy would have liked Ruth, and that is high praise indeed. She turned a page and I saw that she was smiling. As I walked out of the room I gave The Coffee Guy a thumbs-up. He didn't respond, but I was pretty sure Ruth watched me do it.

15.

I sat behind Ruth Anderson for an entire year, just two seats away, watching her work, listening to her in class, and then saw her almost every day through winter training and, of course, in the boat. Why I was so drawn to her remains a mystery to me. My memory of her is of a girl far more complex than she ever could have been, given how young we were and the restricted environment we lived in.

Even though I was something alien and new to the team, at least I could earn acceptance in the traditional ways respected by rowers. But Ruth, the first female coxswain of the God Four, had to forge her own way into that rarified world. No other sport at Fenton had girls competing equally alongside the boys. We would be the closest thing she could call friends, but even once she was valued as a full-fledged member of the team, she remained something of an outsider. While I could wander over to West Dorm to shoot the breeze with Jumbo or play cellar soccer with Wadsworth after study hall, Ruth was literally not allowed that closeness with us as teammates. The boys' dorms were off-limits to girls after dinner, our rooms always forbidden territory for members of the opposite sex. She made that exclusion seem utterly natural, a privilege she bore with grim pride. I admired her for that and always thought of her more as a quiet ally than a buddy or even a girlfriend. She had been swallowed whole by the crew but had still managed to stamp her own identity upon it.

I'd look for that kind of independence in the women I met after Fenton, and would find it in Carolyn. In the five years I lived with Carolyn, I never once thought she'd want to share her life with anyone but me. But I always felt I was competing against that instinctive solitude.

Autumn began to turn relentlessly into winter at Fenton. Every morning I would open the curtains in my dorm room and bathe in the symphony of color that the fall brought to the valley. Those millions upon millions of turning leaves marked the end of the season. The brilliant colors in the cold light against those gothic buildings and the darkening grass seemed at once beautiful and forbidding. Real cold was coming soon but the leaves held against it. Route 7 was a flaming tunnel of overhanging leaves. They blew across the practice fields in golden red swirls, sprites searching for summer. They floated down the river in pockets of yellow and brown and gathered in huge, inviting piles all around the campus. The boardwalk began to smell of arboreal decay. For the first time, I felt that a significant portion of my life was ending, and that the ending was natural.

I knew that I had started falling for Ruth just a day before the strength testing for the God Four really began. I had run along Route 7 to the boathouse and was stretching in the drive when I saw Ruth and Connor walking across the field by the river. Connor was on the riverside, bundled up against the cold in a long camel coat and a plaid scarf and boots, kicking leaves as he went. Ruth was dressed almost identically, her long, black hair streaming behind her and ubiquitous leather satchel slung across her body like some kind of armor. The leaves scattered across the fields glowed ethereally in the half light of the afternoon. The whole tableau was like a glimpse into another world I was not meant to see. A mirage of privilege.

The two of them might have been speaking about anything but it seemed to me, looking at them from a distance, that they were commiserating. They could have been talking about rowing. Or New York. Or Paris. Or how to arrange a private flight to Cape Cod, or possibly just about the video showing in the dining hall that night. But seeing them from two soccer fields away I felt an exclusion that I had never felt in my life. Fenton would be the closest I'd ever come to an existence they took for granted, to everything I hadn't even known was there to aspire to. Rowing had brought me here, washed me up against these people and given me that blushing afternoon when I watched my two teammates walking beside a darkening river. It was a day, I am sure, of no consequence to them, but it is one of my strongest memories of the school.

As they shrunk into the distance I wondered if there was anything between them, then pushed the thought away. I still had to beat Connor on the bench pull test. Acknowledging the idea that there was something else he could take from me was not going to help.

———

The bench pull station is a marvel of Inquisition engineering.

It's a thick wooden plank, shaped like an ironing board mounted on stout wooden legs. You climb up on the bench and lie facedown, your chin against the grooved, bitten, blood and spit-stained tapered edge of the wood. The board is narrow enough so your arms hang on either side. If you drop your hands down your fingers just touch the floor and your shoulders are fully extended.

You reach down and pick up a seventy-five pound bar. You are meant to pull the bar all the way to your body and knock it against the bottom of the bench. Any pull that doesn't knock, doesn't count. If you lift your chin from the bench at any-time, the pull doesn't count. If you lift your feet from the bench, the pull doesn't count. Everytime you pull the weight up into the plank, it jolts your stomach and bashes the wood into your jaw with a dull thump. That Saturday we had five minutes to pro-duce as many pulls as possible. Seventy-five pounds isn't very heavy for an oarsman. It's deceptively light. I could reach down and crack the bar into the bench ten, fifteen, twenty times be-fore the task became difficult.

But everyone on the team wanted to go for at least a hundred pulls. If you went out too fast, lactic acid built up in your mus-cles and within a minute your shoulders felt as if they were on fire. I have seen kids who started out with sixty pulls in the first minute drop to thirty in the second, ten in the third, and then lie there, red-faced and straining, unable to move the bar at all for the last two minutes.

Connor and I filed into the basement of the boathouse where two bench pull stations had been set next to each other in the erg room. Connor was slated to take his test right next to me. Like an opera singer trained in the arias of torture, Ruth was drinking lemon tea for the sake of her precious voice. She had a yellow le-gal pad on the bench before her. Channing was simply waiting, idling away the time, drawing on his immense reserves of pa-tience. The basement was cold; all the steel in the place made it look and feel like an industrial storage locker. I stripped off my down coat, my hat and gloves, threw them in the corner. I was wearing my sweat suit for the test. Connor, in a Russian bearskin hat only he could wear without looking ridiculous, had on his trau and FSBC sweatshirt under his charcoal coat and plaid scarf.

"Good to see you two," Ruth said. She looked different in an atypically tight red sweat suit I had never seen before, though I knew better than to make any sort of comment. She held her white Styrofoam cup in both hands as if praying to whatever pagan god evil little coxswains worshipped. She regarded us through the steam. Connor began to exhale heavily, stretching his arms to stuff oxygen into his muscles. I did the same. Perry would compete against Wadsworth next, but the two of them had been told to wait upstairs. Members of the lesser orders would file down later.

Channing gave us a few moments while we wheezed and puffed in the concrete gloom, then spoke. "Gentlemen, I would like to see you both go over a hundred and seventy pulls today. I will count for Mr. Payne. Ruth will count for you, Robert. Is that acceptable?" It was not a rhetorical question. "I'd appreciate some competition," he added and smiled his yellow, carious smile. Connor rolled his neck, shoved his sleeves up over his forearms. Ruth carefully set her tea on the floor and unhooked her timer that was clipped to the waistband of her sweatpants. "Okay. Five minutes of fun and diverting entertainment. Let's see what you guys can do."

Channing stepped away from the stations, his hands in his pockets. He had a magical way of disappearing into the scenery when the pain began. And the more grueling things were set to be, the more pleasant the man became. I could have sworn he was humming to himself.

I straddled my station and gave my arms one last shake before lying down and reaching to the floor for the bright steel bar. I lifted it with loose fingers, testing. I rested my chin on the end of the board and inhaled the icy air. I pressed my legs together and looked to my right, straight at Connor. Connor got into position, regarded me without interest, his eyes dull. I took three more deep breaths, felt the cold settle into my lungs.

Ruth squatted down into our line of vision. "You guys both ready?"

Connor moved his gaze straight ahead, his eyes blank pools. I grunted out an affirmative, felt my neck stretch as I tried to talk, my head heavy on my jaw.

"Both of you know that you can't move your chin or your legs. You have to connect with the bar every time, then go back to full extension of the arms. No getting up. No quitting. Five minutes."

I took up the weight and waited for the command.

Ruth shifted her feet. "Ready? Let's go!"

I drew the bar up to my chin, bashed it into the board under my jaw with a jolt. I dropped the weight and began counting off a cadence in my head. One—hit. Two—hit. Three. . . . I tried to knock the bench lightly to conserve power.

Connor was hitting his board with the regularity of a machine gun. I filled in the spaces between each of his hits. Hit—hit. Hit—hit. *Bang—bang*. The sounds knocked around the inside of the boathouse. The room sounded like a workshop where clumsy joiners had been assigned iron mallets to pound planks apart for kindling. Channing cleared his throat. "Thirty seconds."

Ruth's voice cut through the racket, "Let's go, Carrey. You missed that one. You have an even twenty, don't miss again."

I lowered the weight, yanked it up to my chin. There was a sharp stab of heat in my upper back now. I went back to banging away, intent on making forty good lifts before Connor. I moved my head until I could see the bar. *Bang. Bang.* Hit. Hit. *Thud. Thud.* I shut my eyes to it.

"That's a minute and you're on thirty-five, Carrey," Ruth hissed. "Wimp." I vaguely heard Channing uttering venom at Connor, standing over him as he lay prone, laboring away.

The sharp points of heat were expanding like two big, white spiders stretching their legs over my shoulder blades. My muscles were stiffening. I would drop the bar to full extension, then pull up. Drop, pull. But I couldn't tell where it was on its ascent anymore. The upper part of the motion was lost in a dead numbness.

"One minute fifteen, Rob, and you have thirty-nine, don't you lose me."

Connor was juddering away on his side, an even series of bangs. I tried to block him out but because I couldn't resist, opened an eye and peeked over as I pulled the bar to the wood. Connor's hair had fallen in front of his face. I could hear him grunting with every hit. Ruth jammed the watch in front of his eyes, then mine. "We're twenty-five seconds into minute number two boys, now you get this going. Connor has forty-seven, Rob has forty-three. Go! Now go!"

Nearly halfway through the second minute, the danger minute, the panic minute. I kept the pace even, fell into step behind Connor again. I heard him grunt in displeasure as I echoed him for thirty seconds, then hammered out two quick ones, ruining his concentration.

"You're up, Rob. Fifty-eight to fifty-six. Don't let it get this close, you take him. You don't lose by one stroke, ever, not at this school. Now go. Two minutes down and buried."

I snapped off two quick ones and tried for a third, missed. The bar came within an inch of the board and dropped. I took a breath and pounded in two more, then fell into a slower step behind Connor. *Thud—thud*. Pause. Breathe. *Thud—thud*. Pause. Breathe. *Thud—thud*. Then Connor pushed through three fast ones and waited for me to fall out of step. He was following me now, answering every hit with one of his own. I was losing count of how many lifts we had. The fat, white spiders had sunk their fangs into the middle of my shoulders and were digging the hooks of their legs into my sides and the center of my back. The long veins standing out of my pink biceps were filled with blue poison. I took a deep breath and pounded into minute four.

"One ten on the dot. Connor, you're at one thirteen, two up on Rob. Finish this," Channing growled.

"Hear that, Rob?" Ruth asked me. "Coach says you're fading.

Now show him you're not." I saw Ruth's sneakers move as she looked over at Channing. She was duck-toed, I realized, and for some reason that was immensely amusing.

I had fallen into step again behind Connor, tongue between my teeth. Nothing existed except the prospect of beating him. I was only one behind now. I dropped the bar, spread my fingers, and willed the aching poison to move away from my arms. I cocked my head and picked up the bar again, slapped off two, three, four. The clusters of bones in my wrists were expanding and contracting with each pull, the long bones of my fingers stretching apart from one another as I brought the bar up into the wood.

Then Connor coughed and dropped his weight.

Ruth laughed. It was shrill, horrible. "He's losing it. Carrey, you are one up. Fifteen seconds more of this minute and you have him. Give me three more and this minute is history, and that's one . . . and that's two . . . and . . . lift it, lift it, c'mon, don't you die on me, that's it. Three." Ruth thrust the watch in my face again. "Four-oh-one. One fifty on the dot. Now, last minute."

The bones in my hands weren't springing back anymore. As I pulled I felt my vertebrae crunching together. Blue, toxic blood from my arms washed over the deadened muscles. I closed my eyes, banged off three, four, ten.

Connor had recovered and was rapping them out on his side. Channing barked out, "Connor you are at one sixty-seven. You can do this. Carrey's exhausted." I slammed the bar up to my chin, the two fistfuls of muscle in my shoulders contracting and colliding. The bar was coming up unevenly now. The sound of metal hitting wood became frenzied.

I was favoring my right arm. I felt the juices in my elbows freeze and each time I dropped the weight I felt the tendons on my forearms begin to tear. The spiders on my back were heavy now.

"Fifteen seconds. Rob, you have one seventy. Go for six more and you're over. C'mon. Don't leave me hanging."

Connor grunted. I glanced up through a blur of sweat and saw him lay into the bar, bring it crashing to the wood.

"One seven five, Connor, keep going. Dig in," Channing intoned.

"You're just about there, Rob. Go. Go," Ruth said."

But Connor was ripping the bar up to his chin now. I managed two more hits and time was up. I dropped the bar to the floor and took a long breath, the two fat spiders sucking on my shoulders resting with me. Ruth marked something on her pad and stepped away. I pushed myself up and looked over at Connor, who was still hugging the board like a surfer waiting for a wave. A thread of glistening spit stretched down from the end of his board to a round puddle on the floor. When he pushed himself up, I saw a pink stripe of blood across his chin and lower lip.

Ruth turned to Channing. "Rob was at one seventy-seven. I counted one eighty for Payne, is that right?"

Channing looked directly at Connor. "No. His back rose off the table for the last three. These two oarsmen are tied, dead finish." Channing shook his head and then laid his dark eyes on Connor. "You looked like a fish out of water, Mr. Payne, flopping around like that."

Connor looked down at the floor and wiped the blood on his face away with the palm of his hand. Two icy, sated spiders scuttled off through the lights dancing before my eyes as I hopped off my station. Connor tuned his back to me, breathing easily, rubbing his arms. I picked up my gear and left the room in that dead silence after nodding once to Channing and once to Ruth. I stood out in the adjoining weight room and wiped my face and eyes and adjusted to the dark, focused on the weak, white rays of late autumn light filtering through the grimy basement windows. It felt hot and prickly under my arms and at the base of my neck and in the back of my throat. I believed I might collapse, but the feeling passed. It was only hours later, that night, that I knew I'd be all right.

16.

I had been drinking for almost twenty years and I had never been a good drunk. But after my phone call to Carolyn from Zambia, and my frantic attempts to call her back after she hung up on me, I had gone down to the hotel restaurant with the intention of getting very, very drunk. I sat under the umbrellas around the pool at my own table, in the corner, by the tall wall that was meant to keep out the beggars on the street who you could hear shouting at the traffic. I sat in the sun and started out with scotch and sodas, which I drank one after the other until I was hungry, and then I ordered dinner—a leathery steak and canned vegetables—and drank a few glasses of wine with that. I then moved to the bar and ran into a sunburned produce buyer from a chain of markets in London, and I bought him warm, oily martinis while I drank more scotch. The two of us hatched a plan to meet some of the leggy flight attendants who were drifting in and out of the lounge.

Later I would see a therapist, upon Carolyn's insistence, after a drunken fight during which she had not only hit me, but had also managed to smash an entire set of dinner plates against a wall behind me, flinging them inaccurately at my head and then kicking me quite accurately in the shins. He would point out that binge drinkers like me have nasty habits of falling in front of cars, or driving cars into other cars. Binge drinkers have trouble with relationships because they make what he called "poor socially induced interpersonal relationship choices," meaning they wind up sleeping with the wrong people. A man who routinely binge drinks forgets a great deal of what happens to him, but I have a fairly good recollection of the night when I was in the middle of a full-blown binge in the Taj Pomodzi Hotel in Zambia. The bartender thought this was fine; people came into his bar from all over the world and had no problem drinking all night, which is what I intended to do. The English produce buyer and I stayed there until eleven, by which time I was clearly and obviously very drunk. Stupidly, moronically, dangerously drunk. The women whom we had sent drinks to at the bar had left us long ago. The buyer finished his martini and wanted to go, too. I told him to stay. I reminded him, a few times, that I was buying. He shook his head and smiled. "Maybe you should go to bed, mate."

I grabbed his arm and leaned over the bar, asked the bartender to pour this guy another shitty martini. The man removed his arm from my grasp and made a sign at the bartender. The bartender laughed and I smacked the bar with my open hand. "This isn't *funny*," I informed him. "I'm not sitting here alone."

The man, who might have been a shade older than me, heavy-set and used to serious farm work, wearing a khaki outfit and sandals, slapped me on the back. Hard. "There's a good bloke. How about you call it a night, mate?"

"Fuck you."

The guy left the bar and I ordered another scotch and the bartender, amazingly, poured me a fresh drink and I sat there, fuming, stewing, sipping from the glass, then adding water to it between sips so I could get it down faster. I was poisoning myself. I glared at the bartender, who had probably seen every kind of sordid behavior on this green earth. "What are you looking at?"

I doubt he even understood me, but he had no problem understanding the tone of my voice. He walked over to the register and picked up the phone calmly. Soon after, two security guards slipped into the bar and stood on either side of me.

One of them asked, "Maybe you have had enough, sir?" As if he was providing me a service. "Maybe now we can bring you to your room?"

I looked at one, then the other. I didn't move. Finally, as if on cue, the two of them each took an arm and eased me off the stool. Once I stood up, my vision tunneled. Both men were smiling at each other I thought. "You go to your room now?" the one on the right, who had been doing all the talking, asked.

I smiled back at both of them, and then I could have sworn I heard a voice, heard it in a hissed whisper, the way I'd hear it when we rowed. "Do it. Do it now," and I swung at the smaller one, the silent young guard who was probably getting his first crash course in dealing with drunken guests. The guard could not have been more than eighteen, his uniform was really only a red blazer that hung off the peaks of his shoulders and draped over his knuckles. He was looking at me gravely and seriously when I connected and sent him sprawling into one of the tables.

The two of them dragged me out of the bar and beat me up in the fire stairwell. They did it the way cops do, so they wouldn't leave a mark, the young, skinny one with the bad fitting blazer linking his arms in mine, the other working me over with his fists to the belly, the sternum, the ribs. They searched me and found my key, which had my room number on it—there were no keycards in that part of Africa—and dragged me up the stairs. By then I was no longer resisting, being covered in puke and blood as I was and unable to even see my feet, much less stand on them. They opened the door to my room, tossed me in, and slammed it shut, leaving me in the humid dark. I lay there for quite awhile, retching and bleeding.

———●———

I had been running religiously at dawn and putting in time at Channing's little debacle of a guesthouse/office in the late afternoons on average three times a week. I had sanded the outside and inside of the place and painted the woodwork, such as it was. One evening I just stayed out there past dinner until Channing came out and kicked me off his property. I had worked off my twenty hours in less than two weeks but I kept coming back whenever I couldn't bear the thought of the boathouse or Connor or the rest of them. Whenever I felt homesick. The tools in the toolbox, the paint lined up on newspaper, the piles of fresh wood and the soaking brushes waiting for me; these were things I knew. I stored the tools and the brushes exactly the way I would on a project at home, covered the wood with a tarp and generally brought the whole site up to speed. Any good builder who went out to inspect my work would know a pro had been operating there.

Channing hardly ever put in an appearance. Half the time his wreck of a station wagon, its browning ferry passes to Martha's Vineyard peeling from the windows, wasn't in the driveway. When he was home, he ignored me, although one time I looked up from varnishing his window frames and saw his shadow on that sunken porch. I didn't wave and he didn't either. By the time we were approaching Thanksgiving break, I'd put in over fifty additional hours of work there. Although we never talked, he did leave evidence that he was inspecting what was going on: tracks in the mud from his boots, one time an empty glass. Whenever I needed more sandpaper, paint, thinners, wood or wedges, smaller screwdrivers, even wiring, I dropped him a note in his mailbox and the stuff would be there in a neatly folded brown bag the next time I showed up.

I arrived one afternoon to find that a branch from the lone tree in his yard had blown right through a windowpane. The wind whistled through the displaced frame—glass and dirt were scattered across the floor and the wall itself was torn. I stood there in the freezing cold, swearing. He had left me a brush and paint and a blank order form for a new sash window and more Rhino Board. He'd also left a note on the worktable in his arrogant, fountain pen scrawl that I'd recognize anywhere:

> . . . *I'd ask to know*
> *What I was walling in or walling out,*
> *And to whom I was like to give offense.*
> *Something there is that doesn't love a wall,*
> *That wants it down.*

I found a pencil in the toolbox and added Tyvek and bevel siding to the order form. Under Channing's poem I wrote, *Am building a house, not a wall.*

The next week the Tyvek, Rhino Board, and siding were there in a neat pile.

Also a note that read, simply, *Fool.*

17.

I awoke late one night to find Perry shaking me. My small room smelled like bandages, sweat and iodine and I listened to his whisperings in a half fog, as if he were part of a bad dream that refused to go away. Finally I pushed him aside and swung my feet to the cold floor, sat on the edge of the bed hugging myself. Perry smelled of beer and the cold outside. I looked at the glowing numerals on the clock. A little after three in the morning.

Perry walked to the window, peered around the curtain at the wasteland beyond. "Did you hear me, Carrey? Connor hijacked the rowing truck. He says you have to come. He's waiting for you down by the football field. Get something else on, it's freezing out there."

I put my hands on my hips and stretched, tried to wake myself up. "Is he crazy?"

"Not as crazy as he thinks he is. Ruth and Wads are also there. He's got beers, dude."

I pulled on my T-shirt and sweatshirt and jeans. Perry watched me dumbly in the dark while I yanked a sweater over my head, slammed my already socked feet into my sneakers and found my jacket and hat. I walked out into the hallway. It seemed obscenely bright. The torn linoleum floor was streaked with Perry's wet footprints. He was a sight to behold in a long, formal coat, snowmobile boots, and a neon green hat. His face had turned bright red in the steam heat of the dorm. When he shoved me through the main doors out into the cold, the night wind howled right through me.

It had snowed. A white revelation of it was like a blanket over the leaves sparkling in the starlight. It clung to the exterior walls of the dorm in flashes, to the wooden fences lining the walkways, had streaked the trees with white. The air seemed to contain the dormant energy of that early snowfall. We started walking fast, me with my arms flat against my sides, my fists balled in my pockets. The dusting of snow on the main drive seeped into the bottoms of my sneakers so that by the time we'd crossed over Route 7, my socks were damp and my feet freezing. Perry and I walked along in silence, until finally he said, "Channing was impressed by your bench pull testing. Connor couldn't believe it. Dude, you almost kicked his ass. There he is over there. Check it out."

I could just make Connor out in the long strip of snow before the field house. The football field. His back was to us, his form shimmering and fading as he threw something deliberately and quickly into the darkness. Ruth was standing near him, small and motionless in a cobalt blue ski jacket that hung off her narrow shoulders. Perry looked at Connor and said to me, "He has a good arm. He's making thirty, forty yards even though he's buzzed."

We had walked up to the end zone near the road. Connor had a bag of footballs open beside him. He'd bend, fade two steps, and feign right, then throw directly for the goalposts. The footballs spiraled into the stars, then dropped like birds below the posts. He seemed to be talking to himself, or else counting. I could hear him grunting out there while he repeated the same movements, again and again. Perry clapped me on the shoulder. "Security will be by sooner or later. Just so you know. Convince him to get out of here fast, okay?"

"Me? Do you really think I can tell the guy to do anything?"

"You can try."

Far off I heard the sound of a trailer rig laboring down the road that led away from us, a black ribbon through the white fields. We walked across the slick, whitened grass to Connor, whose breath was misting in the dark. I stood next to him and he didn't pause, acted as if he hadn't noticed me. I made eye contact with Ruth and half-waved a greeting. She pursed her lips in a kind of grimace by way of answer and hunched deeper into her jacket. Connor launched the next ball downfield. He breathed easy through the release, catching his breath as the ball soared into the black sky. "I found these inside the gym. The doors aren't locked."

"Are you drunk?"

"Am I throwing like I'm drunk?"

"I don't know."

"Perry, give the man a drink."

"They catch me drinking they'll send me home."

"Carrey, you are such a *ridiculous* and *absurd* pussy. Do you want a drink or not?"

Perry held out a six-pack of cans covered in snow. I twisted one off and cracked it, the barley smell strong, the foam icy and familiar on my fingers. Perry tore one off as well. I sipped the beer and couldn't taste it in the cold, just smelled that intense scent, felt it go right down my throat in a searing trickle. I sipped it again and coughed up some. Connor reached down into the snow and picked up his own can easily, tipped it into his mouth and wiped his lips with his free arm, shaking out his gloveless fingers. "Know what?"

"What?"

"It's fucking freezing out here." Connor launched another football downfield, which settled into the end zone without a sound. He snatched up another, threw it hard and it did not arc up into the sky, but bulleted across the white expanse and disappeared. He kicked the empty bag and burped. "That's not bad throwing. Even Jumbo has to admit it. My family has a football game every summer on Cape Cod and I'm always quarterback. I'm undefeatable."

I finished my beer. "Let's go. Jumbo says security's coming soon."

"Security? You mean that rent-a-cop sleeping in the library? I'm always amazed by you Carrey. You're so conscious about rules. Just like Ruthie here. I'm the one from the sheltered background, after all." He reached into his jacket, pulled out a pack of cigarettes, bent over, shook one out and, still bent over, lit it. The smoke was crisp and warm in the dark. I watched him inhale. Of course he was a natural at it. "All right," he said. "I need some coffee."

"There's a gas station in town," I offered. "They'll sell us coffee." I squinted down the drive toward the school. Connor was right; we were alone. For now.

Connor turned around, looked at Ruth. "Hear that, Ruth? Care for an espresso?"

Ruth looked at the three of us and shrugged. She was now smoking, too, and drinking a beer. I wondered if he had woken her or Perry up first. If I was an afterthought. Where was Wadsworth?

"Come on," I said. "Let's get out of here. You have to keep moving if you don't want to get busted."

"Do you want to drive the truck?" Ruth's voice slurred slightly.

"Thought you'd never ask. Where are the keys?"

She dipped her tiny hands into her coat and came out with a jingling wad of keys she must have stolen from the boathouse.

"Think fast, Carrey." She tossed them over the snow, right at my head, and I caught them easily. "Carrey drives, Connor. You're drunk."

Connor laughed. "*I'm* drunk? You've been matching me beer for beer and you're half my size."

We walked through the snow under the clear sky to the road. You could see the stars stretched out forever up there, blue and cool and quiet. Connor inhaled, looked up as if counting them, as if surprised they were there. He blew smoke upward. The truck was a silent hump parked in the shoulder covered in a light frosting of ice.

I swung open the driver's side and got in while Connor stood with his back to me pissing into the snow. Ruth got in behind me, and so did Perry. Wadsworth was snoring in the corner. Perry shoved him and he woke up. "Dude, stop it."

"Carrey's here, Wads," Ruth said quietly.

Wadsworth squinted at me. "So he is. Greetings, Carrey."

I nodded. So I was the last one to be called.

There was a thin ring of blue light over the mountains behind the school fields. Connor zipped up, swung open the passenger door and jumped in, clanged it shut. "God*damn* it, that felt good."

I started the truck and it grunted to life. The dim lights over the dials came up. Connor was still smoking, leaning against the door. I drove slowly toward town, over the steel bridge, praying that it hadn't iced over in the new snow. The truck had hard, awkward steering and the shocks were pretty jacked out—you felt every crack in that road. The river hadn't frozen yet. It cut a deep, black groove through the fields and then through the pastures and the forests beyond. Connor took a last drag on his cigarette, then stiffly wound the window down a crack to flick out the glowing butt that was whisked away by the wind. We labored up the hill into town, and the streetlights made me squint. Only the main road was lit up. We passed by the closed package store and the tourist shops until we came to the gas station and I pulled in. Connor gently felt his pockets for more cigarettes, like a man checking for wounds.

There was a small shop with florescent lights connected to the station. "Give me a few bucks for the coffee, Connor."

He hoisted himself up in the seat, reached into his front pocket. "Get us something to eat, too, Carrey. I haven't had anything since lunch. Here." He shoved a bill in my hand.

"What the hell is this?"

"It's all I have."

"A hundred-dollar bill to buy coffee and donuts? These people won't cash this."

Connor giggled. "I'll give you my credit card if they don't make change. They may surprise you, Carrey. This isn't Kansas, you know."

I glanced into the backseat. Wadsworth looked like he was on the nod again. "Ruth, ask Wads if he wants something."

She nudged him. "Chris. Wake up."

Wadsworth snorted, looked at her, grinned, threw an arm around her. And leaned back into the seat. She shook him off. "Rob's getting coffee."

"Good for him," Wadsworth mumbled.

What about you, Ruth?

She nodded her head. "Just coffee."

"Jumbo?"

"Candy bars, man. We're also down to our last five beers. In case anyone wants to know."

"Keep Wadsworth awake, Jumbo. I'm not helping you carry him into your dorm later."

"He's cool."

"How much have you guys had?"

"Like, eight or nine beers. I dunno."

"Thanks for inviting me."

"We did, dude."

I swung open the door. The hum of the gas station lights was almost unbearably loud. I walked round to the passenger window and tapped on it, and Connor cranked it down halfway. "Can we help you?"

"Pass out that thermos. There, on the floor next to you."

He looked on the floor, pushed aside some newspapers and a clipboard, picked up the silver flask and poked it out through the window. "You're going to want to clean that out."

I walked into the store and nodded to the tired old woman behind the counter. She stared back at me as if I was the harbinger of bad news. I went into the small bathroom in back and poured out the stale coffee in the grimy sink. I rinsed out the thermos as best as I could and set it down by the faucet. There was an open can of scouring soap on the sink and the floor smelled old and muddy. I looked at myself in the mirror, winked, and the kid I saw winked back. I walked out into the light and over to the coffee station, poured half the coffee jug in and about ten creamers. I sugared the thermos and shut it, shook it. I looked up at the woman. "Do you have a microwave here?"

She shook her head. I found two sandwiches in the refrigerator, picked out a fistful of candy bars, grabbed some paper cups and brought it all over to the counter. The woman rang it up, checked the pumps. Up close I saw that she was not so much old as old-looking; not so much tired as plain weary. "You kids are out late for a weekday, aren't you?"

"It's like a field trip."

"Like a field trip," she repeated. "That'll be twenty-one fifty."

I put the hundred on the counter and she set it up on the register, counted out the change in two piles, then watched me while I scraped it into my hand and shoved it in my pocket. "It's a late night for you, too, I guess."

"Some people have to work in this world."

"That's true."

"Yes. It is."

I picked up everything off the counter, walked back out to the truck, opened up the door, and threw everything in. Connor was still leaning against the window. Perry looked stricken and Wads was snoring again. Ruth sat stone-faced staring at nothing. Connor was looking at her intently, and it was obvious from the atmosphere in the cab that they had been arguing while I was in the shop.

"What's going on?" I asked.

Ruth glanced at me. "Nothing. Just drive, Carrey."

I started up the truck and drove out of town into the early morning dark. We stopped at a spot overlooking the river and the fields and the school. I piled the food on the dash and the coffee made a welt of steam on the inside of the windshield. The five of us sat there eating and drinking coffee until the sun began to glow behind the mountains, until we could see the shape of the river and the tiny ripples in the current. I slowly drank down my coffee and shook the cup out the window. Then Connor handed us each a beer and I drank the first dawn drink of my life.

"Have you shown Carrey the covered bridge yet?" Wadsworth asked.

Ruth looked at him impassively. "Let's leave it alone this time. Come on. Don't give Connor ideas."

Connor grinned. "A fine idea, Wadsworth. Let's see if we can get the truck down there."

Perry was calmly drinking his beer. It hurt that they'd been up so long without me, drinking, but I also knew that this was a kind of induction. "It's cool with me," I said. Ruth just sighed and rolled her green eyes.

Connor gave the directions and I drove down Bulls Run along the river for a few miles. The road to the bridge was impossibly narrow and dark and broken in spots, and I navigated it with the brights on, trying not to steer the truck into the water. The old heap rattled as we drove and I took a few of the potholes pretty hard. The seats were stiff, with sharp edges where the springs were working their way through. It was 5:00 A.M.

We came to the covered bridge and I parked with the lights shining into it. I'd have to reverse out of there—the road carried on south, away from the school. The river was too shallow for the boats here. It was pocked with slimy rocks that poked through the flat movement of the water. The bridge was a single lane—you'd have to wait for the person on the bridge to drive through before you could drive into it yourself. Inside, it looked wet and dark and ancient. Sitting in the truck before the yawning entrance you could see fairly far down the river. You could see the hills near the school, but not the school itself.

The five of us got out and stood in the rank darkness. Connor reached into the back of the truck and came up grinning with a leather backpack in his hands. Wordlessly he pulled out a bottle of champagne, then five champagne glasses. It was pathetic how good I felt to note there were five.

"All right, the dude!" Perry yelled. "Now we're talking."

Connor still said nothing. He shoved the bottle in one pocket of his baggy coat, the glasses in the other as we trooped into the bridge. He hopped up onto the rail and held on to one of the supports. The drop below him was fifty feet, maybe only forty, and the rocks snouted through the water with evil intent. Connor let go of the railing and looked at me. "I've come here every year since freshman year. If you look down, you can see the water is deeper than you think. Take a look. You could jump off the bridge and make it."

By way of reply, Perry looked over the bridge and spat a spinning yellow gob.

"Gross, Jumbo," Ruth mumbled.

"Dude, I've told you before," Wadsworth said. "There is no way I'd ever jump off this bridge. You always say you could make it. You couldn't. You'd have to be crazy to try it."

Connor's face went dark. "That's not the attitude to have, Wads. You *could* make the jump. One, two seconds in the air . . ."

I climbed up next to him, hooked an arm around the support and reached down to pull Ruth up. She hugged the bridge, her face red and chapped. Looking down between her boots, she shook her head. "This is silly. I'm getting down. We have to get back to the dorms." She looked at me, then Connor. "Take me home." Her voice was petulant and a little desperate. It sounded wrong coming from her.

Connor ignored her, looked at me evenly, the wind whipping through his hair now. I look back on this and see him so clearly— that white, wispy hair, that red, narrow face, his eyes streaming from the wind. "I'll jump if you do it. I swear to God I will jump on the count of three. You count, Carrey. Come on." He smiled, and then he was not smiling. "Do it, Carrey." He sounded almost serious.

I looked down. In that dim early light you could only see the whitecaps on the rocks. The smell of the freezing water was all around me, and it seemed like the river was moving heavily enough so that you might survive the fall. I leaned over, holding onto the railing with one hand, and finished my beer. I cast the can into the waves and it was pulled under. Connor swung back and forth, the glasses clinking in his pocket. "For three years I've wanted to jump off this bridge, and these guys have never wanted to join me. I was sure you'd try it, Carrey. Before the river freezes. Come on, what do you think?"

"What do I think? I'm thinking that before every dumb thing I've ever done, there was always that moment of knowing it was a dumb thing. You know what I mean, Connor?"

"If we made the jump, we'd be legendary. The first kids to do it. Think about it, Rob. It'd be more amazing than winning the Warwick Race."

Perry leaned over. "He loves this stupid bridge. He seriously thinks he could survive the fall."

"I don't think it, I *know* I could. I've come here a thousand times. I've seen it from the water. It's at least twenty feet deep right under the bridge."

"Unless you hit a rock," Perry pointed out. "Then you're pretty much dead."

"You can *see* the rocks, Jumbo."

Wadsworth grinned. "Don't do it, Connor. You can't tell where you'll fall."

Newly energized, Ruth leaned over the bridge. "Even if you survived the jump, you'd still have to get out of the water. It's a pretty good swim to the shore in this cold." She took a long drink from her can, cast it in. She jumped up on the railing between Connor and me, extended her arms, balanced, her eyes on Connor. For a second I saw something flash between them. Perry climbed up heavily, stood awkwardly on the railing, his feet misshapen and clownish. Finally Wadsworth jumped up, surprisingly agile. The five of us stood on the rail. Connor turned, lost his balance for one moment and flexed his legs. An artist on the high wire. He pulled the bottle from his pocket and dramatically twisted off the cork. Champagne fizzed over onto the bridge.

Slipping his hand into his jacket pocket, Connor took out a glass with a flourish, filled it with champagne, and passed it to Ruth, who carefully passed it to me, who just as gingerly passed it to Perry. And so on, Connor not missing a beat, pouring, passing the drinks, until we all had a glass, and we were all balanced over that churning water, the sulphur smell of French champagne mixing with the foamy smell of the rapids under the bridge. Connor took a gulp from the bottle, belched, and flung it into the river.

He held up his glass. "I propose a toast. To those heinous losers at Warwick." And we drank to it, all of us, the best champagne I'd ever taste. Connor finished his, dropped the glass into the rolling foam, belched again. "Looks like Carrey's one of us now." I had to force myself not to grin. Ruth tipped her glass into the waves, pirouetted on her railing, then jumped into the safety of the bridge. Two more glasses smashed on the rocks below and Wadsworth stepped back into the darkness with Perry flopping down after him.

Connor was still not holding the support. He balanced like a bird of prey, poised to fly. I stood only a few feet away, willing myself not to touch the supporting beam. I drank my champagne down, flicked the glass into the river, waited for Connor. The others started walking to the truck. Ruth finally glanced back, "We need to go, guys. It's time. Stop being jerks."

Connor grinned, bayed into the morning. It was getting bright out. The water was blue in the channels beneath our feet now, much faster than when we arrived.

"Jump, Carrey. Let's do it." I knew he'd follow me down if I accepted his dare.

A breeze howled down the river, caught me, and I grabbed the beam, swung around and leapt down to the road. The impact jammed hard into my heels.

Connor chuckled, shrugged and lightly sprung off the bridge to the cement. He followed me to the truck. I felt his eyes on my back and he was grinning when I turned around. Just before he got into the truck, behind the wheel, he mouthed, "You're a *wicked* loser, Carrey."

I poked my head into the driver's side. He stank of beer but he had sobered up on that bridge all right. "Are you going to smash this thing, Connor?"

He shook his head and flashed me that lopsided crazy smile. Then his dark eyes flicked to the rearview mirror, where I could see Ruth sandwiched between Jumbo who was staring drunkenly out his window and Wadsworth, who was, incredibly, fast asleep like a freakish baby. She examined the two of us from inside the protection of the upturned collar of her ski jacket. Her eyes were red.

"Are you okay, Ruth?" I asked.

"Carrey, we have to get this truck back. She's just pissed off, as usual," Connor said.

"I want to hear it from her."

He regarded me evenly and then raised his hands from the steering wheel in a gesture of exasperation. "Have it your way."

I poked my head in and asked her one last time. She looked at me and simply said, "I'm fine, Rob. We need to go back."

Connor smiled at me. "See? She's fine. Let go of the door. Get in."

"I'll run it."

"Oh, God. How virtuous," he spat out contemptuously. He lurched the truck into gear and was off in a haze of vapor and sand from the shoulder where he'd spun the wheels after dropping the clutch too hard on that shoddy first gear. I could still see the small figure of Ruth hunched in the back, staring vacantly out at the riverbanks which were covered in a crusty, windblown layer of snow. I wondered if I would ever find out what had gone on between her and Connor that night.

I turned and started out at an easy lope. I kept pace for a couple of miles, until I was only a sprint away from the school and then I started a flat-out run. The more I ran the more I felt my life coursing through me and I was electric. I could have shot into that school like a meteor. Man, I must have been something to see.

And when I got to the school road, out of breath, my hands moist, the taste of no sleep and beer and coffee and champagne in my mouth, there was Channing against the steel sky, walking toward me in his flowing black coat. When he saw me he didn't wave or smile. I waited for him to cross to my side, my red, moist hands on my hips. I was pretending to catch my breath.

He was on the walkway beside the bridge, and I was standing in the middle of the road.

Finally he acknowledged me. "Oft I have run o'er meadow an' vale, t'ward what tho', I know not."

I thought for a second. "Wordsworth?"

"Charles Channing. Not damned bad, either."

"The little known poet."

"What brings you out on such a foul morning, Carrey?"

"Don't know. Fresh air, maybe."

"You look terrible. I don't advise fresh air today. But maybe you have a better excuse than I for needing it."

"Which is?"

"Old men are cursed with morning." He looked over the fields at the sleeping school, then at me. "Did you know that there is no verb 'to crew' as it applies to rowing? You may crew a sailboat, but the word only has use as a noun when one rows. Perhaps this use emphasizes the camaraderie of the sport."

"It's called teamwork."

"I don't see my team anywhere near. I often see you work alone, Carrey." The snow was in his hair now. It seemed to be getting colder out as the morning wore on. I stamped my feet. I was getting stiff, standing there and talking to him. He turned and gazed up the black furrow of road breaking the white rise of land before the town. The single light hanging above the mouth of the bridge idly changed from green to yellow. "There might be more to all this life than rowing," he said.

"Not much."

"But then again . . ." He held a finger up for silence, and then cocked an ear. We listened to the morning around us, cold as it was. "The ink painting blowing through the pines. Who hears it?"

"Another one by Charles Channing?"

"No. Should have been, though." He looked back down the road. "Tell that damned Connor Payne to leave his hands off the school's vehicles. Remind him that if he's caught drinking we'll throw him out of school, no matter who his father is." He glanced at me significantly. "The same applies to you. And the others."

He trudged on. Nobody had shoveled the sidewalk and there were crazy pits in the snow leading from the main road to the bridge: his own footprints.

18.

Carolyn had the framework of the shark documentary up by the end of the day. She went through the script with me, showed me some scenes she had put together that would make up the introduction. I wondered if we should find a music track for any of this. The scenes looked good, the piece had begun to take shape, but it was not how I had imagined it. The sharks I filmed needed saving from thrill-seeking sport fishermen. Yet the thrill seeker I had chosen to interview, a woman, looked bright and cheerful on camera. She sounded too modulated and sincere. Of course her sport didn't affect shark numbers, she claimed. Commercial fishing was responsible for that. People pay hundreds of dollars to fish these waters, she pointed out, why should they get a marlin and not a shark? The marlin were nowhere near as plentiful, she was at pains to add, particularly black marlin that tourists from Australia and the UK caught and posed beside like Hemingway.

Carolyn had done a good job. The Natal Sharks Board was indignant enough, the aerial shots we had of the ocean, where you could see the sharks coming in to feast on the school of sardines that ran down the coast at that time of year, were magnificent. The work clearly put Carolyn in a good frame of mind. She opened up a bottle of wine and downed a glass, then another, toasted me and then the sharks while she devoured most of the dolmades and salad we had ordered in. We were now practicing the professional relationship we were meant to cultivate from here on in.

I looked at the video and thought of the weeks it had taken to get it. The time in the water, waiting for the sharks to come out of the gloom in that dense quiet, the feel and taste of the rubber breather in my mouth, the chemical taste of the O_2. The neverending mist on my diving mask and on the camera's eyepiece. Frankly, it was the easiest part of the entire shoot, not that I looked forward to it. When I was twenty-six, underwater filming was a charge. Now it was routine, it was mundane, hours of work you did on top of the hours of work you did putting together the proposal, getting the interview subjects on board, then getting the equipment and the boat rentals and the crew and then driving to the shoot in a 4×4 or in a van; endless driving, eating out of fast-food restaurants and saving the receipts to work into the expenses—including the receipts for the coffee you gave the crew. The hotels that awaited you were the fleabags that small seaside places excelled in, or else overly quaint bed and breakfast houses run by overly concerned proprietors who never had enough space to stow all the gear. I was getting tired of sleeping off filming days under flowery quilts on lumpy beds with Old Mother Hubbard skirting.

In the last year I had taken on more and more shoots inside South Africa, which was comfortable, in many ways easier to navigate than the States. I had quietly turned down shoots in Russia (tiger); India (tiger again); and most recently, one in the Himalayas (tahr) purely because getting myself there with all my equipment, working out the visas and the food and the overland travel was just too uncomfortable. I had been doing the hardcore assignments for a while and I'd had enough.

Instead, I took on pieces like the sardine run off of the very developed city of Durban (really just a more run-down version of Miami), a shoot I could have easily outsourced to a South African crew but May in Durban was *far* nicer than May in rainy Cape Town. My next shoots were going to be on Table Mountain (kwagga) and maybe—*maybe*—in the Kruger National Park (an elephant relocation that would take place not far from the clean, air-conditioned chalets they offered visitors). It was easy work. Dream work. But watching Carolyn edit the shark footage, I felt no yearning whatsoever to be anywhere but where I was. With her, steps away from a shower and a comfortable bed. Our bed.

My current self would have disgusted my younger self.

But I wasn't about to tell Car any of this, just out of pure, dog-stupid stubbornness.

———

Fall term was suddenly over and it was time to write the first exams of the year. The mood on campus shifted and everyone became preoccupied and brooding. Connor holed up in the Rowing Cottage desperately trying to pass all his courses. Even if he was a quadruple legacy to Harvard and a Junior National team member, they could not take him if he was actually failing classes, and his board scores were a complete joke.

I spent this down time studying, sleeping, running and studying some more. The exams were harder than any of the tests I'd taken back at home and I wasn't taking any chances. After I finished the last of them—AP chemistry, an upgrade of the course I had taken in Niccalsetti Senior School—I wandered into town, hoping I'd find somebody on the team to hang out with. I hit it lucky. Ruth was in the Station Shop, alone and reading. The Station Shop was Fenton's idea of a café: it served all the usual coffee concoctions and also ice cream and snacks for the tourists. Most of the kids preferred the Pizza Garden, where they could get away with smoking if they were careful. At this time of year the teachers were too swamped to come into town and patrol the place. For all they cared we could be ordering shots and shooting up in the corners. I knew better than to look for Ruth there.

A jagged row of icicles outside the Station Shop window dripped and sparkled in the weak, white sun. I could hear the fat, melting drops slapping the wet snow. I came into the shop wet from the cold and Ruth turned away from me when she saw me. She was poring over a black-spined Penguin paperback. *The Brothers Karamazov.* She was actually reading it on her own steam. I knew this because our English exams were over. I sat down in front of her and she tried to ignore me, then looked up and sighed. "Can we please, please, please not talk about crew? Or the team? Or training?"

"Okay . . . Are you done with all your exams?"

"Yes, but I don't want to talk about them either."

"What are you doing over Thanksgiving break?"

"Definitely not a good topic for discussion."

"Tell me something I don't know about you then," I said in exasperation. "You know all about me. I don't know anything about you."

She didn't say anything, just looked at the square of light on the floor. "Like what?"

"Anything."

"Just sit there for a second, Rob. I'm busy reading this. I have one more page and it's over."

I liked watching her read. She looked pale and exhausted and she moved with a quiet deliberation. I wanted to reach out and touch her but resisted the impulse. After a few minutes she closed her book, slipped it in her bag, then took a breath. "I think I love my father more than my mother."

It was a surprise to hear that. I was expecting her to tell me to go away. "Yeah? And, so . . . ? How come?"

She stood up abruptly, clearly ready to go. I followed her outside into the afternoon cold. The flagstones leading from the shop door were dark and muddy with footprints. We walked a little way along the road and then headed toward the school. We cut across the last lawns in front of the town and started down the hill leading to the river.

"What do you want out of life?" Ruth suddenly asked me.

Her questions were all over the place but the answer was easy. "I want to be untouchable, the way the guys on the team are untouchable. The way Connor is untouchable."

"Why is he?"

"The same way you are. Because you're rich. Because you're smart and have connections and tradition and you're everything everyone aspires to back home only they can't even visualize or imagine it so they'll never have it."

"It's just luck, Rob. It's not about being special at all."

"Do you want to know something I've found out in the last month?"

"No. You're going to talk about crew and I can't bear it."

"People want something more and more the closer it gets to them. As long as it's just out of reach, you want it like you've never wanted anything, because you can see it so clearly. You can smell it. Until you can't imagine wanting anything else."

"You think being on a team is like that?"

"I think winning is like that. And leaving home behind. Leaving the past behind and starting again, somewhere else. Being a whole new person."

"Do you really think you can leave the past behind just like that?" She smiled, as if she pitied me. "And what happens if you get what you want? What happens then?"

"The past is dead, Ruth. It's over. You have to be able to dump it."

"I hope so. For both our sakes." She stopped midway down the hill, her fingers hooked in the cuffs of her coat. I looked over the river with her, saw the school in a sparkling haze through the trees.

"Here's what I know about leaving the past behind and being close to things you want," she said. She still hadn't turned her eyes to me. "When my parents got divorced—separated, sorry, they got divorced later—they told me right before a cocktail party they were throwing for some German conductor. I was in the kitchen of the old apartment in New York and my mother came in with a big smile on her face. She asked me what time it was. Then she asked me what I thought about her leaving Daddy."

I wasn't sure what to say. I was holding my balance, facing her on the wet hill.

"I should have pulled her hair out. Instead, I said that I thought her leaving Daddy was a bad idea. There were all these people walking in and out who were there to help with the bar and the hors d'oevres and everything. Then the caterers arrived and my father came out of his room and I thought that if I pretended my mother hadn't asked me that question, then everything would be fine. And since Mom was doing the exact same thing, and Daddy didn't even know we'd spoken, we could *all* pretend things were fine, and that's what we did." Ruth's face was getting red in the cold.

The good thing was that I'd found something to say. "Ruth?"
"What?"

"I once went to this funeral where the dead person's brother got into a fight with one of the mourners. The brother hit him so hard that the guy threw up."

"That's pretty unreal, Carrey."

The story was true. Tom hit me so hard that I had to go out behind the hearse we'd rented for Wendy and puke while they finished putting dirt all over her.

I was walking backward now and pulling Ruth down the hill with me. She was having trouble with her balance. I was lower than her now, my boots digging into the snow. I was unbuttoning her coat. Her lips were cold and her mouth was warm and tasted like coffee and something else. Hope, maybe. I slipped and we fell but it's funny how sometimes you don't mind the cold.

Connor received a video in the mail from Warwick a few days after we came back from Thanksgiving break. The five of us assembled in the Rowing Cottage to watch it.

"Warwick has three Junior National team guys on the boat," Connor informed us in a monotone. "Eddie McFarlane, a cox named Brendan Cooper, who is a total psycho, but that's beside the point, and Tony Brickman, the captain, who has hated my guts since we went to Trinity together in kindergarten. I hate to admit it but Brickman is good—he has a place near my parents' house in Osterville and he's a beast, he's the *missing link*. Their coach, by the way, is on his way to Princeton to take over the freshman crew."

The video flickered to life on the TV screen. It had been shot from the bow of a coaching launch. You could see how fast Warwick's crew was by the distance between the puddles left by their oars in the water. They were smooth and ominous looking. There was absolutely no sound, just frame after relentless frame of their perfect form. I allowed myself to consider if we were up to competing against a boatful of champion returners.

We watched for two minutes and then Connor shut off the machine, popped out the video and dropped it in the garbage. The message was clear. It had been a mistake to watch that video and see how good their boat was when the Fenton God Four hadn't even been formed. I hadn't rowed one stroke with these kids. I hadn't even been officially selected yet. It was too late, though. I looked around the Rowing Cottage. Everyone was subdued. The video had done exactly what Warwick intended; we were intimidated.

WINTER

19.

Only two rowers came back from Christmas break early; Connor Payne and me. My father didn't raise an eyebrow when I said I was going back a week before the start of winter term. He handed me some cash, told me to call the bus station myself and not to ask for any more operating capital until the end of February.

I took the bus out to Albany with my bag next to me on the seat. The bus smelled like old, stale food. The seats were mostly empty but a guy got on and came and sat directly across the aisle from me. He put his boots up on the seat next to him and pulled his wool watchman's cap down over his eyes. It was snowing outside while we cut through the darkness. Once, the guy rolled his hat up and gave me that deadeye look you get from ex-cons. Finally he asked if I had a cigarette and when I shrugged and shook my head, he rolled the hat back down and went back to sleep. I had to switch to two more buses before I got to Fenton. Fifteen hours of travel in all, half of it through sleet.

When we hit the town, I was let off opposite the Fox and Fiddle Inn. I could look right across the street at the glowing windows and the people inside dressed up at the bar. I walked down the main road swinging my bag, thankful for the fresh air. I crossed the front soccer fields to the school in the clear dark and the air had a real bite to it. I ate in the snack bar, collapsed into bed and slept for eighteen hours straight. I awoke to watch the numbers on my bedside clock flip by 6:00 P.M. I swung my feet to the floor and shed my blanket, felt the freezing dusk air brush away the warmth of my long sleep. I pulled on my stiff running pants, my T-shirt, sweatshirt, and running shoes, and trudged into the weirdly silent hall breathing the odor of old showers and Lysol that would probably never leave that building until they tore it down.

I ran stiffly down the main walk and passed the Rowing Cottage. There was Connor, sitting idly on the front steps leading into the cottage, as if he was enjoying a warm sunny day rather than the blustery cold of late December in Fenton, Connecticut. He looked up at me as if he barely recognized me or remembered me.

"Carrey. Long time no see."

"What are you doing back here?"

He reached into his sweatshirt, pulled out a letter. "Reading the mail. Catching up with my affairs of state. How was your vacation?"

"It was all right."

"You have a good time with the folks?"

"Yeah. What about you?"

"Do you really use that word?"

"What word?"

" 'Folks.' I asked you how your *folks* were and you didn't call me on it. Where'd they find you, Carrey?" He squinted in a sudden hard gust of wind that came off the river, and stood up. He held out the letter as if looking at it for some sign of hidden value. He waved it in the air. "From my dad. What a man. What a towering figure. Fuck him." Connor stuffed the missive into the pocket of his sweatpants. "Let's run to the boathouse, see if Channing opened it for us."

We started out at half speed, the wind blowing against us. Connor labored beside me, slipped once and swore. When we hit the main drive of the school leading to Route 7, I pushed up our pace. I felt the air in my chest flow ragged suddenly and I pressed by him but I knew he was directly behind me. I could hear his quick, harsh breaths. When I saw the boathouse rising out of its own narrow, unplowed drive, I made for it, my arms swinging, my hands unclenched and free. Behind me, Connor slipped again and a quick, rasping sound escaped from his throat. In ten paces I had beaten him. I touched the boathouse door and rattled the icy lock. He bent over, put his hands on his knees, and sucked the air in rattling gulps. Then he stood, patted my shoulder. "Good job." He tried the lock himself, clearly irritated. "Channing told me he'd open this up for me."

"He probably forgot. Who wants to work out in this weather anyway?"

"True. We're supposed to be on vacation." His nose was running and he pushed his hand across it. He walked away from the boathouse doors, looked out at the lonely drop to where the dock would be in a few months' time. The gray sky seemed hushed and expectant above. Connor stared at the river, which had yet to freeze, mesmerized by the black water running by us. I breathed its cool, living smell.

"So what did it say?"

"What did what say?"

"The letter you were waving around."

"Oh, that. My father dropped me a note. He wished me well for the winter term and informed me that he and my mom will be in London for the foreseeable future. If I need anything, I'm welcome at my grandmother's. I love that."

"Where does your grandmother live?"

"New York, where else? But she'll be out in Osterville soon. If I need a break from this place, I can go hang out there. You're welcome to join us, Carrey." He looked at me with a suddenly sincere face.

"Might need to take a rain check on that."

"I'm thinking I'll fly to London instead. Surprise my parents."

"Just like that? You'd hop on a plane and leave all this?"

"I checked out airline fares. They seem surprisingly affordable."

"Are your parents coming back for the Warwick Race?"

"They will fly back for that. Of course. They wouldn't miss it for the world. That's their plan."

A light rain that felt like it wanted to become snow started to fall. The river was running high. I tried to listen to its flow but the harder I listened the more I heard my own heart.

Connor looked up at the white sky. "I have a question to ask you."

"Ask it."

"Did you fuck Ruth? It's totally cool if you did. She's worth it, I have to say. I think you banged her. That's what I think."

I didn't even bother looking at him. "Nice, Connor. What kind of question is that? I wouldn't tell you if I did."

"When she was a freshman, she did the old captain of the team, Bruce. It's why she was made coxswain, in my humble opinion. She's been around the block, our Ruth. I've always been shocked by her behavior." He was trying hard for a reaction he wasn't going to get.

"I'm going home. You are so full of shit, Connor, and you're an asshole. If you were my kid, I'd ship you off to boarding school and move to another country, too."

He laughed. "You're going 'home'? To where? Niccalsetti?" He turned to the river. "Niccalsetti, New York. Home of Rob Carrey."

"Keep talking to yourself. It's a good sign. Knock yourself out."

"Look how defensive you are about her, Carrey! You're a romantic at heart. Like me. We're the last of the poets."

"Right. Some poets."

"Okay, okay. I'm sorry. I am. Okay? I'll grant you the fact that I'm an asshole. But you need to at least admit you're a cheese dog. You really are. And you have, like, no sense of humor. Nada."

"Be funny, and I'll laugh."

"I'll tell you one thing I am serious about. I can make the jump off the covered bridge. You could, too. You're crazy enough to try it. I know you are. You pretend you're not, but it's still a temptation."

"The covered bridge? Are you kidding? You can't make the jump. It's not something you're meant to make. It's not like you can just decide to miss those rocks on your way down, Connor."

"We could do the jump right now. The water's not frozen yet. Think about it. Even if we win the race, some other crew will have a faster time. But *nobody* wants to make the jump. It's the stuff of legends."

"It's freezing out here. Even if you didn't die jumping off the bridge, the water would kill you."

"Us! You'd be with me! We would *not* freeze, goof. We can swim for two minutes to the shore. Come on, Rob. You have the balls to do it. I promise, if you say the word we'll do it."

"You really want to run down to the covered bridge and jump? Now? In the dark?"

"It's not dark! I can see perfectly."

"In half an hour you won't even be able to see the water off the bridge."

"So what? I'm not kidding, Rob. We could do this. We could make the jump. *Ruth* would do it. She'd think it was cool *you* did it. She wouldn't say so, but she'd think it."

"She's not that dumb. And she would never even try it."

"That's where you're dead wrong, *mon ami*. She's the one

who's most likely to do it. Before you came along, I was fairly sure she'd go over with me."

"She changed her mind?"

"Something like that." He grimaced. "Listen. This is your last chance. We can start down there now and be back for dinner. The river will be frozen soon and then we have to wait until spring. It's now or never."

"Nobody would believe we did it, even if we did. Which we won't."

"Carrey, they know I wouldn't lie about jumping off the covered bridge. And I'd have you to back me up. You're as honest as they come."

"If you were going to jump off that bridge, you would have done it long before I came here. And I don't want you to kill yourself, Connor. If you do, Leonsis gets moved up into your seat. And if that happens, we lose against Warwick."

He smirked, a Cheshire cat in the gathering shadows.

"I saw the video just like you did. We need you around for a few more months. Just until we beat Warwick. Then you can feel free to jump off the Golden Gate Bridge, for all I care."

"Just remember that it would never even occur to Leonsis to jump off the covered bridge. That's what sets him apart from you and me."

"It would never occur to me, either. This is *your* weird thing."

"So, keeping me alive is Robert Carrey's public service. Your selfish nobility humbles me."

"Connor, you don't know anything about dying."

"I think you'd be surprised at what I know."

"You don't know jack crap."

———

The trip back from Zambia was unadulterated hell. I arrived in New York after a total of thirty-two grueling hours of travel.

Ten hours from Lusaka to London. A twelve-hour layover in Heathrow. Ten hours to Kennedy. My entire body ached from the pounding I had been given and I had a screeching hangover, the desperate kind that makes you chew aspirin, tear up cocktail napkins, toss back water two bottles at a time. I had eaten nothing. The meals on the flights revolted me. Halfway across the ocean I finally vomited, standing in the small closet of a bathroom, retching water and snot into the steel bowl. It was almost a relief. I tried to call Carolyn from Lusaka International, then again from London. Nothing. I called her father and mother, both of whom had moved to Boca Raton a year before, and asked if they had heard from Carolyn. They were puzzled by my call and I realized she had not told them what had happened, and that was a bad sign. I told them she had miscarried and I had not been with her. She had gone to the hospital and been discharged, and I was on my way back to be with her. I promised to call them when I got into the city, I was sure everything would be fine. Their thirty-two-year-old daughter was in good hands, she'd call them if she needed them.

I edited out a few facts. The pathetic condition I was in; the hammering headache, the dry lips, the shaking. My bruised, possibly fractured, ribs. Everything was not going to be fine.

I also omitted the things *I* didn't know yet. That Carolyn had woken on a sheet painted with blood at 2:00 A.M. a week before, had called the ambulance. The ambulance guys had come in through the fire escape because they couldn't get the gurney into the freight elevator. Carolyn wouldn't send it down to them as she was passing in and out of consciousness on the floor and was half hysterical with fear. They eventually loaded her onto a seated gurney and carried her down the stairs covered in blankets with an IV in her arm. Carolyn was howling. The neighbors, even the sweatshop workers, were out in the street to see her. Under the sheet, her legs were smeared with blood. She was in the middle of a hemorrhaging miscarriage, this woman who had started to sustain herself by dreaming about a baby that was now trickling out of her.

They had her in the hospital within half an hour and the procedure was finished while she was sedated. Carolyn did it all alone. When it was over, she wanted to continue to be alone. It was just that simple.

When I finally touched down at JFK, I practically ran to the taxi stand and sat through the interminable drive into the city, dreading what I would find. I dialed the number to the loft ten times on the way in and got the same cheery answering machine each time, finally crushing the cell phone in my hands in frustration. I had no idea who else to call. I just did not have the numbers for the rest of the people we knew in New York—those were in a book by the phone in the loft.

When I let myself in, after calling Carolyn's name all the way through the agonizingly slow ride up the elevator, I was confronted by carnage. The smell of congealing food, four days old, struck me first. And the god-awful mess; her clothes, pajamas, bills, papers. The detritus of a life scattered across the workstation and the kitchen and the tables and the floor. I felt as if the dust from a million years of grief had settled on the scattered cushions and unevenly pulled shades and crumpled rug. Carolyn was curled in bed, wearing a sweatshirt of mine and my boxers. I went to the bed, lowered myself next to her with the same helpless horror you feel when you find a grievously and senselessly wounded animal. When she awoke she took my hand, brought it to her mouth, and began to gnaw and make sounds that were like crying.

I nursed her as best I could. She was wearing a kind of heavy pad that she continued to bleed into, that had to be changed like a battle dressing. For a week I emptied out the small, stained cotton pillows that piled up in the steel wastepaper basket in the bathroom. I dressed her, undressed her, bathed her. I didn't leave the apartment. I cleaned up, made food. She ate, she took pills, she cried, she took different pills. I started to forget to clean up, I stopped making meals. I'd move from her bed to the couch, listening always to the way she breathed, to the undulation of her crying, alert for her hysterical rage, terrified I'd fall asleep and she'd hurt herself.

I unplugged the phone, then the computer. We lived like people hiding in a war. We slept. She limped around the apartment. We drank. She kept filling the bandages and I kept throwing them away. I wrapped them in the plastic bags they delivered the food in from Huang's Real New York Chinese Delivery.

I was the messenger. The messages were not very encouraging.

I called Carolyn's parents from my cell phone every morning, standing in the hall and whispering my updates while Carolyn slept. I reported their daughter's progress while sitting on the steel steps leading down to the sweatshop. I called them from the coffee takeout, from the sidewalk standing under the shepherd's crook streetlamp in the evening.

She'll pull out of it, I told them.

Things were kind of hard now but she was 'making progress,' I assured them.

I thought she was getting stronger by the day, I lied.

She was more like her old self, I fabricated.

In fact, she was listless and she was drugged and also, of course, drinking. We had a pretty considerable stash of valium (thanks to my constant flying), and she was pretty much through it. We also had the painkillers the hospital gave her. And wine. And vodka.

I didn't mention the saturated pads of blood to her parents. That was her business, I reasoned. Women bleed, I told myself, and Carolyn had been scraped out. The bleeding would stop as it always did. I didn't need to share that.

Of course, now I have a recurring dream that I switched on the computer during one of those long, listless afternoons and did a search for post-DNC bleeding. Or typed in "bleeding miscarriage" or "miscarriage infection" or "miscarriage care for patient." I dream that I did a mere half hour of surfing, just to pass the time, just to make certain all this blood was normal.

I have another dream that I pick up the damn phone and call the gynecologist and ask a few hard questions. But I did not. I trusted the woman who slept next to me to know her body. Even my drugged out, drunk, sleeping partner who might have been shedding her own skin in there, who might have been losing her vision or her teeth or her sense of touch or slowly suffocating and was in no state to draw my attention to it. We traveled through those days in a dead funk. Two ghost ships drifting aimlessly on a dead, red sea.

Carolyn and I did not say things to each other that were comforting. We did not say, for instance, we could always have another baby. We could try again. We had time. I did not say I loved her. She and I spoke only about the drugs that were running out and where we could get prescriptions for new ones, especially the painkillers. She slept fifteen hours a day. The same person who for years had worked long, crazy hours weeks at a time, the sleepless life of the Indie filmmaker. We drank the things she had not been permitted two weeks before. Coffee. Wine. Scotch. Vodka. She continued to bleed.

Finally, I put a call in for her doctor, who called back five hours later to listen to me ask for more painkillers and hint about where I could find some more of those supersize bandages. The doctor blew up, demanded I bring her in immediately. The bleeding should have stopped days ago. There could be only one reason for what was happening now: infection. Had I looked at the blood? Was it dark blood or pink blood or was it blood and pus? What did it smell like? How the fuck was I supposed to know? The doctor repeated to me again to bring her in, right now, and slammed the phone down.

So I took Carolyn back to Lennox Hill. And as the taxi negotiated uptown on a busy Monday, she slept in my arms. Then we waited in the green waiting area, Carolyn nodding off, both of us looking like junkies. The doctor took one look at her, kicked me out, examined her, called me into her office, and curtly told us that a massive infection had set in and Carolyn was lucky to be alive. I realized we both smelled of booze as the doctor chewed us out. I was sweating it. Carolyn was running on pain-killers, junk food, and wine. If the round of intravenous antibi-otics the doctor prescribed for her did not work, there would have to be more surgery. Carolyn was checked in for observa-tion and possibly for a procedure to halt the infection. I could stay during visiting hours but no longer because I was not a relative (live-in partners are really—when it comes down to the brass tacks of life—nothing). The doctor suggested I go home because I looked terrible and there was nothing that I could do for Carolyn now except let her sleep. I could come back tomor-row between two and five. It was more than a suggestion.

Before I agreed to leave, a nurse who couldn't have been more than twenty-one, hooked her up to a drip, refusing to make eye contact with me. Carolyn was asleep in seconds. I watched her drift off, her lips set as if she was stating a categori-cal refusal to pretty much everything.

Then I left her there.

For the first time in my life I drank completely alone. I drank with no aim in mind but to listen to ice cubes pop and melt in the darkness.

You *wicked* loser, Carrey.

I'd smile and then the vicious voice would ask me what I was smiling about. Losers don't smile. Losers take the long way home. Losers give up their shirts. Losers empty trash baskets full of a woman's blood and sleep on couches, drunk.

What's she doing with a guy like you?

You.

Wicked loser.

20.

Snow began to fall in earnest and with pure malevolence—almost every day throughout the first weeks of January. The boardwalk drifted over, Route 7 became a frosty tunnel and the mountains behind the school turned white. Huge daggers of ice hung from the gutters of the Schoolhouse. During the occasional thaws there was a distracting cacophony of dripping and the snow turned into sticky rain that glued itself to the trees. When the snow assaulted us once more, the trees transformed into a huge and spectacular menagerie of delicate glass sculptures shimmering in the brief, weak sun.

I got busted throwing snowballs at Ruth's window one night. The teacher who ran Middle Dorm, Mrs. Horeline, caught me standing out on the backfield launching perfect bull's-eyes at the third floor, the snowballs exploding satisfyingly against Ruth's storm window.

Horeline let me off lightly with a warning not to be caught up after lights-out again. And no more throwing snowballs at windows. Ruth blew me off in chemistry the next day, wouldn't even look at me. Then she beaned me with a perfect head shot at twenty feet when I was walking out of the labs. When I reeled around, swearing, snow and ice drifting down my collar, she was grinning wickedly and I knew I was forgiven.

One afternoon I walked over to Channing's, trudged behind his house to the shed. I had rehung the door properly just a few weeks before; I'm the only person on earth who can do that job alone. I pushed through the door, stood in the sawdust, and switched on the lights—the electric worked fine. I'd done the wiring, chased the wires to the two light sockets under the ceiling. If you closed the door, the room was a refuge from the cold. No dusting of snow lay near the windows or by the doorway's arch. The tools were carefully lined up where I had left them, the cans of paint removed by me to Channing's garage. Beside the bags of nails and the coiled extension cord was one of his notes, stiff with cold, *Go away, Carrey.*

He'd left a lowball in the shed, the amber liquid inside it completely frozen. I stood still in the wooden quiet for a few minutes, grinning. Then I picked up Channing's glass and brought it outside with me, set it on his small porch. Let him wonder, I thought.

And still the training ground on. As did the testing.

The last ergometer test before the official selection of the God Four and other Fenton boats pitted Connor against me. We had mostly been avoiding each other since our altercation and we warmed up wordlessly on our machines for five minutes. Ruth stood behind us, waiting, as Channing watched the preliminary sequence. I could have sworn he was trying not to grin. He sat there as if he had been looking forward to this moment all day long.

Fluid rushed through the pipes above our heads. I could tell just by listening to the pulse in my ears that my heart rate was already way up past one hundred and fifty. I stopped rowing, crouched at the start of my slide. Connor did the same. Our two flywheels kept ticking, spinning. Ruth knelt in front of us, tiny supplicant to this communion, and said, "Are you two ready?"

I nodded, Connor cleared his throat.

She slowly examined first Connor, then me, as if she might be thinking of some reason to prevent this from happening. It was then that Connor took his hand off the erg handle and tapped my arm. "Good luck, Carrey."

I quickly slapped his fingertips.

Ruth zeroed the computers.

I focused on the wall behind Channing. I breathed. I relaxed. Satellites of dust twirled lazily in the weak winter sunbeams that had somehow managed to penetrate the dirty basement windows. Coiled up and ready, only half-listening to Ruth go over the start procedure, I thought about finally beating him today in this little room.

The ceremony began. Ruth counted off each five hundred segment as we completed it. "First five hundred, rowers even. Time: one minute and forty seconds." Fifty more strokes, then Ruth's voice rising behind us again, "Second five hundred, rowers still even. Time: three minutes and twenty seconds." Ruth counted and the sound of the flywheels ground on and on. And all Connor Payne did for two and a half thousand meters was match me stroke for stroke. I set the pace and Connor mirrored it. When I slowed the rating, he did, too. When I sped up, he did, too. Every time I tried to break away and bring the rating up from a thirty-two to a thirty-five, he followed and didn't miss a stroke.

And then the war inside my own head began. One voice, angry and loud, shouted at me to take control of the duel, jack up the rating. The other, confident and level, insisted that Connor wouldn't follow then blithely reported that yes, he was indeed following me, better drop the rating.

He's reading my mind, I thought.

Shut up, I told myself.

I was tempted to stop dead for a moment just to see what he

would do but to sacrifice even a second would be suicide. I pulled the rating up to an even thirty-six and he followed.

Thirty-seven now and I could feel my lungs protest, the blood begin to rush to my head. It was an insane rating, especially in the middle of a piece. I forced myself to look straight ahead as I rowed, to follow the long cracks in the wall that looked like roads on a road map, roads that met, crossed, carried on through little white chips in the paint. The chips were imaginary towns. I started thinking up names for the towns just as I dropped the rating abruptly to thirty and held it there. It was like flipping a switch, cutting oxygen off from a gushing heart and feeling the poison back up purple and painful.

Channing shifted in his seat, frowning over the fact that we had made a personal battle out of what was meant to be a formal execution. The others looked on in the same impassive way you might witness a stranger's burial. I glanced at them and suddenly wanted to laugh through my pain. Then I felt a tiny, hard bulb of pulse fire off in my skull and I didn't want to laugh anymore.

The numbers on the bottom of the computer screen ticked over to two thousand. I liked the brief look of goose egg perfection in all those zeros. Ruth cleared her throat. "Two thousand, rowers even. Time: six minutes and forty seconds. Five hundred meters to go—now you two rowers show us what you've got."

Only five hundred meters to find a winner. The entire race was down to the last forty-five strokes. Only Connor would try it.

It wasn't just the exhaustion. It wasn't just that my lungs were raw and my legs felt like marble or that the black oar handle was just a vague blur off in the distance where my hands were. The pain, the sound, even the little atlas on the wall, those things were floating away from me now. As I pulled the numbers down, as I brought the five hundred split from one minute forty to one minute thirty-eight, then thirty-seven, I knew Connor was doing the same thing. And I hated him. I hated that he had lain in bed last night and planned this, actually strategized this face-off. Ten strokes into the last five hundred meters I felt the air suddenly turn solid in my lungs. I was rowing ragged, choking, ripping the handle from the erg and slamming back up the slide. It was absolutely no consolation that Connor was doing the same thing. I could hear him hammering away, see mad, spasmodic movement in the corner of my eye.

"Payne's ahead now, one stroke. C'mon Carrey." Ruth said it in a clipped, quiet voice. Each word punched holes in the membrane of concentration around my mind.

Payne's ahead.

The numbers dropped. Good.

My lips peeled back from my teeth and the air whistled through, cold. I felt tiny electric shocks behind my eyes. I was Rob Carrey the astronaut, suffering the worst Gs ever recorded, plummeting out of control toward some planet I'd never seen.

The astronaut called back to ground control, asked for more power. Our hero checked the map on the wall again but saw only endless, ancient lunar rivers leading nowhere. Ruth's voice crackled through the broken radio playing in my mind. "Carrey, he's only one stroke ahead. Last ten strokes. C'mon. Don't die."

Lungs breaking up. Legs and arms on phosphorescent fire, fingers already gone. Eyes going electric.

"Connor has it now, Carrey. Last twenty meters—go. Go."

Two strokes.

Breathe.

Last one.

Breathe.

———

Carolyn could move through digitized film faster than any editor I have ever known, and her concentration was far superior to mine. By the end of the week I was tired of seeing the same sequences of sharks and divers and boats, listening to the same sound-ups, hearing the same ambient noise. A video editor is a special breed of person.

On Friday I started packing up my things. We made it easy on each other, pretended I was packing for just another shoot, but we both knew that this was it. I was boxing up what I owned in the studio, which I discovered wasn't much. This was her place, and I had always been her visitor.

The studio now had a flat, sad feel. Most of the possessions in there were shared, but I was not in the mood to fight over a cappuccino maker bought in a moment of romantic extravagance three years ago, or the toaster, or the photos on the wall, most of which were from Africa and which I could reproduce anyway. Carolyn was right; I probably did have more personal stuff in Cape Town. *Naked unto this loft I came,* I thought, and *close to naked I shall return hither.*

I had no pots and pans of my own, for instance. No plates. The microwave was technically mine, but I wasn't about to claim it. I had no silverware. True, I had bought some of her chairs—faux antique, colonial dining room chairs that sat, unused, around our narrow dining room table, waiting for parties that were never held; we ate in the kitchen or in front of the edit suite. How was I supposed to take them even if I wanted them? I had bought her the afghan throw under the modular couch but I didn't want it. There was an old coffeemaker of mine packed away somewhere but I had no idea where, and in any case I couldn't bring myself to leave carrying only a coffeemaker.

I did want to keep my books. I walked down to the liquor store and begged a few strong boxes. As I neared the freight elevator on my way back to the loft, two kids walked by me, both wearing sweatshirts from New England schools I'd beaten on the water at Fenton. One of them was my height, slight, with wispy blond hair, deep blue eyes, and pale, aristocratic skin. When I saw him I thought, there he is. But Connor Payne would be older now. He'd have gained weight. He wouldn't be wearing

Timberland boots and baggy, gangsta jeans, a torn, rust colored T-shirt, and a Tag Heuer watch. Connor would be an adult, like me. The two kids shouldered by me, agile as ghosts.

There were books that were mine and books that we had bought together, novels we had shared. Poetry books she had bought me that were part of the apartment as well. I put those aside, unwilling to provoke a fight. Then it occurred to me as I was taping the boxes that I did not want her sharing Rilke and Neruda with some other man—the many men she was likely to meet in this business. I confiscated Neruda and Rilke and then Frost and Catullus and Sappho and then an expensive cloth-bound book of Shakespeare's sonnets. I took back *Tropic of Cancer*, which had made her laugh while she read it at my insistence.

I packed these books separately. I sealed them in bubble wrap and plastic. Her next lover would not plunder them like a looter stumbling across the archives of a vanished romance. But I would not open them either, not without her. I knew that already. I could seal these books away easily somewhere: in the bottom of a New York closet, in a storage room, in a crawl space. I had half a mind to send them on a slow boat to Cape Town but they would only gather dust there. Their meaning, I knew, lay here in this studio with her. I wanted them nonetheless.

I went online and printed the invitation to the reunion. I zipped open my hanging bag and packed for the return to Fenton School. I started by laying out clothes suitable for a memorial service—not a difficult task when you work in an industry where black is de rigueur for almost everything. I am a man incredibly well prepared to attend a memorial. I packed a dark shirt and slacks and black shoes. I did not own a tie. These were clothes that I usually wore to cocktail functions in this very neighborhood. To gallery openings. I stuffed in a couple of casual button-down shirts, jeans, and khakis, boots and shoes and then a blazer. These were the essentials of my New York uniform, and had never left the country with me.

I wondered if the others might be wearing their rowing blazers. I had lost mine years ago. It would never have fit anyway, even if I could have brought myself to wear it. I had gained forty pounds since high school. Nonetheless I wore a thirty-six waist and was probably in better shape than half of the returning class, given the nature of my job. Possibly some of the alumni simply reordered the blazers in their adult sizes for these get-togethers so they could look like a team once more. Insanity. I wound up surprising myself, though. Just before I zipped up, I packed a T-shirt and shorts and my Nikes. They might want us to row, I thought. And behind that thought, some part of me still yearned to be out on the river. And dreaded it.

I stood and looked at myself in Carolyn's full-length mirror and wondered how my frame could have coped with being forty pounds lighter. My bones would have been newer and less pounded by gravity and time. My arteries and veins almost pristine. Back then I could count the muscles on my abdomen, trace the obliques beside them, the jutting plates of my chest. I was *the thing itself*, as Channing might say, and that body would never be mine again. I missed that body, missed its clarity, missed not worrying about cancer and heart attacks and addiction and secondary smoke and cholesterol. Could my thirty-five-year-old vertebrae, hips, joints, lungs, fingers, and knees handle even one FSBC workout? Could I even run seven or eight blocks down the street without being winded? What would that kid of fifteen years ago say if he could see me now, balding, fatter, weaker, full of scars and aches? I could close my eyes and remember that old self, feel the way the blood used to course in my ears and the way my heart pumped through the night.

Somewhere I had a team photo from those days, a copy of which was on the boathouse wall beside a hundred similar pictures. Wadsworth, Perry, myself and Connor standing in a row with Ruth sitting cross-legged in front of us wearing her sunglasses. All of us unsmiling. Wraiths looking out into time. Killers.

21.

Connor's time was a second and a half ahead of mine. He beat me by one stroke, exactly one stroke. I had to keep wiping my eyes after the test to see him. We were both hunched over our machines. I don't think I passed out but for a moment the world was just a stranger. Connor got up with me and we walked upstairs to the cold boats to get our stuff. Neither of us looked at the other rowers or at Ruth conferring with Channing.

I tried to talk a few times, but my throat was ragged. We walked through the wet snow with heavy feet for what seemed like a long, long time. It was very cold and as I walked I realized I was thin enough so that the air seemed to blow right through me. Connor was looking up, over the fields, almost to the sky while he walked. He finally broke the silence. "That was a spur of the moment idea. I wanted to see if I could keep up with you." When I didn't say anything in reply he just carried on talking. "You moved the rating all over the place. We both lost time because you did that. You should have ignored me."

"I couldn't." My throat felt like I had swallowed a handful of new silver nails.

"You should have expected that I'd try to follow you. In any case you did really well. We both did. I'm not sure why you're so pissed. You're obviously going to be chosen for the first boat so quit being such a sore loser. One stroke, man, there was nothing in it."

It was getting properly, industrially dark. All the kids from the sports buildings were heading back now, bundled up, hats on, backpacks and gym bags swinging; lines of ragged soldiers returning from the front. Through the big windows in the field house you could see the rows of lights up above the basketball courts still shining lonely and bright. A few of the squash players came by, batting snowballs at each other. Connor stepped out of their way to scrutinize me. "You just can't help it, can you? You have to compete."

"That's right. Especially against you."

We walked the rest of the way to the school in silence. Before we reached the Rowing Cottage, Connor turned to me and said, "That last second was the best I had. I couldn't have beaten you by any more."

"But you wanted me to think you could. You were just making a point."

"Sure. So what? It's called winning, Carrey. You know the score. I'm not going to apologize. You want to beat me so badly, fine. Bring it on. But don't have a fit when you lose."

"You want to know what gets me?"

"Not really."

"You don't even need to impress anybody. You don't even need it."

"I'm always amazed when you say ridiculous things like that. What are you saying? I should have let you win? You're the one with something to prove here, Rob. I have nothing to prove. I just want to win for the sake of it. And because it gives me a buzz to beat you. That's all. It's easier to have simple reasons for doing things."

"Let me tell you something."

"I'm listening."

A sudden wave of dizziness and nausea washed over me and I turned away from him, sure I was going to throw up. But I just needed to breathe. I walked over to the shore through snow that had been scoured here, only ankle deep and crusty. I examined the ice on the river, which was discolored and brown from the wind. "Get down here, Connor."

"Look, Rob, I'll admit it. If you had popped up the rating a few strokes I would never have beaten you. I would have followed too late."

"I think we could make the run across the river."

"What?" He looked nonplussed for a second, then slid down to me. "No way. I mean, it's a noble thought, but the middle isn't solid."

"What do you know about snow? I'm the one from Niccalsetti. I grew up dealing with blizzards. It doesn't even snow in Cape Cod."

"It does. And I grew up here, Carrey. That's moving water out there." He laughed. "Look, Rob, good effort, I swear. But I'm telling you . . ."

"When running on thin ice, Connor, your safety lies in speed."

"There's no point in it."

"There's a lot of point in it." But I would have found it difficult to articulate just why I wanted to do something so reckless all of a sudden. All I do know is that the impulse was overwhelming. I took a few more steps toward the water and slipped on the slick surface of the snowy embankment. I regained my footing on an exposed grassy area. The river smelled of cold and vegetation and frozen earth. The wind whipped across the ice and bit through our clothes.

Connor looked at me and wiped his eyes. "How far would you say it is to the other side?"

"A hundred feet."

"Wrong. A hundred and twelve at this point. The whole river averages that until the bend, when you get another fifty feet."

"So a hundred and twelve feet. That's nothing. That's a sprint."

"You can't even see the other side."

"You *can* see the other side. *I* can see it."

The other shore was a smudge rising out of the line of snow that was the river. The middle was what worried me—what might lie under only a few inches of snow and ice. I stood very still, holding my breath. Connor was right. I could feel the movement of the water beneath the ice, immense and relentless.

But I still started running.

I got fifteen feet across, making strong strides, snow swirling around me like a cloud. I ran blindly and it was slow going. Connor shouted out to me, swore, started following—I could hear his footfalls behind me—though he wouldn't catch me. As I neared the dark middle of the river I allowed myself to think I'd make the other side in thirty seconds; it was a long, steeper shore there.

I fell as I tried to charge forward, away from Connor. I had only a few moments to register that the snow was wet and heavy. I'm not sure if I slipped or if my foot broke through to the river and I was thrown down. But I crashed into the ice and snow hard, banged my forehead with enough force so that my breath was choked out of me. I pushed myself back to my hands and knees and felt blood starting to flow down my face, warm against the frigid cold and wet. I shook my head like a dog and tried to rise back up to my feet. A spatter pattern appeared as if by magic, the redness of my blood shocking in all that white. The wind screamed.

And ice just collapsed around me. There was no sound.

At first I thought that I couldn't have been swallowed into nothing so quickly. I opened my eyes to a murky light. I was not cold and I pushed my hands out in front of me like a man wandering in the dark. My feet did not touch bottom and I felt the water running through my fingers. It seemed oddly warm and quiet. I was not swimming so much as waving my arms. I kicked and my feet felt leaden.

This must have been what Wendy experienced, I thought. It wasn't such an awful way to die; like stepping through an unexpected door. I closed my eyes and only then felt the cold, as if I was being pulled apart. I felt myself smiling. The sheer ridiculousness of my situation was not lost on me.

Connor got my hair first, yanked hard, and the pain woke me from that black doze. I shouted out in the water and it sounded like a burp of bubbles. Then he had my neck and a bunch of clothing at my shoulder. He was in the water, hunched over me, had just followed me in. I felt the rush of water on my face as he kicked us upward. We broke through, both exhaling in the frozen wind, the cold on my hands and feet and neck so awful that I howled. Connor pushed me to the side of the ice. I rested against it and the ice gave, then gave again and, horribly, again, until finally it was firm. I felt an irresistible urge to rest for just a few more minutes. Slip back through that door.

I opened my eyes and blood flowed into them. Connor was mouthing something next to me. He dragged himself halfway out of the water and then pulled me as I started to sink again, yanking my sodden sweatshirt up my chest. Then I was lying on the ice, choking and vomiting. I tried to move on my own steam. I cannot remember how he horsed me away from the hole in the river, or how we made it to the school's embankment. I slid trying to get up to the road and hit the ground hard enough to believe that I might not get up. Then I fell back through that silent door again. My last inconceivable thought was that if I returned I'd owe Connor Payne for saving my life.

The dream was so real it was like going back in time and re-living it all. About a week after Wendy died, the phone rang in the house at 2:30 A.M. I waited for one of my parents to pick up but when no one did, I hauled my ass out of bed and walked down the upstairs hallway to the phone in Wendy's room. I was sitting there on the bed that we hadn't even stripped yet, feeling like Wendy was going to walk in any minute and ask me what I was doing there, thinking I could still smell her.

"Hello?"

It was a cop. I could hear radios and people yelling at each other in the background. I heard a woman repeating, "I don't know *nothing* about that. I told you people, I don't know *nothing* about that." It was a heavy accent from South Niccalsetti and everytime she said it, her voice rose a level, as if saying it loud enough might make them believe her.

"Is this the Robert F. Carrey residence?" The cop sounded bored.

"Yeah. That's us."

"We have a Mr. Robert Carrey down here. Picked him up on a DWI on the Skendal Parkway. He's sleeping it off downstairs."

"Robert Carrey's my dad. You must mean *Tom* Carrey, my brother?" I looked out into the night for my dad's truck but it wasn't parked in front of the garage, which didn't mean any-thing because he usually locked it up at night. Snow had fallen and settled over the drive like a baby's blanket.

"He gave us this telephone number. I have his wallet and ID here. He was driving a Ford pickup, New York State tags." He read the number and it sounded close enough.

"That's my father. He doesn't drink."

"He did tonight."

"Is he all right?"

"Driving erratically and refused to pull over when he was flashed. Didn't resist arrest but failed the Breathalyzer. Failed big-time."

"Where is he?"

"We charged him. His driving record was clean. Couldn't leave him on the street. The truck's out on the Parkway now, somebody's been sent to tow her."

"Did you grab the tools out of the back of that truck?"

"You going to come and get the guy or what, kid?"

"I'll come get him."

"Bring him some clothes. The officer who brought him in had to clear his air passages on the way in."

"Just don't touch him."

"Nobody's touching him. Precinct fifteen downtown, all right? You got that?"

"Don't touch him."

He hung up.

I got a Niccalsetti Senior High gym bag from my closet and went to my folks' bedroom. My mother was curled up like a kid on her side of the bed. She'd been lying there like that for most of the week, drugged into semiconsciousness by the strong tranquilizers she had been prescribed. I listened to her breathing while I went through my father's bureau, grabbing his freshly folded and pressed clothes in the dark. Their window shade was still open and the blue moonlight spilled over the bed. I quickly checked Tom's room. Empty, of course. We'd hardly seen him since the funeral. I prayed he hadn't taken my mom's car.

Downstairs I pulled on my father's leather site coat with the big pockets sewn on the outside for tools, the shoulders all worn down. It smelled strongly of him and coffee and sawdust and pine sap. I shoved my bare feet into my boots and walked out the front door into the cold and ice and rock salt and down to my mother's station wagon. Tom hadn't taken it, thank God. He'd obviously walked to the bars and wouldn't be home for at least another hour. I drove downtown at about a hundred miles an hour, skidding on the new snow even on Main Street, and when I got to the station house it was all lit up, and there was a line of those humped Crown Vics the cops use outside, all snowed on so they looked like sleeping animals.

The place wasn't as busy as I thought it would be. There was a desk at the top of the stairs and a bench where two guys in puffy yellow ascent jackets were sitting and looking at the wall like they were thinking about taking it down. It smelled just like the waiting room in the bus station, like bored people waiting to go from one place they hated to some other place they liked even less. The night officer saw me and came up to the desk and I was surprised to see it wasn't like at the drugstore where the pharmacist is always a little higher than you. He looked me up and down and rubbed his face expectantly.

"I'm here to pick up Robert Carrey."

"All right. I think I just called you. Must have woken you up."

"Yeah."

"You bring his clothes?" I shoved the bag on the table and remembered I hadn't even brought him a comb or soap. The cop took the duffel bag off the counter, clutching it in a ball in his hands. "Your father's just filling out some forms. He's going to pay a fine and the judge will probably suspend his license later. He wants to change. I'll come back and get you in a minute."

He went through a door to the side that closed slowly with a heavy click. I stood in the lights for a second and then leaned against the counter. I could feel the guys on the bench watching me and when I turned around I caught the eyes of the smaller one who looked straight at me and then away, grinning hard at the wall. He was missing one of his teeth. He could have been my age, he could have been twice my age. His friend looked right through me. I shifted my feet in the brown puddle of melted slush on the floor. I was sixteen years old and I was bailing my dad out of the Niccasletti drunk tank.

More like ten minutes later, the cop came back through the door and opened the flap on the counter for me. It flopped open with a dead, dull wooden sound. "C'mon."

I followed him into a longer hallway. There was another desk back there and a bunch of glassed-in offices. At the end of the hallway was a door that looked like part of a fence and another long bench. My father was standing in front of a metal desk alongside another cop. He was wearing the clothes I had brought him and had splashed his face with water somewhere and plastered his hair down so it looked stiff and stood up from the hard skin stretched over his scalp. His hair was dripping down his sweatshirt. The cop next to him was a big guy who wasn't smiling. He had tightly curled, red, sheepskin hair and he was holding my father's hand over an ink pad. He glanced up and looked me over with his shifty cop eyes.

My father saw me and nodded, then looked at the cop. "He's my son."

"We can't get prints off of him," was all the sheep-head cop said to my cop.

My father's thumbprints on the sheet were black smears. He actually smiled at me and said, "No ridges at all in these fingers, Rob. Nothing."

I looked at sheep head. "He doesn't have fingerprints?"

"See them every week. There's no oil in them anymore. No contours. No ridges or whorls. Nothing." He gave up and jerked the sheet of paper away. "Go on. Get out of here. Drive him home. And take that bag with you." The duffel was full of his old clothes and a wet patch was spreading through the side from something he'd put in there. My father picked it up when I reached for it.

My cop lifted his chin. "Tell him to stay off the roads. He's the BAC high score for the night."

My father turned around and said tiredly, "I can hear you just fine, Officer."

The cop didn't even look at him, just at me. "You make sure and tell him."

I tried to sit up in the early morning dark. The pain in my head felt like I'd been pasted good and hard with a socket wrench and I lay back down with a groan. I was in the infirmary and I was sweating. The river and snow and ice were still out there, but the room was cloyingly hot. A sauna. I sank back into feverish sleep.

I dreamed I saw Wendy on the boardwalk watching me and Connor staggering along, dripping wet, frozen, covered in blood. My head was throbbing, my lungs filled with needles of ice. I reached out to hug her, tried to talk, to ask her to help me.

She shook her head and turned away from me.

The ice had done a pretty good number on me. My scalp had been sliced open and enough blood had poured down the front of my face and shirt so that when the nurse on duty took us in, she thought that my skull had been bashed in. I had hit my head hard enough to pass out and had inhaled water. When Connor dragged me into the infirmary, he had been laughing hysterically.

We had both been treated for hypothermia. Connor had been sent back to the Rowing Cottage to recover after they had bandaged up his cuts and ice burns. The gash in my head had required ten stitches. I lay there thinking that I had blown it.

When Channing came to check on me two days later I was feeling well enough to be thinking about getting out of the infirmary. I had a plan to find my clothes and sneak back to my room. I was alone in the ward and figured I could make a break for it. Channing stood at the edge of the bed and looked me over like I had been caught stealing drugs from the place. "How are you feeling?"

"Better."

"I'm not going to ask why you thought you could get across that river."

I blinked, moved up in the pillows. He looked at me expectantly.

"It was my idea. I thought I could make it."

"It was an *exceptionally stupid* idea."

"I know. Connor told me the water might not be frozen solid—"

"Connor saved your life, it seems."

"How many hours of work do we get for this?"

Channing sighed and shook his head. "How do we punish you for being reckless and stupid? Should we advertise that you two have obviously decided to compete to see who is the bigger fool? We do not punish students for accidently falling into the river, Carrey."

"Coach, I didn't think the ice would break. I thought I'd know if it was unsafe."

"Carrey, losing a race is nothing. Losing an ergometer competition is less than nothing. But losing my respect is something you cannot afford, and you are close to it."

"All right. I'm sorry. I am. It was my fault. He didn't want to run across."

"I asked you at the start of the year to watch yourself. To be careful. You do not seem able to do this. I could suggest that you be sent home. For your own good. Fighting. Reckless behavior. Threatening the welfare of my rowers and yourself. The pressure at Fenton might be too much for you, Carrey."

"It isn't. Mr. Channing, I swear I can handle whatever you have. It was a hundred feet across and it looked *easy*! I know it was stupid."

"Understand that you have proven *nothing* to Connor. Or to me."

"I know it."

"And you *will* lose some more in life. I regret to tell you this. More than a simple test on a rowing machine. You will lose things. People. Jobs. And everything else there is to lose. When you do, there will be no river to run to. There will only be the loss. You will lose far, far more than you will win, in the end."

"But not now."

"Had you died, it would have been for nothing. It would have been a source of humor for some. Had you brought Connor with you, it would have been even less amusing."

"Why? Because he's the captain of the God Four? Because people like me die every day?"

"No, you arrogant fool. Because he would have died trying to save your life. You may hate him, but he is the only person on this team with wits and courage enough to rescue you, and I am not sure how he managed to do it."

"It's something I'm trying to forget."

"You shouldn't forget it. He shouldn't let you forget. I certainly will not." He stepped away from the bed, put his hands behind his back and cleared his throat. He made as if to add something else, then thought better of it.

"Coach, do you know where my clothes are?"

"You can get your clothes from the front desk."

"I don't really remember how I got here."

"You two walked in here soaking wet and partly frozen. Connor was delirious. You were half-conscious. You both were duly tested for drugs and alcohol."

"I don't remember it."

"Learn to take better care of yourself, Carrey."

"I'm trying."

"Try harder."

22.

On the day I left New York for Perry's service at Fenton, I got up early to get over to my parking storage on Eighth, a dubious long-term garage with what I had thought, back in the winter when I parked the car and flew to South Africa, had the best rates. For the first time in I did not know how long, Carolyn and I had breakfast together: omelets, toast, and bacon I thawed in her microwave. Even fresh orange juice. Sitting in the open kitchen, where so many things had transpired between us, I felt our past like a physical presence at the table. I looked at her eating and felt the same feeling I once had with my parents; the inability to speak, a crushing, silent weight on my heart. I had the same divided feelings I suppose every couple that breaks up endures, the feeling that something might yet be done. We'd had five years together. She was no longer the same luminous woman she had been when we met. Her face showed the effects of the work, and the loss and the craziness after. It was a face that had seen pleasure and pain, and some small recovery. It was a face you could still fall hopelessly in love with. But we were at the wrong end of our youth. *In media res.*

She was perched on her stool, gazing through the cracked open window at the sky and morning clouds, at the haggard SoHo pigeons already up and calling to each other beyond the glass. I took her hand and she flinched but she didn't move it away. We sat there for a long time before she stood up, claimed her fingers back from mine and gathered the plates.

It took me almost two hours to get the Jeep out of its dusty storage, pay for the months it had been there, and drive it back to Broome. I was frankly surprised it started, and I had to fight through the morning traffic to make it back to the apartment, the entire time listening to the radio blaring because I had taken all of my CDs out of the car when I had left it there.

The Jeep smelled old, disused, muggy. A layer of steamy grime had settled over it, and I was sure that there was a manifold problem that would cost to repair. I pointed the car down Seventh Avenue with the air conditioner breathing on my knees, the sun raging down on me as I crawled with the maddening traffic into the West Village. Past the fire escapes and the old tenements of Varick, the congested entrance to the Holland Tunnel, the tangle of impossible audio and electronics stores and fast-food joints on Canal Street; the shops crammed together into a cacophony of cheap advertising, a mother lode of video equipment and sound equipment and blank digital tapes and rip-offs and slashed-price sales that I could never resist. It took me almost ten minutes to drive up from Centre to the converted police building across from the loft, where every day I saw a new supermodel stalking though the doors. I was forced to park the Jeep in the first free gallery loading bay, yards away from the entrance to our building. I was sweating, swearing at the traffic, dead set on the job at hand. I had piled up my boxes, the dusty computer equipment, my tapes and the hard cases of camera equipment next to the freight elevator before Carolyn had woken up.

Two brutal trips up and down later and the car was full.

There was nothing left save for one awkward chair that didn't fit and a suitcase full of winter clothes I would not need any time soon sitting by the elevator door up there. I was winded by the effort, and angrier than I had been when I started, knowing that the anger didn't come from the impossible, steamy traffic of the New York summer but from the fact that the day had begun as innocuously as any other. I gave half a thought to slipping behind the wheel, twisting the car into the traffic and leaving all this behind without a look back. I sat in the driver's seat instead and slammed my head against the headrest, grit my teeth and pushed open the door. There was nothing else to do but go. I'd just ride the elevator up one last time, say good-bye to her, leave.

But she was already on the sidewalk in front of the graffitied door, shading her eyes to see where my car was. I caught my breath, hands on my hips, my shirt sticking to my shoulders. And then walked to her, hugged her gently, formally. She placed her palm on my shoulder, patted me as if she was making sure I had been something real and alive.

"Bye, Rob. Call me when you get to the school. Please. Okay?"

I nodded, and then thought of kissing her. But I just touched her shoulder back, a mutual acknowledgement of love and loss and five years. I turned away and walked back to the car, fast, ripped open the door, slid inside and twisted the key. Reversed hard out of the loading bay into the one way traffic, glared into the morass of cars and taxis and filthy trucks and then, despite all efforts, glanced back up the sidewalk to our door to see her still standing there, hugging herself in the merciless sun as if an arctic wind had blown down around her.

Ground the gears. Shoved the car back into its space, threw it into park, pushed open the door and scowled back at the guy in the *Art NY* T-shirt looking critically at the obtuse Jeep hanging over the yellow lines into the cars, strode back down the sidewalk under those same lamps I had banished myself to all those months ago to see her looking away from me, her hands up by her throat, palms out, eyes down, already gently shaking her head. And I had her by the arms. "I miss our little girl as much as you do. Do you hear me? Are you listening? I know I wasn't here for you. But I loved her, too. And I love you."

She still wasn't looking at me but she held firm, smaller in my hands than I remembered. And I knew this was a last minute appeal and doomed to failure but the words kept coming out. "I know I left you. After. To work. To escape. You can blame me for it. But the whole fucking world is full of people who need each other and babies and then there's you and me."

And she was just shaking her head and tears were dripping down her face and I knew there was a right thing to say if I could only think it up and I dug my fingers into her arms and bent down so my eyes were level with hers. "Whatever happened, I can fix it. I can fix it for you and for me. And she wouldn't want us to do this."

Carolyn looked up at me sharply. "You tell me how you know that, Rob."

"You tell me how I know anything."

"What was in that stupid African ocean that was so *impor-tant*?" She balled her hands into fists and mashed them into my shoulder, drew back and then battered them into me again, hard enough to make me take a step back. "And why didn't you pro-tect me?"

I looked away, back at the car, realized the front wheel was edged up on the curb, that I had somehow pushed it in at an ob-scure, impossible angle. Lowered my hands from her shoulders and waited for her to hit me again, but she had simply turned away. I opened my own palms. "I tried to. I thought I did."

Then she shook her head. "You were wrong."

"Do you think I don't know that? That I don't live with it?"

"Why are you only saying all this now, Rob? It's too late. I've been waiting for you to stop running away from it, from me."

"It's not too late. I don't need to keep traveling. I can stay here. Wherever you want. Whatever it takes." It was the wrong thing to say.

She smiled vacantly. "You need to move that poor vehicle, Rob."

Tears running down my own face now, I stared into her anguished eyes and knew I could not bear losing her. "Can you forgive me?"

23.

I ran into Connor on the boardwalk the day after they let me out of the infirmary. I had dreaded seeing him but when he recognized me he grinned. "He lives. Nice head wound, Carrey. Nice. Very nice." He was bundled up against the cold in a long blue coat, a plaid scarf, mirrored sunglasses.

"Channing visited me. He read me the riot act."

"He's not a happy camper. I got the same treatment. He blames me for your being such a dumb-ass." He smirked. "I was going to come visit you, bring flowers. It was at the top of my to-do list."

"Thanks, Connor."

He looked at me blankly. "For what?"

———————

I trained alone through the first weeks of February. There was a sudden break in the cold before we were plunged into frozen weather again, but the unexpected flash of warmth was enough to thaw that tenuous layer of ice on the river. Cracks formed along its surface and ruptured chunks rested upon one another.

Connor sought me out. I had been avoiding him and brooding about how he would use the fact he had saved my life against me. But he didn't mention the ice or the infirmary or the healing cut on my scalp when he fell into step with me. "What's with the silent treatment? You're a hard man to find. Listen, you need to go see Channing. Today. At his house." He looked at me, looked again. "You just went completely pale. They're not going to kick you out or anything. It's not that. If the school wanted you out for being a bonehead, you'd be gone by now. It's something else."

"What?"

"No idea. Don't look at me like that. I really have no idea. He told me to find you and make sure you showed up right after classes. Today."

"The river's broken. We'll be on the water soon."

"It'll be awhile before all the ice floes are melted."

"How long?"

"A few weeks. At least. We're not finished with winter yet. I'll see you around, Rob. Don't be a stranger."

———————

When I ran out to Channing's house I dropped the mile in under seven minutes and wasn't even winded when I hit his driveway. The last part of the run was downhill. I stopped by the shed. It was in good shape. It could endure the elements because the basics were right. I had come out twice a week to check on it, had even waterproofed the seals and the interior. I stood in its sawdust silence, and the turmoil of the previous weeks seemed far away; done with. I opened the shed door and looked over at Channing's house, less weatherproofed, peeling in the weak sunlight of the afternoon. I waited, coughed, stamped my feet. If he was in there he didn't know I was here, and I didn't feel like freezing to death while waiting to be acknowledged.

I walked back to the far side of the house to find his garage door open. He'd just left it that way. There was zero crime in Fenton. Not that Channing had anything worth stealing in that garage, unless somebody had a jones for rusted garden tools, battered garbage cans and rows of rotting paint cans.

He kept things. Hellmann's mayonnaise and Peter Pan Peanut Butter jars. Stacks and stacks of the *New York Times*, all tied up in string and forgotten. He had a surf-casting set in there and an old Schwinn bike hanging up, rusted solid. And boxes. All kinds of them. Majestic Van Lines boxes, boxes marked *Summer House* and *Clothes,* and one or two with just 'Cape Cod' in his handwriting. They were covered in dust and dirt and rat shit and some must have been infested with mice and weevils and whatever else lives in garages people never clean out. No legal books. Maybe he'd thrown them all out when they chucked him from the firm. I stood amidst all his junk and saw how hc only *just* had enough room for his old Chevy Estate station wagon, a Brush Hog, a lawnmower and a Weed Eater that was out of twine.

I tried the door leading from the garage to the house itself. It practically fell open and there I was looking into Channing's kitchen.

"Mr. Channing? Coach?"

He had old, brown roll-on linoleum stuck to the kitchen floor and an ancient sink set into a chipped, green Formica counter that was dotted with burn marks. His pots and pans hung off hooks and there were rows of dusty cookbooks above the sagging white electric stove. Dingy, flowery wallpaper was peeling up against the ceiling where the steam from the stove had stained it in brown clouds. The cupboards matched the counters at one time, but were now falling apart, right out of the walls. I searched for a light switch, snapped it on, and a three-bar florescent light flickered and hummed to life above me. And then one of the light tubes winked off.

I'd worked on a few jobs where the previous owner had died

and nobody had known anything about him. You'd just throw all his stuff away and start over with new plumbing and new plug points for the next renter or buyer. This was that kind of kitchen. Two guys could set to work in a kitchen like this with a crowbar and a sledgehammer and rip it all out in an hour. You could tear the whole thing apart before lunch and leave it in the driveway for the junk truck—you'd never be able to resell or reuse any of it. The afternoon light flooded into the room and I held my breath. I hated to imagine Channing sitting here with his back to the window drinking his Sanka from the half-full jar by the sink and thinking about nothing while he did it, like any old guy killing time before work.

I walked through that awful kitchen and into the living room, which at least had a couple of comfortable-looking over-stuffed chairs in it, even if they didn't match the room. He'd set a black and white TV on a bench before the dusty fireplace and a bunch of TV guides were stacked next to his chair with two empty highball glasses balancing on top of them. There was a desk in the corner, positioned so if he sat there his back would be to the window and the road beyond. The desk might not have been a desk at all; it looked like it might have once been a dining room table. Two pictures were stranded on top of it. One was of a kid standing on a wooden sailboat deck shading his eyes to look at the camera. The edges of the picture were frayed with age and the color washed out. The kid was maybe twelve or thirteen years old. Next to it was a picture of a different sailboat, also taken a long time ago with a cheap camera.

A newspaper clipping had been stuck on the wallpaper be-side the desk. It was faded and greasy the way newspaper gets when it's been around a long time. There was a cluster of pin-holes right above the clipping and reddish marks where he'd taped it in different places over the years. It took me a few sec-onds to recognize that the darkened picture on that curled paper was of two rowing shells crossing a finish line. The photo was of the Harvard boat crossing the line first against Yale at Gales Ferry. It was snapped just before the winners would have pumped their arms in the air in victory. The coxswains were both hunched in the back of the boats, and both teams were wearing white tank tops. You could see the backs of people watching the race in the foreground. The caption read, *Harvard takes Yale by one half length at Gales Ferry*, and beneath it were the names of the rowers in each boat. I could barely read them, but finally saw, *C.Channing*. He'd rowed six-seat. I could not see his face. I looked around the room again for more pictures, but there was no further evidence that this was a rower's study, a rowing coach's study. No other news clippings, no oar over the full bookcase, no framed photographs, no cups, medals, or trophies. Nothing.

Somewhere he must have the Yale shirt he'd taken off the other six man, the one the losers traditionally hand over in defeat. I took another look at the clipping on the wall; just a random race result between some college kids in New London, Connecticut. But it was the biggest race in college rowing. I pushed the clipping flat with my fingers. It felt like a skin shed years ago and salvaged.

"What are you doing in here, Carrey?"

He was standing in the doorway with his hands in his pockets. I was busted. Hadn't even heard him.

"Nothing. Just looking for you, Coach. You asked me to drop by?"

"How long were you in here, Carrey?"

"Five minutes. Max. I didn't take anything—I didn't even move anything."

He made a big show of looking around the room carefully. The dark furniture and walls and desk seemed to suck the sunlight from the air. "I certainly hope you weren't pilfering books. I have a valuable collection."

"I didn't touch anything, Mr. Channing, I swear."

I waited to see what he would do, but he just stood there.

"Coach, can I please ask one thing?"

"Ask it."

"Where are all the trophies? All your rowing things?"

"Many of my belongings have been lost, sold, stolen, or litigated away from me over the years."

"You don't keep any of the stuff you win for Fenton?"

He paused, then said, "The trappings of victory are not mine to keep. They are at the school. In my office at the boathouse. On the walls in the banquet room. You know this, Carrey."

"But your own stuff, I mean. Your own medals."

"Carrey, have you ever noticed that the minute you put a trophy in a case, it becomes impossibly old? I do not know why. The luster of victory wears off quickly, I suppose." He looked at me, suddenly old and frail himself. "The thought for the day is not about trophies. It is about this: *ubi concodia, ibi victoria*."

"Where there is unity, there is victory."

"Carrey, I am surprised. By God, you remembered a line of Latin. And who said this?"

"No idea."

"Publilius Syrus. A writer who started out as a slave and found a kind of freedom. *Where there is unity, there is victory.* Every rower knows this because without total unity in the boat, you will only find defeat."

"I'd like to be a unified force of one."

"Carrey, if you agree to think of Publilius Syrus every day from now on, I will agree to have you on the God Four."

"Fine." I said it quickly. There was always the chance he wasn't just joking.

"Then you are on the team. Barring some misfortune that kills you."

"I'm really on the God Four? Just like that?"

"You will be in the boat, but the world is yours to lose."

I didn't know what to say. I stood in his living room, speech-less. Grinning like an idiot. Finally, something did occur to me. *"Ubi maior, minor ceasat."*

"And what on earth does that mean, Carrey?"

"The weak die before the strong."

"The last word is *'cessat.'* Fool. Its real meaning is that what is important brushes away what is not important. Like, for in-stance, the importance of your learning how to row with the others. Getting along with them. This is more important than whatever you have achieved in your scull."

"I'm improving."

"You are getting stronger. Whether you are improving as a rower remains to be seen."

"Do the others know?"

"You will find out. But I want to remind you that nothing is permanent in rowing. I can remove you at any time. I can do it even if you only irritate me. Do you have any more questions, Carrey?"

"Just one, Coach."

"Then ask it and leave. I have things to do."

"Did you go to law school? At Harvard?"

"An idiotic question. Why would you think that?"

"I'm just asking."

"Carrey, let me tell you something I teach all my English stu-dents. Are you ready for it?"

"Okay."

"Don't believe everything you read. Don't believe half of it. And none of what you hear."

———

I had lost enough weight so when I looked in the bathroom mir-ror I could follow the network of veins down my shoulders and arms. If I made a fist, the muscles in my shoulder cuff pumped up and expanded like a fan beneath my skin. I was in the best physical condition of my life. Wadsworth looked much the same as me—lean and mean—and Perry, who had dropped at least twenty pounds of fat but none of his muscle, looked downright menacing.

By the time we were six weeks off the spring racing season, I might not have recognized Connor. His clothes hung from his body and his newly cut short hair only emphasized the fact that you could clearly see the outline of his skull. I had come to believe he was running at night after all the communal training was over. Ruth was not only skeletal, but also undernourished. We could virtually eat what we liked—our training was so intense that we were burning up thousands of calories every day. But she was thin to begin with and had to deprive herself of a lot of food to drop even more weight off her small frame. How she managed to keep up with us on our training runs on the meager rations she allotted herself I do not know. In fact I had no idea just how dangerously underweight she was. The year after we graduated, the school would set a minimum weight for coxswains.

I was eating food supplements, painkillers and vitamins throughout every day—we all were. Three white tablets after morning practice, washed down before the powdery taste coated my tongue. Then a Tylenol, followed by an anti-inflammatory bumblebee-shaped horse pill for my knees. Then two vitamin Cs to ward off winter sickness and flu. A supplement for stress. Two more complex vitamins. Lecithin. A marblelike tablet full of bitter gelatin. A jar of translucent pills stood by my window, golden tears of soft amber. Then two amino acid pills. These were meant to help my body build red, aerobic muscle but instead made my sweat smell like rotting flowers. My dessert was a tiny anti-asthma pill that kept my throat and nasal passages from closing in the cold air. It dried my sinuses and gave me a hollow feeling for the duration of the early morning.

It was now the end of February. Five days of weak sun had melted the snow on the road and the hold-out ice floes on the river drifted by the school like wreckage. The crew started running together outside, long runs down the roads behind Fenton, through the sheep mud of this unexpected spring. We trod on piles of dark leaves covered with old, dirty snow, kicked them aside. River Road was slick and streaked with muddy tire tracks and we ran through the wet and occasional cold gusts with anticipation thinking that winter was over.

One afternoon I joined Connor, Ruth, Perry, and Wadsworth who were all on the main school bridge looking down at the black water running hard in-between the broken floes. Connor leaned over and spat far into the depths below. He turned and folded his arms theatrically. "Your captain declares it time for the God Four to have its first on-the-water practice," and a collective whoop went up. It was the first time I felt truly one of them.

Connor opened the boathouse doors to reveal the slumbering boats. We pulled out the Fenton first boat, flipped it into its cradle and brought out the riggers. Working quickly, we assembled it wordlessly, cranking on the riggers and sliding the seats into place. When that was finished, Ruth stood at the bow formally and made us wait before making the classic coxswain's call, "Reach down . . . and up . . . and over the heads."

We flipped the boat over our heads and maneuvered it out into the cold. Ruth had us walk it forward and then drop it to our shoulders without looking back. I smelled the plastic and grease smell of the rowing shell and then the river and then the wind off the river and excitement surged through me. Ruth led us down to the long wooden dock—still covered in a thin, wind-dappled layer of ice—where we cranked the boat over our heads and flipped it down into the water. She held it firmly while we ran up for the oars, the boat straining against her, looking like it wanted to pull away and take to the water itself.

I picked my oar out of the snow and glanced at Perry. Connor stood next to me for a second, his breath puffs of vapor before us. "What are you thinking?" he asked me, his voice sharp. "You have that look on your face."

"I'm thinking that right before everything good that's ever happened to me, something went wrong."

"Nothing's going wrong. You have to learn to enjoy this sport, Carrey. Remember when you used to enjoy rowing? You'll enjoy it today."

"I know it."

"You have to love the arrogance of it. We're about to illegally take out twenty thousand dollars worth of school property. How does that make you feel?"

"Like I'm taking a joyride in someone else's Porsche."

"This will be better. Take my word on it."

We pushed off the dock and the boat seemed to find itself and graft to the current. Hunched over our oars we let the boat take us down the river while Ruth settled into the stern. She leaned out over the water and sighted the curves, then breathed into her microphone and commanded us to keep our heads in the boat. Our first few strokes fought the speed of the water until we were rowing hard enough for the boat to be steered in the current, and with the current we flew down the river, past the school. Were you to look out the window that day, glance up while packing your books, cleaning up your desk, getting ready for that late winter dusk, you'd see four bodies laying back and that boat catching speed; a thing woken from hibernation and bounding away in exhilaration.

"Oh, man," Wadsworth purred.

"All right!" Perry yelled.

"Quiet in the boat," Ruth admonished, failing to disguise the smile in her voice.

I rowed behind Connor and after the first three strokes I didn't feel the cold; after the first power twenty I didn't even feel the speed. I'm pretty sure I closed my eyes the entire way. Ruth didn't put us through our paces. She just let us bring the boat down to the dam where we dragged it to a stop and sat, hunched over our oars, breathing heavily, light-headed and euphoric. Hunks of ice and logs and other flotsam that had crowded along the boom surrounded us and nudged the boat. My oar was tin-seled with tiny icicles.

Ruth finally spoke into the headset and her voice cracked up around us, an electric, confiding tone. "Carrey's one of us, guys. Channing says we have to be nice to him now."

Connor turned, flashed me a grin, and Perry pounded me on the back hard enough to knock the wind out of me. Wadsworth murmured, "Way to go, Rob." I hate to admit how good it felt.

Then Ruth's stern coxswain voice restored order, "Let's touch it and start half slide in two, people. We need to get back." Ruth hated to break rules. Deep down, she just didn't have the criminal spirit.

Connor's shoulders heaved as he sighed in irritation. "What's the big rush, cox?"

Ruth leaned out of the boat, glanced at Connor, then her voice rose up. "Quiet in the boat. Bow pair, touch it and start half strokes; stern pair, join in on three, that's one . . . and two . . ."

We turned and rowed back in the half darkness, Ruth sighting our way and standing in the stern every so often to look for the deadheads and logs and trash. Even fighting the current the boat had a warrior spirit. When we reached the dock, Connor once again turned to me with a look and I knew what I'd known all along; we were fast and had power and there was nothing except God Himself that would stop us. And even then He'd have to pull something pretty serious.

Which, naturally, He did.

24.

The FSBC crew went in for ultra-colorful rowing garb; hazard yellow climbing jackets and warm-up pants in violent reds, loud blues, deep purples, and various shades of black. We liked to wear tractor caps, too, pulled down low with the bills kneaded until they curled just right and you looked out on the world with tunnel vision. On practice days I wore my *Carrey's Joinery* cap and I fit right in with those kids advertising CAT and John Deere on theirs, though none of them had ever used a mini-dozer, power shovel, or tractor in their lives. Certainly none had had to face the wrath of a contractor when a worker arrived on site still shitfaced and broke a five-thousand-dollar piece of equipment by driving it over building rubble or smashing into a wall.

We practiced at Fenton through the spring vacation. Day after day of it; and every morning the God Four was the first to hit the water. Two weeks of rowing through that wet cold and we felt invincible. We rowed set pieces between landmarks beside the river and the times we clocked were almost perfect. We could not be sure of what other teams were doing, of course, or how the water and wind would affect us in a real race, but we could dependably make the boat run fast enough so that we began to believe we were unstoppable; that we could be walking into an undefeated season. Channing was patient with our confidence, fully aware it was premature but allowing it because of the team spirit we were building. By the time the rest of the school returned from their ski trips in Vail and holidays in Florida and Europe, we were itching for competition.

But then things went wrong.

Rowing is like any sport that melds a human to a machine—like cycling, like kayaking, like race car driving—the key to peak performance lies in the tiny details. And Channing was a tinkerer. He spent every day of spring vacation looking for flaws in the machine, not trusting, from years of experience, that he had such a perfect four. He finally found one; not that he wanted to, it gave him no happiness for his suspicions to be validated. Especially this close to race day.

The practice that signaled the end of our honeymoon period began right after class on an afternoon when the weather was finally warming up. Ruth was waiting for us in the boathouse as we filed in and took our places in front of the long, blue Vespoli four and pulled it from its rack.

"Hands on this boat, gentlemen."

We hoisted the boat to our shoulders at her instruction and balanced it for a quiet moment in the gloom while Channing headed down to the launch dock. In the silence you could hear the rattle in Perry's throat. We stood there, adjusting to the weight, waiting for Ruth's next command. When she gave it, in her distracted, soft voice, we inched out of the boathouse, an awkward caterpillar. Ruth backed away from us to check the riggers as we moved through the doors and finally the boat was birthed from the boathouse and we were following her to the river.

Channing was already waiting in the swirls beneath the bridge, sitting in the stern of the coach's launch and watching our progress. We brought the boat down to the edge of the dock where Ruth gave us the commands to lay it down easy against the surface of the water and run up for the oars, which had been fanned against the side of the hill. We kicked off our shoes while we lowered the oars into the riggers and screwed them down. The damp chill of the dock seeped into my feet. I stood lined up against the boat while Ruth counted us down and then ordered in the starboard side and then the port. To get in the boat I balanced between the tracks and lowered myself like an acrobat into the sliding seat. The weight of the oars stretched across the dock held the boat in place. All the while, Channing watched us from the water, already critiquing as we hunched over to tie in, adjusted the foot stretchers and ran our bodies up the slides before pushing off in one motion.

There was a momentary pause. Ruth leaned out of the boat, dark glasses on, headset strapped over her face; a diminutive pilot. Her voice cracked through the speakers below us. "Three, take half a stroke. Jumbo, touch it," and then the inertia of the boat and its weight and size gave way to the current and the river had us. The boat's bow pushed downstream and I felt myself limbering up, the flat of the oar blade skipping over the water while the bow pair pulled us away from shore and Ruth half stood in the boat looking for the debris of winter being flushed down the Housatonic to greater seas.

Channing's launch chugged into speed behind us and he followed at a respectful distance, always beginning fifty yards down the river from the boat, trying to see us as one small unit he could pick up and hold in his hands. You could look over Connor's shoulder and see him enveloped in a haze of diesel fumes. The boat passed under the town bridge and the splashes and drips echoed and sounded hollow and subterranean.

Ruth leaned out of the boat again and exhaled into the microphone, a long scratchy growl that rose out of the bottom of the boat. "Touch it, and let the bow pair join in. Wads I want you to take it easy on these strokes. Jumbo, you'll be rowing with arms only. On two, and that's one . . . and two . . ."

Connor hunched over in his seat and looked down the port side of the boat for a second, then turned around and felt the rhythm of those strokes as they pulled his torso gently backward. I sat there breathing hard, crouched over my oar, which I balanced on my thighs and held down lightly with my palm, getting ready to have Ruth feed us into the bow pair's cadence.

The command came down. "Stern pair, join in, hands only, on three," and she counted and I looked up directly into the fine white hairs on Connor's neck and we slotted into the cadence. The boat slowly picked up speed. Ruth leaned from side to side, watching the oars, measuring catches.

And part of me wasn't there. Part of me wanted to be in my single scull, doing the same exercises, feeling the smaller boat run out on its own steam. I rowed with only my fingertips, feeling the motion of Connor's back and arms. Ruth leaned out, watched our oars on the starboard side, exhaled. "Carrey, follow Connor. Get the oar out of the water faster. Quick catches here. C'mon." Another exhale into the microphone. "Okay. Add the bodies in three . . ." and in three strokes we were bent at the waist, rowing awkwardly with stiff legs, holding the sliding seats in place by bracing with our thighs. I felt each stroke in the cables of muscle running down my spine and into my pelvis, crunching my guts together. The sound of the launch buzzed to a greater speed and the boat was moving fast enough so I could feel the force of the air parting before us.

"And moving into half slides." Upon the command the launch behind her growled louder and Channing came up the stern to watch what happened next. The port-side rowers had to match each other perfectly. Same with the starboard. In addition, both sides had to be in unison. But the only way an oarsman could tell what his mates on the other side of the boat were doing was to literally feel what the body in front of him was doing, and to glance over the moving bodies at the stroke.

Channing would have seen us for what we were, four preco-cious kids in an expensive boat wearing motley weather gear for about ten cents' worth of crappy weather. He would also have figured we were fast as hell, or could be, and when Ruth had us move to full strokes you could hear the oarlocks straining against the riggers as we knifed up the river. I could feel the power, feel it like you were holding down a gear on a locomotive, one of the Canadian Pacific Freight trains that used to slide over the Black Rock Canal bridge back home during morning practice. That boat was barely in control at resting speed. It had taken five years of rowing in the Black Rock Canal for me to be leaning back into the late winter wind in this boat. It was only four hundred miles away, but really a world apart.

"Carrey, lengthen," called Ruth, and she said it evenly, with-out the usual biting tone of command, so that I knew she was doing it for my sake as the launch came up the river off the star-board of the boat.

"Carrey, follow Connor's lead," Ruth repeated, more urgency in her voice now.

We were cruising at an easy twenty-four strokes a minute and I lengthened my stroke.

"Slow on the last phase of the stroke, Carrey," Channing com-manded. "Don't dump, you're not in a single. Ruth, check Con-nor's rating. I have him all over the place, don't rate him over twenty-five, do you hear me?"

I followed Connor for the two strokes it would take Ruth to read his rating through the computer. "Twenty-four, Connor, good." Pause. "That's twenty-five, not so good. Hang in there. Easy. Carrey, you're rushing Connor. Slow it down you two, this is just one practice."

I could feel the sweat starting under my hat.

"Carrey, dig into this," Ruth warned. "Jumbo, baby, don't slack up out there, we're going to be watching you next."

Channing was standing in the launch now, the sound of the motor an incessant buzz. Connor had lengthened enough, I guessed, but Channing stood there in silence, glowering at the erratic rating. It was now uneven enough so that I could feel the boat's catches get weak and sloppy. "Ruth, make Carrey watch the rating."

"C'mon, Carrey."

Channing's voice now, irritated, "You're going to pull this up to full pressure now. Full pressure any way you want to do it, coxswain, and then it will be fifty strokes to see how you can sustain it. Full power."

Ruth's voice barked through the loudspeakers loud enough to flag us awake. "All right, you heard Channing. We're keeping the same rating but you *will* build to three-quarter pressure in three and then full pressure on my count." She paused exactly two strokes to let that sink in and I heard somebody wheezing on each inhale and realized it was me; the boat had already started to speed up when Channing had handed down the command to Ruth.

"Building in three to three-quarters, and that's one . . ." and the speed began to pick up immediately. But now there was something else. Something uncontained. "That's two . . ." I threw all of my concentration into following Connor. But I knew I was off, and I was throwing the others off. "That's three. And we're on three-quarters pressure, thank you."

Connor muttered something to Ruth and Ruth spoke into the microphone, "Slow those damned slides, guys. Especially you, Carrey. Slow them right down, you *dorks*. Twenty-four. We are *not* building the rating."

The boat was moving good and strong but we were all crashing into the stern on our recoveries. Every stroke you could feel it, almost see it in our wake, a slight jerk to the stern from all that loose human freight shifting backward. "Slow down, Carrey. Nice and easy, apply full pressure in three and I want all of you guys to hold it together on this one. And that's one . . ."

Out of the corner of my eye, I saw Channing pull a stopwatch from his coat. He was looking behind the boat, at the distance between the puddles, then marking where we began.

Ruth counted to three, and on each count you could feel the strength of the boat and the incredible effort we were using to keep it together, to keep things from falling apart. We were literally pushing against our own backward inertia.

Channing finally swore, his voice cracking across the water through the megaphone. "Goddamn it, Carrey. Goddamn it to *hell*—slow that slide down. Slow it right now."

Ruth sighed into the microphone. "You heard it. Slow on three."

Channing watched awhile longer. "What is Connor's rating?"

Ruth clicked in, waited another stroke. "Twenty-six."

"Carrey, you are not following Connor. *Don't look out of the boat, Carrey!*"

I grit my teeth, willed myself to fall into pace behind Connor. It was a matter of inches. A reflexive dip of the oar I just could not execute with Channing right there and four hundred pounds of human meat rolling around behind me. My seat banged up twice against the slide. I finally fell into place with Connor for ten strokes and the boat began to lift out of the water. Channing watched us impassively, and then my blade shoveled into the river and the boat shuddered while I pried it out. Connor glanced to port. "Get it together, Carrey," he whispered, and I swore back at him.

The launch stopped buzzing next to us and fell back. I moved my head enough to see Channing drop the megaphone and sit back down, steering the boat with one hand and staring at me with what looked like hatred. He then turned the throttle and sank back behind us, glaring at us all in frustration. Ruth didn't turn in her seat, just breathed into the microphone and said, "That's it. Wayne-up on three," and on three the oars came up out of the water together and turned. The boat glided down the river on its own momentum until we had the command to touch the oars to the water and roll the boat to a halt.

Ruth put her finger on the mike and exchanged glances with Connor. Then she leaned out of the boat to send me a withering stare. I could barely look back at her. Channing had found the weakness in the boat—the almost invisible distance between Connor and me that I was unable to close—and had zeroed right in on it. Connor's head hung between the twin axes of his shoulder blades, his hair wet and porcupined out. He looked to his right at the coach's launch, which had come up next to the boat and was idling, drifting with us. Channing was studying a clipboard, making us wait. He finally looked up from his numbers quickly, as if remembering we were there. "Terrible rating and short spaces. Your time for that piece was absolutely unacceptable. Do you realize the racing season is upon us? We row against Dover next week! You have ten more power pieces to go today. Spin the boat."

———

I got lost twice cutting up New York, blanked out the Robert F. Kennedy Bridge. And by the time I got there I knew I was either going to tear the steering wheel out of the dash or scream. So I decided to scream. Just screamed my head off the whole way across the bridge, and by the time I was driving upstate I was shaking. My heart was writhing, and I was sweating. And something else: I had the eerie, sinking sensation that I had forgotten something important. I did a mental inventory of what I had packed, listed to myself the equipment I had brought, ran over in my mind every box I had loaded out of the freight elevator. I couldn't put my finger on it, but the feeling was overwhelming.

I finally had to stop to fill up the Jeep at the service station on the Hutch in White Plains, breathing as if I had run a mile. I got out of the Jeep and was engulfed by greenery, stood in front of the quaint stone building filling up my car and supporting myself against it at the same time. When I was finished I got back in and just sat there next to the gas pump, my keys in my hand, unsure if I could drive. I shook the steering wheel, then opened the door again, got out and walked to the grass. I steadied myself against a tree, forcing myself to breathe.

Something was edging itself into my memory, a darkness. I closed my eyes, waited for it. Breaking through the river. Crashing helplessly into that black cold and feeling myself give way to it. The temptation to breathe in the water. I hadn't thought about being in that river for years, but the sudden sensation of wanting to let go came back as I stood there. I had spent years scuba diving and had never thought about that fall through the ice, never thought about that hard feeling in my chest of the oxygen being used up and replaced with that desperate vacuum.

I took a loud gulp of air, turned, and saw a teenager in a blue and red uniform standing next to my car, looking at me quizzically. I had left the door open and I walked back to it, nodded at him to show everything was all right.

"You okay?" he asked. He was no more than eighteen, if that. Tall, gangling, his face a horror of acne.

I nodded again. "Just needed to catch my breath."

He didn't look convinced but he shrugged, walked away, glanced back at me before going back into the building.

I couldn't go to Perry's memorial. No way. I was going to put these boxes in storage and just fly back to Cape Town. Only it was winter in South Africa now. Cape Town would be gray and blustery and damp, windy and then stormy. Working there would be a write off for the next few months. I considered going to Washington, DC, and meeting with my commissioning editor at *National Geographic* to nail down another commission. Now would be a good time to find something out west, or in Canada, or Europe. Even getting attached to a film team would do. I had no desire at all to go to Fenton, which was now only a little over an hour away and no longer just a memory but a looming reality.

I rumbled the engine to life and pulled out from the shelter of the pumps, still dead set on rerouting to DC. And then I was confronted by a freak of nature: a mammoth pine towering over the other trees, far too narrow and perfect. A poorly disguised mobile phone antenna. I laughed out loud. Carolyn had pointed one out to me just like it when we drove through Arizona's Painted Desert. She had been offended by its colossal absurdity, dubbed it a giant mascara brush, demanded that I stop the car—this car—so she could photograph it. She was furious, stood defiant by the side of the highway in her shorts and white tank top, snapping pictures against the never-ending motley hills. And with this memory I realized with gut-wrenching clarity what I had left behind in New York. I could still smell her hair and the Navajo sand. I decided to head north to Fenton. I couldn't keep running away. She was right. I had to move toward something.

SPRING

25.

We met the Dover School crew about five hundred meters before the start. As we warmed up beside them, Ruth's voice came down a notch from its usual shrillness. It was serious but undemanding, cool and even—a perfect voice for us now. She sounded almost bored, her corrections to our techniques perfunctory. "Jumbo, nice and easy on the slide, niceneeezy. Good. That's it." Or, "Wads, get the oar out of the water, up and out, out, yeah, thanks." The snap came back in the boat, that rushing feeling under us during the return.

"Eyes in the boat, gentlemen, they are not there. Don't look at them, eyes in the boat. C'mon now."

Mea culpa. She had caught me looking, watching their slow recoveries, their smooth drive. They were a strong four, dressed in scarlet racing shirts. It was hypnotic, their quick slide over the water, their release, as if the Dover boat was just gliding along, its every stroke kicking up a cool burst of speed.

An icy finger pressed into my back while I rowed.

The minutes ticked by. I wondered how long we had to prepare. No command was given while we tightened and practiced, even when the coach's launch appeared. But finally, Dover glided down past the stake boats and backed up. We gave them time, then followed to our own stake boat. A freshman named Charlie lay prone on the tiny floating wooden island, his hands hovering over the water for the boat, his face red with concentration while we backed into him. I saw the coach's launch ten meters up the river, and the shimmering water all around.

Feel something, I told myself.

Anything.

We rolled up the slides to the start, buried our blades in the water and the same breeze wafted down the river; the same trees waved and swayed on shore as they had over the days of unsuccessful practice. I reached out and patted the exact center of Connor's back. "Good luck." He nodded once, his eyes locked with Ruth's.

I closed mine, opened them.

"Dover's hand is down." Channing was speaking into the bullhorn, casual at first. "Fenton's hand is down. Both hands are down." Now his voice boomed over the water, "Are you ready? Row."

I don't remember the first ten strokes of the race. In my mind's eye I can only see them as part of the roaring water around me. It must have been a standard start, though, no different than a thousand others we had practiced. I was dizzy, rowing with my mouth wide open at first, then with my teeth clenched and my lips drawn back. Ruth began to screech in the barbaric coxswain language of counting and commanding—harsh, guttural gibberish that meant something to some part of me, meant that we had taken them but by the end of the start they were coming back. We had taken a tiny lead, nothing to bank on, and they were holding us.

Twenty, thirty strokes in and we hadn't moved on them and they hadn't been able to pull through us. We were two boats, practically dead even, roaring down the coarse, neither coxswain willing to risk a power twenty just yet. Ruth was leaning far out of the boat, jamming the rudder in short bursts. I noticed that her sunglasses had fallen down her nose, a comical sight. I might have smiled as I rowed.

I realized the stroke was higher than we were used to when Ruth put in for a move, gave the command for a power twenty in three and I felt something sharp and warm move in my guts when she said it. "I want twenty power strokes to move, Fenton, in three. And that's one . . . that's two . . . that's three . . . on this one."

Connor brought the rating up over the twenty and Ruth didn't call him on it. Twelve strokes in, I felt my ears pop. The boat was in pain, running ragged and we hadn't even hit the halfway point yet. Ruth hunched over in the boat, her head turning quickly to see what we had taken off Dover. "I have their deck, I'm sitting on their stroke. You're going to give me that seat, Fenton. Three more out of this twenty and settle. Row for their stroke seat, Fenton. Take it now . . ."

But we didn't take their stroke seat. Once you had brought your coxswain even with the stroke of the opposing team, you had an edge and Dover knew it. They were digging in, an ominous, quiet opponent, their coxswain's voice not traveling over to us.

Ruth leaned out and must have sighted the thousand meter buoy. "I want that stroke seat by the thousand meter mark, guys. I want them to bleed. You wanna make Dover bleed, don't you?"

She ordered another ten power strokes. I didn't feel out of breath, just all the pain that comes from being out of breath— the heavy, leaden heat in my legs, the burn in my back, the pounding blood in my ears and the bite in my arms. *The rating's too high*, I thought. *We're blowing it all just to take a seat before the halfway mark*. We passed the red buoy without taking the seat. I prayed she wasn't going to push for another power ten, and I started counting down in my head, just as Ruth would.

Ten strokes after the buoy, and, just as I feared, "This is it, FSBC, another power ten to pull through them, in three. And that's one . . . that's two . . . and three . . . go."

Each stroke was torn from us; brutal, hard, fast strokes that felt like shocks. The boat lost its set for one stroke, and still we passed the thirteen hundred mark without giving Ruth her damned seat. The Dover boat began to pick up speed right beside us for the turn in the river and now I could hear the sound of their coxswain's voice, counting out their set. Ruth had no choice but to demand another ten from us in response, ten more power strokes from a bleeding boat. I could feel the wind in my throat. "I want another power ten now, now, on this one . . ."

No warning or countdown, just a sudden burst from the boat, the surprise attack. I had no idea where the power was coming from, where we found that store of energy for a third time. But still they held us off. There were ten strokes to go before the pink buoy that marked the last five hundred of the race and just before we reached it, Connor went insane by bringing the rating up to a thirty-nine, a rating that could leave us scraping the water right before the final sprint. And once again, Ruth didn't stop him. I couldn't believe it.

We took the five-hundred mark clearly ahead of Dover. But they responded to our attack and closed quickly and were close now, the oars from each boat almost touching. Any moment I expected to hear Channing's voice booming out over the river instructing one coxswain to peel off, but the warning never came.

This close, I could hear Dover's seats moving back and forth, hear the sound of their coxswain, his voice a subdued scream. "Okay, guys, we're going to pull through them in twenty on two, and that's one . . . that's two . . . pull."

Ruth's bitter voice cut through him, "Take a power fifty in three Fenton, let's trash these people." We were up for it, our boat moving now at thirty-seven strokes, Dover matching us, but both boats just barely under control. We started the power piece, Connor driving into the water, sending white puddles that linked with mine behind the boat.

"That's it FSBC. They're dying. I see them dying, they're dying on us. They can't hold it and I see the finish, I see it, and *they can't take it*." Ruth's voice rose out of the boat, horrible. "Dig for this last twenty and the race is ours, you dig in now," and wham, another ten strokes gone.

Then the Dover coxswain, his voice firm and cold, "Twenty on this next one to move, Dover. Now . . ."

And Ruth counted, and the other coxswain counted. They counted out the final strokes of that race even as Dover took our stern deck, their coxswain's shrill and urgent voice carrying clearly over the animal sounds of the crowd on shore, and the Fenton School Boat Club crossed the finish line one stroke behind.

"I have a crooked room you should see," Carolyn had said. "It's a studio on Broome Street."

There are days you remember in their entirety, hours you know transformed you.

I now knew a beautiful woman with a crooked room in New York and on that early evening when rain was threatening down the East River, when clouds rolled over the streets, I had spent two lazy hours having dinner with her alone in a restaurant before the night-time rush. Her mention of the crooked room was the beginning of a storm of love. We were walking up Mulberry Street like tourists, holding hands, a bottle of wine left empty for our shyly grinning waiter on the white tablecloth. I remember every step.

Her unspoken question to me was not really a question, and we turned into Broome Street and walked past the galleries and the brick walls, under the hooked lamps and by the drunken graffiti and the tired traffic with me one half step behind her, wanting to savor this moment when the stars aligned and life was perfect. Walking along that old, broad sidewalk I knew I was sailing into something more than a relationship, something more than a love affair. Half-drunk, half in love, full of lust, I followed her without pause into the elevator. We stood there not touching each other, our eyes forward, Carolyn idly humming, pleased with herself, a formality between us still, as if there was a contract that had yet to be defined and signed and sealed.

It took a full minute for the doors to shut and the elevator to begin its scraping ascent. I felt her close to me, inches away. A dramatic face with deep eyes, a severe face, possibly. A woman who might be a shade too tall, too strong, her center of gravity too low, as if she was set to push you away. And she was strong— God, did I learn that—strong enough to bear whatever came our way, strong enough to tear that place to pieces. I had to turn my head and pretend to examine the three numbers on the faded elevator panel because it was hard to breath when I looked at her. She knew I was struggling and she was loving it.

When the doors opened to the loft, I was confronted with her life as it was then lived: the cavern of space, the pushed open windows, the lone couch from her parents' summer house in the center of the room, the worktable and her equipment, the make-shift kitchen we would tear out a year later with the double bed beside it, unmade, her shoes jettisoned at the end. The air that rushed in over us was cold with the rain that had burst down on the street below and brushed against the windows, the traffic hissing against that summer cloudburst.

Undressing her sitting on that bed of hers, I chased her body as she leaned over me to pick up the blankets and the sheets off the floor. I gazed at her face as I explored her, Carolyn's face all seriousness, as if she had found me herself and was discovering me methodically and carefully. I knew that somehow the two of us had carelessly joined hands and jumped into whatever was next in our lives, into that nothingness of the future. What was being done now was going to be impossible to undo without the greatest loss. This virtual stranger with the heat rising from her naked body, her shoulders round and graceful, neck bones perfect, her face close to mine, on those cool sheets. More. Her long arms and legs, the muscles of her forearms that stood out and shifted and twirled as she held my hand. The surprise of her fingers and palms which were rough, her nails clipped down for work. When I felt the mysterious subterranean muscles of her belly shifting under me, I was seized by a rush of love and longing so powerful I gasped, and she pulled her face from mine quizzically and I shook my head.

And what I wanted to whisper to her, if I had the words (if such thoughts come to a man so utterly overwhelmed), was that she could have this section of my life right now, and the rest, too, if she wanted it. It was the crazy, silent deal you make with yourself when you suddenly touch the woman who was made for you and feel that searing terror of loneliness after years of living by yourself. It happened to me in a crooked room against a body I yearn for like nothing else, need more than water, or blood or breathing.

"Just enjoy it," she whispered. "I don't want to hear you." It was an urgent whisper. What do lovers do when they are confronted by that ocean of life, that electric field that develops between two people maybe once in a lifetime and mostly never? Where does all that power go? I learned that day it is not graceful, it isn't even romantic. It's two people clinging on for dear life. Afterward, with her lying next to me, breathing gently into sleep, the evening now fully upon us, the white light I would come to know so well making squares on the marred floor, I knew only that the worst fate in the world would be to lose her. I'd love her no matter what. So long as I had this I'd take whatever came.

I have a crooked room, she had said. Come and enter.

And so came her pregnancy, and so came the blood, and so came the doctors, and so came the news in the doctor's office that Carolyn did indeed require surgery; that the infection was catastrophic and severe and had forever damaged her. She'd have her life but there would be no more. It was the best they could do, we were told, in that quiet office. In that awful place where I took her hand before she began to weep when we were politely left alone. Where she scraped her nails against my hands and then against my arms and then across my chest and then over my face as if scribbling me out. Where she wept and wept and then pushed me away.

26.

Channing watched the race from the coach's launch, which traveled behind the two crews. When we crossed the finish he pulled the throttle and the boat cruised by us imperiously. He didn't look at us, or make any sign that he'd registered our defeat. Connor was leaning out of the boat and retching. I knew I had done damage to the fibrous muscles around my back. Ruth's voice was subdued as she ordered the boat turned around for the row back. Wadsworth threw up then and I realized that Perry had pissed his pants; the urine slopped along the bottom of the boat as we rowed.

At the dock, Connor slipped out of the boat and stood on shaking red legs. I tried not to think of the human effluent rolling in the hull. The Dover crew was already celebrating. They threw their cox in the water and looked away from us as we rose out of our boat.

We had lost even though we had driven the rating to thirty-nine. What I felt wasn't anger. It was the urge to destroy something, a viciousness that I'd never outgrow. We had hit that high rating and been unable to move past Dover. We'd still been beaten.

Channing stood near the boathouse doors looking down at us while we stripped off our shirts and handed them over in the traditional signal of defeat. Connor went first and the Dover stroke received his dripping offering like it was something freshly killed. Connor stood pale and gangling in the sun, a scarecrow devoid of power. I ripped mine off next and handed it over wordlessly. Then Perry gave his soaked shirt to a giant of equal size from Dover, who contemptuously squeezed it out on the dock. Wadsworth shook hands with the Dover bow man as he gave up his.

When it came to Ruth's turn, Connor faced her impassively. "Take it off, Ruth."

She didn't miss a beat, pulled off her shirt quickly, easily. She was wearing only a thin bra underneath and looked emaciated. You could count every rib and see the sharp outlines of her shoulder blades. The dark points of her nipples stood out shockingly in the cold. Her legs stuck out of her rowing trau like sticks. She handed her shirt over to the Dover coxswain in silence, Jumbo staring hard at every one of their crew, daring them to laugh. They did not. They looked on in stunned horror. Stripped, Ruth looked like a vulnerable child, skeletal and beaten. Pale with humiliation, she turned and walked by us with as much dignity as she could muster. Nobody said anything as we all watched her on her solitary journey back to the boathouse.

The vicious feeling passed. I lined up by the boat to swab it out and then flip it up on Connor's command. We were showered with fouled water and loss. Ruth had already left the boathouse by the time we got the boat back up there, as had Channing. Connor sighed, glanced at me before his gaze returned to the jubilant Dover four. "Nice race, Carrey."

"Yeah, right. We couldn't move on them even on the high ratings. If we can't beat Dover, we can't beat Warwick."

Connor looked, for the first time, like he might really lose his temper. It came on in a flash. "*You're* not following me in the boat, Rob. *You're still too fast on the recovery.* And Perry and Wads follow *you*." He took a deep, ragged breath. "Just forget it."

I spun him around. "Are you blaming this on me? Are you? You're the one who pushed that rating up so high. And Ruth is so damned scared of you she didn't push it back down."

"Okay, so that was a surprise. But you guys were *good* for it." He flashed me that elusive grin of his. "When you rush your recovery, Carrey, there's something like half a ton of human weight—you, Jumbo and Wads—pushing us the wrong way for about half a second. There are two hundred strokes in a race. That's a hundred seconds of us being pushed back because you can't recover. We lost this race by less than two seconds. Just think about it." He pointed at the Dover crew piling into their van. "Do you know why they are so happy? Because they didn't expect to win. Yet there they go."

He pushed by me and I watched the Dover van drive away, then looked out at the river and the dock. The Dover coxswain had left Ruth's shirt there, a tiny sodden ball of indictment.

I wasn't outraged by Connor's treatment of Ruth. It was just one of his many transgressions. I might have felt indignant for thirty seconds. Less. I reminded myself that my own success at rowing was dependent upon my ability to tolerate cruelty. I heaped it upon myself for that entire year. I allowed it to happen all around me. I embraced it. *Ruth's tough*, I thought. *She can take it. It's not a big deal.*

Winning was a big deal, and we had lost.

Life at prep school is not something that can be idealized. Anyway, I figured, nothing the kids at Fenton went through could compare with what it was like at Niccalsetti Senior School, where you rode your bike seven miles to crew practice, where kids drank half jacks in the hallways, beat the living shit out of each other in the empty swimming pool during winter.

I would never have believed back then that in fifteen years I would care deeply that I had permitted people who meant something to me to be pushed around. Ruth was tough, I told myself. Perry was tough. I was tough. And the small cruelties of Connor Payne were not going to kill anybody.

Wadsworth and Perry dropped by my room after lights-out, midway through the following miserable week's practice. I was sitting in the dark at my desk with ice on my knees, thinking I might sleep that way. They crowded into my room and looked down at me. Wadsworth was carrying a golf club. Perry held a glowing garbage bag.

Perry looked at me, shook his head. "Dude, you're in bad shape."

Wadsworth switched on my desk lamp. "This place smells like rubbing ointment, Carrey." He pulled me up and my knees creaked. "You'll stiffen up sitting there like that. You need exercise."

"That's no problem, because I'm never rowing again." It seemed like a good idea. Channing was killing us in preparation for Warwick, dragging us through endless power pieces and starts. And I was getting the brunt of his displeasure.

"Yeah. We thought you might be a little bummed," noted Perry. "Especially after Channing told you that a slave in a Greek galley could row better than you."

"Still," said Wadsworth, "you need to keep moving. Our times on the water were pretty fast, Ruth says."

"Ruth didn't tell me." In fact, she had pretty much ostracized me all week. Had taken gleeful pleasure in announcing to the boat that my catches were off, or, as always, I was rushing my slide.

"Come on."

"Where?"

Perry picked up the mysteriously glowing bag and hustled me out the door. "You'll see. Just go."

"Wads, why do you have a golf club?"

"It's a driver."

"And what's in the bag?"

Perry shrugged. "Nothing. What bag?"

I followed them out to the fire escape stairs, up to the roof. Wadsworth pushed open the door and we were suddenly on top of the world, looking down at the river, the farmland, the town, the endless trees. "Have you ever been up here, Carrey?"

"No. The fire door is supposed to have an alarm on it."

"Maybe ten years ago. We figured after Channing yelled at you, you might need to be inducted into our club. So feel privileged."

Perry nodded. "We're the only ones who are allowed to drive golf balls off the roof." He shook the bag. "We used to use regular balls but it wasn't as much fun as these. This is a super secret club, by the way. The Society of Glowing Golf Balls. We're the founding members."

"The school lets you drive golf balls up here?"

"No, but let's just say that they turn a blind eye. And the rest of the kids in this dorm stay off the roof."

"Maybe because we're not allowed on the roof and all," I noted.

"Yeah. That, too. But the point is, you can actually hit balls into the river. I've *cleared* the river a few times."

I looked out into the darkness, saw the lights of the town beyond the snakelike shape of the river. Perry pulled a portable practice tee from the bag. He set it up, rummaged inside the bag. Inside there were a few dozen, multicolored, mysteriously glowing golf balls. He pointed. "It takes forever to get the little glow sticks in those things, but it's worth it. Trust me. I save these for emergencies."

"We loaded fifty of those babies," said Wadsworth solemnly. It was cold up there, but he shrugged off his coat and rolled up the sleeves to his sweater. He picked up the driver, peered out into the darkness, then plucked a glowing neon green ball out of the bag. "Yup. The river is about fifty yards off the roof. When you hit the ball, it makes quite an effect."

Perry nodded in affirmation. "You need to take the oath."

"What oath?"

He held up a joint, lit it theatrically and took a hit, swiping the smoke away from his face with a paw. He handed it to me. "The oath is, you swear on Bob Marley's grave never to tell anyone about the Society of Glowing Golf Balls. Membership is restricted."

"I swear. Gimmie that before you hurt somebody, Jumbo."

"Swear on his dreadlocked soul."

I snatched the joint from him.

"Careful, Carrey," Perry warned. "This stuff has a kick."

"You guys are smoking weed six days before the Warwick Race?"

Wadsworth shrugged. "Looks like you are, too."

I inhaled on the joint, felt the effect of it cloud into my capillaries. Sure enough it hit me almost immediately. I inhaled again while Wadsworth drew back the driver and crushed the eerily glowing ball. It streaked off into the darkness and arched towards the water, settling into the dark shapes of the brush near the river. Perry watched, I watched, Wadsworth watched. None of us said anything. I handed the joint to Wadsworth and he took a drag.

"That was far," Perry said. "Inaccurate but far, man. Let me show you how a pro does it." He took the driver from Wads, bent down, and set a pink ball up on the tee. It glowed innocently, a ruby in the blackness, as he adjusted his bulk over it. He glanced up at me. "This is how you address the ball, dude."

Wadsworth waved at it. "Hello, ball."

Perry drew back and slapped the ball into the night. It missiled off the roof toward the fields, and I watched it disappear into what I thought might be the river. The thought of the ball resting on the river bottom, emitting that comforting rosy glow, was extremely soothing.

Perry was saying something. I looked at him, perplexed. "Your turn," he repeated.

"I don't play." I didn't mention that there seemed to be something fundamentally wrong about hitting those beautiful dimpled orbs. My knees were sore, my arms were sore, but the pain seemed much less acute up here. Perry handed me the driver. "Give it a try. Go on."

I bowed over a yellow ball. Tried to set it on the tee. It rolled off. Set it up again and everything was cool.

"Dude, terrible stance." Perry snatched the driver from me. "Hold it like this. Arms straight, wrists firm." He handed me the club and I tried to adjust myself. "Okay, Rob. Close enough. Let 'er rip."

I wound back and whacked at the ball, missed entirely. Wadsworth laughed, "Again! Again!"

I connected with the ball on my fourth try, and it was more of a slapshot than a drive. Still, the ball streaked off into the darkness.

Into outer space. Gone.

Perry cheered. "Slice! Dude, slice!" He teed up another ball, a blue one this time. "Fore!"

After three false tries, I slapped it again. I dropped the driver, stood back on my heels and watched the ball bounce in impossible parabolas down the main drive of the school. When was the last time I smoked pot? I looked at the bag of glowing balls, chose a martian green one, pitched it into the darkness where it sailed toward the river and abruptly disappeared.

Wadsworth picked up the driver, launched a red ball into the gloom. It traced the green trail mine had left behind. "You need to relax, Carrey. Just slow down your slide in the boat. Your recovery is way too fast. Just chill. Then Connor will be happy. Channing will be happy. The boat will be faster. It'll be all good."

I picked up another red ball, whipped it far out toward the science building, where it bounced along the roof in cheerful zigzags. "It's not like I don't want to."

Perry accepted the driver from Wads and bent over a glowing golden orb. He drew back, smacked it, and it beelined toward the water, then abruptly arched upward into the stars. I watched in amazement. A quantum leap, a defiance of gravity. Perry glanced at me. "You have nothing to lose."

"Rowing in the four is different than rowing in the single."

"Ya think? Damn. That's deep."

Wadsworth claimed back the driver, stood back and consulted the heavens. "Of course it's different. It's way faster. And you're not in charge. But the key to speed in the four . . . is . . . following."

"Following *Connor* might be the problem."

"Connor is . . . wise, dude," Wads said.

Perry giggled. "Yeah. Like, you know. Wise."

Wadsworth set up a purple ball, blasted it into the purple horizon. "If you just relax for one race, we'll go faster. It's that easy."

"But, we have no idea how to make you do that," Perry added.

"Nope. No clue." Wadsworth sighed. Teed up a glowing, ice blue ball. Drove it all the way back to Superman's fortress.

27.

Ten miles away from Fenton, I parked the Jeep outside one of the pizza/bar/coffee places that dot that area of New England. I walked into the small shop and found it almost empty. It was the kind of spot you frequented as a prep school kid, serving the gamut from milk shakes and sodas to pizzas, hot dogs and hamburgers to pasta to bogus vegetarian meals and salads to desserts with names like "Mac's Surprise."

I ordered a cup of coffee at the counter from a young woman wearing a flannel shirt that reached her knees, which looked like bumps sticking out of legs packed into tight black leggings. She had long, tired brown hair and sausage fingers and chatted perfunctorily with the cook through the serving window as she stood at her post in front of the register. She was wearing gaudy running shoes, incongruously, and as I paid I thought about what Connor would have made of her had we stopped by a decade and a half ago. I imagined the casual names we'd have used to describe her, the snobbery of the rich and the beautiful when having dealings with the poor and the plain. She smiled at me when she gave me my change and I smiled back. "You going to the reunion?"

"Yes."

"You're the third person who came in today. Two other guys came in and ordered beers. They looked like they were getting ready to have a good time over there."

Or they were bracing themselves, I thought.

She told me to sit down anywhere and I chose one of the two booths, sat looking out at the hard packed gravel drive and the dark road. She served the coffee with the same brilliant smile, and I sipped it, accepted a refill and sipped some more, looking out at the road, knowing just what the soft shoulder would feel like when you ran down it early in the morning.

I had made decisions at that school. Decisions that were with me now and would remain with me. I had decided, for instance, that no matter what I did in college, and in life, I would do nothing that required me to work on a team, or in any kind of team environment. I would never work directly under an authority figure, either, or select a job where I had to compete head to head with others. Documentary filmmaking fit the bill for this. As far as I was concerned, it was not really a collaborative effort. I could choose what projects I wanted to work on and was in charge of my own shoots. Even when I worked with Carolyn, I had her create the final cut for me from my scripts. The people I filmed, when I did film people, were small and distant figures down an eyepiece. You can film terrible things when your mind is fooled into thinking it's happening on TV.

I lingered over my coffee. The woman behind the register disappeared into the back. I thought, seriously, of ordering a beer, and knew if I did I wouldn't leave the place.

One thing that people in my industry had to learn in order to get ahead was how to be nice. They *schmoozed*, they *took meetings*, they *traded contacts*, they *beamed each other* and *shot each other e-mail*. Carolyn was a great connector, she was good with people in a way I could never be. Being unable to deal with people, even with people in my own profession, certainly meant I would never go big-time, would never run my own production company or get a contract for a really serious string of shows.

I would not make much more money than my father did, and that had irked him. I'd be small-time, like he was. Unlike him though, sooner or later I'd have to find a job that didn't beat my body up so much, and I had some options to do so. I could write, or teach. I had taught before, after Carolyn had forced me to do it, given informal talks at small colleges and film schools about the business, short presentations at film festivals. The first time I had done this, I had realized something I had not known before: Teaching is a lonely pursuit. The podium acts like the viewfinder, and the faces in the class seem to meld into each other. You prepare the talk, you give the presentation, you take the questions and move on. I was attracted to the idea. Teaching would allow me to be my own boss, in a manner of speaking. The more you taught, in a strange way, the more disconnected you became from your charges.

Channing must have liked that as well.

———————

I tied into the single my father made for me, clamped down the sculls and concentrated on breathing hard. I was still allowed to use it on the condition I had Channing's permission, which I did not. As I pushed off and tapped the boat into the current I watched the winter detritus from far upriver float down the exact middle of the bed. Old logs, dead trees, clumps of grass, and mud that we called "clong", all tossed aside by the brown water that moved now with resolve and strength. It was still cold out, the cold could hang on until May even, but it was a good cold. I worked into the piece, thinking about gaining length as I rowed down the river toward the town bridge. I could smell it as I approached—wet winter steel—and I looked back to see it and align myself. The darkness below it came on quickly and as I passed under, I glanced up at the support beams and cross-bars, took two more strokes, and ran out.

"Solid rowing."

Channing's voice startled me and I looked sharply to the shore to see nothing but the banks sloping into the water, covered in leaves. Then I looked up on the bridge and there he was, his elbows on the railing. I brought the scull to an awkward stop. "You have a weak recovery, Carrey. You're pulling the blades out too soon. You do it in the four as well."

"I'm working on it." I looked up at him.

"I've told you all week, all year, that your recoveries have to change if you want more speed."

"You can judge my recoveries from up there, too?"

"I can, yes."

I rowed away from him, left him there watching me. He cupped his hands over his mouth and shouted down across the river. "You're bringing your hands too close to your body, and hunching over to pull the oars from the water. Fool."

I ignored him, rowed all the way down the river until it bent. From the bend you could get in fifty more strokes and then the river dammed up in front of the covered bridge and you had to turn around. I spun the boat and thought about my hands being too close to my body. I leveled them out and flattened and pulled. I rowed back up the river and when I turned the corner I checked my line and then looked up at the bridge. He was still up there, waiting. I turned back and settled into the oars, twenty fast strokes.

"You're rowing like you're strapped to a bowling ball," he called. "You have short strokes."

I carried on rowing and as I got closer I could hear him muttering to himself. "Bad stroke. Bad, bad. Good stroke, good one, good. Bad. Bad." He coughed. I slipped back under the bridge and rowed a further fifteen strokes before stopping. He shaded his eyes when I did. "Look at the Harvard man, hunched over his oars."

I laid my oars flat on the water and felt the current push me away from him. I turned the oar, palmed some water with my blade and pulled, gently, running out beneath him.

"Go ahead. I want to see one perfect stroke, Carrey. Just one."

I came up the slide slowly and turned the sculls until they dug into the river, set the blades and snapped off a stroke into the current, leaning back and tapping the sculls out of the water. I moved five meters down the river and quickly turned to see what was coming at me. Channing watched for a moment and shook his head. "You pull with your lower back. I'm not sure how you stay on your feet after a race. And you duck your head. How on earth are you so fast on the water?"

"Luck."

"It's not luck. It's power. It's strength. Do you think you'll have it forever?"

I shrugged. "Long enough."

"You have no discipline, Carrey. You row like you're chopping wood or sawing or laying down track. Power is cheap in this world, Carrey. Very, very cheap."

I looked up at him and snapped off another stroke. He shaded his eyes again, watched, shook his head again. "You look like you're doing a job."

"It is a job."

"It's not. Not a soul will pay you."

"Rowing this way has got me pretty far."

"Roll forward on the slide. Do it."

I rolled forward and the boat began to rock in the current. Balled up at the end of the tracks I was vulnerable, my arms spread out over the water.

"Chin up, now."

He was right, I was looking down at the bow deck. I looked up and felt my spine settle into my back, the bones pile into one another, connecting, and the muscles in my forearms stretch out.

"Get those blades off the water and hold them. Then turn the oar handles and don't bend your arms until I give the command."

For one second I was free and balanced over the water while I turned the blades over the current. Poised this way in space, I could place the oars exactly and when they cleaved the water, I pushed with my legs and fell backward, my arms burning to pull into my body. He waited for a moment and then said, finally, "Row," and my arms bent and the oars came into my chest. I might have gained a foot of run. My body felt taller, stronger.

He nodded as if finding resolution to some debate he'd been having with himself. He looked down from the bridge. Deep inside the structure you could hear drips of water falling hollowly.

"There are scullers older than you and faster and less likely to do idiotic things. Harvard wants to see rowers who have the ability to bring magic into a team. That's what they are looking for. The only thing you have on your side is youth and power. If you do not progress, you're nothing."

"How do you know all this?"

"I'm your advisor. I'm advising."

"Tell me about the picture on the wall of your house, Coach."

"What picture, Carrey?"

"The newspaper photo. You at Gales Ferry, rowing against Yale."

"It's of another person, a long time ago. He'd have little to offer you."

"I'd still like to know."

"I appreciate your interest, Carrey, but I'm in the future business, not the past. And unless you keep your hands higher into your chest at the finish you won't be rowing anywhere once the year finishes. One person alone cannot make that much difference, but two rowers, you and Payne, can. The four has the speed, it has the potential. Learn to exploit it."

"There's not much time left; only three days until the race."

"I'm well aware of that. Use what you have, Carrey. Use what you have. You need to solve this problem. Now. Do whatever is necessary. And if I see you out in the single again without my say-so, I will kick you off the team."

"Yes, sir."

"And you *will* learn to row with the others. Right now. You will think of nothing else. Or the Rob Carrey story will be over."

"Got it."

"I'll see you and the others on the water tomorrow. And again on Sunday, immediately after chapel. I need improvement, Carrey. Get ready for two long days."

28.

Later that evening I walked across the campus to the Rowing Cottage. It was two hours until lights-out and there was a movie showing in the auditorium, a band playing in the coffee room. A dwindling light still glowed over the mountains. I walked up the stairs and when I stepped into his living room, Connor looked up at me from the couch where he was crouched under a long brass lamp, carefully pulling tape from his fingers. He was dressed in an achingly white button-down Brooks Brothers shirt, khakis, and black loafers. He was also wearing wire glasses I had never seen on him before.

"Did you ever hear of knocking, Carrey?"

"We've got to get the boat to work, Connor. I need to be able to follow you on the water. I'm not able to do it."

"Talk to Channing. He's the coach. Every time I criticize your rowing I wind up getting insulted or hit."

"Channing says if I don't learn to row with you and the others I'm off the team, but I have no idea how to do it anymore. I don't want to get dumped from the team, or lose the Warwick Race. If I can follow you, then Jumbo and Wadsworth will fall right into place behind me, and we'll beat Warwick." I waited. "But I just can't follow you. I've tried everything. Even when I'm sure I'm doing it, I'm still off."

"I could have told you that back in the fall, when we were rowing in the tanks. Wait a minute, I did tell you that."

"I know. Channing bet on the fact that I was just as strong as you, but it's not working."

"You're not as strong as me. Not quite."

"Close enough."

He looked at me for a few long seconds and I held his gaze. Then he nodded. "You're losing six inches of finish with each stroke, pulling out of the water early and jerking the first two inches of your slide." Connor held his hands in front of his face and tested his fingers, gingerly making fists. "The way you rush up the slide screws up my rating."

"I know. I *know*. But how do I get the length? What do I need to do?"

He looked up at me over his glasses, a frighteningly mature look. "Are you seriously asking me? Me? Seriously?"

"Serious as cancer."

Connor thought for a second. "Sit down on the floor."

"What for?"

"Look. I'm going to tell you something. Something you need to understand. You're a good rower. No. You're a great rower. The best I've seen in four years, maybe even the best—"

"Outside of yourself, you mean."

"Shut up and listen, Carrey. You have one flaw. When you're sitting in the boat you have no flexibility in the last phase of the stroke. And it's easy to—"

"But—"

"Are you going to sit down and listen or not?" His usual sarcastic tone was gone. He was confiding in me, and the earnestness in his voice was unnerving.

I sat down on the threadbare Persian carpet and looked up at him. "All right. I'm listening."

"It's easy to fix, but you need to trust me. What I'm about to tell you to do won't feel right to you because you're a sculler, which is why your hands are too fast, but it will work in the four."

He stood, reached for the long brass lamp and unscrewed the linen shade which had stains on it—speckles of champagne or else something vile—from God knows what rituals. He set the lampshade aside, pulled the cord out of the wall, twirled off the dusty bulb, and lay the brass rod across my knees. I examined it. "This thing is supposed to look like a long piece of brass bamboo. What is it with rich people and fake bamboo furniture?"

"That's supposed to be bamboo? I had no idea. It's not like I go out and buy this stuff myself, Carrey."

I held the lamp, and using the heavy base as a fulcrum, jiggled it up and down. It had almost the exact diameter of an oar.

"Lean back," he said. "Tap the end down. Like you do in the boat."

I obeyed, but I lost my balance, just a touch.

"See?" He sounded almost triumphant.

"See what?"

"You're pushing the oar handle away from you already, sliding it out. Tap the oar out of the water leaning *back*."

I tapped out, sitting on the floor, legs out in front of me, leaning back maybe one hundred and twenty degrees, looking dead forward. I felt the pull across the tight stomach muscles clinging to my ribs.

"Do it again. Ease it out of the water and take your time."

"How many times do you want me to do this, Connor?"

"Until it looks like you know what you're doing. Tap it out. Now. Right now while you're leaning back."

I tapped out and bent forward at my waist, just slightly. He shook his head, scratched it and looked around. Then he walked toward his bedroom, glancing down at me as he went. "Don't stop."

"Where are you going?" I was sweating from keeping my back at full extension, but my finishes were looking slightly better.

Connor came back and set something next to me. "That's called a metronome."

I tried to keep my voice from sounding winded. " I know what it is. Did you steal it out of the music department?"

"No, from the chapel. Father Davis uses it to keep time on the piano, or used to, to get an even count. Like, twenty-eight beats a minute."

"Or thirty-five."

"I'm setting it at twenty-eight for now. You worry about pushing down on the oar handle, releasing, and moving your body forward just before your knees come up. That's it. Those inches at the release are where you're losing the beat and losing your length."

"We should go to the tanks and do this."

"They're locked. It doesn't matter where we do this. I'm talking about six inches of movement. Be quiet and concentrate. Just think about doing this correctly." He set the small weight and the metronome began to tick over, a hollow, tinny sound.

"You stole something from a chapel, Connor, so you could improve your rowing. A *chapel*. This cannot be ignored." I tapped out the shaft of the lamp, leaned back, and it was a strangely familiar sensation. The pull at the back of my legs was deeper, and I almost felt the motion of the boat.

"Do you want to make this team work or not?"

"Tell me what to do."

"I've told you. Just a few inches on your release. Like you're doing right now. If you do that, then we're not losing anymore races this year. We're winning. But you need to trust it. You keep wanting to get the oar out of the water and charge up the slide. I can feel you back there, just hacking away."

I followed the beat, and then he reset the metronome to a higher cadence. Even sitting on the floor of his living room I started to miss strokes. I felt it. "How much longer do I have to do this?"

"Until you know what you're doing. Stop being impatient, okay? I'm going to tell you something, Carrey. Channing knows a high rating isn't the answer. He's right. We *can* hit a high rating but we don't need to. I've been hitting those high ratings for him for years now. Years. Ruth won't let us go past thirty-five strokes per minute again."

I nodded absently. I could feel myself falling into the cadence. The metronome ticked away until I didn't hear it, just felt myself slide into its rhythm.

"Look, you're doing it. You're following it just fine now. Anyone can do it. But you need to *trust* it."

I stopped, held the oar out at the release and followed through. I was sweating hard. Connor looked at the arm of the metronome, then at me. "The boat is fast, Carrey. Ruth panicked against Dover and you were rushing the release. But it's fast." He paused. "If you wait just half a second when you tap the oar out, you and I will drive this boat over the limit."

"How do you know? How can you be so sure?"

"I'm sure. You know it, too. The others will feel the power and catch on. If you just wait, the boat will lift out of the water with each stroke. It's not a matter of showing you what to do. It's a matter of you trusting what you have to do. That's it."

"I'm going to have to take it on faith."

"And you're going to have to trust Ruth. She's the best coxswain you'll ever meet."

"*I* have to trust Ruth! I can't believe what I'm hearing. *You* didn't trust her against Dover. *You* jacked our rating sky high, twice, not Ruth. What happened to trusting the cox to control the boat? And you were the one who told her to take off her shirt. Not me."

"You didn't stop me. You blamed her for the Dover Race, too."

"Okay, I know, I blamed you both. I was mad at you for taking the rating up and at her for not calling you on it."

"So we both need to trust her. After the race I went over to Middle Dorm and left her a note. I tried to say I was sorry, but she needs to hear it from you. Why haven't you spoken to her? She expects me to be a bastard. She doesn't expect it from you."

"Believe me, I've tried speaking to her. She's totally blowing me off."

Connor sat in front of me, leaned back until he was at the oar's release. I copied him, tapped out the lamp and waited that millisecond before he moved his torso forward. I followed through and we paused for the strokes and then the recovery until we were leaning back, mirroring each other. "Let's hit thirty-five for five minutes. If you can do it here, you can follow me in the boat. I guarantee it."

"It's that simple?"

He twisted around and looked at me. "Rob, trusting something that doesn't feel right is not simple. You'll either do it or not. But if you don't try it, we're dead. That's what's simple."

"I'll do it." And I meant it.

"Ruth, wait for me."

Of course she ignored me. She had ignored me since the Dover Race. She'd made sure to abuse me on the water, but a silence had hung between us in the boathouse and now again in chemistry, the last class of the day. Students were filing out of the sulphuric labs into the warm hallways and outside into the bright sun. Ruth didn't even look back at me as I tried to catch up with her. She could move surprisingly fast when she wanted to, even carrying that heavy leather bag of hers and wearing the regulation-length skirt and shoes they forced the girls to wear. I finally got next to her and she still refused to even look at me, managed to increase her pace so I almost had to jog along beside her.

"Listen, Ruth. Wait. Please. Just hear me out. Give me five minutes of your precious time, okay?"

"I'm busy, Rob. Do you understand? I'm busy."

"You are *not*. That was the last class of the day. Practice isn't for an hour. You have five minutes."

"You have no idea how busy I am when it comes to you, Carrey. Go away."

But she slowed down just a little to hear me out. We were headed for her dorm and I gently took her elbow and guided her away, toward the island in the school parking. The trees around the school were bursting into a furious green and the omnipresent cut-grass smell was overpowering. It was Monday, the day before the Warwick Race and the kids who saw us walking together made way. Some of the freshmen high-fived both of us as I tried to steer her someplace where we could talk. She didn't look at me but she didn't pull away from me either.

We crossed the quad in front of the Schoolhouse and then passed the dining hall toward the back sports fields. The tennis courts were a giant circuit board of fenced-in red and green and white in front of the squat, gray tennis club. Some kids were already out there, warming up before practice, and I could hear the *thwack* of the balls being hit from player to player in what looked like lazy, slow-motion strikes. I had never been here, never knew that the clubhouse had a solid Plexiglas front behind which were comfortable-looking couches, a widescreen TV, soft drink machines, and pale wooden tables. The room had the privileged smell of tennis balls, and the walls were lined with rows and rows of framed pictures of kids in white, holding rackets.

"Ruth, I'm sorry about what happened after the Dover Race, I really am."

She set her mouth, looked out at the courts, back at me. "Right, Rob. You're so sorry yet you didn't even *say* anything, let alone do something. None of you did. I really thought you guys had my back. Especially you."

"I was so furious because we had lost. I wasn't thinking straight. What can I say? I was wrong. I know it."

"And you're the last one to apologize to me, you know. Even Connor's apologized. But not you."

"That's not fair. I've been trying to get you to talk to me all week, Ruth, you know I have. I'm apologizing now, okay? I really am. I should have done something. I blew it. I always blow it." I wanted her to get away from the glass, but she was immovable. I swung my backpack down onto one of the pedestal tables, unzipped it and pulled out a small, tight bundle; her rowing shirt. I handed it to her like a folded flag of surrender.

She took it from me, shook it out. I couldn't read her expression. "How did you get this?"

I didn't answer her question, ashamed to admit that the Dover cox had left it behind, disgusted by our behavior. I wished I could tell her that I had come to my senses once she had walked away, had taken it from him to give back to her, but I had not. Instead I could only promise, "No one will ask you to do it again."

"No, they will not. Because we're not going to lose again. Especially not tomorrow." She opened up her satchel and pulled out a notebook, flipped through it while she nibbled the end of a piece of her hair. I had rarely been alone with Ruth when she was in dress code. Her dark hair hung loose over her collar and she looked amazingly well put together. She found what she was looking for, a carefully compiled graph of dates and times. She pointed at yesterday's date, the Sunday that Channing had insisted we get back on the water after torturing us all Saturday morning. "Look at this. The boat really started to pick up in the middle of practice, but we started out ahead anyway."

I had gone on the water both days with the single aim of copying Connor perfectly. Saturday had passed without Channing making one comment about my efforts. The entire practice had been nerve wracking. I found myself biting the inside of my mouth to keep my recoveries slow and I knew Connor was exaggerating his releases for my benefit. On Sunday my determination seemed to start paying off. Within a few minutes of that morning practice Connor and I were matching each other stroke for stroke. Watching from the stern of his boat, Channing followed us wordlessly down the river again. The boat had not felt faster to me, but it had felt lighter.

But, as usual, Ruth had kept track of all the times, and I saw that each piece we had rowed on Sunday was incrementally faster than the one before it and definitely faster than any on Saturday and the week before. Ruth absently reached into her bag and snapped open a hard case, slipped her sunglasses on and looked at me. "At first I thought the current of the river might be helping us, and then I realized that you had found a way to follow Connor. I kept waiting for Channing to say something but he's not going to and I know why. He thinks you're doing it unconsciously and if he comments on it, you'll stop. I can't see why it's working but it's working. So keep doing it. I'd love to know how Connor finally convinced you to stop rowing like a sculler and start following him."

"I went and asked him for help. I don't want to lose this race, Ruth, just as much as you and the others don't."

"The times are fast. Channing might not trust them. He might not want to jinx this. Or he might think you'll get cocky and screw up if you know the boat is flying."

I gently pushed the notebook away. "The times don't mean anything now, Ruth. Just tell me how it feels. How does the boat feel?"

She thought. "It feels like you guys are rowing together. It feels fast. It feels like you know there's nothing to lose." She hugged the notebook to her. "Channing wants to meet us an hour or so before the race. He'll be going over all the equipment tonight and will give us last-minute instructions later. Speaking of which . . . we'd better head back. I need to eat something before practice."

"Warwick beat Brooks Academy."

"I know. By three boat lengths. I didn't even look at the times. But they were rowing on their lake—we have a current here and they won't be used to it." Kids were walking toward the courts, would be invading this weird club soon. "In just over twenty-four hours it will all be over. It won't matter anymore."

"I know."

She let me hold her hand and we walked the whole way back to her dorm in complete silence.

29.

It was raining steadily as Channing spoke to us before we laid hands on the boat. We were in the wooden meeting room next to his office where I had been inducted into the team all those months before. The small, round windows were thrown open to the mountain and overlooked the palatial tent that had been erected that morning, inhabited now by nervous parents, somber members of the Board of Trustees and pink-faced alumni of all kinds and ages ranging from the eager, recently graduated to the jaded, middle-aged-running-to-fat, to the seen-it-all-stooped-and-wrinkled, all helping themselves to drinks at the bar.

Channing had plotted the race on the blackboard and led us through every stroke. When he was finished, he looked out a window and motioned for us to come to the sill and watch the Warwick team walking their pale blue boat down to the dock, their coach and assistant coach striding assuredly behind them. There was squat, psychotic coxswain Cooper, barking orders. There was Brickman, huge and ominous in the three seat. The infamous Warwick crew—subject of our collective obsession for so long. As they stripped down in preparation for battle, I could have sworn I saw Cooper look directly up at us, although I doubt he had the vantage to see us.

Channing pointed with contempt. "Look at them. Take a good look now because I do not want any of you glancing over in the boat during the race. There they are, four arrogant young men and that disgrace of an individual they call a coxswain, the one who crashed an Empacher shell at the Head of the Charles two years ago. Look down upon them, all of you. Look upon them from a vaunted height."

Connor glowered menacingly out the window but I couldn't help noticing how impossibly thin and frail he seemed compared to Brickman. The rain suddenly blew into the room, blew out. Next to Connor, Wadsworth stood angular and awkward and Perry looked massive and unwieldy alongside Chris. Ruth hovered pale and ghostly just behind me, her mirrored sunglasses on despite the utter absence of sun. We contemplated the Warwick team, the ease and confidence with which they flipped the boat into the water, their size, their disregard for the rain, the arrogant way they ignored the small band of Warwick supporters clapping and cheering for them. All five of them were wearing identical white baseball hats to ward off the rain.

Looking at that boat, I suddenly felt like throwing up. Each rower seemed taller, stronger, more intimidating than the Dover kids. And inside that tent somewhere, where jovial laughter rose up to us with the wind, was the Harvard coach. Students dressed in slickers and rain gear were starting to line the way to the water. There would be many more of them at the finish, crowded under the shelter of trees.

Channing coughed. "They are no better than you. Their equipment is the same. They can be beaten. They can be beaten because they are so sure they *cannot* be beaten. They can be beaten because I have timed you for months now and in the last few days your times have been superior to any boat I have coached on that river. That same river that you know far better than they do,

remember. Let them lose a second on a turn, let them fail to ne-
gotiate the new current, let them misjudge the wind—our
wind—and they are done for. Look upon them and know that
their confidence in themselves is misplaced."

He glanced at us, looked us over with a kind of crazed aston-
ishment. "They know about John Perry, the strong giant on our
crew from the football team. And, oh yes, they feel fear. They
know about the indefatigable Chris Wadsworth, who like Connor and Perry, has rowed with us for four years. And they fear
this experience, too. They have heard that we have scoured the
earth and come up with a trump card in Rob Carrey, a recruit.
They have no recruits. This eats at their imaginations. They are
very aware that our coxswain is twenty pounds lighter than
theirs, has never crashed a boat into anything, and knows their
strategy as well as I do. And I can assure you that all of them
know of Connor Payne and wish they did not."

He grinned suddenly, looking at the Warwick four as they
ran their oars to the water, Cooper squatting and holding the
boat to the dock. "They have not raced in rain yet, but we have
practiced in the snow." He lowered his voice and seemed to hiss.
"This might be my last race against this particular team. And I
have never felt surer of victory."

He glanced at the rafters, as if dragging up his own memory.
"Fifteen hundred years ago, we are told, a small band of three
hundred Spartans and seven hundred allies faced an invading
army of two hundred and fifty thousand Persians. A spy was
sent out by the invading king to scout them and was astonished
to find them not cowering in fear at their imminent annihilation,
but calmly sitting upon the ground combing their hair. The Persian king was informed that this meant that the Greeks were
preparing for a fine battle. Incensed, the Persian king sent an
emissary to boast that his army was so great that the arrows of
his soldiers would blot out the sky." Channing coughed again.
"His Spartan opposite simply replied, 'Then we shall fight in the

shade.'" Channing turned to us. "But today we face enemies of equal size. We are fighting with home advantage, on a river we know by heart in difficult weather." He looked at Ruth. "Use the current when it serves, Ruth. That team has never rowed on this river when it is high. It might look flat but the current beneath is significant as you well know and Brendan Cooper will misjudge it." Channing put his back to it. "Just remember that you cannot control what they do out there. You can only control what you do. And understand that if you row your best race, they will not beat you. It is now up to you to find out what that race is. It's time, Fenton. The die is cast."

And we proceeded down the stairs to the boathouse, where inquiring lines of alumni and students peered into the darkness while we unracked the shell and followed Ruth, who walked in front of us on stick legs into the warm rain, as if we were heading out to yet anther practice. Channing stood just inside the sliding doors and I glanced at him as we passed. He was looking not at the river, but at the tent and the fields and the school and the mountains beyond.

The small crowd began to clap as we walked by. The rest of the school would be at the start, and vanloads of this group would follow down the road to the finish line as soon as we had launched. It was not a huge crowd, I observed. In the long buildup to this day it had often seemed as if the entire world would be watching, such was its import, but this was not the case. I forced myself not to smile, to focus on Ruth and pick my way carefully to the water, where we would line up against the lip of the dock, raise the boat over our heads, and flip it down to kiss the river.

The rain was falling in straight lines on the water. We were soaked through by the time we got to the stake boats to meet Warwick, when their coxswain told them to let their oars fly and they drifted in perfect precision into the waiting hands of the freshman assigned to hold their stern for the countdown. Then, eerily, the rain suddenly stopped, as if a curtain had been pulled aside, as if the weather itself was holding its breath. With the end of the rain, the water became utterly flat, a mirror to the heavens.

Despite Channing's instruction I glanced over to see our rivals glaring straight ahead for the start. Cooper was hunched deep into the boat and grumbled incessantly at his rowers. His voice sounded like the snarls and barks of a small but particularly vicious dog. Although it had now abated, rainwater still dripped from my hair down my face and down my back. I looked again at the reflection of the trees on the river and then I smiled. Ruth sighted the course, her hand up, then whispered something to Connor, who whispered something back and then turned swiftly in his seat to flash us that insane, cocky grin. Channing steered up in the coach's launch with the young Warwick coach beside him. He held the megaphone to his lips and readied the boats. Ruth lowered her hand, and then Brendan Cooper dropped his.

Channing shouted the start and we surged into the river.

Warwick had us by half a boat length within fifteen strokes and started to pull away through the first fifty. I could see their stern deck jerking back and forth in the water and Ruth screamed into the microphone and kicked the rating up. We burned into the race at an impossible cadence and took back one seat.

The boats torpedoed toward the halfway point—one thousand meters—in a suspended silence, as if the thunder clouds still threatening us above had drawn the sound from the coxswains' lungs. Ruth was almost whispering to us as we charged down the course and Cooper seemed to be yowling into his microphone. Noting that the two boats were spread apart on the water and in no danger of running into each other, the coaches sank back, farther away than they might otherwise have been.

As we took the seat back Ruth's voice, calm and almost reassuring, rose out of the boat. "We'll be dropping the rating in three."

Perry swore. To drop the rating now would mean giving up

the seat we had just taken, letting Warwick jet in front of us. I bit my lip and pulled, made myself focus on the race. All I heard was the oiled movement of the riggers, the splash of our oars on the water and the grunts and struggles of bodies depleting.

Ruth breathed carefully into the mike and said, "We *will* drop in three, and this is one . . . and this is two . . . and this is three." And the rating did drop, possibly only by two strokes a minute, although at that speed it seemed like an immense drop, and Warwick immediately snatched back their seat.

Connor held the rating. I forced myself to tap out the oar with him, mirror the movement, and hold the slide while the boat surged forward. Wadsworth and Perry hooked into the new pace, and finally, at exactly one thousand meters, we hit our stride, behind Warwick but suddenly flying. One hundred strokes to go, and it felt as if the boat had found some kind of grace, like a giant bird expanding its wings and folding them against the sky. Ruth would have been looking at the speed of the boat when she spoke into the mike. "You will not increase the rating but you will give me ten hard strokes in three."

And she counted down, and the desire to rush the slide and grab back the seat, for me, was almost irresistible. I willed myself to follow the agonizingly slow rating and when we dug in, the boat seemed to surge out of the water. I glimpsed Ruth crouching down into her seat to avoid being thrown backward with each stroke.

We had not made the seat back. Warwick remained ahead.

I felt the first stirrings of panic. We had barely held on to them through the power ten. In the next hundred strokes we might have three more power tens in us and a sprint over the finish line. Ruth jetted the rudder, tried another route, pushing the boat closer to Warwick as she did so. The move gained us perhaps half a meter on their boat, but as we neared the Warwick four we could hear the excitement in Cooper's voice as he held us off and bore down on the last five hundred meters of the race. Water, or sweat, or both, ran into my eyes and I blinked it away, tried to focus on Connor, to grit my teeth through the maddeningly slow rating.

Cooper screeched into the mike, insulting Ruth as we neared his boat. "Back off, Fenton, don't touch our oars." But Ruth held her course, our oars less than two meters away from theirs now, enough for the coach's boat to churn closer and for Channing to lean forward, ready to ward us off them. Even one small touch of the oars would skew the result, possibly nullify the race, and we were as close now as either coach would allow.

Cooper was sitting just level with me and I could see him glancing down the course and then over at us. I realized that they had never been held this long and that he was desperate to sight the five hundred meter buoy; that Ruth knew this and that Connor would catch scent of their fear and it would electrify us.

Then Ruth's cool voice. "Power through in ten, and rating up one in three." Bringing that rating up was pure relief and as she counted I knew the others wanted to drive it up even higher, but that one beat a minute was enough to pull us further into Warwick, enough so that I could see Cooper perfectly now, leaning back against the drive of his boat, startled that we had driven almost level in just ten strokes. He called for a power ten as we cruised by the five hundred meter buoy, a sure sign that he had been waiting to pull out another burst of power.

I yearned for Ruth to match him, but she forced us to wait again as we took back half a seat, and only then, "Power twenty, Fenton, to pass them in three. And that's one . . ."

She wasn't changing the rating. We were running at possibly thirty strokes a minute and Cooper would have jammed his boys up five strokes higher. If we were going to pass Warwick we had to mine it, using our strength only, and we dug deeply into each one as she counted. After the first three strokes the boat felt unnaturally heavy, like it was filled with sand or water. I grit my teeth and pulled, and by the end of the fifth stroke I knew that the heaviness was the acceleration of the boat, its natural resistance to a sudden increase in speed. Our combined weights had to catch up to the boat's propulsion; the same problem a bird faced becoming airborne, looking for liftoff. By our tenth stroke Cooper was already on his fifteenth, gibbering into his mike, almost standing up.

"Twenty-five more strokes to go, Fenton," Ruth intoned, almost offhandedly. "Step on it."

Almost imperceptibly, Connor increased his length yet further. Ruth powered us into it and for the next ten strokes we flew like we knew we were able to. We reached a crescendo of speed and the exhilaration behind our exhaustion was something to cling to.

And then Connor grunted and pulled five impossibly strong strokes; a silent push that Cooper would not expect or hear, that Ruth could never ask of him, that he knew we would follow. It was as if we had caught the boat a millisecond ahead of the rating and launched it out of the river. I felt the bones of my vertebrae grate together through each one of those scrapes of the water. Cooper responded to the move too late and howled. Our oars reached out into the final gap that lay before the finish of the race. I rowed through a blue haze of exhaustion, deaf to Ruth's banshee countdown of the last ten strokes as we tore through them.

We crossed the line and leaned back into the warm exhalation of the fresh breeze. Gasping for oxygen, I looked to the port shore and there was Wendy standing apart from the crowd, waving at me for a perfect moment before she vanished into the insane bellow of the students who had braved the broken weather to witness the Fenton God Four defeat Warwick by the length of a human body.

30.

This is what I told the police later. The race took place on Tuesday, as was the tradition. After Channing had raised his arm signaling the end of the contest, we rowed to the dock and collected our shirts, an exhausted, oddly somber quintet shaking hands with an equally depleted and noticeably diminished Warwick. To the Fenton crowd's delight, Connor accepted a tarnished silver trophy—the cherished Tuesday Cup—that would be proudly and prominently displayed in the dean's office for the next year. We threw Ruth in the water, as was also the tradition, and jumped in after her, which was not. Drunk and euphoric alumni sprayed us with champagne and we were hardly able to move through the crowd to put the boat back. There was a party for us at Fenton afterward and then various dinners in town. We were finally able to revel in our victory. The Payne family held court for the entire crew at the Fox and Fiddle Inn. Channing did not come out at all. He had been whisked away almost immediately after the race by the headmaster and whoever else funded the machine that was Fenton. In his absence and on Connor's father's tab, all five of us got thoroughly drunk, quickly intoxicated by the potent mix of expensive alcohol of various kinds and our own success.

Early on in the evening, I stole away from the fracas to call home with the news from the phone in the coatroom of the inn. But when my father took my call in his workshop I found I had no idea what to say, other than we had won a very important race. He waited, and then said, "That's not news, son. That's business as usual, as far as we're concerned. What did they expect?"

I tried to tell him about the significance of the race, about the Harvard coach conferring with Channing in the boathouse and then shaking all of our hands. I described the near riot in the spectator's tent when the students came back from the finish line. I wanted him to be able to picture Channing's face as I had glimpsed it when we poured ourselves over the finish; the way he had thrown the megaphone out of the boat and hugged himself before punching the sky that was swollen with the rain that would fall upon us as we rowed back ahead of the crushed Warwick boat. But the race was over, and my father was too far away, and I was on a pay phone with the time running out. "It's a big win, Dad. The most important one. I wanted you to know." I knew he'd take my word for it, but he'd disbelieve that the race would change my life, and in that he was wrong.

I hung up the phone and went back into the dining room of the inn to find that the team had moved away from the main table and was sitting outside on the porch. The celebrations were winding down. Connor had brought along an ice bucket and champagne. A tray of glistening champagne glasses, all perfectly full, stood in the middle of the table. Jumbo had brought his own bottle out of which he was taking generous slugs while slumped back in his seat. He offered it to me as I sat down, smiling crookedly, and I took it by the neck, swallowed what was left.

"We did it. We did it by half a length." Jumbo grinned at the table. Then at the stars.

Ruth reached out, placed a glass of champagne in front of her.

Wadsworth was drinking, amazingly, a Coke. Perry prodded him. "The rest of the year will be a cakewalk. When the other schools hear we took down Warwick, they will fall at our feet. They will beg for mercy. The poor *bastards*." Jumbo reached over to Connor's bottle, helped himself to a long draught. Connor regarded him with a rare half smile. Was he really wearing a white dinner jacket? Connor took up his own champagne flute, examined the liquid within as if counting the bubbles.

Wadsworth snatched the bottle from Perry. "Careful, big guy. Even if we did win the Warwick Race, we're still not supposed to come back to campus completely blotto."

Perry laughed. "Let them try to kick me out. They wouldn't dare. We're untouchable. Remember? We're Gods! Gods are *not* expelled!"

Ruth laughed. "Some 'god'. Look at you. Drunkard. We have another race coming up, Jumbo."

"Yeah? Bring it." Perry burped, grabbed back the bottle from Wadsworth and stood unsteadily, held it aloft in his paw. "Here's to the flat water on the Tuesday race. Here's to defeating Warwick. Finally. Here's to flat water Tuesday!"

Connor grunted, put up his glass. "Flat water Tuesday it is." And we all drank to it.

But then Connor stood and held up his half-full glass before us again. "And let's also have a toast to all that comes next." We all looked at him expectantly. He thought for a few seconds. "What does come next? Could anything possibly come after the Warwick Race? Oh, yes! There's the Exeter Race, The Holy Spirit Race, The Andover Race, etcetera, etcetera, till the end of the season. Then the National Championships." He paused. I did not like to hear the bitter tone in his voice. "Then we graduate. But don't worry. There's plenty more to look forward to. Here's to making the Harvard heavy eight. Ladies and gentlemen, I give you The Head of the Charles and The Head of the Schuylkill! And let's not forget the good old Harvard–Yale Race." He drank off the glass, took the bottle from Jumbo, poured his glass full again, drank a sip, held it before him. "Then hoist up your loving cups to the National Team selection camp. After that, we can all drink a last one to . . . the Olympics!"

Connor drained the glass and flung it against the wall of the inn, where it shattered into tiny, glinting shards. He collapsed into his chair. "Maybe then my dad will be happy. I'll have definitely shown him." He raised his hand for the waiter, pointed at the bottle, spun his finger round. Gazing straight ahead, he said, "Drink up, Fenton School Boat Club. The drinks, and the laughs, are on me."

Silence descended. Connor contemplated the remaining glasses scattered across the table; pieces in a game he was endlessly playing against an adversary only he could see. On that evening, you could look in on the five privileged kids sitting in the light spilling out of the dining room sharing a careless pensive moment while Connor regarded a future of infinite competition. I knew for sure that rowing was slowly coming to an end for me, that the race against Warwick had been a kind of coda to this segment of my life, a part of my life that had been closing for months now. Looking around the table, I became aware that I was not alone. Ruth and Wadsworth both seemed suddenly older; they looked at this evening with a kind of bemused irony, as if they had walked into a party they had not been invited to but to which they had been warmly welcomed. And Perry had always been an outsider to this, perhaps even more than I. Whatever I had to prove to Connor had been proven. It was clear to me that Connor had no such release. He would always be looking for the next stretch of water to prove himself on, always searching for the last test, the final selection, the ultimate victory. And each triumph for him, I knew, would mean less and less, until that day when he stood alone with his laurels, all the cheering and applause forever silenced by an adulthood which was closing in upon him; the searching, relentless bow of a boat he could never leave in the golden wake of his glorious youth.

And then the waiter came with yet another linen-wrapped bottle and another set of glasses. Jumbo plucked it off the waiter's tray and twisted the cork out of it in one massive turn, spilling an amber froth down his wrist and arm. "Hell, I'll drink to that."

Connor grinned. I held out my own glass, he held out his. Ruth found hers. Even Wadsworth partook.

———

School had to continue. The crowds dispersed. The Payne family and other parents left us at the dorms and disappeared back into New York and Cape Cod and elsewhere. The tent was taken down. We had classes and the next race, against Exeter, to think about. It was scheduled to take place on the following Friday. We had a week and a half to recover and prepare. Channing had decreed that we could have the Wednesday following the Warwick Race off, but that we had to go for a light run to ward off the effects of our revelry the night before.

Connor was the one who enforced this decision. Naturally.

Rain continued to fall on Tuesday night and on and off on Wednesday. We gathered at the boathouse after classes ended and stood in the doorway to wait for it to stop. Sore and stiff with lactic acid from the exertions of the race, sluggish and bloated from the rich food we had gorged ourselves on and hungover as all hell from who knows what combination of drinks we had downed, we were all, even Ruth—especially Ruth—hoping that Connor would tell us to forget it. Channing hadn't appeared to see if we would actually do the run. As usual, it was a matter of honor, of the sport's relentless probing of a rower's pain threshold. The river was dotted with endless dimples of raindrops over raindrops. Detritus lazily spun and flowed in the brown water. The close, muggy heat exacerbated our discomfort.

Miserable and desperate to get it over with, we initiated a communal lope through the drizzle. Connor led, Ruth pushed a tight pace next to a flat-footed and wheezing Perry, who pounded beside Wadsworth. We were slow, the efforts and indulgences of the day before had taken their toll.

Connor ran well. I took up the pace behind him, then ran alongside him. We had pulled away from the others when the covered bridge appeared at the end of the road, a yawning cavern. The two of us knifed through the rain until we reached its darkness. I sprinted by him to find that the floor of the bridge was dry. Wadsworth jogged into the bridge's mouth, then Perry, then Ruth, Ruth's breaths coming in quick rasps. She was soaked through. Her hair hung long and wet and crazy around her face. A witch's hair. Her eyes were red rimmed from the run and you could see the lines of blue veins in her hands as she stood there, clenching and unclenching her fingers. She was wearing running shorts and a Fenton T-shirt. Her heaving chest was almost as flat as mine.

Connor looked directly at Perry. "Rob beat me but we still kicked your fat ass, Jumbo."

"Good for you, dude."

Connor spat over the side of the bridge, then got up onto the rail and stared into the mist and the river. He spat again and turned, his eyes roving over us. "The river's high now, it's deeper."

Wadsworth looked at him evenly from his side of the bridge. "Get off the railing, Connor," he said. "Get off now." And I heard it for sure. The irritation of a mature person dealing with a kid.

Connor looked at him. "C'mon, Wads. I want to make the jump. I'm thinking there'll never be a better time. We could all do it. A victory leap. We can do anything now."

Perry looked at Connor evenly, stood up to his full height. Connor was gently swinging himself back and forth over the water, forward and back, supported by the bridge strut. He was humming, a tuneless song that rose and fell in the dark. The rain blew into the bridge. Finally Perry said, simply, "Do it, then. Why don't you just jump? I am so sick of hearing you talk about it."

Connor looked at Perry, surprised. "I know I can make it."

Ruth crouched down on the other end of the bridge, hugging her bare legs. It was cold now, the humid heat not reaching us in here. She said, "Jumbo's right. I can't do this today, Connor. I think I'm going to throw up. Just jump. See what you're made of. Jump or get down and let's go back." She hugged her legs harder.

Perry smiled and for Ruth's benefit said, "He's just a lot of talk."

Connor continued to hum, then began whistling just as tunelessly. It echoed in the bridge's interior and sounded like wind. He looked at me. "And what do you think, Roberto?"

It was infuriating, the way he simply did not give up, or change. Here we were, the five us, having shared that conversion on the water. Performed a miracle. But it was never enough. Not for him. So what I said was, "I don't care, Connor. None of us do. Do you know what this is? This is a joke that's been told once too often."

Connor looked at Wadsworth. "What'll you give me if I jump?"

Ruth groaned loudly and Wadsworth began stretching for the run back. He shrugged. "What will I *give* you? Seriously? Jump, Connor. We don't give a shit anymore."

Connor looked slowly at each of us and his face split into that cocky grin of his. I would later come to think of it as a smile of benediction. Still grinning, he took an easy step backward and plummeted into the rain.

31.

I drove past crisp, green fields ringed by mountains as I approached Fenton. The campus looked serene and sedate, abandoned, as I drove toward it, the chapel protruding above the rest of the buildings. I glanced in the direction of the boathouse but could not make it out yet. I passed the modern field house and the football fields, then the practice fields, and finally arrived at the walled entrance of the school. It had been enlarged since I was here, and also modernized a little bit—the old-fashioned wrought-iron gates replaced with what looked to me like lighter weight, decorative ones that were never closed. The road leading into the school dipped and then found its way upward, and I drove by a few of the year-round ground staff walking along the flagstones beside the administrative buildings. There was a banner stretched over the road between the trees, welcoming back our class and two others, one ten years behind us, one ten years ahead. I pulled into the packed main lot and parked next to a Volvo with a PROUD FENTON FAMILY sticker on the back window. I switched off the engine and remained in the car, staring out at the river that was deep blue, almost black, murky and ever shifting. I never thought I would see it again.

I had a program for the day I had downloaded off the Web site. There were a series of presentations in the morning, which I had missed, and a lunch in the dining hall that I had also missed. A slide show and talk were in progress, with a break scheduled in one of the common rooms. I walked through the parking lot and didn't see anyone at all, then turned toward the labs and made my way up the stairs and through the open front doors where student desks had been pushed together to form a kind of ad-hoc registration area. A woman wearing a bright pink polo shirt and pearls smiled brightly when I approached. A stick-on name tag curved over her right breast: "Hi! I'm Charlotte" and her year of graduation, which was after mine. An alumnae volunteer.

"It's great to see so many members of your class here," she noted enthusiastically as I signed in and accepted a registration packet.

"I haven't been back in a while."

"Well, you can get a beer in the common area of North Dorm. Do you remember where that is?" She was aggressively friendly in a PR kind of way. She'd have a firm, eager handshake, I thought.

"I remember."

"Good!" Big smile. Then she looked at me expectantly and I started to walk away.

The smell from the labs had not changed, a smell of students and chemicals and preserved, dead things. It brought back unpleasant memories of standardized tests and dissections. I looked at the next day's schedule for my reason for being here, and found it. It read, "Chapel Service: 9:00 A.M."

I considered going into the common room of North Dorm, thought better of it, and headed for the stairs. I found my assigned room on the first floor, a room that had been occupied by a kid named David Kenner when I'd gone to Fenton. His name had escaped me until I opened the door. Someone had neatly piled clean sheets and cotton blankets on the lower mattress of the bunk bed pushed into the corner of the room. A photocopied schedule identical to the one I had downloaded was on one of the two small desks. I sat down on the lower bunk and felt the springs give in the mattress, and then give some more. I'd wake up sore tomorrow, I could already tell.

It was hot and stuffy in the room and I opened the window. Written in pencil, next to the window, was a list of numbers. Below them, the writer had scrawled in neat, sloping handwriting, "Jill Dopkins Has a Great Ass." He'd written it there as if to remind himself of the fact.

I had a great view of the river and of the soccer fields. Two kids would make their home here next year. It seemed impossibly small, like a prison cell, but this would be one of the more desirable rooms. The mattress in the bunk above me was rolled up in a ball. I would not have a roommate tonight, I noted with relief.

There was no phone in the room and my cell phone was out of juice, of course, since I hadn't charged it the night before. I took it out, plugged it in, and left it on the tiny desk. I walked back out into the hallway and looked for a pay phone—every dorm used to have pay phones at the end of the halls—but perhaps they were considered redundant now. I found one installed in a disused closet and crammed into the small, confined area. There was no light switch, so I let the door hang open and called the city. I punched in my credit card number and finally the phone rang in the studio. Carolyn picked up after five rings, and when she did she sounded tired, and annoyed.

"I'm here."

"Is it like you remember?"

"Smaller. Smellier."

"Where are you sleeping?"

"They gave me a dorm room."

"That sounds horrible."

"It will be fine for one night." I paused, trying to think of what to say next, wanting her to stay on the line.

"What's wrong?"

"Nothing. Everything. How is the edit?"

"The sound on one of the interviews is fucked up. But some parts are usable. You have to test that LAV mike, Rob. I think one of the channels isn't recording."

An awkward silence again. "Thanks. Thanks for dealing with that." I paused, then added, "I miss you."

She waited. "Do you?"

"Yes." And it was true. I had a strong urge to go and fetch my bag, to just leave the registration pack in the room, get in the car and drive away. "The memorial service is first thing tomorrow. I'll call you right after before I take off."

"You don't have to. But, good. Okay." There was resignation in her voice. I told her I had to go and she said that's fine, and hung up. I stayed on the line a few seconds longer, studying the initials hacked into the black metal paint. Someone had written on the door: "1-800-GOD-FOUR."

———————

The next item on the reunion program was a talk by the head-master about the importance of a prep school education in the new millennium. I just wasn't up for it. Instead, I returned to my room, pulled a towel and shaving kit out of my bag and headed for the showers in the boys' bathroom down the hall. The shower rooms and sinks were surprisingly clean. There were no mold and spit stalactites in evidence anywhere, although the school might have made a special effort for the alumni visit and removed them. I shaved in one of the sinks and when I was finished, I went back to my room half-naked, the towel around my waist, and got dressed. I chose a black shirt and crisp chinos, a canvas belt and boat shoes. I'd play the part. I checked my watch: 4:00 P.M. Practice time.

I decided to walk over to the Schoolhouse, the humid heat of the New England summer making me break out into an immediate sweat. The dining hall had been modernized and enlarged. The library had grown an extension. There were more, and better, computers, in fact a huge computer center with lines of flat screens. A writing center was attached to the English department now. It was locked. I looked in the narrow window and saw rows of tables. They looked like conference tables, the kind you find in college workshops. The old wooden desks were long gone. The blackboard had been replaced with a whiteboard and I could see an overhead projector in there.

Channing didn't last much longer after our year. They ran an article about his retirement in the alumni magazine, which my parents continued to receive for years after I had left the school. The article mentioned his contributions to the rowing team and to the English department. He had retired from teaching to pursue his many other, varied interests. The article did not elaborate on what those other interests were. A few years after that, my brother made a rare long-distance call to me in New Guinea, where I had been filming the ghost fleet at the bottom of the Truk Lagoon, to say he'd happened to read that Channing had died and there would be a service at the school for him. He'd faxed me the article, which was entitled *Charles Channing, An Appreciation*, and featured a picture of him at Henley, and another black-and-white, staged shot of him, much younger, teaching. The students in the picture looked interested and engaged with no hint of terror in their faces. The article did not specify how he had died, or if it had been unexpected. There were quotes from a few former students and one from the headmaster praising his commitment and dedication to the great tradition of Fenton rowing.

I walked down the hallway to the stairs and then out of the building onto the impossibly green quad. The doors to the new auditorium were flung open and people were milling out. For a fleeting moment I thought they were students, and then I realized they were, of course, alumni. I stood on the grass verge and braced myself. I tried to recognize faces, sifted through the thinning hair, the loose-fitting sundresses, the strollers and sensible shoes and toddlers and tucked-in polo shirts. America's executives on a weekend outing.

I waited until I saw her, and I recognized her before she recognized me.

———

Ruth and Perry stayed with Connor while Wadsworth and I sprinted back to the school, the two of us clicking off three back-to-back six-minute miles in the rain.

We ran to the admissions office, of all places, the first building with a phone, and told them there'd been an accident and we needed to call Mr. Channing at home. The office was quiet and sedate and tastefully decorated to look like the living area of an expensive house. This gave parents the impression that they were sending their kids off to a kind of refined New England resort, not drafting them into a low-level war.

We exploded into this usually serene space and stood there dripping water and mud all over the well-treated wood floor. We were wild-eyed, shaking and incoherent at first. Frantic. The woman behind the reception desk looked at us with what might have been terror or incredulity. Admissions officers didn't deal with students after the tuition check had been signed—we were invaders. Our commotion brought the head of admissions, Mr. Mantisorri, out from his office with his glasses down his nose and his bow tie askew. He immediately demanded to know what we thought we were doing, and it was Wadsworth who said,

"There's been an accident . . . an emergency . . . and we need to call Mr. Channing, right now." That had been our only plan: Call Channing first. We had no idea what would happen beyond that.

"What on earth has happened?"

The receptionist held up the phone and I realized I had no idea what Channing's number was. I asked her to look it up. My lips had turned blue and I was trembling violently. While she looked up the number, Mr. Mantisorri came over to us and said, quietly, "We'll call Mr. Channing. Just tell me what's wrong."

"A student has drowned, sir," Wadsworth replied. He was unnaturally composed. "You should call an ambulance. And we have to call Mr. Channing. Please."

He nodded once to the woman, who dialed the number and held the phone out to both of us. I was the one who took it. Channing came on after four or five rings.

"Channing."

I opened my mouth but I couldn't get it out.

"Hello?"

I tried again. I took a breath, a long audible breath, and Wadsworth looked at me quizzically, impatiently, and mouthed, "What?"

"Who is this?"

Finally, "Mr. Channing, Connor fell off the covered bridge and I think he's dead." My voice didn't sound like mine.

The line cracked in the rain. "Carrey? Is that you?"

"Yeah. Yes, Coach, it is."

"Repeat what you just said."

I whispered into the receiver. "I think he's dead. Mr. Channing, I'm pretty sure—"

"Carrey. Listen to me. Listen to me carefully. Where are you?"

"In the admissions office."

"Where is he?"

"Who?"

"Connor Payne, where is he?"

"Jumbo and Ruth are with him, near the covered bridge, on the school side of the river."

A pause. "Have Mr. Mantisorri place a call to the headmaster, and tell them exactly what you told me."

"I already have. Mr. Channing?"

But he had clicked off. The receptionist ushered us into Mr. Mantisorri's office. He was on the phone to the sheriff, urgently explaining where the covered bridge was. The headmaster and paramedics had already been notified. A paramedic team arrived from the town within minutes.

We were put into the ambulance and Mr. Mantisorri directed the paramedics back to the bridge. The vehicle's sirens were off. Its lights flashed red, blue, white while the headlights alternated. It took longer to drive than I would have thought. Mr. Mantisorri kept saying, "It's all right. Everything's going to be fine, boys."

But everything was not fine. Connor's body was in the overgrown grass by the water. Ruth and Perry were kneeling near him, Ruth in the same crouch she'd been in on the bridge, Perry as if in prayer. When he saw the lights of the ambulance Perry stood up and stumbled toward us. He was pushed aside by the paramedics, who ran down to Connor carrying what looked to me like a toolbox and an oversized tackle box. One of the men stripped off his jacket and hunched over the body, breathed into it, and then pushed on the stomach.

The sheriff appeared in a brown Dodge. I can't remember what Perry said to me, if anything. Mr. Mantisorri walked over to Ruth and helped her up. She was pale and shaking and kept saying she was fine and not to touch her. When she saw Wadsworth and me she burst into tears and came over and folded herself into me, keening sobs racking through her. We stood there and watched them work over Connor's rag-doll form. After a while they covered his face and lifted his body onto a stretcher. Ruth was still clinging to me when Channing and the dean arrived and got us out of there.

———

Even though we told them all what had happened, several times, the police insisted on formal and separate interviews. When we arrived back at school, Ruth was gently led away by a police-woman to her dorm to shower, warm up and change. Wadsworth and I were also told to get cleaned up and dry and to report to the headmaster's study as soon as we had finished. Perry was taken directly to the infirmary. I didn't know why then, but he was treated for hypothermia and shock. Later I'd learn Ruth had to be treated for shock as well. That meant they gave you a ma-jor pill, a true-blue chill pill.

The sheriff interviewed me first with the headmaster, dean, and Mr. Channing present. The headmaster seemed extremely uncomfortable and made it clear he wanted the interview to be over as quickly as possible. The dean didn't say a single word and just sat there looking shell-shocked. Channing was still wearing his rain gear over his faded khakis and his boots, and looked as if he had aged by ten years. He had the presence of mind to point out that I had a choice; I was entitled to refuse the interview. I should take my time to decide. I was nineteen years old—no longer a minor—but Channing also reminded me that the school was still acting *in loco parentis*. I agreed to answer the sheriff's questions.

He asked me to describe events from our meeting at the boat-house, through the run and our stop for shelter on the covered bridge. He tried to have me explain in detail about why Connor had jumped on the railing but Channing interjected. "The boy was behaving immaturely and recklessly. That's it."

Did anyone tell Connor Payne to get off the railing? *Yes.*

Did Connor Payne routinely engage in this sort of dangerous behavior in front of his friends? *No.*

Was anyone else on the railing with or near Connor Payne? *No.*

Why was I so sure Connor Payne had jumped off the bridge and not slipped? *He told us he was going to jump and we saw him do it.*

He told us and we watched him do it? Why did no one stop him? *He had said he wanted to make the jump on several occasions, but never did. We didn't think he would ever actually do it.*

Why had none of us reported Connor's suicidal behavior to one of our teachers? *We didn't think he was suicidal. It was just something he always did, almost a tradition, a ritual. Connor would hop onto the railing and say he would like to make the jump. We would all say it was impossible. He would insist it wasn't. We would tell him to get down and, eventually, he always did and we'd run back to the boathouse.*

On and on and on until the headmaster objected.

The sheriff nodded and then looked at me. "When Connor Payne jumped off the bridge he was on the side facing the school, am I right?"

"That's right."

"His body was downstream, had traveled under the bridge and then into the rocks. How did he get to the shore?"

"I pulled him in. Jumbo helped me."

"Jumbo?"

Channing interjected again. "John Perry. He was with Ruth Anderson when Robert and Chris reported the accident, Frank."

The headmaster shifted in his seat and cleared his throat in an irritated way. The sheriff was running out of time.

"Okay, Robert, we're almost done here. I need to be clear about something. Before you ran down to the river, did you actually *see* the body when it came out the other side of the bridge, carried by the current?"

"Yes."

Another pause, another scratch in his notebook. He looked at me, and then his eyes flickered over to Channing, and I knew damn well what was coming.

The sheriff finally asked it. "Do you think Connor Payne was alive after he splashed down?"

Channing exploded. "For the love of God, Frank, what more do you want from this kid?"

The headmaster stood up and said, "This interview is over, Sheriff. Robert Carrey has more than co-operated with you and needs time now to recover from this very traumatic incident."

The sheriff shut his notebook in acquiescence but all four adults continued to look at me.

I looked back at them, and shook my head.

32.

Wadsworth's interview went pretty much the same as mine. The girl's dean terminated Ruth's before it even started. Incoherent and clearly traumatized, she was in no state to be interrogated. Perry spoke briefly to the headmaster and to Channing in the infirmary, but I never found out what he said. Our parents were called and we were all sent home for a week. We missed the race against Exeter. The JV four stood in for us, and lost, but not disgracefully. Ruth and Perry agreed to be questioned in the presence of a lawyer once they were sufficiently recovered, and that was it. Nobody ever asked me for another interview. I spent most of my time at home sleeping. Of course I spoke to my parents about what had happened and they were concerned about me but there was only so much comfort they could provide about the death of someone else's child.

Everyone in the school knew what had happened within a day or so. The headmaster made an announcement in chapel—Connor had drowned in a tragic and regrettable accident—but the rumors about us had already flown around. Upon our return,

Fenton held a memorial service and Connor's family attended. They filed into the front of the chapel in dark, well-cut suits and frozen expressions and none could hold my eye when I glanced at each of them from my pew. Were these really the people who loomed so large in his life? They seemed too ordinary. Perfectly groomed and obviously wealthy, yes, but nothing like the monsters of my imagination. There were two parents, each with new deferential partners, and the matriarchal grandmother in ivory and black. They glanced around the chapel discretely and they looked, if anything, perplexed. The only thing I knew for sure was that they clearly had not known their son and grandson.

Connor was buried in Osterville. We heard about it from Channing. It was a private service.

We all spent ten days off the water. I had no idea how the others were doing or what they were feeling. We did not contact each other while we were at home, and we did not sit together on the day of the memorial service. Later in the week, I had had enough. I walked down to Middle Dorm and knocked on the window until Mrs. Horeline came to the door and gave me the same look the rest of the teachers had been giving me since my return—a mixture of pity and contempt. I asked if she could get Ruth and she disappeared into the building. I waited on the stairs for a while and finally Ruth came down. She was wearing jeans and a button-down shirt and loafers. She opened the door and stepped out into the sunlight, blinking.

We didn't speak to each other right away. Instead, we walked into town, past the Station Shop and the Fox and Fiddle to the diner. We sat at a table, alone, near the window, looking out into the main road of Fenton at the Jeeps and BMWs from the city. We ordered coffee. She drank hers black and I dumped sugar and milk into mine. She was wearing makeup, I realized, just a little. A clear gloss shone on her lips and her cheeks were rosy with a hint of blush. Her dark hair was loose but swept back off her face with a tortoiseshell comb. Her green eyes looked huge, intense, haunted. She was beautiful. Sitting there I could not think of her screaming obscenities at us in the boathouse.

She had brought a purse with her into town, the first time I'd seen her with one of those as well. She unzipped it, dug around and fished out a piece of paper that she handed to me wordlessly. She watched my face as I read it. It was from Yale, an acceptance letter. I wasn't sure how to react or what to say. I read it to the end—the words of congratulation, the invitation to come to the school—and then I folded it twice and set it between us.

"I knew you'd get in. I knew it."

"It came today. You're the first person I've told."

I couldn't help myself. "Have you heard from Harvard?"

She waved her hand at the room, dismissing rowing, us, Harvard, everything. "I don't think I will, Rob. I think I'm going to Yale and I'm allowed to be happy about it."

"I'm happy for you."

"What are your plans?"

"I have no idea. Really, no idea at all."

"The police asked me a bunch of questions."

"Me, too."

"Have they said anything else to you?"

"Nope. It doesn't matter, anyway. We told them what happened."

She looked at her coffee, sipped it, looked at the table next to us, at the waitress by the serving counter, then at me. "Did we?"

"Yes, we did. I did. Whatever I left out, they wouldn't understand. We've got nothing to hide, Ruth. I wouldn't care if they interviewed me again."

"They wouldn't dare."

"Are you still going to cox the four?"

"I don't know. Channing sent me a note. He's moving Phil Leonsis up from the JV boat into the bow and Wads will move to stroke. Perry will stay at two and you'll still be the three seat.

If that doesn't work they'll put you on the stroke seat. I haven't written Channing back."

"You should."

She shrugged, looked at me, her eyes different than only a minute ago. "I keep seeing Connor, Carrey. Lying there. You two left us with him, you jerks. Perry had no idea what to do. I didn't either."

"He was gone when I got him out of the water."

She thought about that, nodded. "He was. There was nothing we could have done."

"Absolutely nothing. And that's the end of it. You have to believe it and try and put it behind you." *Why did I sound so angry?* "I'm going to tell Perry and Wadsworth I want to row again. I want them to row again, too. And I want you to cox us."

"That's a lot of wants, Rob."

"We worked hard this year, Ruth. I've never been on a faster boat. Connor or no Connor."

"You don't know that for sure. We haven't rowed without him yet." Her eyes teared up as she said it and instead of compassion I felt another flash of rage that I swallowed with the last gulp of my coffee.

"It seems kind of silly now, doesn't it? This dumb, prep-school thing."

I looked around the restaurant quickly, then at her. "That's not why we have to keep rowing. And you know it."

She finished her coffee, looked at the cup and looked at me, set the cup in the saucer. "Have you ever really wanted a drink, Rob?"

"You mean a real drink? I've wanted one pretty badly, sure. But I've never *needed* one, yet."

"I think I could really use one right about now."

We walked back onto campus, Ruth next to me, close, but we were already separating from each other. I could feel it. That letter in her purse meant that she was free from here in five or six weeks. I studied her and admitted to myself that in the end we had nothing in common except rowing and a secret. And the fact that maybe she knew I'd loved her from the first time I saw her. But that was plenty. When we got to her dorm I glanced in the window. Horeline wasn't at her desk. I took Ruth's hand and pushed open the door. She pulled away, looked behind her, then back at me. "I think you read my mind, Carrey."

"I hope so."

"Just be careful with me, okay?"

———

She hasn't changed much, I tell myself as we walk toward each other on the long, green expanse of lawn. Put her into the school dress code, give her back that famous leather satchel of hers, and she might be able to pass for eighteen again, at least from a distance. As I neared her I saw the signs of age. Her face had matured, had become, if possible, more beautiful. Her hair, still dark, was swept back from her ears and her eyes were still intense and piercingly green. She'd always been poised, and she came toward me with the confident gait of a woman used to being watched. She looked casually elegant in a black, sleeveless sweater, choker string of pearls, white Bermuda shorts, and flat, black patent sandals. She smiled when she saw me and we hugged, close, her body firm and reedlike in my arms.

After our embrace she continued to hold onto me, as if to confirm I was really there. Her hands were the hands of an older woman, but they were the same hands, with carefully manicured fingernails now rather than ragged cuticles. It was startling how fine and smooth her skin was. It felt good to see her again.

When we began to talk, I realized we were doing it while walking away from the rest of the class—the surreptitiousness of the past coming back to us, unconsciously.

"I'm so glad you made it back, Rob," she said. "It's not a bad weekend. I'm handling it."

I gave her a sideways look. She shrugged. "I am. You don't get to do these things too often. I'll never have a fifteenth re-union again. And I have to say it, the school looks good."

"True. I can't believe how much we hated it back then."

"You hate everything at that age. Nothing's cool."

"Have you been here since the start of the activities?"

"I have. I'll admit it. It's mostly been the hard sell on the quali-ties and growth and values of the school, you know, all that stuff, but I guess if I ever have kids, I'd be happy to send them here." She smiled again, ruefully. "Although the having kids part is starting to seem less and less likely."

It was an opening but I wasn't sure I was ready to exchange that information yet. Neither of us had good news for the other in that department, it could wait. They'd give us booze soon and we'd get into it then. She looked at me. "Chris Wadsworth didn't make it. He sent me an e-mail and said there was no way. His wife had a baby ten days ago or something. Or so he claims."

"Where is he living?"

"He's in Florida. In Tampa. So it's a plane ride for him, not just a few hours in the car."

The school has many quiet nooks. Benches under trees with vantage points into the mountains. I didn't remember these—when you're a teenager there's no time to sit.

She was half my size, I realized. A very tiny woman. Her voice had a huskiness to it I did not recall. We sat for a few beats in silence, me thinking that I was looking at a woman who had become, essentially, the person she'd envisioned she'd be in high school. I envied that.

She said, "I have to say one thing, I never saw you going into the film industry."

"It's not really the film industry the way you think of it. It's documentary film. We're more highbrow, which means we don't make much money."

"It sounds exciting. I never could see you in a suit, Carrey."

"I couldn't either."

"You get to travel all over the world, I guess. That must be something."

"It's better when you're just out of college, or film school."

"Did you go to film school?"

"No." I laughed. "Can you see me trying to pass a class in film theory or postmodern cinema? I came into it by mistake. I needed money and I wanted to see the world and a crew was hiring."

"Another crew." She reached into her shorts, pulled out a soft pack of Marlboros, and gave me a guilty look. "Do you mind?"

"Christ, no."

"It's such a dumb habit. So dumb. I started the minute I got into law school. I've quit a few times, naturally. Then I took it up again about six months ago. I think because of the stress of leaving my husband. I'm weak."

"I've never thought of you as weak."

"I'm a lawyer and yet I never realized, at, you know, a kinetic level, the toll of a divorce. It goes on forever. Never get divorced, it truly sucks."

"How long were you married?"

"We got married six years ago. My ex and I knew each other in college. And then he went to business school at Yale and I went to the law school. It seemed like a good fit. It was, for a while." She lit the cigarette, inhaled, breathed out through her nose tilting her head away from me awkwardly to redirect the smoke. "God, I feel like I'm going to get caught any minute now for smoking on campus."

"Twenty hours of work if they bust you."

"It's so worth it."

"So will you stay in New York?"

"Yeah, definitely. He's the one who has to find a place to live.

It won't be hard. He was one of those people who got hooked up into the dot-com thing and it lasted through the first crash. The second time around he wasn't so lucky. But he just lost a company and a job—he got to keep the money. Unlike everybody else we knew."

"Sounds like a good profile for a documentary."

"His name is Walter. He's a great guy, he really and truly is. He's wonderful. Even with all the shit we're in, he's great." This sounded rehearsed, polished, as if she'd said it to a few people. Practiced it in front of a mirror.

I almost asked her what happened, why the marriage blew up, but I didn't. We weren't in enough sync yet to trade war stories. Somewhere along the line I'd lost the appetite for bad news and firsthand gossip. I leaned back on the bench and admired her neck. I could count the rise of the vertebrae leading into her sweater.

She leaned forward, sucked a last gasp from the cigarette and stepped on it, ground it into the grass with the toe of her shoe. "I'm having a weird time. I'm hanging out with people I just do not remember. Isn't that strange? We spent all that time with only a hundred or so measly people and I have no recollection of some of them. I'm drawing total blanks when people come up to me. They're older, for one, and that's depressing because it means I'm older."

"You don't look it."

"I've been told that ten times already. I *do* look my age. I *want* to look it. I *deserve* to look it, after what I've been through."

"What's it like, in there?" I gestured at the dining hall, where people were filing in now. You could hear good-natured laughter from across the quad. The restrained, polite, adult laughter of people on their way to drinks.

"Do you know what?" she turned, looked at me, her eyes widening a little, but now she could make a point and be emphatic about it. "We went to school with some interesting people. I thought all the interesting ones would be at Yale. I still see those people, but never really thought my boarding school friends would be as nice. Turns out I was wrong." She checked her watch, a platinum Cartier, with roman numerals. Last time I'd seen her she was wearing a waterproof digital that was too big for her wrist. "They're going to serve us drinks. I'm dying for one."

It turned out I was, too.

33.

The boat still moved fast in the water even after they moved up Leonsis. We were strong, but we arrived to practice like mercenaries, people doing a job. Leonsis coped well in the bow and Wads was a solid stroke who worked really well with Ruth. I rowed in the three seat in front of Perry as I always had, but I was more aware of him now, perhaps because I was no longer so focused on Connor. Perry was stronger than I had thought but he had changed, we all had. He was harder, I suppose. Less like the stuffed bear Connor had made him out to be. I watched him rise out of the boat after practice, well over six five, his mass apelike, powerful, and could not see how Connor had found it so easy to treat Perry so badly.

I remember those last weeks like they were one long practice, the five of us working steadfastly to create a boat that was ever more impressive. Against expectation, we performed well that season, winning four of our remaining six races. But there was a heaviness to the boat we could not rid ourselves of. The feeling of flying, the passion and aggression, the soul of the boat had disappeared with Connor. The fact was, nothing was the same without him. Although we seldom spoke of him, we felt his absence acutely. Rowing was not as exciting for me anymore, it was simply an exhausting sport that demanded a lot of hard work and sacrifice and now offered dubious rewards. I started to look forward to graduation. Walking out of the boathouse with Perry one day, I said to him what we'd all known for a while. "It feels so different." I didn't add *without Connor*, but it hung in the air as if I had.

He just shrugged. "What did you expect? It's a tough sport. We're getting tired. And we've been through a lot."

I felt the exhaustion more and more, felt the pain in my back and my knees, across my shoulders. At the end of each practice I realized I was leaving blood on the oar handle, and the ripped blisters and ruptures on my palms were taking their toll. I felt as if I were trapped in an old man's body at the end of the day.

DeKress showed up one late afternoon just as I was starting the ritual of laying ice on my knees, sitting hunched over my bed, chewing Tylenol. The sour taste of the pills was going right into my blood, and I was waiting for the dull feeling to reach my legs. DeKress told me Channing had called the dean's office and wanted me to stop by his house before dinner. "He says you have to go, dude."

I closed my eyes and counted to a hundred, then got up and pulled on my sweatshirt. I hobbled for the first few steps, feeling my muscles start to widen and warm up again as I walked down the stairs, and then out the door. It was a mile to Channing's house, at least, so I took it slowly, thinking he'd better have a good reason for calling me. I had a pretty good idea what it was about, though, and it kept me going.

And then it started to rain. Hard. The clouds that had been sitting fat and heavy over the school just opened up, and I kept walking along, the rain warm and humid on my face. It was over in a few minutes but by the time I reached Channing's, the pathway down to the shed was practically a river and part of the site was yellow-brown clay.

I looked in and saw that Channing had started to move his stuff into the shed; an old desk, a stack of pictures and his file cabinet. He had divided the back part out and his gardening tools and crap were out there, bags of fertilizer and the spades and the pitchfork and everything he'd need. It was a good shed. Solid. The basics were there and I'd started from nothing. Just a frame, a badly built one at that.

"What are you doing, Carrey?"

It was him. He was standing on the porch. I could just see his outline behind the rusted screen of the door. He looked out at me tentatively, as if I was some sort of official come to investigate his outbuildings. "It's customary to knock on the front door when you visit somebody."

"I wasn't visiting." I started making my way through the mud and over the wet grass until I was at the foot of his sagging stairs. "You called. I came."

"Indeed. Come inside and get dry." I was struck again by how dilapidated his kitchen looked. He opened the freezer door and I heard him rattling ice cubes, scraping trays against the gaseous frost. "Do you drink, Carrey?"

"If you're buying."

Channing grunted and poured me a shot of whiskey in one of the glasses he kept on top of the freezer, threw ice on top of it, and passed it behind himself. "Make it last, Carrey. I give this to you with complete deniability attached."

I knew if I had one sip I'd feel it. Good. I sipped. Channing poured scotch over the ice cubes in his own glass, set the drink down on the counter, looked at it. "The picture in my office was taken at Gales Ferry. I was in six-seat. They moved me back from the stroke. We won by half a boat length. Not clear water, but enough to break them. It was one year before an Olympic year. Back then the selection was different. Much more arbitrary. We didn't have the machines you have. Nothing, really, except boats."

"You were the power seat."

"We were snot nose brats. I've timed your boat. On good days you people could have taken us on the short run, just the four of you. Two men smoked on my freshman team, if you can believe that."

"Did you go to the Olympics?"

"It was a different time, Carrey. I wanted to go to Henley, and we did, and we won there as well."

"And then?"

"I believed I wanted to work. I went to law school at Harvard. Practiced law, briefly." He smiled. "I was never disbarred. Or sued. I despise those rumors but at times they are useful. No, I simply quietly left the profession to teach. And coach. There was nothing untoward or dishonorable about it."

"Thank you for telling me. I'll keep mum about it."

"I would appreciate that."

He reached into his breast pocket and pulled out a small card, no bigger than an index card, folded in half. It was cream colored, with a single crimson stripe across the top. He pushed it toward me but I didn't open it. I looked at the embossed, heavy paper, then back at him. "What is it?"

"I am the messenger of greater things, Carrey."

I unfolded it.

Charles,
Please ask Mr. Carrey if he would be interested in joining us
next year.

I knew the signature, which wasn't really a signature, just the printed first name of the Harvard coach.

"They know I'm interested. They've known for a year."

"You deserve it, you know."

"It's because of you."

"They'd seek you out."

"They have no idea what happened on that bridge. Not really. I'm not sure they'd want any of us if they did."

"Listen to me now, Carrey. Connor Payne was a prodigious rowing talent, one of my best, but a very troubled young man. I coached that boy for four years and I am deeply saddened by his death. I am angered by it. But I am not surprised by it. Do you hear me? And you should know that there was only one note sent to me from Cambridge. This one."

"What about the others?"

"Neither Perry nor Wadsworth applied, it seems. And our Ruth has already said yes to New Haven. Much to Harvard's eternal dismay."

"What should I do?"

"No, Carrey. This is up to you. This is your decision alone."

I looked at it again, then folded it along the crease. Channing waited. He did not look impatient, merely curious.

"Can I keep this?" I asked.

"You may."

"It will be something to have."

"They'll be sorry to lose you. Do not be overly hasty in your decision, Carrey. What you have experienced has been very trying. Understand what you are turning down. Perhaps you need to take some time. You might feel differently after the summer."

"I know what you're saying, Mr. Channing, but I really think I may be finished with this sport."

"Possibly you'll change your mind."

"I don't think so."

"I am obliged to remind you that you do not need to row if you accept their invitation, Carrey. Harvard is, in the end, an institution of learning."

"I don't work that way. You don't either."

He gazed out at the darkening mountains, at the land that had been here long before the houses, and the school. "Let's drink to arcane principles."

We stood on his porch drinking from those two old tumblers, a pretty hefty shot of whiskey each. He was doing it to give me time to reconsider, I knew, but I had made up my mind. I kept the letter, read it again, alone, in my dorm room, and then mailed it to my father. Years later I'd find it tacked up over his workbench, next to the debt I still owed him for the scull. My father would attach it using carpentry pins, one pounded into each corner. It would still be there when I cleared away those tools for good.

34.

I realized by the time Ruth and I walked into the dining hall that she had seconded me to be her date for the evening. I didn't mind. Most of the other alumni were with their spouses. Toddlers lurked in the corners, bedtimes looming. They had set up two bars and there were sections of tables for each year. Ruth and I headed straight for one of the bars. She ordered a double scotch, I ordered a beer, and we stood at the periphery of three classes of Fenton students getting oiled up for the weekend. It was an oddly formal affair because half of the people there had never been to Fenton. There were a number of overdressed wives with strollers and portable bassinets and unfamiliar-looking men with Kangapouches for babies who had come with their alumnae wives. The drinks were served in plastic cups with the Fenton crest, and there was a surprisingly good selection of booze for a school that frowned on drinking. Ruth scanned the crowd, the plastic glass half up to her lips.

The headmaster was filtering through the alumni, in a khaki suit, smiling, genial, more of a salesman than I remembered from years back. He also seemed smaller, and of course, older. He made his way around to Ruth and me and didn't miss a beat. "Rob Carrey and Ruth Anderson. How have you been?"

"I'm surprised you remember us, Headmaster." Ruth smiled at him as she said it and he gave her a look.

"Well, it would be hard to forget you both, now, I suppose. Did either of you go on to row in college?"

I shook my head, and Ruth, after a moment, shook hers. "I decided I didn't want to worry about my weight anymore."

"The coxswain's lament," he said.

"The protest of the compulsive anorexic, actually."

His eyebrows shot up for a moment. He looked at me, rose on his toes, as if trying to match my height. He had rowed for Fenton as well, and had rowed at Princeton. "I'm surprised you chose to stop rowing, Rob. I remember you had big plans."

"I tried some other sports."

"I see. I always wished I had been good at other sports as well. I would actually like to play golf better than I do."

"I hear it's easy to pick up," Ruth chipped in. She gazed at him, as if sizing him up. "What kind of alumni have our class been?"

"Your class has been very loyal. Very supportive of the school."

"I don't see many of us here today."

"This is an awkward time in people's lives. They have children, they are in the middle of their careers, time is precious. They return to the school when things have reached a more even keel." His gaze swept the room once, hopefully, and then returned to her.

"When they have something to show for it, you mean."

"That's perhaps one way of putting it, yes." He seemed to sigh. "I have been writing about John Perry this week. I have been trying to say something about his character."

"You can say he was a very kind person." Ruth looked at the headmaster evenly. "You can say he was a fine oarsman."

"He went on to Penn State. Did either of you ever hear from him?"

"He went to U Penn, Headmaster." Ruth looked at me as if for confirmation, then said, "We never really spoke after Fenton. I think everybody lost touch."

"U Penn? Yes, of course. That's correct." He lifted himself on his toes again, as if physically registering the mistake. "He did not row, I learned." The headmaster looked skyward. "The other boy from your year, Wadsworth, he did. He rowed at Williams. For two years. And the boy who joined you in the middle of the season, Mr. Leonsis, he rowed on the first four in Henley, after you graduated, and then went on to Trinity College in Hartford. I think he captained the team there."

Ruth swirled the ice in her glass. I sensed her move slightly closer to me. I glanced over at her and thought I saw color high on her cheeks, her eyes a little brighter. I wanted to reach out and steady her, just touch her elbow so I'd be there for her. The headmaster looked at each of us, then at the room. "It's sad that the tragedy of your year probably colors your memory of Fenton."

Ruth giggled then. Really giggled, and took my arm, her fingers slipping down my forearm, as if to ensure I'd heard. Then she laughed, loud enough so that a few of the older alumni looked in our direction amiably, wondering what the joke was. She covered her mouth and looked away. "God," she gasped. "Sad." She squeezed my forearm then, hard, dug her nails into me.

He looked at us, from one to the other, and smiled. "Well, I hope this weekend helps bring you closer to the school." And he walked away. Ruth watched him go, the man's shoulders slightly rounded, looking for another group to descend upon, finding it only a few yards away from where we stood, two couples with strollers. Without taking her eyes off him, Ruth said to me, "I need another drink. Dewar's, on the rocks. Like, right now."

It turned out most of the rowers from our year did come back, kids from the JV and club boats, as well as quite a few from classes that were not officially part of the reunion—rowers from a year or two behind and ahead of us who remembered John with affection. I had simply not recognized them, but as the night wore on, and dinner was served and speeches made, a few of them stopped by our table, all of them with drinks in their hands. I was able to put the names to the faces only after a while, and most of them wanted to see Ruth anyway, who had gained a degree of notoriety as the only girl to ever cox the Fenton God Four. I also realized, with a sudden rush of admiration for his living memory, that almost all of the guys on John's football team had shown up to pay their respects. He was well loved.

The rowers there had all gone on to row in college, it seemed. Harvard. Naval Academy. Princeton, Cornell, Trinity, Amherst. Some had rowed out of places I did not even know had rowing teams, like the University of Colorado and Colgate University. We'd gained weight, as a crew. Lost hair. Become less intense. The dropouts, the people who quit the sport, were not in attendance. Save for Ruth and me.

Ruth enjoyed the attention. She was also becoming swiftly less and less popular with the wives and female friends almost all of these guys had brought in tow. Ruth's angularity, her swift New York humor, the fact she was getting almost raucously drunk, and the fact she looked like a college student, really did not sit well with the more sedate crowd that had shown up for the chapel service—the women in muted pastels and sensible shoes and baby daypacks with lukewarm bottles in the expandable netting under the block initials.

At one point, one of the guys, Bruce Ferry, who was wearing the prerequisite khakis and boat shoes and a canvas belt with red lobsters on it, collared me. He was radiantly healthy, badly sunburned, almost bald, the skin under the wisps of his blond hair peeling. He pressed a beer in my hand and made a show of slipping an arm around my shoulders and conspiratorially whispering in my ear, "Are you here with her? I didn't remember her being so good looking. I always figured she was kind of, you know, out there . . ." He looked at me significantly, raised his eyebrows over his glasses. Then he examined me again, carefully, as if suddenly noticing he'd been talking to the wrong person, a stranger who had appeared bearing the name of a long ago face. We were all giving each other those looks, age making us strangers to each other, the bonds of memory faded with time and adulthood and now drink. "You ever go to the Olympics, Carrey?"

"Not even close."

"Connor used to tell us you were the only Olympian we were likely to meet. It pissed him off." He glanced over at Ruth, who was talking to a rower from a year behind us named David Forester, who went on to Brown. Her hand was on his shoulder and David's partner, a woman in long, tan slacks and a red halter neck top, was shifting her purse from hand to shoulder while Ruth laughed. "Where did you, you know, go to college?" asked Bruce.

"I sort of took time off after I left Fenton."

He nodded, not listening, his eyes on Ruth, in good humor, backslappingly drunk. "Keep an eye on her, okay? She's getting hammered." He grinned. "Don't do anything I wouldn't do, right Carrey?" He looked down at his watch—one of those luminous Timexes that I coveted—before scanning the crowd while he took a pull from his bottle. He set it down and sighed heavily. "I have to find my wife. I'll see you tomorrow. We're staying in town and we have the baby. Full house at the inn." He shook his head, walked away, slinging his seersucker blazer over his shoulder. I slid next to Ruth, who gave me a look and set her head gently on my shoulder, still looking at David, who was telling her something about property prices in New York since the crash. David looked at me and nodded once. It made me feel like an outsider to their clan, and I guess I was, the hired gun, the mercenary they had needed for one year. Most of the others had been through four years together at Fenton.

Ruth was crunching the ice from her empty cup. "David's been telling me he can find me a great one bedroom on the East Side for a song. We're talking under a million. I'm so tempted. I need a change."

David smiled, looked pleased with himself and reached into his blazer. He took out a silver card holder and proffered a card to her between his index and middle finger . . . a strangely inappropriate gesture that clearly annoyed the woman in red. "I'm really not kidding. Call me. Whenever, okay?"

He backed away from Ruth, responding, finally, to his date, who was tugging playfully but insistently on his fingers, drawing him toward her. Ruth watched him go, breathed out. "I think I need some air."

The room was suddenly hot with the press of bodies. I watched as she licked her lips, arranged the cocktail stirrer, napkin, and plastic tumbler on a table beside us, took her purse methodically from the back of a chair, shook her hair back, and grinned up at me as if she had accomplished something. Her hand slipped under my arm again, and I was conscious of how small it was, how aristocratic. She held on to me while I guided her through the crowd, through the sixty percent of the reunion attendees who did not remember us, me clearing the way. We stopped at the bar and she pointed at the bartender, who looked at us quizzically, and then realized she was pointing at a bottle of white wine behind him. "My husband wants a bottle of wine, bartender." The kid smiled, and I realized it was just some student from Fenton, or maybe a townie they had drafted in. Seventeen years old. He grabbed the bottle by the neck and set it between us, pulled out the cork before handing it to me along with two wineglasses. Ruth smiled at the kid and took my arm, waiting for me to part the crowd for her again. I wondered if she should be drinking. If I should, for that matter.

When we got outside to the porch where the smokers were, I noticed the headmaster standing on the grass, rising once again to his tiptoes as he spoke to two young women who were laughing, probably too hard, at what he had to say. They were new alumni, only five years out of Fenton, fresh from college, enjoying the novelty of drinking on the school property. Ruth let me watch them for a second, her lips were pressed together and she was breathing deeply. One hand was against the top of her chest. "Walk me somewhere," she said, but she wound up leading the way, across the quad, past Middle Dorm and then North Dorm. We stopped so she could take off her sandals and she walked the rest of the way barefoot. The dining hall behind us seemed like a dark ship on a sea of blue-green night grass, lit up, full of strangers.

We were heading toward the Rowing Cottage, which had a station wagon parked in front of it. The cottage had been converted into faculty housing the year after we graduated. There were new steps leading up to the door and the whole building had been repainted a duck egg blue.

"It seems smaller," Ruth said. "I can't believe they let students sleep in a house right there on the water. Especially Connor. My God, the faith they must have had in us. That place has *lawsuit* written all over it." She squinted at the cottage, stood straighter to see it.

I had something I wanted to ask her, but wasn't sure exactly how to phrase it. Standing there in the coolness of the evening the exact words wouldn't come. It was partly because it was so disconcerting having her next to me—the first time I had been close to another woman, alone, in a long while. I thought about Carolyn. She would be editing my work at this very moment, stuck in front of the Mac. I hoped she was, at least. Maybe she had abandoned that project as well. I looked over at the glowing buildings and wondered how I could have fallen so far from the expectations of this place. I felt like a fraud, coming back here, my life in exactly the kind of mess the school was supposed to teach you to avoid.

"I want another drink, Carrey." Ruth looked up at me, blinking.

"Tell me more about the guy you married."

I gently handed her one of the glasses and drew the bottle out from under my arm, filled her glass halfway. "Keep still, Ruth, you're going to spill."

"I'm paying attention. Don't worry." She took a sip. "My ex-husband was from a public school, for starters. You know, like one of those schools that are just a number. PS 345 or whatever." She kicked grass with her toe, then touched it gently with the flat of her foot, as if she was trying to leave an impression. The grass was freshly cut. "He had a start-up. Internet security for credit card transactions. He sold it when there were still buyers. You've probably seen the little badge on a million Web sites."

"So you're filthy rich?"

"He is. I'm not rich anymore. You stop being rich when they dump you. Anyway, there were other people who made more than he did. He should have cut his losses, but he didn't."

She handed me her wineglass, reached into the pocket of her white shorts, and extracted the package of cigarettes. Tapped one out. She was winded from walking up the hill. Ruth inhaled on the cigarette. "I swear these things taste better here. Maybe because we weren't allowed to smoke." She inhaled again, took back her wine.

"What was he like?" I poured my own drink. I sat down on the ground and she lowered herself down next to me, always careful of herself now, the instinctive care you take in the dark when you are used to drinking. She sat with her legs crossed before her, the end of her cigarette like a beacon, her drink twisted into the grass beside her hand.

"I told you already. A nice guy. A nerd. He grew up in Bend, Oregon, for God's sake. When he started making money we used to take little romantic trips from New York to the shore, you know? So eventually he bought a house near Chatham, which I had to furnish and which he hated but made sure remained his in the settlement." She inhaled again and folded her arms, looked down at her wine as if discovering something unexpected and adorable, picked up the glass and almost drained it. "And here I am."

I glanced over at Ruth's silhouette in the dark and wondered how to form the question I wanted to ask. There were lights on the second floor of the Rowing Cottage. Somebody was carrying a baby around in there. I could not imagine that front room covered in baby toys and pictures, with a TV and cartoons.

Finally I just came out with it. "How are you doing with all this?"

Ruth looked at me and her eyes welled up. "I just can't believe Jumbo is dead, too. That we're back here to say good-bye and attend *another* memorial service. It seems . . . unreal. It's brought it all back. That whole year." She took a sip of her wine. "He jumped off a bridge. A *bridge*. Do you think it was some kind of message?"

"A message? To us? No. Perry was a mess. You read his letter."

"I wish I had written back. Or called him. Something. I keep thinking that maybe if I had—"

"He might not have killed himself? I doubt it. He would have liked to have heard from you, sure, but it wouldn't have made that big a difference if he was in such a bad place. I didn't call him either. I don't feel great about it, but whatever was going on in his life was beyond us."

"I hope so. I really do."

"Ruth, Connor was another mess. We never really knew him, not really—"

"I knew him better than you did."

"Okay, fair enough. Then you knew the kind of world he lived in. About his father. About what it was like growing up under all that pressure to be the best. To be . . . superior. I think now about how driven he was. It was unnatural. There was something obscene about it."

"But we were *all* like that back then."

"For all the good it did us. We had nothing to do with Connor's death, either, Ruth. We just had the bad fortune to be there when he finally decided to jump."

"Then why do I feel so guilty when I think about it? I don't think any of us really got over it.

"Perry and you were stuck with Connor on the shore for a long time."

"I can still remember him floating in the water, you know? I still see it sometimes. It haunted me for years."

"I don't think I ever told you I was sorry for leaving you there."

"Well, you and Wads could run faster. It was the only logical thing to do, anyway. We were all in shock." She inhaled hard on the cigarette and I remembered John Perry's letter; he had taken up smoking, too. "I had never seen a dead person. I'll never forget that look on his face." She bit her top lip. "Poor Perry. Do you know what he kept saying to me the whole time we were waiting?"

I sipped my drink, waited for it. Drank again and realized the wine was almost warm now. I had been gripping the top of the glass.

" 'We shouldn't have done it, Ruth, we shouldn't have done it. It's all our fault. It's all our fault.' That's what he said. Over and over and over. And I just ignored him, you know, the way you do when a boy is crying, but I can remember him saying that. He kept saying it until the ambulance came with you and Wads and then he shut up. He put his hands over his mouth to make himself keep quiet, like this," and she showed me, her fingers en-twined over her lips.

"We didn't *do* anything. We didn't cause Connor's death, Ruth."

"That's what I should have said to Jumbo. He needed me to say it, to comfort him. But I didn't. Would you like to know what I did instead?"

"Yes."

"I just kept nodding, hard, again and again. I kept nodding but I was whispering something, too. It was the word 'yes.' Every time he said we shouldn't have done it, I said yes. Every time he said it was our fault, I said yes. This deranged, incessant mantra. And I do not think . . ." She looked away to compose herself. "Anyway. I told my mother about it, you know, in detail, a year or so later. How responsible I felt, what Perry had said and what I said back. All she told me was that we were lucky I wasn't an adult. I was just seventeen." She shivered. "My mother has a horror of lawsuits. Well, who doesn't, I suppose? But that was the extent of her empathy."

"I was nineteen."

"I know. Bad things happen when you are a teenager. But when you are that age they haven't happened before."

"Did you and Connor ever . . ."

"No. And yes. We were young. I don't need to tell you he had a certain kind of attraction. I knew him longer than you did, Rob. We were both outsiders. Until you came along."

I refilled her glass all the way to the rim, in the dark, hardly able to see it.

35.

Had Connor fallen a foot farther beneath the bridge, he would have missed the rocks and he would have lived. But they told us later that he died almost instantly. He landed at an angle on a rock, hard. We saw him floating face up in the water, which was clear and metallic in the spring cold. His arms were extended behind his body, not as in a crucifixion but down deep, as if he was thrusting his chest upward, trying to levitate over the surface of the river. He was still grinning, the water just covering his jaws, and then he floated away from us as if he was knuckling himself along the bottom. We ran down the right hand side of the river and I was the one who left the shore and waded through the current to him, falling twice, three times, the cold tearing through my clothes, dropping my body heat. When I got to him I was shoulder deep. I wound up hugging him around his neck in order to hold his face above the water but it was a futile effort because he was now nothing more than a sodden bag of meat and bone.

I tried to pull him through the current but his body was like lead, his feet, made heavy by his sneakers, dangling behind me.

I finally towed him by his shirt to the shore and then Perry was next to me, whimpering and wheezing but swimming hard, and he grabbed Connor's waist and the two of us heaved him out the river and hauled him up to the mud and reeds and grass on the bank where we knelt beside him.

I think about that day and wonder if any of us had known CPR, or how to do mouth to mouth, if we would have tried it. I like to tell myself that of course we would have. We would have had the presence of mind to touch that body. But nothing we could have done would have saved him. The back of his skull was crushed. He broke his neck as well, fractured two of his seven cervical vertebrae. I have never forgotten that term, *cervical vertebrae*. It was revealed to us by one of the trauma counselors brought in from New Milford. She told us that the impact had smashed the *atlas* and the *axis*, the bones responsible for stabilizing the head. This is why as he lay on the grass beside the river, still grinning up at us, blood and water tricking from his mouth, Connor's head had flopped backward at an unnatural, truly dead angle.

I have filmed the hundreds of mutilated bodies that washed up beside the Kagera River in Rwanda after the massacres, bodies emaciated by HIV/AIDS and tuberculosis in clinics across Zambia and Swaziland, the tortured bodies of poachers that we found in Botswana wrapped in razor wire and burned beyond recognition, and bodies macabrely outfitted in evening wear and squeezed into old-fashioned, rent-by-the-day, faux mahogany open coffins in the sprawling cemeteries outside Soweto in South Africa. Every time I witnessed those corpses, the rag-doll uselessness of their twisted limbs, their dead, fish-eyed stare, I thought of Connor.

Ruth had been kneeling in the wet grass when we dragged him to shore. She nudged her way between us, stared in horror at Connor's head and face and started retching and groaning at the same time. Perry was mewling like an animal in agony. Wadsworth had taken one look and started sprinting for the road,

screaming at me to come with him. I jumped up and followed
him and didn't look back.

By the time we got back with the ambulance, Connor was lying in a pool of pink froth. Ruth and Perry were covered in it.
They had stayed next to him the whole time; two kids who had
never been so close to death, immobilized by it in the rain.

———————

Ruth pulled her knees up to her chest. "Have you been back to
the boathouse, Rob?"

"What do you think?"

"No. I haven't either. I don't want to. I never set foot in Yale's
boathouse, can you believe that? I wanted to drop you a line a
few times, find out if you were rowing."

"I gave it up, too."

"Did you keep that wooden scull of yours?"

"Yes. In my father's workshop. Actually, he took it from me
when I came back from school, never said a word about it. I was
only home for a couple of weeks after that, then I got a job. My
dad said he wouldn't hire me if I didn't go to college and he kept
to it. My parents were pretty disappointed I turned down Harvard. In fact, they were furious."

"What did you do?"

"I traveled up to Canada. Got a job near Vancouver. I wound
up working as a fix-it guy for a small documentary film company—
sort of a carpenter and general skivvy. I'd drive the vans, haul
equipment around, that sort of thing. One day they offered to
teach me how to use one of the cameras, and that was it for me. I
wound up doing my own filming, working with a really tight Canadian film crew called Mercenary Productions that got sent all
around the world doing doccie stuff and news fillers."

"Doccie?"

"Documentary film work. Whenever a big outfit needed shots in someplace in the middle of nowhere, they'd call us up. We once spent six months filming a team trying to get a beached tanker off an island in Newfoundland. We got sent out to the Yukon to film Inuit people in reservations. The crew I worked with did underwater filming. Nasty stuff. If a TV channel or production house needed shots of fishing nets underwater, or the bottom of a boat, or even shipwrecks that were leaking oil into the sea, we were the guys they called. I was twenty-one years old, the other three guys were almost thirty. I got PADIS certified, learned about the equipment, edited on an old Avid system in this craphole studio they had in Vancouver, just outside the Gaslight District in an old railroad siding. Then digital video came along and I got into that."

"Do you keep in touch?"

"I wound up doing a year at the University of Vancouver to get up to speed on some of the business aspects of filming. I couldn't even do a spreadsheet. While I was studying, one of the guys died on a shoot."

"What, did he drown?"

"Nope. He had a heart attack at thirty-one. After that, the other two just threw in the towel. I bought some of their equipment; their sound stuff and a Sony Beta SP, which I still use when customers insist on Beta. And then I was my own operator. *National Geographic* started buying more and more of my footage and then they started commissioning pieces. It's mostly been pretty good. I never regretted saying no to Harvard, but my dad never really forgave me. It was always between us."

"Then you met the woman you live with."

"Yes. Carolyn. Five years ago."

"Is she in the business?"

"She's an editor and writer."

"Why isn't she with you?"

"The short answer is she's working, editing my latest shoot."

"And the long answer?"

"The long answer is she's working."

"Okay, I get it. It's complicated." There was a brief silence as she drained the last of her wine. A million unspoken possibilities passed between us and then Ruth gracefully let the subject drop. "You used to write pretty well."

"But you have to learn to write like a documentarian. Channing wouldn't have approved." I grinned. "Short, punchy, repetitive sentences. No equivocation."

"Like sales copy."

"Yeah."

"So here you are." She carefully set down her wineglass on the lawn, pressed it into the grass as if planting it, let go. The glass toppled over. She stood up and reached out, gripped my shoulder for balance. "Which way is your dorm?"

"The one I'm in tonight?"

"Uh-huh. I remember where you used to stay. In North Dorm. Where are you tonight?"

"I'm back in North Dorm."

"Me, too. That's where we're going."

I stood up and she took my arm, leaned against me while we picked our way blindly across the field in the dark. I wondered what would happen if I let her go. We'd left the glasses and wine bottle behind for Buildings and Grounds to find the next morning. We reached my old dorm and went in through the back entrance. When we came to my room she flicked on the light and squinted. "I love what you've done to the place."

She sat on the bare mattress, picked up one of the folded blankets, and opened it before her, stood, and tossed it back on the bunk. "I need to use the bathroom. And get changed. I need something warm to sleep in. I need socks."

"Demanding woman."

"Make your bed, Carrey. I'm damn well not sleeping alone

tonight if you're around. I'm going to be back here in ten minutes and this place better be ready."

"Good night, Ruth."

"It's not good night. I told you I'll see you in ten minutes, sailor." She grinned, that crooked grin that she had saved for years, and reached up to me, her wrists dry on my neck, and kissed me quickly, theatrically, drunkenly, her eyes closed. Then she took an unsteady step back, turned, and slipped out the door. I heard two guys talking loudly in the hallway, laughing. They greeted her and demanded to know why she was sneaking around like this, wanted to know who she was visiting. Ruth played up to it, swore she'd never tell, told the two of them to go to bed, which they found hilarious.

I sat on the bed and let that warm feeling of expectation dissipate. She wasn't coming back.

I pulled the sheets over the mattress, stuffed the tired pillow into the white case, threw the blanket on the bed. I stripped off my clothes, hung them over one of the desk chairs and wrapped my towel around my waist again, before heading for the bathroom with my toiletry kit. I walked over to the middle sink, leaned against it, checked my watch. It was after 11:00 P.M. I brushed my teeth, spat, then hunched over the faucet and began rehydrating.

"Hey, who's there?"

I stood up, wiped my mouth. "Rob Carrey." I announced my class year, too, like an idiot, looking around me. The bathroom was empty. Then I saw two loafers sticking out from beneath the end stall.

"Jeez, can you look in one of these stalls for a roll of toilet paper? This one's all out. I'm stranded."

I laughed, searched around, opened up one of the roll dispensers in a vacant stall (real toilet paper dispensers!) and tossed a sealed roll over the stall door. I heard the guy inside fumble it.

The hallway was dark now and I padded along the wall, counting doors until I came to my room. I flicked on the overhead light and found Ruth in the bed, small and curled up under the sheets. I switched the light off, shuffled across the room and found a pair of shorts and a T-shirt that I slipped on quickly and furtively. I sat on the bed next to Ruth and listened to her breathing. She stirred when the mattress shifted with my weight, mumbled and pulled the blankets over her shoulders. A faint white light was coming through the naked, curtainless window from the floodlights on the corner of the building that illuminated the front lawn. She had neatly stacked her contact case and a toiletry kit on the desk by the bed. A pair of eyeglasses lay open next to her purse and a half-full glass of water. Her cell phone was next to it all.

I squeezed myself down next to her gently. The bed was impossibly tiny. When had I last slept in a single bed? She started, turned over quickly and touched me, blindly. She made some kind of affirmative sound and pressed her head against my chest and relaxed. I waited for a few minutes, then I closed my eyes.

In the middle of the night I woke up to find Ruth propped up next to me, reaching over me for her purse. "Sorry, Carrey, I need something in there." Then she paused. "God, you're warm."

She was wearing a T-shirt that hung off her sharp shoulders. She pulled her bag across me, rummaged inside and came out with something she palmed. She chucked the purse off the bed and lay back "I grind my teeth. I have this guard I have to wear. It's not really attractive. If you're going to make a move, do it now."

"I'm still thinking about it."

"Then hand me that glass of water. I can't see anything."

I took the warm glass and handed it over. She tentatively pushed her hand toward me and I took it, pressed it against the glass, waited for her to finish the water, took it back. She fell back in bed, pulled me to her.

"Go to sleep, Ruth."

"I'm trying."

36.

Just before sunrise I was still holding her. It had not been a comfortable sleep. My left arm was completely numb and my back was killing me. I pulled myself out of bed and sat up. Ruth spread her arms when I left the sheets. It was 5:30 A.M., three and a half hours before the service for John. I covered her gently and stood by the window watching her sleep. The river was brooding blue, the hills indigo. All around the grass fields were vibrant and green. You could feel that strange energy coming from them, the ground having absorbed hundreds of games of soccer and lacrosse, field hockey and football, baseball and rugby; the energy of youth pounded into the earth, released at dawn.

I went to the bathroom and slipped on a pair of shorts, went back to the room and found my running shoes. I hadn't run in weeks. No, months. They were stiff with disuse.

Ruth sighed and curled up. I wondered if she was really sleeping or half-awake, waiting for me to leave the room so she could make her exit. I'd see her later in the chapel, after the service, trade numbers and e-mails with her. We'd hug good-bye, tear up a bit, and we'd promise, *promise* to stay in touch, although we knew we wouldn't. Not really.

I slipped my cell phone into my shorts, eased out of the door without clicking it, and walked down the hall through the open front door into the light of morning.

By the time I reached the road I was already out of breath but I had a good pace. I felt limber, more powerful than I thought I would. I jogged along the river, away from the school and the boathouse. By the end of the first mile I was going strong, by the second I was winded, almost walking. I pushed through another half mile and stopped. I turned and looked up the river.

The sun shone across its surface and the water glinted and winked. I had to shade my eyes to look far down where the river turned east, toward the school. I breathed deeply and evenly knowing that this iridescent light would not last. And then, a miracle. A boat was making its way down to me. A small scull, the oars pressing into the water evenly, rhythmically, driven by a good hand. I waited to hear the sounds of the oarlocks, hear the exhalation of the rower, the backsplash of the blades, but it moved in silence.

It wasn't a sculler. It was a bird flying out of the sun and over the surface of the water, skimming it, just touching, before lifting up and out of the river valley. I watched it fly over the mountains, wings beating. I looked once again at the river but the sunlight had shifted, and the surface had become a cool shadow. And I knew for sure that the bird would continue on and make its way to the ocean. On its journey it would fly over millions of us. It would soar over broken hearts and broken bodies and ended relationships and new beginnings and sons and daughters and parents and rivers and boats and schools and kids free for the summer and it would just keep going. It would fly over cemeteries and cars and houses and fields and roads and highways and then into the clouds, through shame and longing and regret and grief and forgiveness and laughter and childless love.

I would never come back. I would not think about this place much, either. A year later, Ruth would send me a letter announcing a new marriage. Wadsworth would write a short e-mail to her reveling in the birth of his second son, William, and she'd send that on.

On that last day at Fenton, however, I would open the phone and call Carolyn. I'd wake her up. At first she wouldn't be sure it was me, and then she'd ask why I was out of breath. I'd say it was because I had been running and I was in pretty bad shape but that wasn't important now.

She'd want me to tell her what *was* important. And I'd reply I didn't know. But that was not really true. I knew that it was important to remember that time was impossible to stop. I knew that if we could have one piece of it back, just the briefest hour of our choosing, we would find each other. And we would hold on against the future.

We would find each other and hold on.

But on that brilliant morning she'd sigh and yawn and ask me when I was coming home without any guarantee in her voice.

And I'd tell her.

AUTHOR'S NOTE

This is a work of fiction, but it is partly about the fine sport of rowing. The tragic events described herein are in no way meant to disparage that brilliant pursuit, but instead to provide a record of the exhilaration of a fast boat and the tremendous toll it takes upon those who move it. Rowing, like love, asks much of the human spirit over time and distance.

This novel has made friends over the many years it took for me to write it. Katie Gilligan, its editor at St. Martin's Press in New York, has shown unflagging enthusiasm ever since I sprung the idea of a love-struck rower on her over lunch in Cape Town. Tris Coburn, its agent, was also my roommate at Kent School; he's a much finer oar than I and a partner in crime.

I owe much to Tim Scott and Mimi Dow, who introduced me to the world of writing. I also wish to thank the Centre for Film and Media at the University of Cape Town for providing me the time, space, and wherewithal to write this novel.

The greatest debts are to my family, particularly to my father, whose deep love of books has become my own. And to Emma and Sarah, who have put up with so many unexplained absences. And to my lovely wife, Jacqueline, who always believed and made it possible.

Reading
Group
Gold

FLAT WATER TUESDAY

by Ron Irwin

About the Author

- A Conversation with Ron Irwin

Behind the Novel

- "The Memories of the Water Do Not Fade"
An Original Essay by the Author

Keep on Reading

- Recommended Reading
- Reading Group Questions

*A
Reading
Group Gold
Selection*

For more reading group suggestions,
visit www.readinggroupgold.com.

ST. MARTIN'S GRIFFIN

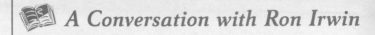

Could you tell us a little bit about your background, and when you decided that you wanted to lead a literary life?

I have always wanted to be a writer. I grew up in Buffalo, New York, and my parents both encouraged me to read widely. I remember being in the hospital for what seemed like weeks with pneumonia and I must have read *The Call of the Wild* by Jack London a hundred times: The Yukon seemed like a much better place than my hospital room. In high school, I became fascinated by Ernest Hemingway and his life, a fascination that endures today. The idea of living overseas and writing appeared to be a very good idea, so after I graduated from college I moved to South Africa. I had no idea if I would be a novelist but I knew I would write . . . something.

After college I taught at a school in South Africa for severely underprivileged children who came mostly from Soweto. I had never been exposed to such crushing poverty and it was humbling. I had grown up in a well-to-do American household that valued education, and to meet talented, brilliant kids who could not afford shoes or books was a shock. I began to realize that the worst poverty in life was not really financial hardship. It was being so poor, so limited, that you were unable to express yourself, to leave your mark on the world. It was then that I decided that I wanted to leave behind something unique, to do something that would, in a sense, justify the advantages I had been given simply by having the good fortune of being born the son of an investment banker. So I got my hands on an old computer and started writing in the small flat I shared with my girlfriend in a funky part of Johannesburg. My first office was a converted kitchenette with a broken sink in the corner. I loved it. I lived in the artistic section of the city and many of my friends were writers and photographers and painters. My landlord and his wife were sculptors. I think our rent was the equivalent of eighty dollars a month. It was a pretty stripped down existence, balanced on the birth of the New South Africa, a heady time indeed.

That year in the little room was really my introduction
to the world of writing. I read everything I could about
the book trade and haunted a used bookstore down the
road, where I devoured all of the new fiction I could
find and bought classics by the boxful. I had majored in
English in college, but I wanted to expand my knowledge, to live and think like a writer rather than as a
student of literature. It meant reexamining lots of good
books not with the aim of writing character analyses or
essays, but to see how the authors had achieved what
they had, to find out what makes good fiction tick. I
knew I had to find my voice as a novelist, and to do
that I had to open myself up to finding characters to
inhabit my fiction. While I read, I wrote.

I was thousands of miles from home, doing exactly
what I wanted to do. Reading with the goal of
becoming a writer was a liberating experience. And
there were no distractions. We didn't own a stereo or
television because we couldn't afford those things.
This was before the days of the Internet and the mobile
phone. We only had one battered rotary telephone in
the apartment and half the time it didn't work. It was
really there that I found my voice as a writer and a
creative person.

**Is there a book that most influenced your life or
inspired you to become a writer?**

I don't think there is one book that really influenced
me to become a writer. There are a number of books
that I read and admired that prompted me to think
that I could be a professional writer. Any novel that you
voluntarily want to read ten or fifteen times is probably trying to tell you something about how you should
write and think. Writers have to learn to stop thinking
about good versus bad fiction and instead focus on
effective versus ineffective fiction.

I did my graduate work at the University of Cape Town under Professor J. M. Coetzee and had the privilege of speaking with him quite often about his work. One of his most important novels is *Waiting for the Barbarians*, which was written during the height of apartheid. It easily could have gotten him thrown in jail. Coetzee was the first person I ever met who wrote knowing that his novels could get him or members of his family incarcerated, or worse, and he went ahead and wrote them anyway. He was the person who made me believe that being a writer was a serious business, literally a matter of life and death.

What was the inspiration for *Flat Water Tuesday*?

I grew up rowing. From the very first time I got into a boat the sport had an almost supernatural effect on me. When I went away to Kent School in Kent, Connecticut, (my local school in Buffalo wouldn't support me being a rower, so I left) I discovered just how tribal rowing was. I was out of my depth at Kent as an athlete, but for a long time I existed in that very closed world of rowing, and admired the discipline and teamwork that went into making a boat go fast. Being in a fast boat is just as exciting and transcendent as skiing down a mountain on a beautiful powder day or catching that perfect wave on a surfboard. Once a boat flies there are not enough superlatives to describe the feeling. It is something you never forget, and I hope I have communicated it well in the novel.

Flat Water Tuesday is also a love story. I wanted to record what it was like to hang onto somebody you love despite tragedy, despite reality, despite everything. The loft where Carolyn and Rob live is a real place in New York. And the subject of miscarriage was interesting to me, not least because I feared it. I noticed that it was a tragedy that many couples I knew bore silently, an unspoken horror that people were afraid or ashamed to bring up. True love, sadly, always seems to exist in the shadow of disaster and loss. I have no idea why that's the case, but it is.

Take readers into the process of writing your novel. What challenges did you face in terms of plotting and structure, for example? How did you manage to create the distinct voices of each main character?

The first version of *Flat Water Tuesday* was really a memoir about my experiences as a rower. I had to learn how to shape that into the dramatic urgency of a novel. But to do that I had to reexamine my own past, to mine it for many of the bad memories . . . and good memories . . . I retained from boarding school.

The novel changed over time, partly because I got older. In one sense, *Flat Water Tuesday* is ultimately not a rowing novel at all. It is, as I've said, a love story. It was very painful to write that tragic love affair into the novel. I truly believe that the characters come to the writer. They aren't really "created." Carolyn is a very real person to me. I have a very good idea of who she is, what she looks like, what she smells like, and what she loves and what breaks her heart. Knowing that character allowed me to write about her with a sense of realism, and that of course gives her a distinct voice.

Connor Payne is another character I know well. I have met many rowers who are like Connor, and I used those memories to form that character and the relationship he has with Rob Carrey. Connor is, to me, a fascinating character, partly because he comes from so much wealth. The idea that money can shield you from the things that strike the rest of us down is an inherently American belief that has fascinated many American writers and certainly fascinates me. When I was at Kent, I met lots of kids who knew that they could do whatever they wanted with their lives and money would never be an issue. They did not need to row to get a scholarship into college. So here were these rowers at boarding school who could have really been living it up and instead they were pushing themselves to excel at a sport the average person has never even heard of. There was something pure about that. Rob Carrey is a great sculler, but he knows he has to pay his way into college and rowing is his ticket. Connor Payne, on the other hand, is an even better oarsman . . . and he is guaranteed a place at Harvard no matter what he does. And Connor is ultimately more mature and harder working and heroic than hotheaded Rob. Why?

About the Author

The structure of *Flat Water Tuesday* is relatively complex. On the one hand there is the story of boarding school, which happens in the past, and on the other there is the love story between Carolyn and Rob unraveling in the present. The two stories depend on each other because the reader only knows that whatever happened back in boarding school hangs over Rob the adult. You are always told in boarding school that hardships are "character building experiences," and I wanted to see just what kind of adult character the hardship of scholastic rowing created.

I wanted the entire novel to reach a triple dénouement. Firstly, the reader would find out if Rob and Carolyn stay together, and then they would find out what exactly was the tragedy that haunts Rob from his teenage years. Finally, the reader would discover if Fenton wins the all-important race against Warwick. The entire novel had to be structured in such a way so that the reader is kept in the dark about all three of these issues and has to keep turning the pages to find out how it all turns out.

I was not sure as I was finishing the novel if Rob would get to keep Carolyn and in many ways I leave that open. I explored that rowing, while being a wonderful sport, encourages people to think extremely literally about emotional issues. They run the danger of trying to solve every problem using physical effort. Many of the subtleties that are required for deep romance are lost if you keep thinking in terms of trying to prevail over the other person. Rowers tend to think that a massive effort can literally change everything, and on the water they are right, but in love they are often wrong.

Are you currently working on another book? And if so, what—or who—is your subject?

Sure. As was the case with *Flat Water Tuesday*, I am not starting with the subject but with the character. This is a female character who doesn't seem to want to go away, so I think I will listen to what she has to say. I think that I already have the ending of the novel figured out. I just have to decide how to begin it.

"The Memories of the Water Do Not Fade"
by Ron Irwin

I was recently giving a reading of *Flat Water Tuesday* at the Glenridge retirement complex in Sarasota, Florida, when a man approached me holding a set of large photos. He told me he had rowed at Kent, the school I attended, in an undefeated boat but missed his chance to go to the Royal Henley Regatta in England because of the war, and the regret was still in his voice. His photos were not photos of his team, or even of his boat, but simply poignant shots of where it all happened: the stretch of the Housatonic River that runs through the school. He had held on to these photos for seventy years, and now he wanted me to have them. Me, an utter stranger who was bound to him only through a passion for rowing and a novel. Those photos of the river called me back to the school decades after I had left that world and moved to South Africa. That stretch of brooding water captured in sepia still haunted his dreams.

The Kent School's crew program is legendary. On spring days you can look out on the river and count down the hours until you will row on it. My novel may provide a dark look at the vicious side of the sport and indeed the dangers of competition, but the school's crew program prompted me to go on to row for four additional years after graduating. The gently meandering course of the Housatonic River changed the course of my life, leading me to many wins as a rower in college and in Buffalo, New York. That river led me to hundreds of friendships, and of course to the novel you now hold in your hands. And, in turn, the novel is deeply connected to the school. My U.S. agent, Tris Coburn, was my roommate at Kent and a fellow rower and sculler from those days. The film rights to *Flat Water Tuesday* are held by Lars Winther, another Kent rower. It was Tris and Lars who called me in the middle of the night at my house in Cape Town when our legendary coach at Kent died and asked that I finish the manuscript of *Flat Water Tuesday* and bring to life our memories of rowing. Many of those memories I had let go into the current of adulthood. But when I examined them, they were as real and immediate as the beginning of a race, or the electric feeling when a shell kisses the water and those first few strokes cut the surface of sleeping river. Two years after my friends called me, *Flat Water Tuesday* was launched.

Any body of water that is still and flat seems to call out to oarsmen. On those days when we see a really fast crew skim by beneath us as we stand gaping on a bridge, we feel the movement in our spines and our legs and our toes, the lift and settle of the boat, the cut of the oars into the water. The Kent School itself, with its history stretching back to 1906, was founded by Reverend Frederick Sill, a zealous rower, and has offered generations of students that incredible release. And to return to the school after years away, as I have, is to be overwhelmed by that river. To stand beside it is to feel the connection not only to the impossibly swift boats practicing there today, but also to the generations of rowers who have sounded it, dreamed over it, raced and despaired and exulted upon it. The equipment has become sleeker and the school's facilities have grown to world-class level, but behind it all is that transcendent feeling of power and flight. It is a feeling I share with the kids there now, as well as with the man solemnly handing over his pictures at my reading. That sense of flying over the river is what we all yearn for, even when our bodies have begun to crumble and true flight is just a memory . . . or words on a page.

And so the novel has brought me these old pictures. *Flat Water Tuesday* seems to have touched hundreds of former rowers. Yes, it is a tragic story, but it is also a hopeful one. I have been asked many times if I had a chance would I do it all again. Would I go away to Kent again and subject myself to that competition once more? Would I accept a chance to fly again? Yes. In a heartbeat.

 *Recommended Reading*

If readers would like to know more about rowing, I urge them to read *The Amateurs* by David Halberstam. This is an exhilarating look at the men who represented the U.S. in the 1984 Olympic single scull. It is probably the best book ever written about the sport.

I also suggest *The Shell Game* by Stephen Kiesling, his autobiographical account of rowing at Yale. They might also pick up Daniel Brown's recently published *The Boys in the Boat*, a vivid portrayal of the men who rowed the eight-oared shell in the 1936 Olympics. Also of note is *True Blue* by Daniel Topolski, about an eventful year in the build up to the Oxford-Cambridge Boat Race, the most famous race in the rowing world. This book was turned into a good film, too.

Books about boarding school are many, and at the top of the list is *The Catcher in the Rye* by J. D. Salinger, as well as *A Separate Peace* by John Knowles.

Behind the Novel

Laurie Hooper, Kent School, Class of '43

Haunting view of the Housatonic River near The Kent School in Kent, Connecticut (circa 1943).

Eric Houston

Kent School Rowers at the 2010 Henley Royal Regatta.

Eric Houston

The Kent School Boat Club's first boat, the inspiration for the God Four in *Flat Water Tuesday*.

Behind the Novel

Elijah Engleke

A sculler on flat water. This shot is one of the finalists for the *Flat Water Tuesday* picture competition held at RowingRelated.com.

# Reading Group Questions

1. How did you experience the novel? Did you feel it was a love story or a rowing story—or both?

2. The main character's voice switches often between being that of an adolescent and that of an adult. How did the author do this, and was it effective? Which did you prefer?

3. Did this novel fulfill your expectations? Why or why not?

4. Do the main characters in *Flat Water Tuesday* change throughout the novel? How does this change occur?

5. Did the actions of the main characters seem believable?

6. Many readers know nothing about the sport of rowing. Did *Flat Water Tuesday*'s rowing sequences engage you?

7. Take a moment to discuss the structure of the novel. Did you enjoy the framed narrative, which switched from the past to the present day? Which did you enjoy more and why?

8. Did you find any passages in the novel that were particularly evocative or moving? Disappointing or depressing? Take a moment to discuss your favorite scenes, background characters, even dialogue.

9. Would you recommend *Flat Water Tuesday* to other readers? What would be your one-sentence pitch?

10. We are taught, as young readers, that every story has a "moral." What, do you think, is the moral of *Flat Water Tuesday*? What can be learned from this novel—about our world, about our own selves?

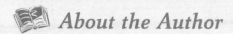 *About the Author*

Ron Irwin is an American writer who divides his time between Cape Town, South Africa, and various places in the United States. He grew up in Buffalo, New York, as part of a family of avid readers. His first experience of rowing was at the West Side Rowing Club in Buffalo, where he participated in state competition. He attended boarding school and college in New England, and was part of a number of winning crews.

Ron has worked as a journalist, a documentary filmmaker, and a teacher. He enjoys sailing, hiking, and skiing. He is passionately interested in the conservation of animal life in South Africa and relaxes by trout fishing in the streams near Cape Town. He is married and has three children. He also has a fish named Fiona and a dog named Olive. Ron still rows whenever he can on a stretch of water near his house in Cape Town that is home to flamingoes and pelicans.

Ron currently lectures in the Centre for Film and Media Studies at the University of Cape Town.

Visit him on the Web at www.ronirwin.com.

*Keep on
Reading*

Credit: Bernadine Jones

Glossary of Rowing Terms

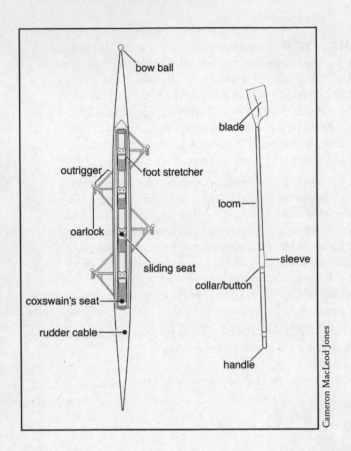

bow ball

blade

outrigger

foot stretcher

loom

oarlock

sleeve

sliding seat

collar/button

coxswain's seat

rudder cable

handle

Cameron MacLeod Jones

The Two Types of Rowing

SWEEP: Rowing with one large oar on one side of the boat.

SCULLING: A single sculler rows with two smaller oars, each mounted on either side of the boat. There are also boats that contain two scullers, called *doubles*, and boats that hold four scullers, called *quads*.

Boats and Parts of the Boats

BOATS (sweeps): There are three different shell sizes in sweep rowing. The biggest boat is called an *eight* (eight rowers and a coxswain). There are also a *four* (four rowers and a coxswain) and a *pair* (two rowers and a coxswain).

A *pair* or a *four* with no coxswain is called a *straight pair* and a *straight four*. (Eights always have coxswains.)

In *Flat Water Tuesday*, the characters row in a four; each rower uses one oar. Rob Carrey, a champion single sculler, finds rowing in the four difficult to master initially for two reasons: He is used to rowing alone and making his own decisions without a coxswain, and he is used to rowing with two oars. The coxswain, Ruth, sits in the stern of the boat. In fact, very few fours place the coxswain in the stern anymore. Modern fours place the coxswain facing forward in the bow of the boat, lying down to decrease wind resistance and provide more stability. Boats with stern-seated coxswains were much more common fifteen years before the publication of the novel, when the school scenes of Fenton were set.

BLADE: The flat part of the oar that goes into the water.

BOW: The part of the boat closest to the direction the boat travels. It is the front of the boat. The bow crosses the finish line first.

BOW BALL: A soft rubber or foam ball attached to the sharp bow of the boat to prevent it from doing damage to other boats.

COXSWAIN: Ruth is the coxswain of the God Four at Fenton. She sits in the stern of the boat. Her most important task is steering, but she also provides race feedback to the team about the boat's position on the course relative to the competitors, and informs the rowers how many strokes they are taking per minute. Remember that rowers cannot see where they are going, so she is the eyes, ears, and brain of the God Four.

COX BOX: A small computer and amplifier that Ruth, the coxswain, uses to amplify her voice. It also gives her information about the speed of the boat and its stroke rating.

FOOT STRETCHER: This is an adjustable section in front of each sliding seat where the shoes are attached. The rower pushes his legs against this at the start of each stroke. It holds the rower's feet and therefore his body in place as the boat picks up speed.

OARLOCK: The latched assembly that holds the oar in place.

PORT: This is the side of the boat to the coxswain's left and to the rowers' right. Rowers who prefer to row on this side are said to *row port*.

RIGGER: An apparatus on the side of the boat that holds the oar in its oarlock away from the rower.

RUDDER: A fin on the bottom of the boat that the coxswain uses to steer.

SEAT: This is often called a *sliding seat*. It is a moving seat on which the rower sits. It slides back and forth so that the rower can use his legs to pull the oar through the water. Each seat in the boat is numbered according to its position, going from bow to stern. In a four the seats are numbered 1 to 4. The #1 seat, the one closest to the bow, is called *bow seat* or just *bow*. The #4 seat, closest to the stern, is referred to as the *stroke seat* or just the *stroke*. Rowers are often called by their seat numbers. In *Flat Water Tuesday*, Connor Payne rows the stroke seat (#4), Rob Carrey rows #3, John (Jumbo) Perry rows #2, and Chris Wadsworth rows bow (#1).

SHELL: Another term for a boat.

SINGLE: A boat for one rower using two oars. Rob Carrey used to row in a single. Single rowers are also called *single scullers* or *scullers*.

SLIDE: The two tracks in which the rolling seat is held in place and on which the seat moves or "slides" back and forth.

SPLIT: A measurement of time to row the equivalent of 500 meters on an ergometer.

STARBOARD: The side of the boat to the coxswain's right and to the rowers' left. Rowers who prefer to row on this side are said to row *starboard*.

STERN: The part of the boat farthest from the direction of travel. It is the back of the boat. Ruth sits in the stern.

Elements of the Stroke

A stroke is one full motion with the oar taken by the rower that moves the boat. The parts of the stroke are the *catch*, the *drive*, and the *recovery*.

CATCH: The very first part of the stroke when the oar enters the water. This must be done crisply and cleanly.

DRIVE: The part of the stroke where the rower pulls the blade through the water using his legs, back, and arms.

FINISH: The part of the stroke when the blade comes out of the water, ready for a new stroke.

RELEASE: Another word for the finish.

FEATHERING: Rotating the oar in the oarlock so that the blade is parallel to the surface of the water. The blade must be held flat as the rower brings it back for another stroke to decrease wind resistance.

RECOVERY: The part of the stroke when the rower comes back up the slide slowly, preparing for a new stroke. The oar is pushed away from the body by extending the arms, reaching the arms and body forward, and compressing the legs.

STROKE RATE: This is a measurement of how many strokes a rower takes per minute.

Rowing Commands and Terms

CATCHING A CRAB: The oar blade slices into the water at an awkward angle. This has thrown rowers out of the boat and can bring a boat to a dead stop in a race.

ERGOMETER (ERG): A rowing machine attached to a small computer that simulates the actual rowing motion. It is used for training off the water and especially for testing the strength of a rower.

"LET IT RUN!": This is the command the coxswain makes to tell the rowers to stop rowing. This allows the boat to glide through the water and coast to a stop.

"POWER 10!": The call to take a set of ten very hard strokes.

"READY ALL, ROW!": The command to begin rowing.

RUSHING THE SLIDE: The rower pushes himself up the slide too quickly, slowing the boat.

TANKS or ROWING TANKS: Many schools like Fenton have an area where a mock boat has been mounted alongside long troughs of circulating water. This allows rowers to practice rowing together and perfect their technique when they cannot actually get on the river, usually due to weather conditions.

"WAY-ENOUGH!": The command to stop rowing.

FLAT WATER TUESDAY

by Ron Irwin
NARRATED BY Holter Graham

AVAILABLE ON CD AND FOR DIGITAL DOWNLOAD

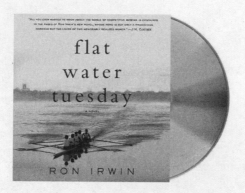

"Actor Holter Graham, who narrates this book, has a knack
for these young-men-on-the-brink stories, and he was spot-on
for Richard Ford's *Canada* and Chad Harbach's *The Art of Fielding*.
His performance is just as satisfying in *Flat Water Tuesday*, and he is
particularly good in the competition sequences, giving Irwin's best
prose the voice it deserves."—*CHICAGO TRIBUNE*

"It may be premature to declare Ron Irwin's *Flat Water Tuesday*
the best audiobook of 2013, but I'll do so without reservation....
If you've never heard Holter Graham read a novel, a delight awaits
you.... In short, Graham makes *Flat Water Tuesday* the best way
to 'read' this memorable novel." —*THE STAR-LEDGER*

Visit www.macmillanaudio.com for audio samples and more!
Follow us on Facebook and Twitter.